The Shadowy Thing

HIPPOCAMPUS PRESS PRESENTS LOVECRAFT'S LIBRARY

The Metal Monster by A. Merritt
The Place Called Dagon by Herbert Gorman
Incredible Adventures by Algernon Blackwood
The House of Sounds and Others by M. P. Shiel
An Exchange of Souls by Barry Pain AND *Lazarus* by Henri Béraud
Cold Harbour by Francis Brett Young AND *Sinister House* by Leland Hall

The Shadowy Thing

H. B. Drake

With an Introduction by S. T. Joshi

Hippocampus Press

New York

Published by Hippocampus Press
P.O. Box 641, New York, NY 10156.
http://www.hippocampuspress.com

Cover art is from *The Shadowy Thing* by H. B. Drake, New York:
A.L. Burt Company (1928 reprint).
Cover design and Lovecraft's Library series logo by Barbara Briggs Silbert.
Hippocampus Press logo designed by Anastasia Damianakos.

First Edition
1 3 5 7 9 8 6 4 2

ISBN 978-0-9824296-8-6

Introduction

Henry Burgess Drake (1893–1964) is a mystery man in Anglo-American letters. He was the author of nine weird and adventure novels, a children's story, a travel book, and several English textbooks, but aside from his dates of birth and death only a single biographical fact about him has emerged: at some point he served as a professor of English at the preparatory school of Keijo Imperial University in Seoul, Korea (an experience that led to his writing of his travelogue, *Korea of the Japanese* [1930]). His first published book dates to 1925, his last to 1959. But today he is known, if at all, for a single work: the weird novel *The Shadowy Thing* (1928).

This work itself was first published in England under the title *The Remedy* (1925), and constituted Drake's first novel. Several adventure novels followed in the 1920s: *The Schooner California* (1926), *Cursed Be the Treasure* (1926), *The Children Reap* (1929), and *Shinju* (1929), the last two of which are set in the Orient and apparently draw further upon Drake's years spent there. Although *The Children Reap* has some elements of weirdness, these novels are rousing adventure tales that evoked reviewers' comparisons with Robert Louis Stevenson and even Joseph Conrad.

In the 1930s Drake was literarily quiescent, issuing only his book on Korea and another novel (*The Captain of the Jehovah*, 1936), and commencing a five-book series, *An Approach to English Literature for Students Abroad*, published by Oxford University Press between 1938 and 1950. In the 1940s all we have is a further textbook, *Foundation Exercises in English*, published by Macmillan in two books in 1941.

In the 1950s Drake resumed fiction writing, producing a children's story, *The Book of Lyonne* (1952), that had the distinction of being illustrated by Mervyn Peake, and three further novels, *Chinese White* (1950), *Hush-a-by Baby* (1952; published in the U.S. as *Children of the Wind*), and *The Woman and the Priest* (1955). *Hush-a-by Baby* is manifestly a weird novel, about a woman haunted by the spirits of her twin unborn babies. I have not read it, but it received good reviews upon its appearance. Drake also produced *The Oxford English Course for Secondary Schools* in three books (1957-59); a fourth book written by another author appeared in 1963, leading one to believe that Drake was dead by this time.

But if Drake had done nothing but write *The Shadowy Thing*, he would deserve to be remembered. Not only is this a strangely compelling supernatural novel, but it clearly influenced H. P. Lovecraft's "The Thing on the

Doorstep" (1933), as both works deal with characters who display anomalous powers of hypnosis and mind-transference. In the revised version of "Supernatural Horror in Literature" he states somewhat vaguely: ". . . H. B. Drake's *The Shadowy Thing* summons up strange and terrible vistas."

An entry in Lovecraft's commonplace book (#158) records the plot-germ of his story:

> Man has terrible wizard friend who gains influence over him. Kills him in defence of his soul—walls body up in ancient cellar—BUT—the dead wizard (who has said strange things about soul lingering in body) *changes bodies with him* . . . leaving him a conscious corpse in cellar.

This is not exactly a description of the plot of *The Shadowy Thing*, but rather an imaginative extrapolation based upon it. In Drake's novel, a man, Avery Booth, does indeed exhibit powers that seem akin to hypnosis, to such a degree that he can oust the mind or personality from another person's body and occupy it. Booth does so on several occasions throughout the novel, and in the final episode he appears to have come back from the dead (he had been killed in a battle in World War I) and occupied the body of a friend and soldier who had himself been horribly mangled in battle. Lovecraft has amended this plot by introducing the notion of *mind-exchange:* whereas Drake does not clarify what happens to the ousted mind when it is taken over by the mind of Booth, Lovecraft envisages an exact transference whereby the ousted mind occupies the body of its possessor. Lovecraft then adds a further twist by envisioning what might happen if the occupier's body were killed and a dispossessed mind was thrust into it. The significant difference between the story and the plot-germ as recorded in the commonplace book is that the "wizard friend" has become the man's wife—a feature that may have been derived from Barry Pain's *An Exchange of Souls* (1911), which Lovecraft had in his library. This element also points to highly revealing autobiographical connexions (for Asenath Waite is clearly a compendium of Lovecraft's wife and his mother) that we cannot pursue here.

Otherwise, much of Lovecraft's story can be found directly in *The Shadowy Thing*. Avery Booth first possesses a weak-willed schoolmate, Gaveston, who is forced into an insane asylum as a result of his aberrant behaviour, just as Asenath Waite (in Edward Derby's body) is confined to the Arkham Sanitarium. Later Gaveston escapes, and the narrator of the novel is forced to shoot him, just as the narrator of "The Thing on the Doorstep" goes to the sanitarium to shoot the body of Edward Derby. When he does so he maintains that he has "purged the earth of a horror whose survival might have loosed untold terrors on all mankind"; in *The*

Shadowy Thing the narrator's sister, Blanche, says of Gaveston, "If he goes under, a power of evil will be let loose in the world that none of us can estimate."

And yet, it would be unfair to claim that *The Shadowy Thing* is solely of interest for its relation to a major Lovecraft story. It is a worthy novel in its own right. Although Lovecraft would probably have discounted it, the romance between the narrator, Dick Bellew, and Katrina Guthrie is delicately handled and integral to the plot; the etching of the other characters—Blanche Bellew, Olave Guthrie, Gaveston, and in particular Avery Booth, who hovers like a dark shadow behind all the events of the novel—is deft and skilful. The work's excellence should lead us to seek out Drake's other weird novel, *Hush-a-by Baby,* and to regret that he did not receive more encouragement to continue in this vein. Although *The Shadowy Thing* garnered relatively cordial reviews, it took three years to receive an American edition—a fact that perhaps led Drake to work in what he felt to be the more lucrative vein of the adventure story. It has been the fate of most weird writers to labour in obscurity, and the result is that minor masterworks like *The Shadowy Thing* must be resurrected by devotees and presented for the delectation of a select audience. Even if Drake's novel must ride Lovecraft's coattails to achieve a tenuous immortality, it is a more welcome fate than many other worthy contributions to our field have endured.

—S. T. JOSHI

To my father and mother

Part I

Gaveston

CHAPTER I

I don't quite know how I'm going to tell my story convincingly, for the simple reason that I'm not at all sure how much of it I believe myself. Looking back it seems to me nothing more than a wild and extravagant dream, though I'm surrounded with plentiful witnesses to the reality of the thing. It's disconcerting enough for a plain man like myself to be entangled in a mystery of any sort; but it's not only disconcerting, but shattering to all one's cherished and settled conceptions of things, to be forced to account for the mystery by an explanation more preposterous and fantastic still. I like to feel the earth firm beneath my feet; but when I find myself yielding to a belief in the only logical solution that seems to fit the events, I feel as though the earth were reeling away from under me, and all about me were fluid and unstable like the shifting substance of a nightmare.

But my best plan is to set the whole matter down as plainly and simply as I can, and leave it to speak for itself. Yet if anyone chooses to call it the fabrication of a demented visionary, I really don't know how I am to convince him that it is sober fact told by as level-headed and commonplace a fellow as he could wish to see; for indeed I should be half inclined to side with him against myself.

And first I had better tell you something about Avery Booth. But at the outset I ought to say that it will be no easy matter for me to be strictly fair to him. The man who cuts in between you and the girl you love . . . But that's anticipating, for the quarrel between us was of older standing than the affair of Katrina. And yet it wasn't exactly a quarrel, for we never came to words even, let alone blows. I suppose it was just a rooted antipathy born of our different natures. From my schooldays at Abbot's Gate I had hated him, though as a boy I had told myself I merely despised him. I can't pretend to analyse my feelings, so I don't know how far jealousy might have come into the matter; for he had amazing powers and was extraordinarily popular, which was natural enough; for he could tell hair-raising stories and do a hundred and one clever tricks, and had a knack with the fiddle, setting simple melodies to haunting and unearthly rhythms. But it always seemed to me that his popularity had something shifty about it. I can see now that it was of that kind that compels by some subterfuge of sinister fascination, for through all the admiration that was lavished upon him—"slobber" I called it in schoolboy slang, for the fawning and the flattery of it all disgusted me—a fear followed him and an uneasiness of distrust. He was petted as one might pet a snake, for its stealthy and subtle attraction rather than for its beauty. And to me, encased I suppose in the conventional prejudice of an English schoolboy, all this was odious because it was perplexing. Not that I stood alone in my antagonism to Avery; but I think I was the chief among the few who refused to come under his sway.

Well, all that is an old tale, and yet it is important too; for it shows that from my earliest knowledge of Avery I loathed and mistrusted him, and so I expect I never did him justice in my heart. But in these pages I must try and put aside my own personal prejudice; so first let me say that even at school there was no doubt at all of his wonderful powers. He delighted and thrilled us, myself included, with his uncanny hypnotic feats. I say myself included, though I affected to discredit the genuineness of the business, declaring it all to be mere clever trickery. Yet even as tricks the thing was wonderful enough, and far beyond my fathoming, so that I came more and more to believe deep in my heart that Avery was possessed of powers that couldn't be explained by any facile reference to ordinary conjuring.

The usual run of things was for him to send a boy to sleep, or put him into a trance as he called it, by some subtle and rhythmic process of his own; and when once under the spell the boy was in his power, controlled by sheer force of will, and obeying him at a word or a nod. And even when the patient had come to, something of his influence still lingered. At first I didn't set much store by these tricks, because Avery could only succeed with those who willingly submitted to him. But little by little his power seemed to grow, and at length there were very few in our dormitory set who had not been under his spell. This rather shook my obstinate disbelief; but outwardly at any rate I still refused to take the thing seriously, for every effort he had made on myself had failed. I think perhaps the whole matter seemed too silly to allow me to respond to his passes and suggestions.

I remember the first time that I allowed myself to be practised on. It was quite against my will, but the voice of the dormitory was insistent, fairly enough too; for I had no right to laugh at the thing if I wouldn't put it to a fair proof. I lay down on my back, and the light was turned low. I was told to look as far back as I could till I could just see my watch which I had hung at the head of my bed, and which Avery had set slowly swinging. And while I followed its motion to and fro he rubbed my brows and kept murmuring drowsily, "You're going to sleep—you're going to sleep—" And indeed I think my eyes did begin blinking sleepily; certainly they felt very heavy and hot. And then I became aware of Avery's black eyes staring very fixedly at me, and he was passing his hands before my face with a strangely rhythmical motion. And at that I came suddenly back to reality; and at the absurdity of it all I fairly burst out laughing. Avery turned sharply away from me, biting his lip. From hearsay I learnt that he accounted for his failure by calling me an obtuse and insensible clod. I think very likely his estimate of me was right enough; but at the time I rejoiced in my victory, and even let him practise upon me a second and third time so that I could have the joy of seeing him again discomfited. And when others, weaker than myself as I imagined, sank easily under his spell, and danced and sang to his will, and declared that their pillows were green or violet, and looking into the looking-glass set the room laughing by calling it the picture of a donkey, and on waking told us seriously that they were the Great Cham or the Emperor of Thibet, I looked disdainfully on and pitied them.

I think I first began to be afraid in my heart that it wasn't all a mere game of bluff when young Gaveston, a nervous enough youngster in any case, and one whom Avery could control more easily than most, became convulsed during one of his trances, and raved as though possessed of a devil. At first everyone began to laugh, thinking it part of the game; but it soon became clear by Avery's drawn face and sharp commands that something terrible had happened. Then there was a breathless hush while we watched the pair, not knowing in the least what was the matter. For Gaveston seemed to have passed clean out of control. He cursed Avery in frightful terms, and fled from him in a sort of angry terror. He would have burst from the room, but Avery shouted to someone to hold the door, and Gaveston turned hissing and rushed for the window. But again he was stayed, and foaming and chattering he faced round at Avery who was stepping slowly up to him with his eyes glaring wide and unblinking, and his hands playing in a smooth rhythm before his face. For a moment it looked as though Gaveston would have sprung at him. He seemed crouched for a leap, and his whole face worked in a spasm of hatred such as I had not thought possible in the kindly little fellow. But as Avery drew near he fell suddenly limp, and sank with a moan to the floor. Avery stooped over him quickly, and I heard him murmur, "Gaveston, Gaveston, come back; it's over, it's all over." Gaveston opened his eyes doubtfully, and asking weakly, "Where am I?" rose on his elbow and looked stupidly about him. Then he fell to crying, and we put him to bed where he was soon asleep. I looked at Avery as he turned away from the bed. He was panting as though after a fight, and there was sweat thick upon his forehead.

For a week or two Gaveston moved about and talked as though half dazed and uncertain of himself. I rather liked the little fellow; and he would often come timidly up to me and ask if he could come with me for a walk, or shyly offer me some cake or some sweets; and so we had struck up a sort of chumship, very condescending, I'm afraid, on my part. So now I naturally tried to get him to tell me what had happened, but he usually just rubbed his eyes and looked up at me blinking as though he had been staring at the sun and couldn't quite see. Then he would shake his head slowly, and his brow would cloud over, and he would say, "I don't know, Dick, I really don't know." Or sometimes with a note of fear in his voice he would whisper more hurriedly, "You mustn't ask me, Dick, you mustn't." And if I pressed him he would say as though in pain, "Oh don't, don't." And he would turn and leave me.

And then an extraordinary rumor began to get about. Avery, it seems, accounted for the affair by saying that during the trance a disembodied spirit trying to return to earth had wrestled with Gaveston for the possession of his body. For during a trance, Avery explained, the bonds that held flesh and spirit together were loosened, and the spirit might even float free. I gathered that Avery had invented this ridiculous fable to increase his own reputation for occult powers, for it was by his strength, it was to be presumed, that Gaveston had won through. And strangely enough that was how the fellows all seemed to look at the affair, as though somehow it redounded to Avery's credit. But to me, and one or two more like me, it all seemed too absurd and extravagant to bother about, otherwise I might have taken it upon myself to report it to the authorities. But its effect upon me was to cut me away from Avery more than ever, and I turned my attention to Gaveston.

For a while he returned to something of his old manner. Then he began to have fits, and would wake up at night screaming terribly. Of course he was put into the doctor's hands, and sometimes he would be better and sometimes worse. But he never regained full confidence in himself during the few months that he remained with us. There was always a haunting fear in his eyes as though he had seen unearthly things that he dared not reveal. It was the look that I would have imagined in the face of one who had died and come alive again, and dreaded to tell what he had seen beyond the grave.

I found Avery had been tampering with him again, telling him that he needed his strength to help him if he wanted to pull through. And at that I made a last bid to get at the root of the matter. I told Gaveston that I must know what was distressing him, and would pay no heed to his evasions. We were out in the fields, I remember, and he gazed about him with great wide eyes. Then seeing the coast clear he clutched me eagerly by the shoulders, and raising his lips whispered brokenly close to my ear, "Oh, Dick, I'm afraid, I'm afraid." And he began sobbing convulsively.

I have reproached myself ever since that my first feeling was not one of sympathy, but of extreme discomfort at my own plight. I suppose I was afraid somebody might see us.

"Good Lord," I said bluntly, "you can't do that kind of thing, you know." And I think my unresponsive coldness steadied him, for he choked down his sobs and said more calmly, "I know I'm a baby, Dick. But it's terrible."

His voice frightened me. It suggested things I could not name.

"Why, what is it?" I asked.

He was silent for a moment while he swallowed the last of his tears, and then facing me dry-eyed he said very solemnly, "Dick, it sounds a lot of rot, I know; but I don't know who I am. I've lost myself somewhere. Or part of myself. Oh, I don't know," he broke out fretfully, rubbing his eyes. "I can't remember, I can't remember, Dick." And his voice became tense again with an unearthly alarm which set I know not what strange chord vibrating uneasily in my heart.

"Look here, old chap," I began stupidly, but he cut in, "Yes, I know it's all rot, but I can't get it out of my head. I think things I don't want to think, and I do things I don't want to do. Oh, why is it, Dick?" he darted the question at me, but went on without waiting for an answer, "And when I go to bed I'm afraid to sleep. Something happens when I'm asleep. I feel myself drifting away; right away. It isn't just like sleeping; it's like, like . . ."

"Dying," I suggested bluntly.

He looked up at me suddenly, and with a catch at his breath said, "Ach, I was afraid to say it. And yet, and yet—" he hesitated, glancing at me inquiringly as though fearing to trust me with his full confidence, but at length exclaiming with a rush, "It's more than that. There's something pushing me out. Something trying to get in. Oh, Dick, there's something terribly evil trying to get in. I'm afraid. It's as though there were a cold thing moving beside me deep in here, right deep in. And I wake up struggling against it, and it clings to me, and then it slips off and glides away. But the next night it's back again, back again. And some morning I shall wake and find it right inside. Or perhaps—perhaps I shan't feel it at all. Perhaps I shan't be there. Ach!" he ended with a shudder that shook his whole frame as though a wind had blown through him. But before I could think of anything to say to such an amazing rush of folly, he smiled up at me and said, "Dick, don't tell anyone. I know it's all rot. I'm all right, you know." And in spite of the whimper in his voice he moved away with a pitiful effort at a swagger of nonchalance.

I didn't follow him, for my mind was unable to cope with such impossible ideas, and I felt tongue-tied and foolish and preferred to keep aloof from things I couldn't understand. But I began to realize in my heart that there were more things in heaven and earth than were dreamt of in my philosophy; for Gaveston's words, or rather the evident terror that vibrated through them, had shaken me more deeply than I cared to confess to myself.

While I still stood there he ran back to say, "You're so strong, Dick." He felt my arm appraisingly, and added in a different tone, "But, Dick, take care." He threw me a quick dark look, and was off again, leaving me to puzzle out the meaning of the little scene. But I found it beyond my fathoming.

I took care to let it be known that Gaveston was under my protection, and accordingly Avery had to leave him alone. But I heard that Avery attributed Gaveston's growing insanity to the ignorance of the doctor attending him, and to my interference. For the doctor was a poor fool of a fellow who couldn't be expected to understand the case; and I was guarding Gaveston from Avery who was the only one who could help him win his battle. Well, perhaps he was right after all; but at the time I felt no least prompting of a doubt concerning my action. It seemed the only thing I could do. But my schoolfellows looked rather askance at me, and some told me openly that I should leave the matter to Avery. For the strange thing about our antagonism was that although it was clear to everyone that we were ranged against each other, yet we never crossed words. All our battling seemed to be done through mediaries. We skirmished with reports and rumours. It was only towards the end that Avery broke through our tacit reticence, and came up to me and said, "Will you let me save Gaveston?"

The question was thrown at me with a blunt suddenness that disconcerted me. There were so many nasty things I could have answered that my shafts of sarcasm crossed confusedly in my mind, and I couldn't put tongue to a word. I tried to express my meaning by my survey of scorn.

"You won't!" he exclaimed, his eyes blazing into mine with a questioning menace. And I must confess I stepped back a pace. There was a power about him which seemed to crush me in as by a heavy atmosphere. "Very well," he said darkly, "you're his own worst enemy, if you'd like to know." He swung away from me, but faced round again rather uncertainly, eyeing me with a slow hesitation, and said with a strangely colourless voice, "I suppose there's such a thing as making up for a mistake."

As far as I could understand the remark I took it for a confession of blame, and my face must have expressed my triumph; for he glared at me with a sudden anger, and I could have sworn the air about me became sensibly hot. "Never a second time," he said. And snapping his fingers, and laughing hardly, he left me. And strangely enough, though I felt the victory was mine, I stood there for a moment too weak and stupid to move. I had never been in such close contact with him before, and it was like entering a charged and electric atmosphere. I drew a deep breath and took myself off. But when I thought over the affair I was shaken by an uneasy doubt. For Avery to have swallowed his pride and appealed to me in such a way meant that the matter must have seemed to him of extraordinarily urgent import. And when I heard he had even besieged the doctor, I felt a pang of dismay. All was not right. The thing was beyond me. But I clung obstinately to my conviction that Avery meant ill to Gaveston, though what had passed between him and the doctor nobody seemed to know.

A few weeks later Gaveston was carried raving to St. Jude's Asylum. I heard occasional reports. Sometimes he was his own meek gentle little self, and sometimes he became a wild mad thing, raging and shouting in his padded cell. I couldn't help thinking of the disembodied spirit theory which Avery had set going. It seemed to me that it fitted the case remarkably well. But always I told myself that it was too utterly ridiculous, and I fortified myself behind a scientific catch-word which of course I didn't understand in the least, calling it a case of "Dual personality." And so I was somewhat reassured. But all the same I felt that I had looked into abysmal things, and had reeled shuddering from the sight.

After this, naturally enough, fellows fought shy of submitting to Avery's spells; for Gaveston's undeniable madness, and the uncanny rumours afloat concerning the affair, effectually daunted the boldest from dabbling again in such mysteries. But what I can't understand now is that no one seemed to think the worse of him. For me, as I have said, I tried to think the whole thing was nonsense. "Dual personality" covered my utter ignorance of Gaveston's case. But why those who really believed in the dispossessed spirit theory didn't rise against Avery and denounce him, or at least shun him and avoid further contamination for their own sakes, it is beyond me to say. I suppose his influence was either too frightening, or too strong to be resisted. But there's the fact of the matter. No one seemed to shrink from him, and certainly no one betrayed him. Not a whisper of the real history of Gaveston's madness ever reached the ears of authority. Perhaps if I had thought over that at the time I should have had greater cause than ever to fear the dark spirit that moved behind those black and piercing eyes.

CHAPTER II

For a time things were quiet enough. I kept myself to my few special chums, and let Avery and his satellites spin on their own way unheeded. It was seldom enough in any case that Avery's path crossed mine, and now we never seemed to touch even in passing. But occasionally I caught a quick gleam from his eyes as he flashed them on me for a moment and away again before I could meet his gaze. I hardly dared own it to myself, but I felt a pang of alarm whenever I caught him glancing at me in this way; for always it seemed as though he had stolen something from me, whisking it away before I could stop him. What he had stolen I did not know; but I always felt suddenly weak and a little dazed, and my breath came thickly as though I had been running. There was the suggestion, too, that I had been napping and he had found me off my guard, and I tried to keep on the alert for him; and then I noticed that if I was prepared his quick flashing look had no effect upon me; in fact, if anything, I seemed to win back something of the strength which he had been stealing from me little by little. And so that strange battle of eyes went on, and I began to feel a nervousness that was quite foreign to me. The truth was that I was afraid of I knew not what. It wasn't the hatred in Avery's eyes that I was afraid of, nor even the desire to do me a hurt. These things I was aware of without the need of such subtle reminders, and I was prepared to face them. It was rather the dark menace of something incomprehensible, something that hovered beyond my circle of view and understanding, and left me vaguely conscious of presences and influences that I couldn't see and measure. It was indeed the dark fear of the unknown which Avery was little by little implanting in my heart; and it worked within me like a subtle poison, weakening my conventional security of thought, and troubling my mind with foolish shadows of doubt and dread and fantastic imaginings which above all things were hateful to me and unsettling to my easy convictions.

I found I wasn't the only one who began to have dark thoughts about Avery. I have said that no one again willingly submitted to him. Even his closest friends had had enough of that. But it grew clearer little by little that fellows were doing strange things quite against their will. It was hinted among us that Avery was at the bottom of it, though some denied that, because he had always insisted that he needed the co-operation of the subject, and without a willing submission he could do nothing. That was all very well, but others declared that they felt their frequent submission to him had weakened their own wills and given him a tremendous control over them; and besides, his power seemed to have developed suddenly since the affair of Gaveston, though no one could explain why. So altogether we were in a fine state of doubt, moving among unpleasant and inexplicable shadows, as though we were living in a haunted atmosphere; and several who had been ardent admirers of Avery fell away from him and joined the opposing camp.

But Avery knew his own game well enough to play it without fault. When he realized the consternation he was causing among his friends he smoothed the whole matter over by confessing frankly to the thing, and using his new powers as a source of fun. And so his party gathered round him again, and it became quite a game among them to get him to set people to all manner of antics; and in spite of my detestation of him I think I enjoyed the humour of the thing as well as anybody. Especially so, I think, as at first I was never made a butt for his tricks. Indeed, in spite of the uneasiness which I felt when I caught his eyes upon me, I prided myself that I was immune from the general disease. I looked upon myself as of stronger and more independent will than my companions; but I have wondered since whether it was not mere dullness and unresponsive lethargy of spirit that protected me, and that Avery was working on my imagination by his subtle and suggestive glances till I should be ripe for his attack.

This sort of thing had been going on for some time, and Gaveston's case had been forgotten, when I began to find myself walking in my sleep. At first I merely awoke sitting up in bed and with a sort of idea in my mind that I had got up to go somewhere. Then one night I woke to find myself out of bed and feeling for my slippers; but coming to my senses I realized my position and told myself I must have been dreaming, though I couldn't remember any dream. I had forgotten the incident when a week or two later I found myself not only out of bed and with my slippers on, but with my dressing-gown about me too. I had even taken a step or two away from my bed before I realized where I was; and feeling a strange dazedness of brain as though I had been holding my breath under water, I turned rather stupidly towards my bed. But as I turned I saw somebody suddenly sink back under his clothes as though he had been half raised to watch me. With a clear mind I deliberately walked to the door, and going to the bathroom drew myself a cup of water, making as much noise as I could to let anyone who might be listening know exactly what I was doing. For I wouldn't have had it thought for the world that I walked in my sleep. The suggestion of freakishness was at this time, and I believe has always been, my greatest aversion.

All this didn't trouble me very much at first, for the occasions were far between, and I had forgotten one before the next one arrived. It's only on looking back that I see them in a developing sequence. But little by little the habit of sleep-walking was growing upon me, till I couldn't blind myself to the fact that there was something wrong somewhere; for at length almost every night I awoke either sitting up in bed or even out of bed, though so far I hadn't repeated the performance I have just described. And the worst of it was that I couldn't account for the thing at all. I suppose I must have suspected the finger of Avery in it, but my pride refused to allow me to set much store by that. Yet questioning the meaning of it I couldn't find answer. I was as healthy as a bull. I don't think I had much in the way of a conscience; certainly not enough to set me roaming at night. There was nothing that I knew of preying on my mind. I didn't suffer from indigestion. In fact there was no reason in nature for my strange desire to go wandering in my sleep.

To combat the thing I took to keeping awake as long as I could. But that didn't help much. Indeed after a while I found myself seized with the absurd desire to get up and go I knew not where, even when still in full possession of my consciousness. At this I began to be worried and a little fretful, and my sleep became broken with disturbing dreams. I tossed about at night, and woke with my clothes in a tumbled confusion.

It was about this time that there was rather a nasty scandal at school. Money had been stolen, and the thief couldn't be found. There was quite a stir, and I suppose most of us had the matter well to the fore in our minds. It was naturally the kind of thing we would discuss, some advancing one theory, some another. And of course rumours made the air thick. Then there came trickling through that Avery knew the thief; and later that he had set a trap to catch him. Matters concerning Avery always came in rumours. Nobody knew where they began, but everybody believed them. And as a rule they proved true enough. So now excitement grew to a height. Avery's power was known, and I suppose nearly everybody believed he would catch the culprit. In fact, it was considered rather a wonder that the fellow didn't immediately confess, instead of awaiting a certain discovery.

That matter was all in the air when one night I suddenly started up more alert than usual, and seemed to catch the fading tones of a voice saying, "But Dick, take care." For a moment I sat up in bed listening, and then I remembered that it was in just such a way that Gaveston had spoken to me when he came running back that day in the fields, and looked at me so strangely, as though he held a secret I couldn't guess. The horrible idea seized me that his disembodied spirit was haunting me, and that I had heard it speak. Perhaps that was the cause of my strangely disturbed nights.

But such a fantastic notion couldn't take a real grip of my belief, and I dismissed it with an irritated sniff and tried to settle myself to sleep again. But the impression of having heard Gaveston's voice was so clear that I couldn't close my ears to it. It seemed to be echoing still. And as I fell from doze to doze I would hear it again and again, "Dick, take care." Then the thought came to me suddenly that Gaveston was warning me against something. Against what? I asked; not realizing that my question implied the belief I would not yield to. But suddenly my mind grew clear. How I had managed to delude myself so long I don't know, but it wasn't till this moment that I really gave in to the belief that Avery was practising his spells upon me. The meaning of his covert glances became clear to me now, though the source of their power was a dark enough secret. I supposed that he had staked his credit before his select band of followers that he would break my will and draw me too into his net. Or perhaps it was merely that he had set himself the task for the satisfaction of his own pride. But I remember that the certainty that his influence lay beneath all my troubled nights made me feel strong again, for now that I knew what was menacing me I told myself I could guard against it. But now I rather think that this conquest of my imagination was the snapping of my last defence. However that may have been, I was soon in a deep sleep. And yet was only a few minutes later, it seemed, that I was dimly aware of rising and throwing on my dressing-gown, and walking out of the room and down the corridor. I knew what I was doing, yet I couldn't prevent myself. Some power not of my own will was drawing me on. It was as though a magnet was tugging at me; I could feel almost a physical compulsion. And wrestling against my weakness, and fretting at heart, I walked forward unsteadily. And then suddenly a cold fear came over me, for I knew where I was going. I was going to Avery's study. I was going to break open his locker, for something told me that there was money inside. I was bound on a journey of burglary, and I knew it and couldn't stop myself. And beating in my mind was all the scandal of the past few days.

The misery of that moment is indescribable. For not merely was the whole idea of theft detestable to me; not only did my whole soul revolt against the thing I was doing; but I could foresee the frightful consequences: I should be expelled. The very word was hateful and horrible. I should be cast out ignominiously, with my name branded and my honour smirched. At the thought of it my whole soul seemed to crumple up as though its very substance were melted and wasted. I had never known such an agony before. But I gathered my strength as well as I might and struggled with the evil thing that was possessing me as though with a living creature. Yet still I crept unwillingly forward, and my hesitation must have seemed remarkably like stealth. For I was sucked on as it were by a slow current that was tugging and dragging me along. And then as I was rounding a corner I heard Gaveston's voice whisper most distinctly in a hushed warning, "Dick, take care."

It was that that saved me, for I woke to a sudden possession of my will. And then in front of me from the shadows I heard a slight rustle. There were fellows there in waiting for me to watch my disgrace. But the game was in my hands now. I stood still and shouted out with a mocking laugh, "You're mighty clever, aren't you, Avery? Well, you see *I'm* not Gaveston."

My voice rang out loudly through the darkness, and for a horrible moment I was afraid I had made a supreme fool of myself. For in front of me no one stirred, and from the dormitory behind I heard voices and movements, and I dreaded that my sleep-walking would now be discovered. Biting my lips in anger I strode forward, putting everything to the hazard; and sure enough I stumbled against a foot in the dark passage, and sweeping out my arm I seized a couple of the spies and knocked their heads together in fine indignation.

Strangely enough Avery was found sleeping serenely in his bed; but it wasn't long before the whole matter leaked out, and it was known that he had pitted his will against mine and I had been more than a match for him. After that I wasn't worried by him any more, though sometimes I caught his eyes upon me. But now I could read nothing there except the hatred which after all was my due. That unnameable suggestion of strange and troubling evil seemed to have melted quite out of them; or perhaps it was that my recovered assurance in myself made me blind to their menace.

What disturbed me now was Gaveston's voice that had warned me. It wasn't a habit of mine to try and account for things. I tended rather to a mute acceptation of everything as it came. But here was a mystery that craved solving. I couldn't leave it alone in my mind. Had Gaveston indeed been hovering near, a spectator of the evil trick? And having fallen a snare to the dark wiles of Avery, had he set himself to save me from the same fate? I couldn't tear my thoughts away from these teasing questions, though I tried to tell myself that I had far better dismiss the whole thing as an oddity and a whim. After all who could explain what happened in sleep?

And the impression of the episode did grow fainter and fainter with time as Avery's path and mine fell further and further apart; and at last the whole affair became so shadowy and when I thought of it at all it seemed so silly and extravagant, that I think I would have forgotten it altogether had not fate thrown me once again into Avery's way and twisted our lives into a more inextricable tangle than ever.

CHAPTER III

It was really due to Blanche that I came into contact with Avery again. Blanche was my sister, a year or two younger than myself. I suppose as a child I took about as much or as little notice of her as brothers usually take of their sisters. But I think we always hit it off well enough together. At any rate, I don't remember any violent quarrels, such as I have heard tell of in some families; and indeed Blanche remains rather a shadowy little figure when I look back upon my boyhood. I suppose I had plenty of friends always about me, and Blanche was of a quiet and rather serious nature, and, unlike so many girls, not inclined to jealousy or interference, so our paths didn't touch very often. The sort of picture I have in my memory is of myself central in some boisterous and exuberant game, with Blanche's gaze quietly falling on me at fleeting intervals from her retired corner.

When my father died Blanche assumed a greater importance in my life; for my mother completely collapsed, and Blanche had to take over the management of things. But it wasn't until I was at Oxford, or to be exact, during my first long vacation, that Blanche suddenly became a living reality in my world. I suppose I was as puffed up with undigested wisdom as the usual student at the end of his first year; and so when on the first evening of my arrival home my mother began rather nervously to talk to me about Blanche, and at last asked me to speak to her about things, as the girl seemed to have got some funny notions into her head, I readily undertook the commission.

"Why, yes, mater," I said easily; "but what's it all about?"

"You see, she goes to these meetings," my mother answered slowly. "She's gone to-night even, and I told her she ought to stay at home for your first evening."

"Oh, she's no cause to stay at home for me," I brushed aside the objection. "But what meetings?"

"Well, that's just what I don't quite know." My mother was obviously troubled at something that was baffling her. She looked unusually tired, too. "The girl's not candid," she said.

"Have you spoken to her?" I asked.

"I've tried to," my mother answered; "but she doesn't give me a straight answer. But don't think there's anything wrong, Dick," she put in hastily; "there's nothing really wrong with her. It's just that I don't quite know what she's at. Of course if she were a silly, flighty girl it would be

25

another matter. But Blanche knows what she's about as a rule. But I don't like all this spiritualistic stuff; do you, Dick?"

"Oh, it's spiritualism, is it?" I said gaily. "She'll get over that, mater. It's just a craze, you know."

"But Blanche doesn't have crazes," said my mother; and we turned to other things. But it wasn't long before my mother said she must be off to bed. I rose to help her from the couch, but she waved me away. "No," she said, with a faint smile, "Blanche says I mustn't be helped. She's very severe with me, Dick."

"I should think so," I replied, putting my arm about her and supporting her to her room.

"Ah," she sighed contentedly, "but it is nice to be helped. You see, Blanche says I don't try enough." And she kissed me good-night.

During the evening while I was waiting for Blanche to come home I suppose I gave more thought to her than I had done during the whole of my life before. And as I called up in my mind the picture of my sister, I was aware for the first time of something strangely elusive about her. She was one of the few people I knew who seemed to live in an atmosphere of their own. Her presence in the room made a difference. The vision of her came to me as a pair of eyes that watched; a steady pair of eyes. And not only did they watch, but a power came out of them; they seemed to move, to inspire, to control. Somehow I thought again of Avery, though my memory had pretty nearly lost the image of him. I remembered how his eyes used to watch me. But Blanche's gaze was different. It was tranquillizing, not unsettling. It gave power, instead of seeming to steal it away drop by drop. It was the difference of health and disease, or of life and death.

I cannot account to myself even now how it was that Blanche seemed to take shape so suddenly in my mind. I suppose it was that all the material lay ready to hand, and an hour's concentration of thought was enough to compose the picture. But I know for a fact that when Blanche arrived at last I looked upon her with very different eyes than before. I saw her as a shape, not as a shadow. And I noticed with appraising pride the steady poise of her body and the strong but light carriage of her head. It is usually, I believe, something of a shock to a man to realize that his sister is beautiful, and the shock in my case was the greater because I had to confess that I had never seen a lovelier girl. Somehow the thing seemed ridiculous. I suppose I had the sort of feeling a man has when he suddenly finds that one of his children is a genius.

You may be sure that I watched her pretty carefully that night as we sat up late and talked. And I began to understand why it was that my mental picture of her had seemed to build itself up around her eyes; for they were indeed the central fact about her beauty. Most people would call them violet; but it was not their colour so much as their depth of colour that made them significant. And yet not quite that, either. There was a force, an expression, a purpose in them, something that I would call a will if I could use the word to mean a subconscious power; for the eyes held me as by a physical spell, and yet without any suggestion of doing so purposely. It was, in fact, just that my sister's amazing force of personality had for the first time made itself felt in my consciousness. I don't know that I found the experience particularly pleasing; for though I felt a wonderful sense of restful confidence, yet somehow this sudden entrance into an unimagined world made my own little world seem by contrast a noisy, futile, meaningless affair without plan or purpose or durability. For it was as though I had caught a glimpse of the unchangeable and the eternal through a rift in the transitory semblances of things. One thing I understood very clearly as I tumbled into bed, and that was that it would be no easy matter for me to fulfil the commission I had undertaken so lightly. A talk with Blanche wouldn't be a big brother's kindly bullying of a little sister. I was strangely apprehensive as I thought of the coming interview, wondering if I should be able to bring myself to broach matters on the morrow.

It wasn't on the morrow, nor yet within a week of morrows, that I summoned the necessary courage to speak. It seemed so unfitting and unworthy of the whole thing to begin with some such question as, "I say, Blanche, what's this mater's been telling me about you?" And I couldn't bring myself to open the subject in a serious parsonic way. It wasn't in my nature to say, "Blanche dear, I should like to have a quiet little talk with you." So I hung irresolute, till Blanche herself came to the rescue, and asked me why I kept on looking at her as I did.

"Why, how?" I asked, terribly nervous at the thought that the moment had come.

"Like this," said Blanche, quizzing up her brows in a questioning way, and so ludicrously like a puzzled dog that I burst out laughing; and Blanche laughed too, and added, "I'm going out again to-night, and if you want to ask me where I'm going, you may do so."

This was said so easily and with such a frank look into my eyes that all my stupid nervousness vanished and I said, "Well, what's it all about, Blanche, anyway? You know you're upsetting mother, and unless it's horribly important I should have thought you might have dropped the thing."

"Yes," she answered me slowly, her face growing very grave, "I know it's upsetting mother. I'm sorry."

"Well then," I pressed.

"But one can't give up one's very life, you know."

That sort of talk was beyond me, and I waited, not very patiently, for something more lucid.

She watched me a moment, and said, "Dick, I suppose it sounds very silly to you. But you know to some people, rowing and boxing even seem a little meaningless."

"Good Lord," I cried, "do you want me to give up . . ."

But she cut me short with a little laugh. "Oh, Dick, Dick, you stupid thing, that was only an analogy. I mean," she continued more seriously, "we all put different values on things. Well, to me spiritualism means life."

"Well then," I said, "tell me what it's about. What is spiritualism?"

"I've just told you," she answered; "it's life itself."

"Yes, but," I began fretfully, "can't you explain what it is? I mean, what do you do?" Her answer gave me some clue as to my mother's meaning when she said Blanche wasn't candid.

She smiled at me enigmatically, and slowly shook her head. "You're like the rest, Dick," she said. "You think it's merely a matter of doing certain things. I suppose you think we perform all manner of mystic rites and secret celebrations, and raise spirits and talk with the dead. Well, what if we do? That's not the heart of the thing. I tell you it's not a matter of doing or believing; it's a way of life."

"Well, what way?" I asked.

"My dear boy," she answered me, "you can only know by living it. You must either be one of us, or you simply mustn't bother your head about us at all." She added with an affectionate little smile, and played with my hand, "For you, Dick, I should say, don't bother your head about us at all. I don't think it's your line."

"But surely," I said, not willing to be put off so, "surely you can tell me what you do believe."

"Look here," she answered in a lighter way, "I can explain it like this, if you'll let me use another analogy." She waited for a half moment, and her eyes twinkled humorously. "May I?" she cried.

"Oh, go on," I said.

"Well then, take Christianity. If anybody asked you why you're a Christian, would you begin explaining the doctrine of the Trinity?"

"Oh, good Lord!" I blurted out, in dismay at the thought of it.

Blanche laughed outright. "And yet you go to church," she said. "And quite right too. You see, Christianity is a way of life, not a creed. For you," she added, again with that humorous twinkle in her eyes, "I should say it would be best named the Higher Decency."

I didn't quite see where the argument had strayed to, and I tried to bring it back to the starting-point. "I don't know about all that," I said. "All I know is that you're upsetting mater."

She dropped her hands to her sides, and gave a little sigh. "Well, I'm sorry, Dick," she said, "but I can't help it. After all, I don't think I'm becoming a freak. I don't pretend to raise people from the dead. I don't preach lunacy as a desirable cult. I don't haunt graveyards. I don't even talk in my sleep. And it really does help me to live my life. That's about as much as I know."

"Well, look here," I said, "don't get carried away by any of these non-sense mongers who do do these things. That's all."

She looked at me with a swift earnestness, but turned away with a little laugh. "Oh, Dick," she said, "when will you learn to sift the evidence before you pass judgment?"

But I couldn't let that go unchallenged, for the memory of Avery came back to me. "Blanche," I said more seriously than before, "I may know more than you think. I tell you there's real danger in meddling with things you don't understand. Sometimes madness comes of it. I tell you I know. And I'm warning you, that's all."

"Yes, Dick," she said more humbly, "I know, too. And I should be glad enough if our people would keep clear of these things altogether. But power is a temptation, you know. I sometimes think Christ must have been the most tempted man that ever lived. And then people ask us for signs. It's not easy to deny them when they're so easily given. It makes an impression, you know, to cure a madman, or . . . well, that kind of thing. But still," she broke off, "I wish we could clear ourselves of all that. Then dear old stupids like you, Dick, wouldn't be able to call us freaks and impostors, and all the rest of it."

She ended up gaily enough, but I could feel that she was troubled at something. However, I had had enough of the argument, and I satisfied myself with saying, "I suppose you're one of the powerful ones, eh? Well, don't fall into temptation and start working miracles."

I spoke, of course, lightly enough, and patted her affectionately on the shoulder as though the matter were settled; but she shot up at me such a vivid and terrified look that my heart gave a thump of alarm.

"Good God!" I exclaimed, "what's the matter, Blanche?"

She gave rather a forced laugh, and answered me with an effort at lightness, "There, that's the end of the business." And she broke away

from me, leaving me with a sense of something incomprehensible troubling my very soul.

"She's afraid," I said to myself, "she's afraid of something." But for
the life of me I couldn't imagine what her fear could mean. I told myself in
baffled annoyance that it was an unhealthy business. I had the picture in
my mind of Avery's sweating brow as he had wrestled with the demon of
madness that had possessed Gaveston. "Power is a temptation," Blanche
had said. That picture and those words seemed to fuse themselves together
in my mind, though I couldn't trace their connection; unless it was that
Avery's tricks were a case in point of power misapplied. But I couldn't get
the thing clear at all. I didn't like it. And yet I had the daily life of Blanche
before me to show how near the earthly could reach to the divine. It all
seemed a monstrous paradox, and I was glad enough to escape to the more
congenial even if more frivolous companionship of my College chums.

CHAPTER IV

Blanche certainly wasn't candid, if candour means telling everybody everything you're doing whether you're asked or not. But I can't blame her for living her own life in a sort of secrecy seeing that she was likely to find little enough sympathy from her mother or her brother. I dare say if father had been alive things might have been different, for her grave reserve was largely an inheritance from him, and I think the two would have made a fine pair of confidants. But it wasn't likely that she would tell either my mother or myself more than was necessary to answer our questions, which, as a matter of fact, were formal rather than inquisitive; for we tended to shut the door upon her affairs, and didn't want to know more than we were bound to. Still, in matters of less importance Blanche maintained this same secrecy, and that rather annoyed me. It wasn't till the day before the event that she told us she was to act in a play. I had never had the least idea that she was interested in theatricals, and it didn't seem to ease things when she said I had never asked her. That's an answer I particularly object to. There's a sort of twist in it that baffles me.

As it happened, Olave Guthrie, a College chum of mine, was staying with me at the time. How we came to be chums has always puzzled me, because our temperaments were so dissimilar. In fact, Olave had something of Blanche's serious dignity of reserve about him, but there was enough of the sportsman in him to make our friendship a companionable affair. But it wasn't a mere field companionship. I could get that in abundance without going to Olave. The difference between our friendship and that with my other innumerable sportsmates was that the tie that bound us was below the surface, as it were. I suppose it was a sort of affinity, in spite of the dissimilarity of our natures.

Well, at the mention of a play Olave pricked up his ears. It was the kind of thing to appeal to him. "May I ask what play, Miss Bellew?" he said.

"The Cenci," Blanche answered him, fixing him with a quiet look.

"What?" I said. "Never heard of it."

But something was taking place between those two. Obviously the thing had a significance for Olave that escaped me.

"The Cenci!" he said very quietly but very expressively. "You, of course, are Beatrice," he went on.

"Yes," said Blanche.

"I've never seen it acted," said Olave.

31

"I've never even heard of it," I repeated.

"Then, Dick," said Blanche, "you'll come to it with a fresh mind. And I think you'll have a surprise," she added, throwing at me an amused but significant look.

"Yes," I answered, "I dare say I shall have a surprise all right."

But Olave didn't seem to like the way I was taking it. "Dick," he said quietly, "I think you'll be even more surprised than you bargain for." Then turning to Blanche he launched out into a discussion of the whole thing which passed beyond me. I busied myself with the morning paper, catching here and there a word or two of the conversation. "I should have thought," said Olave, "the thing would have been too terrible for representation." And again I heard Blanche say, "I look upon it as the struggle between good and evil." And in answer to some objection of Olave's, "Yes, but good isn't always triumphant, is it? And the best motives get distorted sometimes." But at the moment their talk meant little enough to me.

I was deep in some article or other when Blanche's voice cut into my consciousness. "What's that?" I said, suddenly arrested.

"What do you mean?" said Blanche.

"Sorry," I answered, "don't let me interrupt. But I thought you mentioned St. Jude's."

"I did," Blanche said; "the play's in aid of it."

"The Asylum?" I asked.

"Yes," she answered.

"But how," I began . . . I meant to ask what her connection was with St. Jude's Asylum. But I merely said mumblingly, "Hm, good cause, I suppose."

I turned back to my paper, but it was my own thoughts now which shut out the conversation. The mention of St. Jude's had brought Gaveston back suddenly to my memory. I think I had quite forgotten him. Certainly I had never been to see him. Visiting at asylums didn't seem to me exactly the kind of thing I was called upon to do. But what did Blanche know about St. Jude's? And after all, who were these people she was acting with? The fact that I didn't put the question to Blanche shows the reluctance I felt at prying into her affairs. And it may have been too, that I didn't want her to know that St. Jude's meant anything to me.

I heard Olave's voice. "Dick, we're talking to you."

"Good," I said, throwing the paper aside.

"Are you coming with us?" he asked me.

"Of course," I said, "where?"

The realization that somehow I had become the outsider in our party of three was just faintly forming in my mind, when my thoughts were sent scattering by Olave's answer.

"To St. Jude's."

"But, Good God!" I exclaimed, looking foolishly from one to the other.

"Oh, he hasn't been listening to us," said Blanche. Then turning to me, "Dick, dear," she explained as she might have done to a child, "Mr. Guthrie would like to look over the Asylum. As it happens I can introduce him to Doctor Dale. As a matter of fact I do a certain amount of work there. Well, will you come too?" she ended.

"But you've never told me this before," I said. The thought of Gaveston somehow terrified me. I wanted to get out of the expedition if possible.

"It was hardly necessary," said Blanche.

I didn't like to hang back for no reason, and yet I rather dreaded the possible discovery of my being acquainted with a lunatic. I supposed the business of visiting an asylum was all right if Olave was willing to go. I could always trust him to do the proper thing.

"Are you coming?" said Blanche.

"Well, as a matter of fact," I said in desperation, thinking it best to make a clean breast of the thing, "one of my old school chums happens to be there. At least he used to be."

"He still is," said Blanche.

"What?" I cried.

"He's mentioned your name," said Blanche, "but I've never quite known whether he's wanted to see you. But the other day he asked for you."

I turned to Olave with a gesture of abandonment. "You see what a sister I have," I said. But the way in which he looked towards her didn't suggest that he saw her as I had meant him to.

And so we went to St. Jude's; and all the day the feeling of being the outsider strengthened in my mind. It was Olave and Blanche who seemed to be the kindred souls, and I was left out in the cold.

I must say my general impression of the Asylum was one of disgust. Frankly I didn't enjoy the visit at all. It seemed to me that if such things had to be they were best hidden away. There was a suggestion of indecency in drawing the curtain for inquisitive eyes to peep through.

However, I was rather glad to see Gaveston again. Of course he was greatly changed. For one thing he was no longer a boy, though I could hardly call him a man. And strangely enough he was serenely content with his lot. I don't quite know what I had expected to see, but certainly Gaveston didn't resemble in the least my conception of a lunatic. I had seen him at school raving; but here he was calm and placid, and to all appearances perfectly normal. We chatted of old times, though of course I had been told not to mention anything likely to disturb him; so naturally I steered clear of all reference to Avery. It was only when I had turned to go that he clutched me suddenly, making me jump, and looking rather wildly into my eyes he whispered hoarsely, "Don't let them come, Dick; don't let them come."

I suppose I ought to have humoured him, but for the moment I forgot he was mad. "Why, who?" I asked.

A look of terrible fear came into his eyes, and waving his hands as though to keep something away from him he whimpered, "Oh, Dick, I'm so happy; don't let them come, don't let them touch me."

And at that I was taken away, and Doctor Dale explained the case very learnedly to me at great length while I was waiting for Blanche and Olave to join me.

I can't hope to tell you all the doctor said. For one thing it was beyond me, and for another he seemed strangely disturbed and unsatisfied at his own exposition. I remember him repeating over and over in a puzzled way, "It's a curious case, you know, Mr. Bellew; a very curious case."

He pointed out some of the patients. "There," he said, "goes the Empress of China."

"Who?" I exclaimed.

"The Empress of China," he repeated chuckling; as a fat old dame passed haughtily by us shouldering a besom with which she had been sweeping the path. The doctor addressed her as Your Majesty, and sweeping her a bow passed on. I began to wonder whether the attendants were as mad as the patients, but he explained, "You see, that's a simple case. The poor old thing was having too rough a time of it, so she decided to escape from the degrading reality of being Mrs. Sikes by posing as the Empress of China. And then she found the make-belief gave her wonderful consolation, so she persuaded herself to believe the thing was the actual truth. That's quite simple. It's the sort of thing we all do in dreams; and in day-dreams too, if we'd only confess to it. Children, of course, live in a world of their own. Madness, you see, is a carrying into daily life the life of childish or dream-land fantasy. You see that?"

Of course I said, "Yes."

"But then," he went on, his brow puckering as though with annoyance, "your friend's case is different. For days at a time he's just himself. To-day, for instance, anyone might say there's nothing to suggest madness about him. But at other times he's not himself. That is, he becomes an absolutely different personality. And yet if you saw him then you'd still say he wasn't mad. The fact is he's living two lives; but not like the Empress. It's easy to see why she calls herself the Empress of China. It's just because she wants to be something of that sort. But there's no reason for Gaveston wanting to change into his other self. It doesn't serve any purpose of fantasy at all. And the two people are distinct. Neither of them remembers the other."

His voice grew more and more querulous, as though he were trying to beat down some absurd argument that teased him.

"But doesn't he have fits, or anything of that sort?" I asked, remembering the beginning of the affair.

"He used to," he answered, "especially when he was changing. It was as though he were being torn violently from his body. And it was the same when he was coming back to himself. There was the same struggle and upheaval. In fact, it reminded me of," he paused and eyed me doubtfully, "of one of the miracles in the New Testament. You know I sometimes think," he put in confidentially, blushing a little as though not quite at his ease, "I sometimes think they're not all bunkum. At any rate, you remember the account of the lunatic boy, 'And the spirit cried and rent him sore, and came out of him; and he was as one dead.' Well, that's just what it was like with your friend. In fact the old phrase, 'possessed of a devil,' seemed the only explanation."

I felt I was wading in deep waters, and the doctor's evident perplexity didn't reassure me; for I remembered Avery's account of the thing, and I began to wonder whether he had been nearer the truth than I cared to think.

The doctor continued, "But that's all changed. The transitions are still a little difficult, but it looks as though a truce has been called or a bargain struck. It's rather like two quarrelsome children who have learnt to hit it off together. I keep to the dual picture merely as a convenient way of expressing the affair, you understand. But all the same, it's puzzling."

"Any hope of a cure?" I asked, more for the sake of saying something than wanting an answer.

"Well, there again," said the doctor rather fretfully, "it's a difficult case. You see, we can only effect cures with the co-operation of the patients. If we can persuade them to face the facts of the situation they automatically cure themselves. You know," he turned to me with an awkward smile, "that's where your sister comes in useful. She's really rather marvellous. Her ideas are a bit cranky perhaps, but she has a power over some of these people. I can't quite explain it." He paused, gazing out from under his puckered brows, then quickly took up his theme again. "But with Gaveston it's different. He resents interference. I think he's made up his mind to enjoy his half life, instead of making a bid for the whole, which of course would mean an enormous struggle, probably throwing him back into his fits again for a while. But someone with power, now, might do something with him. In fact, your sister would rather like to take the thing in hand. I think she's got someone up her sleeve who would help her."

"What do you mean by power?" I asked. But the arrival of Blanche and Olave cut me off from the answer. And you may be sure I had plenty to think about for the rest of the day, though constantly I tried to rid my mind of the whole matter, telling myself that it was out of my province.

And the day following was the day of the play. I had been promised a surprise, and I got it. First of all, I knew nothing about the play itself. I did learn before the performance that it was by Shelley, but the discovery didn't make the prospect very promising. I expected to be well bored by wearying flights of poetry. So you can understand how the unfolding of the appalling story shook me from my lackadaisical indifference. I was soon in a fine glow of excitement, thrilled to the soul as I had never been before. And yet through it all I felt a strange sense of the unhealthiness of the thing. I didn't want it to stop, but I knew it was bad. It gripped me too powerfully, and I lost all self-control. I was whirled away from my normal world of well-known and well-proved things into a frightful conflict of forces that seemed not human, but symbolic. Blanche's phrase came back to me, "I look upon it as the struggle between good and evil." A strange good, I thought, that was driven to do murder, and a strange evil that in spite of the black and clinging horror that invested it yet drove in with an appeal to the heart, as though calling to kindred impulses long stifled and overlaid, and setting them throbbing once more with old lusts and furies and primal hates.

For gradually the mere story lost its meaning for me, and all my mind was enthralled by the struggle of the Count and Beatrice. I had only a momentary thought to give to Blanche's superb acting. For the time it was not Blanche before me; it was not even Beatrice. It was a visible power wrestling with another visible power; a conflict between the radiance of day and abysmal blackness. And the two were not ranged against each other so much as intertwisted in their combat. It was a writhing grapple of locked forces that somehow oppressed me with the sense of unnameable mystery and immeasurable might. Who were these two terrible antagonists, and what was the significance of their huge strife?

With the death of the Count my interest flagged. At least the feeling of unknown presences and hidden issues in the drama had gone. It became more human. And so I had more leisure to notice Blanche's acting. She had hurled the frightful shadow from her path, and now she was fighting for bare life. There was still a sense of reserve energy behind her words, but the suggestion of strange alliances and baffling influences no longer gave that symbolic significance to all her actions. It was only towards the end that the old thrill set my heart thumping, when she stared down the wretch who would have betrayed her, till he sank dead at her feet.

In fact, looking back, that is the picture most vivid in my memory. I can still feel something of the wonder and horror of the huge struggle I have described, the shock as of electric forces as the two combatants met and closed in their irreconcilable conflict; but even that fades before that one vision of Blanche, drawn tense in her indignation, facing the quailing wretch, and killing him with a look. It seemed to explain the whole play to me. It was only such a force that could meet and vanquish the hellish thing that had risen up against her.

I was rather dazed when the play was over. I don't quite know how I told Blanche what I thought of it all. I expect my words were hopelessly feeble. But it was while I was stuttering out something or other more or less to the purpose, that Olave asked her who took the part of the Count.

"I don't suppose you know him," said Blanche; "he's one of our people. His name's Booth, Avery Booth."

I hadn't the strength to say a word.

It was only when I was alone in my room at last that the strange appropriateness of the thing dawned upon me. Where Avery had appeared from, how he had come to meet Blanche, I didn't question. I merely realized that such a conflict between these two as I had seen that night seemed wonderfully satisfying to my sense of the fitness of things, and that she had ruthlessly killed the evil creature was a climax that thrilled me with a dark content.

CHAPTER V

I knew perfectly well that I ought to slip in a word of warning somehow to put Blanche on her guard against Avery; but though I made many a resolution to do so, even beginning with an, "I say, Blanche," I never succeeded in fulfilling what I knew was just my plain duty. So I went back to Oxford with the word unspoken; but I comforted myself with the thought that Blanche knew well enough how to take care of herself. Her penetrating gaze would bring her to a clearer vision of master Avery's true nature than any words of mine. And then somehow the fact that she had foiled Avery in the play gave me an unreasonable, yet very real, sense of security.

I was glad enough to be back again in sane and care-free surroundings, away from the uneasy restraint of that queer atmosphere which had somehow enveloped my home till everything had become unnaturally tense and constricted. And yet I didn't realize how queer it was until I was free of it, nor how it had teased my nerves, making me curiously sensitive and alert. But it was good to be able to subside into a laxer state of mind, accepting life joyously and easily as I had used to do. And then I had found a new zest in living which for the time effectually banished the memory of Blanche and the mystery that hovered about her.

Olave didn't accompany me back to Oxford. He was senior to me, and had finished his course. For my part, I had no course, properly speaking. I intended to stay as long as the life continued to satisfy me. And for one thing I had made up my mind to win a place in the Eight before I left.

I spent a few days with Olave at Little Hinton before the term began. And there I learnt the secret of my friend's compelling charm. It was just that he was the soul, or the emanation as it were, of his perfectly ordered home. The chaste symmetry of the white stone hall, the satisfying grace of the chestnut avenue sweeping up in a curve to the entrance, and the breadth of smooth lawn sloping away to the circle of woodland cut neatly to a bordering wall—everything was but a reflection of what I already knew of the character of the master himself. It was the perfect harmonizing of grace and strength. And to see Olave among his attendants, or even among his dogs or his horses, was a satisfaction and a delight. There was that complete air of effortless command which is the fine flower of mastership. And so far I had always thought of Olave's rare charm as a triumph of perfect breeding; but now I saw it not so much the outcome of breeding as of breed. For the sense of stability I had always felt behind

38

Olave's tight-knit and shapely but slight little frame was not explained merely by the lands and hall of which he was the master; it was not just the consciousness of possession and the dignity of command which made one aware of underlying forces moving beneath his quiet and reserve; it was this combined with the backing of the generations whose spirit and blood had moulded both the place and the man.

The similarity of our positions struck me as being curious. Olave hadn't told me much about his circumstances, and now I found that, like myself, he had come to his inheritance early; but he had lost his mother as well as his father. Indeed this was the only difference in our positions, for we neither had any brothers, and we each had one sister younger than ourselves.

It was only on my last day at Hinton Hall that I met Olave's sister, for she had been away. I remember now the effect of her coming. Olave and I had just returned from a ride and had sent the horses back to the stables, when she came tripping lightly over the lawn to greet her brother, with a couple of huge bloodhounds leaping beside her. The picture of her slight little figure between those bounding brutes, and the touch of her little hands on their great heads, was a thing to set my heart thumping. She stopped short at the sight of me, and for my part I was devouring her with my eyes. I dare say it was stupid of me, for she was only a child of fifteen or so, with her hair in a great golden plait curling over her shoulder and on to her breast. But child as she was, already the curving delicacy of her body would have been enough to have set a colder heart than mine in a tumult. And her eyes were blue, 1 noticed, like her brother's; but to me they had in them the blue of heaven and the sparkle of the sea. And I know I stood there foolishly enough, gulping in, as it were, the sweet freshness of the picture, till Olave broke the spell.

"Katrina," he said, kissing her, "Mr. Bellew."

She held out her hand to me very frankly, her face lifted full to mine, radiant with a smile of greeting that seemed to be a play of light over every feature. In a strange confusion I clutched the little fingers, and they seemed to crumple up in my grip.

"Ah," she said, her lip quivering, but without turning away her face, "I was told you were strong."

I began to stammer an apology, but she flung an arm round each of the mighty hounds as they nosed up at her face, and said, "I adore strong things."

At that a feeling came to me in a surge of desire that I might have the chance of using my strength to protect this delicious girl from some yet unimagined enemy. My muscles seemed to swell at the thought. I could have prayed for nothing so fervently as for some danger to threaten her that I might have the pride of saving her. For somehow it wasn't merely her loveliness, but her very slightness and delicacy which seemed to set the chords of my whole soul vibrating with an unknown music. And how I envied those huge brutes that bounded at her side! Though how it was they didn't crush her in their boisterous adoration was a marvel to me. But in spite of their leaping and nuzzling they never made her step an inch from her path.

But in a few hours I was away. Yet not before I had lived a lifetime of glory and wonder. The afternoon was radiant with sun and wind, and we spent it for the most part roaming the woods and hills. And I couldn't help comparing the suave gravity of Olave with the rippling lightheartedness of his sister. But the thing that puzzled me was the likeness of the two, rather than their obvious dissimilarity. They had the same blue eyes; yet I was confirmed in my first impression that Katrina's eyes were the very blue of heaven, but Olave's had in them the glint of steel. I think I hit on the mystery of their likeness when I suddenly realized that the secret of Katrina's artless and airy charm was not merely the innocence of maidenhood, nor yet the radiance of health, but the gift of perfect nurture and perfect race.

How it was that I was able to ponder these questions I can't say, for I was supremely conscious all the while of a stupid confusion. And the desire somehow to do battle for Katrina against ogres and dragons and enchanters grew in me like an appetite. I was hungry to do her a service, something violently physical for preference; and I would have given much to have been allowed to jump and play about her like Ravin and Flame, her hounds.

It was the behaviour of these two creatures, I think, which showed me the essential difference between brother and sister, just as the purity of race explained their essential similarity. For they would walk sedately behind Olave, their muzzles low, and their great ears sweeping the earth; but they would run ahead of Katrina, sniffing round angles and corners and tree-trunks and plunging into nooks and shadowy places as though to clear her path of possible dangers.

Well, the parting came all too soon. Katrina had lost something of her gaiety before I had gone, and I chose to regard it as a good sign. And when I said good-bye I took care not to crush her hand again, and she said, "You can be very gentle, Mr. Bellew."

Olave laughed, remarking, "That's not exactly what he's noted for."

At that Katrina threw me a look that set the blood hammering at my ears. I sent a gaze diving into her eyes, but she turned her face away, reddening; and we parted.

So you can understand that I had other matters to think about than Blanche and her affairs. When Olave wrote to me I skimmed the ordinary matter, and plunged for any mention of Katrina. I think he must have seen what was wrong with me, for he cheered me with liberal doses. And I paid a flying visit or two to Hinton Hall, and was greeted with a wonderful welcome by my little lady. I usually found her abroad with Ravin and Flame, and looming mightily in her wake, her attendant Jock, a huge, bearded and kilted Highlander, as dumb and as redoubtable as one of his native mountains. I thought of her words, "I adore strong things." Certainly she was set about with an imposing guard. But I was jealous of Jock and Ravin and Flame; I wanted to supplant them all three, and stand alone her champion confessed against whoever might wish to harm her.

And so I returned to Oxford to dream of Katrina, and train my muscles for the service that might lie ahead. And from Olave's letters I built up a completer picture of her. I even tried, for the first and last time in my life, to write verses. All I learnt was that the poets are right after all in naming girls and flowers in a breath, and setting the expression of love to delicate rhythms. For though of course my own pitiful efforts merely went to choke the grate, yet that much insight into the meaning of poetry I did obtain.

I gathered that Olave had made a journey or two to my home at Chalk Ridge. From suggestions in his letters I might have realized that he was becoming more absorbed in Blanche's spiritualistic concerns than I would have liked. It was the kind of thing I should have known to appeal to him, if I hadn't told myself that his common sense would have kept him aloof. But as a matter of fact I didn't take the trouble to read between the lines. Indeed, I'm afraid I skimmed hastily over everything that didn't center round Katrina. And as to what Blanche and Avery might be up to, I didn't give a single thought.

CHAPTER VI

In spite of all this effervescence of spirits, when I returned to Chalk Ridge the queer atmosphere of the place laid an immediate grip upon me. It had deepened and intensified during the few months I had been away, and I felt it as a palpable thing as soon as I set foot in my home. Perhaps it was because I found my mother more nervous than ever about Blanche's behaviour. But it wasn't her mysterious meetings that troubled her now, nor her peculiar ideas and notions. My mother was worrying more about herself. I thought she was pitying herself a little.

"Oh, Dick," she said, fondling my hand, and smiling weakly up into my face as I stooped to kiss her where she lay on her couch, "Oh, Dick, I'm so glad you've come back. Blanche is so hard, you know," she added. I didn't quite follow the drift of her thought; but I understood when she went on, "You're so much kinder, Dick. You do things for me."

"Ah well, mater," I answered lightly, "Blanche is your nurse, and she knows what's best for you, I dare say. I expect I should spoil you if I had the nursing of you."

"Well," she said wistfully, "it is nice to have things done for you sometimes. But Blanche won't even let me go to bed when I'm tired. Oh, she bullies me dreadfully," she put in smiling. "And yet it's much nicer to lie quietly and do nothing."

"Come," I said, "you'd just fade away if Blanche didn't look after you."

And to tell the truth I was inclined to side with Blanche in this matter. My mother had never rallied since my father had died, and it was clear to me that she would have flickered out long ago if Blanche hadn't taken her in hand. Still, the frail little woman lying there before me, stroking my hand, and fixing me with great eyes full of a nameless fear, rather disturbed me. "Dick," she said, "you won't leave me quite to Blanche, will you?" And she spoke with such a genuine appeal that I fell on my knees beside her and said, "Why, mater, whatever's the matter?"

She put her hands over her eyes, and answered with a little shiver, "Oh, I don't know, Dick; I don't know. But she looks at me."

Well, this sort of thing brought back that old sense of uneasy restraint I had felt before I had left for Oxford that last time. Again I seemed to become strangely alert, jumping stupidly at little noises, and looking behind me in a sudden sort of way as though I thought someone were following me. And it wasn't that I did this kind of thing unconsciously. I was always unpleasantly aware of what I was doing. As I came into a room I would quite deliberately scan every corner of it swiftly to see what might be lurking there, in fact half expecting to see a dipping head pop suddenly down behind the sofa. And sometimes I would throw the door open and step back, as though someone were waiting to spring out at me. But always, as I say, I knew what I was doing, and it was this awareness that troubled me. What was there in the place, I asked myself, to make me behave like a timid child frightened by a ghost story?

I told myself that it must be Blanche's behaviour; but there was nothing in Blanche's behaviour to disturb me in this way. Certainly she seemed to have withdrawn more deeply into herself during the few months that had gone by. There was a rapt look in her eyes, as though she were deep in some mystical meditation; and her words came slowly and gravely, as though her mind were far away, and only travelled back to earth by a deliberate effort. And all this rather upset me. It seemed an unhealthy sort of going on for a girl just touching on twenty. But there was nothing in it to fret me with that sense of alarm which had taken almost immediate possession of me with my return home.

Naturally, my mind turned to Avery. I thought I traced his handiwork. And when I learnt casually from my mother that he had visited the house, I believed I had explained the whole thing. It was his evil influence he had left in the air. I determined to speak to Blanche without fail, and to forbid any further visits from the fellow. Incidentally, I found that others of her queer friends had been hanging round the place; among them Dr. Dale, though I had no particular objection to him. My mother confessed that this partly explained her uneasiness. She didn't like Blanche's friends. She didn't know what they got up to. And Dr. Dale, she said, was as hard as Blanche herself.

Well, I knew this had got to be stopped, but before I had summoned courage to speak to Blanche, she approached me herself on another subject which surprised me enough to shake all thoughts of Avery out of my mind, for the time being at any rate, and which seemed to account largely for Blanche's strange behaviour.

I had noticed her eyes bent queerly on me more than once, and I didn't like the scrutiny. She seemed to be questioning something deep within me. And at last the meaning of it became clear. She said to me one morning, "Dick, I want your help."

"Want my help?" I repeated weakly.

She stood before me, her face lowered, and her fingers playing uneasily together at her breast. But she suddenly drew herself up straight and fixed me with her direct gaze, and said, "I should say, Gaveston needs your help."

"Gaveston!" I exclaimed.

"He needs your help," Blanche repeated simply, but with more emphasis.

"Well, for heaven's sake explain," I cried, for some unknown reason feeling unusually fretful and uncertain of myself.

"Yes, I'll explain," she said quietly. Then again fixing me with that straight gaze she continued, "I'm trying to cure him. It's a hard battle, but he leaves me to do all the fighting. That's no use. He must fight for himself. If you understood the matter, Dick, you'd realize he must fight for himself. It'll mean a terrible struggle for him, I know. But he must be made to brace himself to the effort."

She paused, watching me.

For my part I was left puzzling at the meaning of the thing. "Look here," I said at length, "I simply don't understand a word you're saying."

"Dick, it's simple," she insisted; "just listen to me. I tell you I'm trying to cure Gaveston."

"Well?" I said.

"Oh, I can't go into the whole thing. You wouldn't be able to follow," she said rather wearily, then brightening, went on, "Dick, you can help me."

"Well," I said, shifting my feet uneasily, "what do you want me to do?"

"He's rather fond of you, Dick," she said. "He doesn't like me because I tell him he's got to fight. But he'll listen to you."

"But what have I got to do?" I asked. "Go to him and say, 'Gaveston, old chap, you've got to fight'? Well, what against?"

"He knows what against, well enough," she answered. "He's weak, you see. It's easier letting things stay as they are. And of course there's a risk. He'd have to pass back through his old madness, I expect. But we've power enough to pull him through."

The memory of Gaveston's appeal to me became clear now. And somehow I sympathized with the little fellow. His life had been spoilt by another's meddling, and no wonder if he wasn't willing to submit to further experimenting. What Blanche intended to do, and how she had obtained permission to interfere with the case at all, I didn't know and didn't inquire. But I guessed her treatment, whatever it was, would be drastic enough, from her saying that he would have to pass back through his old madness. And I remembered something of Dr. Dale's exposition of the case which seemed to confirm my impression of a serious time ahead for Gaveston if Blanche were allowed to work her will on him. His words came back to me with pitiful appeal, "Don't let them touch me." It seemed better to leave well alone, so I said, "He's quite contented as he is. Why bother him?"

Something happened behind Blanche's eyes. "That's weakness," she said, "and you know it is."

Strangely enough I did know it. It became startling clear to me that I was taking the coward's part. Yet throbbing deep within me was the feeling that all this tampering with incomprehensible things was monstrous. I tried to express myself, but all I could say was, "Yes, I know."

"Well then," said Blanche, "you'll help me."

But I broke away from her, and immediately saw the case plainly again in a common-sense light. "No," I cried, "no. You're playing with fire."

She waited till I had become calm again, for I had started striding up and down the room. She laid her hands on my shoulders, bringing me to a standstill; and once more looking full into my eyes said, "Dick, you must help me. It's not a matter of saving a life, but a soul. You must help me, Dick, you must help me."

What was happening to me I didn't quite know just at first, but I felt I was going to yield, in spite of a sort of muffled voice deep down in my heart crying out against the wickedness of the thing. Then I remember a horrible suspicion leapt into my mind. Blanche still had her hands on my shoulders, and her eyes were steadily searching mine, but I threw her hands off and pushed her away from me. "Blanche," I cried, digging my fists into my eyes, for somehow I felt dazed and bewildered, "don't play those tricks on me."

When I looked round she had collapsed weakly on to a chair, her hands drooping, and her arms hanging limply at her sides.

"Blanche," I said, going quickly up to her, "what is it?"

She recovered herself, and smiling rather faintly said, "I'm sorry, Dick. I didn't know."

"Didn't know?" I questioned.

"Never mind," she replied with an effort at lightness. "It's just that I find myself doing it when I don't mean to." And suddenly changing her tone to one of sisterly endearment she said, "But you will help me, won't you, Dick?" She stroked my hand and added, "At any rate, you'll come round and see Gaveston?"

Well, I couldn't refuse her that much, so I consented. She rose rather languidly, and sighing said, "Dick, do you ever feel tired? I mean dreadfully tired, weary, so that you almost long for death?"

"Good God!" I exclaimed laughing, though I didn't like the question, "anyone'd think you were an old woman, Blanche."

At that she smiled brightly enough and said, "Oh, well, I do feel like that sometimes, Dick. I did just now. I find things rather exhausting. It's the old story, I suppose, of virtue going out of you." Then she added suddenly, "Dick, do you ever study the miracles? Do you know, I find them perfectly wonderful."

"Well, of course," I said simply, and she broke away laughing like a schoolgirl.

But our visit to St. Jude's was fruitless. Gaveston didn't know me. He had passed to his other self, and I hardly even knew him. It seemed incredible that such a meek, gentle little face could be distorted into such a hideous caricature of itself. For the charm of timid simplicity which had somehow attracted me in him had changed to a loathsome leer of cunning malignity. The little figure, too, was hunched and twisted into a horrible deformity. The fingers were hooked, claw-like, and the wretched creature kept dragging them slowly through his hair, twisting a matted hank half over one eye. And there was something funny about the eyes which I couldn't understand. It wasn't merely that they were fierce and cruel; somehow they weren't the eyes of Gaveston. And the hateful thing peered up at me, and grinned, and bowed its head with fawning deference, and chattered, till I felt physically sick.

Blanche's comment was, "Now you'll help me, won't you, Dick?"

"But I can't understand," I said.

"You see, that's what he's got to fight against," she said.

"Then he hasn't a dog's chance," I replied.

"Yes, if we supply the power," she said; and added, "But he must brace himself for the battle."

But my thought was to escape to Hinton Hall as soon as possible, away from this diseased atmosphere, and freshen my heart again with the sweet, clean fragrance of Katrina.

CHAPTER VII

Next morning I said a rather shame-faced good-bye to my mother, who took a lingering hold of my hand, saying, "You'll come back soon, won't you, Dick?" As I left the house I had to call up the vision of Katrina to drive out the haunting memory of my mother's appealing gaze reaching out after me as I had turned away from her. But driving through the gates and winding out into the open road I drew a mighty breath of relief, and tried to crush down the feeling at my heart that I was running away like a coward. Well, it was good to be racing through the wide country with Katrina at the end of the road.

As I turned into the visitors' room at Hinton Hall I caught the sound of music from somewhere within the house. But it stopped abruptly, I supposed as my arrival was announced, and Katrina herself came running in to greet me.

"Oh, Dick," she cried, "Dick, I am glad you've come."

For the moment the surge of exultation at my heart at hearing my Christian name cried in such a tone of welcome prevented me from noticing the trouble in her voice, and in her eyes too, lifted wildly to mine.

"Katrina!" I exclaimed.

Then I realized that there was something dreadfully wrong.

"Why," I cried in alarm, "what is it?"

"Oh, I don't quite know," she said, and the words seemed strangely familiar. "But I'm glad you've come," she added more brightly, treating me to one of her real smiles. Then she broke lightly away from me and ran to the window. "Look," she cried, "it's splendid outside. Shall we go for a tramp?"

"Rather," I assented.

"I hate indoors," she said, turning to me again. "I feel safer in the open."

"Safer?" I questioned.

"Well, freer," she said.

"Yes, I know what you mean," I replied. "You don't feel there are things behind you."

"Things watching you," she added.

Now all this time there seemed to be something peculiar about Katrina. It wasn't merely that there was something troubling her. That was evident enough, and I promised myself the pleasure of getting her to confide in me when we were well out on our tramp. The thing that puzzled me was rather something that was missing; and while we were speaking, my mind was busy trying to get on the track of it. And suddenly I knew.

"Katrina," I asked, venturing a repetition of the familiar name, "where are the dogs?"

"Poor old things!" she cried. "But we'll have them out again."

"You know," I said, smiling, "you're like a picture out of its frame without them."

"I feel as though I've been left alone all of a sudden balanced on a tight-rope," she replied. Then dancing to the door, "Come," she cried gaily, "I won't have them chained up. It's a shame."

"Chained up?" I asked. "Whatever for?"

She stopped at the door, and opening it slowly stood for a moment listening. Then she closed it again quietly, and coming up to me said in a hushed way, "I'll tell you, Dick. It's because of Olave's new friend. He met him . . . "

"Good God!" I cried, an inexplicable fear at my heart, "Avery!"

"You know him?" she asked.

"Katrina," I exclaimed, "do you mean to say he's here?" But before she could answer I had rushed to the music-room, and flinging the door open broke in. It was empty. I turned, and came face to face with Katrina, who had followed me.

"Where is he?" I cried.

"Dick," she said, "whatever's wrong?"

"Where is he?" was all I could say.

She went to the French window which stood open, and looking out said, "There, he's just disappearing."

I rushed to the window, and saw the vanishing figure merge darkly into the belt of woodland that closed the lawn in like a wall.

I sat down feeling strangely faint. Katrina came and stood in front of me, looking at me questioningly.

"Dick," she said, "you make me feel rather frightened."

"Oh, Katrina, I'm sorry," I cried, springing up. "You mustn't be frightened," I added rather stupidly, not knowing what to say.

"You see," she said seriously, "you behave just like my dogs. I mean," she added quickly with a little laugh, "as soon as they saw him they growled dreadfully. In fact Ravin sprang right at him. But you know . . . But it was rather horrible," she broke off shuddering, and covered her eyes with her hands.

"Katrina," I said, "you must tell me everything."

"Oh yes, Dick, I will," she answered me simply. "But you see he just looked at him. Like that. No, I can't show you how. And the poor old thing just crumpled up and cried. He did indeed, Dick. He crept to my feet and whimpered like a baby. I think he was hurt right in his heart."

"He was afraid," I said.

"Yes," she replied, "but something more. He was hurt. Oh, I don't know what it was. But it was dreadful. So you see I had to chain them up."

"Does he come here often?" I asked.

"He's been twice," she said. "But to-day Olave wasn't in. So I had him to myself. I . . . I rather like him in a way. He has wonderful eyes. But I feel afraid. He plays the violin, you know, and it seems to go right into my soul. Oh, I don't know," she broke off in her bright, girlish way, "It all sounds very silly. Let's go for a good old scamper."

And she was away before I could speak the warning on my lips.

I found her at the kennels, with Ravin and Flame leaping joyously about her, glad to be free. As I turned the corner they came bounding up to me, fiercely enough, I thought, but they recognized me as an old friend and seemed to greet me with unusual zest. So we set off for the hills. And Katrina, turning to look behind her, said, "And there's dear old Jock too. He's always on guard. Now I feel safe again." She seemed to snuggle into herself contentedly, and added, "You know, in bed I never feel safe until I've got the clothes right over my shoulders."

But with the breath of the hills about her she seemed to come out of the strange shadow that had closed her round, and was soon the radiant-hearted creature I had learned to look to for the freshening of my own clouded soul.

We returned through the woods, and it was here that Ravin and Flame, scouting on ahead, simultaneously let out a terrible deep-throated bay. It was so sudden, and not only sudden but so pained and ominous, that Katrina gripped me convulsively, and old Jock, with his huge hand tightened about his stick, lumbered past us after the hounds. I would have followed, but Katrina held to me and said "Stay with me, Dick," in such a frightened voice that I couldn't leave her. And strangely enough, although there seemed nothing to be alarmed at, my heart was thumping uneasily.

"Come," I said lightly, "it's some poacher."

But Katrina answered firmly, "No, it's not that." And we stepped on after Jock whom we could hear beating his way through the undergrowth and calling to the hounds.

And suddenly we came upon them. Jock in a daze was stupidly look-ing down at the hounds, at a loss to understand their antics. For the great creatures were stretched flat to earth, cringing and whimpering as though expecting the lash. Katrina fell on her knees and threw an arm about them, and they lifted their heads and nuzzled up to her, whining piteously; and gradually they rose to their feet, but with their tails curled tight between their legs, and began licking her and digging their great muzzles under her arms.

"You see," said Katrina, raising a serious face to mine, "they're hurt."

"Hurt?" I said. "I don't think so. They're just frightened at something."

"Ah, no," she answered, "I mean they're hurt right in their hearts. I expect they're ashamed at being frightened. But they just can't help it."

She rose and made to move on, but the hounds flung themselves in her path, and began again that unearthly whining. Clearly they scented danger on ahead. So we turned back the way we had come. But Jock wasn't to be daunted. He strode forward into the brushwood, and I wished I could have gone with him, for the longing to do battle for Katrina was strong in me. We waited for him, and he returned in a few minutes. He had scouted to the road, but had seen nothing.

Taking up our path where we had left it we were soon clear of the woods, and before us the lawn sloped graciously up to the Hall. After a few paces I turned to look behind me, and stopped with a sudden thought gripping at my mind. "Katrina," I said, "that's where he vanished."

"Yes," she answered, "I know."

"Well, then?" I was at a loss what to do. It was Avery's trail that had set the hounds whimpering. They simply couldn't follow, though the scent called to them. I would certainly have made after him, but Jock had already scouted to the road, and the coast was clear.

"Didn't you know?" Katrina asked me.

"I'm very dull," I answered. "It hadn't occurred to me."

As we stood there the hounds began circling round us, growling uneasily. I noticed the fear in their upward-peering eyes; and again their tails were drawn in tight between their legs. A sudden impulse mastered me. "Seize him!" I cried to them, and started running back towards the wood. I heard Katrina's voice raised in terrified alarm behind me, calling me back. But the hounds leapt forward ahead of me, nose to earth and baying terribly. I suppose my example had heartened them. But they had hardly reached the edge of the woodland before they stopped and fell to earth cringing and whining as they had done before, and when I called to them they came creeping back so obviously ashamed of themselves that I pitied them from my heart. They circled away from me, afraid of being punished,

I expect, but I called them and patted them, and they trotted off looking more like themselves.

"Dick," said Katrina, "whatever made you do it?"

"I don't quite know," I answered.

"Why," she said, "if they had caught him . . ."

"Well," I replied, with some heat, "I wish to God they would. It would ease my heart of a mighty load, I can tell you. But he doesn't seem in any danger by the look of things," I added bitterly.

"Oh, Dick, what does it all mean?" she asked me, looking up with troubled eyes. "I don't like it, I don't like it."

"Nor do I, Katrina," I said. "But it means that you must steer clear of Avery, that's all. The dogs don't trust him; and that's always a bad sign. You see, he's dangerous."

I might have said more, but just then Olave came out from the Hall to meet us.

"Dick!" he cried. "Splendid! They told me you had come. I was keeping a look-out for you."

So we went in together, and at the first opportunity I opened my heart to him on the happenings of the day. "You've just got to keep your door shut tight against that fellow," I ended.

Olave was quiet a minute or two, and then said, "Well, I never feel quite at my ease with him. But Blanche has a great opinion of him, you know, and I rather put faith in her judgment of people. She has a way of looking right in."

"I suppose she introduced you?" I said.

"Yes," he answered, and told me something of his dealings with Blanche's spiritualistic friends. "Of course," he said, "I'm quite a novice, and I'm afraid I'm inclined to criticize too much. But there's certainly a lot in it. And it helps in one's daily life. You get a sort of power, a grip of things, a steadiness; I don't quite know how to put it."

"It seems to me," I said, "that there's not much steadiness about it. Frankly, Olave, it looks like a cranky craze. It's not healthy. It's not sane."

He answered me gravely enough, "Certainly it's inclined to have such an aspect. There are extremists, of course. But on the whole it's deepening, satisfying."

"Avery," I said, "is one of the extremists, I suppose."

"I should say he's a class apart," Olave replied. "He has power. I don't know that it's quite the kind of power a man ought to have. Still, there it is. In the old days he would certainly have been burnt for having dealings with the Devil."

"The good old days!" I exclaimed.

Olave turned to me very seriously. "Dick," he said, "frankly, do you hate him to that pitch?"

"Hate him?" I cried. But before I could say how much, Olave interrupted, "All right; I see. And perhaps you're right. But I can't turn him down just on hearsay."

"Oh, Olave," I pleaded, "you must. You must shut your doors against him, tight! You must shun him like the plague. If not, then God help us all, for something terrible will come of it."

It was on the tip of my tongue to say what I knew of Gaveston's case, but some scruple of conscience told me that wouldn't be playing the game. So I contented myself with speaking as solemn a warning as I could. After all, the queer business of the hounds' behaviour should have been enough to have put Olave on his guard, and I trusted that that together with his own suspicions of him would prevail to make him steer clear of Avery in future. And meanwhile, I determined that nothing should prevent me from thrashing the whole matter out with Blanche as soon as I got home. I began to see that my cowardly procrastination might have more serious consequences than I had imagined. To tell the truth, I was a little afraid.

Before I left, Olave took me to the Hall Chapel. He wanted to show me a sculptured monument which had just been set in place over his father's tomb. I had never been in the chapel before. It was drawing on towards dusk, and the evening light only filtered dimly through the high windows, giving to the place a strangely shadowy effect. And after the sinister happenings of the day I felt unpleasantly disturbed as I stood there with the white marble figures and ghostly columns about me standing up faintly luminous in the twilight. Indeed I think I shivered as though a cold wind had caught me, and certainly I started almost with a cry as I felt a hand touch me from behind. I sprang round, only to see Katrina, who had crept in after us.

Her eyes seemed to glow darkly through the dusk. She looked up at me and whispered. "You don't like it? Nor do I."

Olave hadn't spoken a word. He simply led on to his father's tomb and waited there, while I followed slowly, peering about me at the shadowy memorials, and feeling a strange sense of hovering presences in the ghost-haunted air. But Katrina's hand upon my arm, and her evident sympathy with my uneasiness, comforted me.

We were soon at the place where Olave awaited us. Without a word he stood aside for me to examine the work. Understanding nothing I read the inscription, and cast an uncomprehending look at the heavy mass of marble that lay like a load upon the tomb. I remember that it was carved about with figures, but what they were I didn't observe. My mind was stupidly numbed by the mysterious atmosphere of the place.

Presently Olave advanced. What he did I don't know, but the whole monument began sliding back to the wall, and I found myself looking down into a dark pit at my feet; and then I realized that something was rising up towards me. It assumed shape, and I saw it was a coffin. It was lying on a stone slab which rose and fitted exactly into the gap in the floor. The whole process was so quiet, almost stealthy, and seemed so like some dark and secret ceremony, that the feeling of dismay deepened at my heart. And then the sight of the coffin rising so mysteriously from the grave, and the thought of the silent figure that lay within, filled me with a sense of disgust. I didn't like it. And it was an immense relief to me when the thing began to sink again, and the monument came sliding back to its place and hid it from my sight.

As I left the chapel I found myself wiping my brow. Olave hadn't spoken a word inside, and he added no comment now. He seemed absorbed, indeed, with his own thoughts. It was Katrina who explained it all to me in a hushed voice. "It was Olave's idea," she said. "He hates the clumsy way coffins are usually lowered. You know, straps and things. When father was buried he just sank into the earth quietly like that. It's rather nice, I think. But it made me dream. It was so mysterious, like a mouth swallowing him."

Well, once in my car, and speeding home through the gathering twilight, I shook off the darker impressions of the day. I fixed my thoughts on Katrina, letting my imagination play about the future. She had called me Dick. She had been glad to see me. The sweet little figure danced before me all the way to Chalk Ridge, deliciously desirable. And her parting words sang like a melody in my heart, "Come again soon, Dick, come again soon."

CHAPTER VIII

It was late enough when I arrived home, and I was surprised to find Dr. Dale with Blanche in the drawing-room. He rose and said he must be going when I entered the room. I was feeling tired, and I dare say a little shaken after the events of the day, and I didn't attempt to hinder his departure. In fact, I stood at the door and held it open for him. But it was clear that he was in no hurry. Also there seemed to be something on his mind that he was trying to get said. He hummed and haed, and then came out with, "Miss Bellew and I have been having a talk."

"Yes," I said, though not very encouragingly.

I threw a glance at Blanche. She stood grave and impassive, and I could read nothing in her countenance.

"It's a matter of psychology," the doctor continued.

"Oh," I cried, "then you'd better leave me out of it."

"Well," he said, "but it concerns you rather nearly."

I saw he intended to stay till he had delivered himself; so I closed the door, drew up a chair, and sat down. The doctor too resumed his seat, but Blanche remained standing. For a moment I thought she was going to leave us alone, but her mind seemed to change; for she took a step towards the door, hesitated, and turned back again, and stood resting one arm on the mantelpiece.

"Well, what is it, doctor?" I asked, wishing to come to grips with the business.

"It's a matter of strain," he said. "Your sister's wearing herself out. Let me tell you, Mr. Bellew," he leant forward and spoke very emphatically, "there's no labour in the world so fatiguing as psychical concentration."

"I'm afraid I've never tried it," I said lightly.

"That's why you're so perfectly fit," he replied; and went on, "I don't suppose I can make myself quite clear to you. In the first place I'm not sure how far I may reveal certain things." He looked to Blanche, but her expression gave him no answer. "Well," he resumed, "I suppose I must confine myself to hinting. There are certain practices which may be quite harmless and even laudable, but they leave the whole mind and body in a state of utter exhaustion, bordering indeed on collapse. Now I've been pleading with your sister to curtail her spiritual labours. Honestly, Mr. Bellew, I'm frightened at what may happen if she indulges, or rather martyrizes, herself as she has been doing lately. You're an athlete, and you know the danger of overtraining. Well, it's something of the same sort of thing, you see. Only a collapse of the psychical forces is apt to be more serious than a strained muscle, or even a strained heart."

"Well," I said, "all this is rather incomprehensible to me. I'm afraid you leave me guessing, doctor." Then turning to Blanche I said, "What's it all about, Blanche?"

She merely raised her brows, and the doctor continued with a little laugh, "There, that's about as much as I can get out of her. When your sister's made up her mind, you know . . ." He didn't finish the sentence.

"Well, look here, doctor," I said, "we'll just pretend she isn't here. Now what's she been doing? What's it you want her to give up?"

He shifted in his seat rather uneasily, throwing an inquiring glance or two at Blanche. I had an idea and asked, "Is it all this business at the Asylum?"

"Well, no," he answered, "that's good, useful work. And really, Mr. Bellew, I must say your sister's perfectly marvellous in matters of that kind. I must confess, it beats me. Though, of course, as an unprejudiced scientific man I can't accept her explanation of things. And it isn't even your mother's case that's bothering me."

"My mother's case?" I asked quickly.

He opened wide eyes on me. "Surely," he said, "you know . . ." and stopped.

"What?" I asked.

He turned a slow gaze on Blanche, and answered.

"Well, of course your mother would have been dead these three years if your sister hadn't kept her alive."

"You mean nursed her?" I said.

"Good God, no!" he cried. "She's just refused to let her die. Willed her to live, if you like. And that means the expense of enormous energy, Mr. Bellew."

"Yes," I said weakly, "I suppose it does."

Blanche, I noticed, had a strange little smile playing about her lips. But somehow I didn't like to look at her. There seemed something unnatural in discussing her in this way before her own silent image.

But the doctor went on. "But that's not the trouble. That's good work, you see. It's all this fancy business. At least," he added quickly, "to my uninitiated mind it seems a fancy business." He threw up a propitiatory look to Blanche, and it wasn't till that moment that I had my first suspicion that the fellow was in love with her. Somehow that seemed to discount his words some ninety per cent., for I thought I could see in them a middle-aged man's fussy attentions to a girl still in the full flush and energy of enthusiastic youth. In fact, I hardly listened to him now. I began to side with Blanche. For if there was anything I hated it was the well-meant warnings of the elderly and debile not to over-exert and overstrain.

He was saying, "She must reserve her strength for the things that matter."

"Well," I put in, hardly restraining a yawn, "what's she been doing? Calling up the dead, or what?"

He stared at me in a sudden, questioning sort of way, and said solemnly enough, "You may be nearer the truth than you think, Mr. Bellew. Though, of course, as an unbiased scientific man . . ."

At that I laughed outright. As a matter of fact, I was tired and had lost control of myself. Also the discovery of his preposterous motive had taken all value out of the thing.

"I suppose you're afraid of a ghost being let loose on you," I chaffed him stupidly. "Well," I went on with a chuckle, "I don't think I should bother. They seem to lie pretty close as a rule." And I quoted,

> "The undiscovered country from whose bourne
>   No traveller returns."

"But," said Blanche very quietly, and the unexpectedness of her voice startled me, "one did return in the very same play. And he had a very real message to deliver."

She was eyeing me strangely, and I felt her words had a meaning that hovered beyond my grasp.

But I answered laughing, "Of course you've got me there, Blanche. I didn't know it came from a play."

The thing seemed to me to belong to some schoolboy memory. I suppose I had heard it in class when I wasn't paying too much attention.

And then the doctor rose at last. "I thought I ought to warn you," he said. "She mustn't overdo it." His fatherly smile and sloppy head-shake confirmed my belief that he was in love with the girl. And as he said goodnight to her I thought I understood how it was that Blanche had managed to get a footing in the Asylum.

Well, I was glad when the door closed behind him.

I would have gone straight to bed, but it seemed that Blanche wanted to say her word now.

"Dick," she said, resting her hands on my shoulders, "you know that's all nonsense, don't you?"

"I'm not so sure," I answered. "You told me yourself that sometimes you feel tired enough to lie down and die. At least it was something of that sort. Now didn't you?"

"But I don't die," she said, smiling frankly enough. "And I don't look very ill, do I?"

"My God, Blanche," 1 exclaimed, "I don't understand you. Sometimes you're as mysterious as the Sphinx, and sometimes you're just as charming a girl as one could wish to see."

"And which do you like best?" she asked, her eyes shining roguishly.

"I can tell you this," I answered. "I haven't heard of a Sphinx winning a husband."

"Ah, a husband!" she said, breathing deeply, and filling the name with such a wonderful music that I exclaimed, "Good Lord, Blanche, are you in love?"

She broke from me laughing. "Not with the doctor, at any rate." At which I laughed too. Then she turned to me again and kissed me with an unusual passion, and drawing back, said, "Now get along to bed. You're looking dreadfully tired. I did want to speak with you, but to-morrow will do."

"And I've a word to say to you as well," I answered. And we separated for the night.

So the next morning there was no need for preliminaries. "Come along," I said to Blanche after breakfast, "let's get on with our confab."

"Very well," she said, "what's it you want to say to me?"

"Oh," I answered, sheering away from the issue, "you begin."

She smiled rather strangely at me, and said, "Well, I suppose it comes to the same thing. You want to speak to me about Avery, don't you?"

"Now, how in the name of wonder did you guess that?" I cried.

"What's it you want to say about him?" she put me off, and she was looking at me very steadily.

"Just that he's an infernal scoundrel," I exclaimed hotly, "and you must have exactly nothing to do with him."

"Oh, well," she answered calmly, "we'd better talk this out. There's to be a battle, I see."

"A battle?" I said. "I hope not, Blanche. You must take my word in this matter. I was at school with him, remember."

"But schoolboy faults shouldn't shadow one's whole life," she answered firmly.

I took a turn up and down the room. "Blanche," I said at length, "what makes you want to stand up for him?"

"Because I know something of the tremendous issues at stake," she answered so quickly that I stopped in my pacing and gazed at her questioningly.

"Well," I said, "what?"

"Oh, just everything," she replied.

"Good God, Blanche," I began to fume, "can't you give me a plain answer? Why will you always veil things up in this way? It's enough to make a fellow distrust your behaviour."

"All right, Dick," she said soothingly. "I won't tease you. But honestly," and the firm note came back to her voice, "absolutely everything's at stake. You ought to know enough of Avery to realize that he can be dangerous."

"But," I said fretfully, "that's just what I want you to understand."

"Yes, Dick, yes, I know," she said, "and I do understand it. But I understand it so well that I want to prevent it. Can't you see that the best way to deal with a dangerous enemy is to make him a friend?"

"Do you mean," I began, hardly trusting my ears, "do you mean . . ." But I couldn't finish the sentence. The implication in Blanche's words of a cowardly fawning to the fellow made me dumb with dismay. But she chimed in with a long-suffering sigh, "Oh, Dick, when will you learn to distinguish analogy from fact? But look here, old stupid, you must understand me; it's so important. Now just listen. I suppose you look upon people as either good or bad."

"Of course," I said.

"Of course," she repeated. "Well, Dick, I suppose there's such a thing as fighting down the evil in one's nature."

"If you mean that Avery," I began. But she took me up with sudden energy, "Yes, Dick, that's just what I do mean. And it's what you've got to understand. The whole issue hangs on that. There are some people who are naturally good, and some who are naturally bad. But there are others who merely have powers which may be swayed by the least little accident either way. And it's the least little accident which determines the whole course of a life. And when you look to the end, and see the frightful gulf which divides the evil and the good in the last resort, well, it makes you realize something of the enormous importance to be set on that little determining accident."

"But, Blanche," I asked, "what's this got to do with Avery?"

"Yes, indeed, what?" she continued with the same fierce energy. "Can't you see, Dick, Avery's still balanced on the ridge. A touch, and over he goes, and nothing will alter his course. And a man with such powers . . . Well, it means the making of an archangel or a devil."

"My dear Blanche," I said, "you needn't fret yourself. He's started on his journey long ago. In fact, I should have thought he'd pretty well reached the end by now."

"Then you're utterly wrong, Dick," she insisted passionately. "You judge by some stupid little schoolboy mistake . . ."

"Pardon me," I broke in more warmly, "I tell you, Blanche—and you needn't trouble to dispute my word—I'm not talking about any little mistake. I'm talking about crime. And indeed crime doesn't cover it. It's real deep-down wickedness. Not moral, merely. But utter naked evil."

"I know, Dick, I know," she said. "You mean about Gaveston."

"Good God!" I cried, starting back. "You know, and you call it a little schoolboy mistake!"

"But, Dick," she took me up, "he didn't know what he was doing. And he wants to repair the wrong."

"What," I cried, "he's still on Gaveston's tracks, is he?" And then something seemed to stir at my memory, something Doctor Dale had said. "Blanche," I exclaimed, seizing her by the wrists, "tell me, is it Avery who's helping you in your experiments on Gaveston?"

"He's helping me to cure him," she replied, facing me steadily.

I dropped her wrists and turned away, for I couldn't endure her eyes. "Well, then," I flung over my shoulder, "you'd better give him warning through me. If he sets foot in St. Jude's again, or attempts in any way to tamper with Gaveston, I'll declare what I know of the business and have him hounded away."

There was silence for a minute or two. I walked to the window, feeling stupidly shaken and indignant. And the worst of it was I knew the battle wasn't over.

"Dick," Blanche said at length, speaking quietly, "you'll think that over and not ask me to give that message."

I swung round on her and cried, "I'll be damned if I'll think it over." And then I felt bitterly ashamed of myself, and mumbled an apology.

Blanche sat down and faced me steadily. She looked weak and limp enough sitting there, her hands drooping at her sides, but the vigour of her gaze told me that her will wasn't conquered.

"Dick," she said in the same quiet way, "you're like a child playing with enormous explosives. Honestly, you simply don't know what you're doing. A word from you now may determine not only the fate of a single soul, though that's a grave enough responsibility, but the fate of thousands of lives, it may be; all those, indeed, who'll ever come in touch with Avery. You know something of his power. But you can't guess at a tithe of its real significance. And all that power you can let loose at a word for unimagined good or unimagined evil. With such a one as Avery there's no middle way."

I must confess my confidence in my own judgment was shaken. Blanche spoke with such conviction, that my memories of Avery at school, the picture of Gaveston's transformation in the Asylum, the events even of the day before at Hinton Hall, could not determine me in a settled opposition to her. I fumed weakly while she watched me with grave steady eyes. And suddenly I stopped in front of her with a sharp suspicion stabbing at my heart. "Blanche," I said hoarsely, "do you love the fellow?"

But she sprang up and exclaimed, "God forbid!" with such fervour that I fell back a pace, gazing at her, and marvelling confusedly at the incomprehensible ways of women.

She sank back on to her chair, unclasping her clenched hands, and said quietly, "No, Dick, no; I don't love him."

Well, I didn't understand the little outburst, but its effect upon me was to break the spell she had cast over me. Again I felt the rightness of my conduct. Blanche's pleading for Avery appeared to me not only unreasonable but useless. Avery had chosen his course years ago. There was no question of sending him to the Devil merely by frustrating him in the matter of Gaveston. And thinking of Gaveston I could hear the little fellow pleading with me not to let them touch him. Well, I would defend him. Avery could practice his evil mysteries elsewhere. I had seen the fruit of his tampering with Gaveston. For all I knew, that hideous transformation was some creature of his own he had summoned from the underworld to second him in his black purposes. Blanche was being duped. He had no intention of undoing his wrong. Rather his scheme was to confirm it, and create for himself a frightful ally for some dark and inscrutable ends of his own.

Well, so I reasoned, any way. And I turned to Blanche and said, "Look here, I've made up my mind, so we needn't discuss the thing any more. You'll just give Avery that warning from me. He's to go."

Blanche sprang towards me and cried, "No, Dick, no. You mustn't, you really mustn't. Oh, Dick, you don't know what'll come of it. It'll be frightful, frightful." She caught my arms, digging her fingers fiercely into me in the intensity of her pleading. But I wouldn't look her into the eyes. I'm afraid I shook myself free none too gently, for she was gripping me with a passion, and leaving the room I put an end to the discussion with an abrupt, "Well, that's my last word."

Half turning as I went I caught sight of her white face very tense and drawn, the lips parted, and the dark eyes straining out in an agony.

Need I say I hesitated, and felt half drawn back to her? But the cry of Gaveston still echoed in my heart, and Katrina's hounds flattened in terror at the mere scent of Avery's trail rose up in a vivid picture before me; and all my disgust of him surged up in my soul. So I took a hold of my resolution, and stepped on.

Behind me I heard Blanche say very faintly, "Oh, Dick!"

CHAPTER IX

But Blanche wasn't to be beaten so easily. I thought I had settled the matter, but I soon found I had a second and a third attack to repulse, for Blanche would return to the conflict with unabated vigour in spite of my protestations that it was all useless. As a matter of fact, I found it difficult enough to remain firm. Blanche had such a way of hinting that dark and terrible issues depended on my single will in the affair that I became nervous in spite of myself, and felt my confidence strangely shaken. But I knew all the while that my mind was made up, and however she would plead and threaten, and though at times I felt a leaning towards concession, the result was inevitable. I had delivered my ultimatum, and I meant to abide by it. And when closely pressed I always had the refuge of firing a parting shot from the door and slamming it behind me.

It was nearly time for me to return to Oxford when I declared that unless Blanche delivered my message to Avery immediately I would reveal all I knew of Gaveston's case to Doctor Dale, and so put an effectual check to Avery's tampering with him any more. And Blanche consented with a sigh, realizing, I suppose, that she had lost the battle. As she left me she turned with her lips parted, and I thought she was about to make a further appeal to me. I stiffened for the attack. But she merely gazed at me sadly, and as it seems to me now as I look back upon it, with a far look of prophecy in her eyes. Then bowing her head as though to an unjust judgment, she turned slowly and left me. And as she went, a terrible prompting came to me to call her back and submit my will to hers after all, but I clenched my fists and set my teeth, and fought down the stupid relenting, which I knew was merely a weak pity; and so I let her go.

But I was unsettled for the rest of the day until she returned, late in the evening, looking utterly shaken and broken in spirit.

"Good God!" I cried, "What is it? What has he done to you?"

She faced me very quietly for a minute, and then said, "I don't quite know what it means, Dick. He merely said, 'Never a second time; tell him that.' He said you'd know what it meant."

She fell limply into a chair, as though weak with fatigue.

For myself, I was living over again that old scene at school when Avery himself had pleaded with me to let him save Gaveston. I knew his words referred to that, and I could aim well enough at their meaning. Why I felt an ominous stirring at my heart I can't say, unless it was the suggestion of finality about the words, as though something had come to an end, or perhaps a chance had been lost which would never return.

Blanche had raised her face to mine, still pale and weak from weariness. "Well," she said in a colourless voice, as though she hardly had the energy to frame the question, "do you know what it means, Dick?"

I moved uneasily, though with an effort of nonchalance, and answered, "Oh, he just means that the whole matter's ended."

"Ah," she sighed, "I could have told you that much." She drooped her head forward into her hands while I paced the room for my better comfort, for I was unpleasantly disturbed by something I couldn't name, and standing still I seemed to become gradually closed about by a clinging atmosphere that oppressed and numbed me till even my fingers stiffened, and I was afraid so much as to turn my head. My only relief was in violent pacing to keep my muscles on the move.

Then Blanche lifted her face again, and I saw that something of her old life and power had returned to her eyes. It was audible in her voice too, when she said, "Dick, I want to know what he meant."

"Why," I answered rather fretfully, "I've told you. I suppose he means that he doesn't intend to make any useless appeal. He knows I mean what I say. That's all."

She looked at me with a growing fire in her eyes, and suddenly springing from her chair she gripped me by the shoulders, and cried, "Oh, Dick, but there may be a chance still. Even if he's too proud to appeal, I'm not. Oh, let me go to him, Dick, and tell him you won't do this thing. Dick, let me. I could go now."

"Blanche," I said in amazement, "you've hardly the strength to get to your room."

"True, Dick," she answered, "if I'm to go there with such a weight on my heart. But I could run back to Avery if it was to tell him . . ."

"Blanche," I cut in sharply, "this is perfectly absurd. You know my mind."

At that I felt her grip relax, and she swung away from me almost in a faint. I caught her in my arms, and set her back again in her chair. Her face was covered, but by the heaving of her shoulders I thought she was crying. I felt unpleasantly guilty as though I had struck her physically. I knelt down beside her, and in a clumsy sort of way did my best to soothe her.

"Blanche," I said, "you're tired. Best get off to bed."

There was no sound of tears in her voice as she answered, "Not tired, Dick. Just utterly exhausted."

"Well, then," I said.

But she didn't move. And I rose and began my pacing again, watching her covertly. Presently she seemed to recover her strength. The weary droop went from her straightening shoulders, and at length she raised her head. She seemed strangely calm as she said, "Dick, I'm sorry if I've troubled you. It's over now. But I've had rather a bad time. He . . . he was terrible, you know."

"Why, Blanche," I cried, frightened in earnest, "what did he do?"

"Oh," she answered, "he didn't do anything. But he looked . . . well, I can't tell how. But it was frightful. I suppose a man might look like that if he were cast out of Heaven. Perhaps that's how Lucifer looked when he fell."

Somehow her words called up Avery's face before me more vividly than I had ever seen it in memory or imagination.

"And I knew what was happening to him," she went on. "I was sorry for him, but I was frightened too. But I did my best. I tried to wrestle with him. And that kind of thing's rather exhausting. I wanted to save him, you see."

"Blanche," I cried, "I don't know what you're talking about. But I know it would need an angel from Heaven to save Avery."

"It would now," she said seriously enough. "At least, that is . . ." she hesitated, "I dare say I could save him yet." And then she suddenly burst out with a strange passion, "Oh, Dick, you've made it cruelly hard for me."

Without warning she had sprung from her chair and swept from the room. I was left in utter amazement. I went dazedly forward and opened the door. But upstairs Blanche's door was closing behind her on a shaken sob.

I stood listening foolishly, then slowly mounted the stairs. For a moment I waited outside her room, at a loss what to do. Then I tapped uncertainly, but not a sound answered me. So I went quietly to my own room, telling myself that the girl had over-excited herself about the silly business. She would be all right the next day. But in spite of this easy reassurance I was absurdly troubled in my mind. I couldn't prevent a sense of heavy foreboding weighing at my heart, I seemed to be caught in a tangle of perplexing things, and as I turned into bed I deliberately shut my eyes as though to hide out the disturbing picture.

But my sleep was unusually shaken with dreams. And at last I awoke, fretful and uneasy, and tossed about in discomfort, unable to settle to sleep again. My bed was in disorder, and I rose and switched on the light, and rearranged the clothes; and before turning in again I made a restless turn or two up and down the room. I couldn't account to myself for the ridiculous activity of my mind. For I seemed to be living over and over again the happenings of the past few days. It was as though there were a problem underlying the whole thing, and I was fumbling about stupidly for a solution. And yet I kept on telling myself that there was no problem at all. It was merely Blanche's superstitious behaviour that had disturbed me. Looked at clearly, there was absolutely nothing to bother about. Avery was dangerous, but having admitted that, all was said. As for Blanche's insistence on immeasurable issues depending on the affair, I dismissed it as mere vapouring and fancy. So I slipped back under the clothes, and said, "I will go to sleep." And I did.

But I awoke again, and for a moment was utterly at a loss to know what was happening to me. Then I realized I was out of bed. In fact I was half dressed, and was slowly walking forward. I stopped with a jerk as I came to consciousness, and with the shock of awaking, nearly fell to the floor. But I put out a hand and gripped the post of a door. Then looking about me in the darkness I asked myself where I was. The door at my side was closed, but I thought I heard a faint sound within. And then at my feet I became aware of a thin line of light. And I knew at once that I was outside Blanche's room, and that she was still up. In front of me were the stairs, and it was clear that I had been making for them. And suddenly I felt a desire to go forward again. There was something calling to me outside in the darkness. I even took a step or two, and then came to a halt, breathing thickly. For a memory came to me of that night at school when I had nearly fallen into Avery's trap. A fear seized me that I was in his power again. But I shook myself wide awake, and said, "I won't." And I turned back, feeling wonderfully relieved.

But I hesitated outside Blanche's door, in two minds whether to knock or not. I guessed the girl hadn't been to bed the whole night, and I felt angry; for her behaviour seemed silly to me. She had been dead tired when she had left me, and needed a night's thorough rest. But I felt it would be useless to remonstrate, so I went on to my room. And I think I fell asleep as soon as my head touched the pillow.

It was natural enough that I should wake late the next morning. But I didn't expect to find that Blanche was already up and out. The news disturbed me, and brought back something of the uneasiness of the night before. And as the day wore on and Blanche didn't return, I became more and more troubled, till at last I had worked myself up into a fine state of nerves, beating about in my mind for every conceivable explanation of her absence. But argue down my fears as I would, I knew she had gone back to Avery. Knowing how she had wrestled with me I guessed that she wouldn't surrender him after one battle only. But what troubled me was her weariness of the night before, and my knowledge that she hadn't been to bed. I could only dimly imagine what her state of collapse would be when she returned after another fruitless conflict. For I couldn't picture her succeeding in the attempt to fight the devil out of Avery's soul.

She came unexpectedly enough while I was still tossing the thing about in my mind. But she didn't come creeping in broken and weary as I had expected. There was a glow and vigour about her which puzzled me. I just uttered her name, waiting for her to speak.

"It's all over," she said.

Then she came up to me and laid her head gently on my shoulder and breathed, "Oh, Dick!"

"Why, Blanche," was all I could say.

"Dick," she went on, moving away to arm's length, and looking me steadily in the eyes, "I said it was all over. But I should have said it's just beginning."

She was watching me intently, as though to see how her words took effect. Then with a little laugh she broke out with, "Poor old thing, how puzzled you look. Well, I suppose you are a bit mystified. But, Dick," and she became grave again, "you see, there was still one way to save him."

At last I found my voice, and said impatiently, "For God's sake, Blanche, if you can explain, then explain. But if you can't, then say so, and stop all this teasing talk."

Again the look of amusement came into her eyes, but only to fade away into a cold, hard gaze as she said, "Well, you see, he . . . he asked me to marry him."

At that I fell back, staring at her.

"That would have saved him, you see," she explained, still with that hard, glittering gaze fixed upon me searchingly.

"And Blanche," I said, forcing myself to speak, "did you?"

She suddenly seemed to collapse, and covering her face sank into a chair.

"Blanche," I cried, stooping over her.

But she only muttered, "God forgive me!"

I stepped back, horrified, exclaiming, "But, Blanche, you mustn't."

"I know, Dick," she answered, "I know. I haven't. But God forgive me, it was his last chance."

I was too relieved at first to speak; then I managed to say, "Look here, you mustn't take things to heart like this. Pity for Avery is just so much waste. He's beyond pity, Blanche. You needn't think you've sent him to the Devil. He was marked for the Devil's own from his birth."

She seemed to have recovered something of the vigour she had shown as she first came in. She rose again, and with a wonderful affection came and kissed me, and said, "You're a dear, good old thing, Dick. And I know you believe what you say. And as a matter of fact, I'm not so sure as I was that you're wrong. There are things that I don't understand. And yet I can't think he was wicked all along. You know, Dick," and her voice sank almost to a whisper, "I saw right into his heart to-day."

"Ha!" I exclaimed.

"Dick," she went on, "it was black, pitch black. Oh, I can't tell you."

"And yet he asked you to marry him," I said in disgust.

"That was yesterday," she answered. "And I went to him to-day to say Yes. Oh, Dick, I had to fight hard before I could bring my heart to do it. But to-day . . . Well, he has changed. All in one night, Dick. Unless you were right after all. But there was a thing he talked of . . . Just black wickedness."

"Blanche," I cried, "do you mean . . ."

"No, no," she said, "not a little thing like that. No, it was to do with Gaveston. I can't tell you what. You'd laugh. Well, it's not a laughing matter. And it made me wonder whether he'd been wicked all along."

"He has," I said.

"I don't know," she answered. "At first, I'm sure, it was just playing with unknown things. It was just chance, I think. And then he began to realize what could be done. There was power for the asking. Unlimited power, Dick. To you it would be like a story from the 'Arabian Nights.' But it was evil, utter evil. Still, the temptation must have been terrible. After all, every great soul has to face the same thing. 'All these things will I give thee if thou wilt fall down and worship me.' Dick, you remember Gaveston when you saw him a few days ago?"

The sudden question, bringing as it did the picture of that hideous creature vividly before my eyes, gave me a clue to Blanche's mysterious meaning.

"Remember him!" I exclaimed.

"Oh, we must save him now," she cried. "Even if it kills him."

There was no sign of weakness about her now. Her eyes were blazing, and for some reason I recalled her acting of Beatrice. I suppose something of the force and courage that had radiated from her then showed in her bearing now.

"Dick," she went on, "I told him it was war. Yesterday I pleaded with him. To-day I challenged him. What he may have been I shall never rightly know, and in any case, it doesn't matter any more. Because I know well enough what he is now. And I mean to fight him, Dick. I shall need help, I know; but I shall get help. I have allies."

"Well," I said, stirred with something of her enthusiasm, but unable to say anything worthy of my feelings, "we are agreed at last then."

"Ah, yes," she said. "And you know it's hurt me, Dick, to have felt you against me. I'm so glad we're on the same side now."

Blanche's sudden changes from the inspired prophetess to the affectionate girl had disconcerted me more than once, and now as she threw her arms about me without warning and kissed me passionately, I was taken aback, and could only return her embrace with a rather patronizing pat on the shoulder, and an awkward, "There, there."

But all the same I felt as though the atmosphere of my home had become strangely eased.

And the next day I had gone.

CHAPTER X

As usual, things assumed a normal and sane perspective as soon as I was among my College chums again. And now I had less time than ever to think of Blanche and Avery and Gaveston, and the shadowing mystery that hovered over them. For I had won my place in the Eight, and was eagerly training for the great struggle ahead. Never, I think, had I known such complete happiness as during those weeks of devoted exertion. It was a thrill and a delight to feel muscles and limbs grow to an ordered harmony of perfect obedience. And naturally enough all the unhealthy business I had left behind me at Chalk Ridge faded right out of my mind, or if I thought of it at all, for instance when I received a letter from Blanche, it was merely to dismiss it with a little half-amused sniff.

But Blanche's letters just kept me in touch with the thing, enough for me to pick up the thread of it again if necessary. I learnt that Avery had vanished, which filled me with immense relief. Then Blanche told me something of Gaveston's condition. He had become rapidly worse; that is, the real Gaveston had given place more and more to that other thing, whatever it might be. But he was beginning to struggle at last. It seemed that Blanche had impressed him somehow with the tremendous importance of the conflict. For my part, I couldn't see that it was any more important than it had been before, and Blanche didn't enlighten me. All she said was, "Gaveston realizes now that he's not merely fighting for himself. If he goes under, a power of evil will be let loose in the world that none of us can estimate. The dear little fellow's not so obstinate as you, Dick, and at any rate, he's trying, though the struggle seems to be breaking his heart. He's shaken off two terrible attacks, and at present he's lying prostrate. I'm afraid the next attack will be too much for him, but at least he'll have two victories to his credit." And the letter went on in the same strain. Later, I heard that he had succumbed as Blanche had feared. "The evil thing is back once more," she wrote. "But what's troubling me is the eyes. I expect you noticed yourself that they had changed colour last time you saw him. It's part of the general transformation. But the disturbing thing is that they don't change back properly to their right colour, even when he's himself again. It suggests that he's losing something of his permanent personality."

I didn't quite know why Blanche wrote to me in this way as though I were her ally, but all through her letters there was the suggestion that somehow we were both mightily concerned with the welfare of Gaveston.

And passages like these might have troubled me if I hadn't been so preoccupied with my own concerns. As it was, I had forgotten them with the stuffing of the letters into my pocket. As for Gaveston's eyes, I remembered that there had been something queer about them. I tried to recall what colour they had been, but could only succeed in calling up a picture of something strangely dark. And that was curious enough, because I knew he had had pale grey eyes at school, kindly, but rather washed out and weak. But I didn't bother my head about the thing, as I had more engaging matters on hand.

I took more notice when Blanche wrote about my mother. She seemed to be failing. And when Blanche wrote, "I haven't the force to spend on her. I need it all for the other fight," I felt acutely alarmed. I remembered Doctor Dale's words, and I knew myself that somehow it was Blanche who had kept my mother's frail little soul from flying away. I merely wrote, "Mother comes first." But she answered, "I'm sorry, Dick, but I have a battle ahead, and it will need all my energy." To tell the truth I didn't understand quite what she meant; and didn't put much faith in what I thought I did understand of it. So I said nothing more.

And then, of course, I went with the rest to Putney to finish my training; and if I thought of anything but the great race to come, it was that Katrina would be there to watch, for Olave had promised to bring her down. And at the anticipation, I don't know whether I felt more nervous or more exultant. But after all, that has no bearing on the story I have to tell. The day came and went. And the sweetest thing, I think, wasn't the victory, but Katrina's hands fingering along my arms, and her voice saying, "Oh, Dick, how perfectly magnificent you are!" If we had been alone at that moment I might have taken advantage of her simple pride in me, for the temptation was terribly strong. But she was still little more than a child, and I told myself I must wait till she could know her own mind. But I noticed that her hair was no longer gathered into the golden, girlish plait I had learnt to know so well; and that was like the passing of a milestone on the way. Meanwhile, I was forced to content myself with delicious draughts from the wells of anticipation, for I had promised myself that some day I would claim all that loveliness for my own. And the thought of it set my breast heaving mightily.

I was surprised to find that Blanche had been able to leave mother and had come to watch the race. In the excitement of the hour there was little enough time for talking, but I managed to gather that mother had rather welcomed Blanche's absence as a relief. Blanche smiled faintly as she told me that. "You see," she said in a strangely bitter way, "she can just die at her leisure if I don't bother her."

"Blanche!" I cried; but I was torn away, and I didn't like to renew the subject.

The next day we all drove off in Olave's car for Hinton Hall where we were to spend a few days together. And it was a wonderful relief to lean back in the great seat and watch the landscape swing easily by. And I didn't realize till then how weary I was after the strain of the race, and I became extraordinarily sleepy. All I knew was that the motion of the huge car was luxuriously comforting; and it was wonderfully delightful to gaze across at Katrina through half shut eyes, and feel as in a dream the trees and fields racing away on either hand. Also I remember old Jock sitting up in front, the huge mass of his shoulders brawnily butting out half the landscape.

I believe I was even asleep as the car rounded the corner into the drive at Hinton Hall. At all events I remember no warning as the great thing lurched and swerved. But for a sickening instant I was terribly aware of it slithering helplessly from side to side. And suddenly in front of me loomed up the massive stonework of the entrance, for all the world like a huge wave poised to break. And rather than our rushing in against it, it seemed to smash over us. And everything became horribly still.

It had happened suddenly, like the climax to a dream, and for a moment I lay dazed with a buzzing at my ears. Then I felt wide awake and master of my senses. I stirred, and shook myself free of the wreckage, and without much effort was out of it and on my feet, unhurt as far as I knew. I felt just a pang of disgust at the sight that met me. An indescribable mass of ruin showed dimly through a fog of dust, heaving and subsiding as though moved by some strange current. And there was a sickening sound of moaning. But the next instant I was tearing and straining at the débris; for the thought that all that I held dearest on earth was lying buried there, hurt, mangled, perhaps dead, worked like a frenzy in my heart. But soon Olave was free, and though he limped he was able to help me lever up the twisted mass; for by now I realized that the thing had somehow turned a somersault, and Blanche and Katrina were pinned helplessly beneath it. But we soon found it wasn't safe to work blindly, so we cleared away the loose fragments of wood and metal-work, and then peering below I met the open eyes of Katrina. She just whispered, "I can't move," and I felt a wonderful pride that she should lie there so calmly. I strained at the imprisoning wreckage, but couldn't stir it. Then I called to Olave, and creeping underneath I gradually levered the mass up on my back, while he pulled at Katrina, slowly working her free. It took some time, and my endurance was almost exhausted before she was safe. I crept out, aching and sore, but proudly conscious that at last I had been able to put my strength at the service of my darling.

As I crept out I saw that a crowd had gathered. Also, somehow Blanche had been extricated, and was being carried into the house. "Nothing serious, I think," Olave said as he saw me start after her. And turning to Katrina my eyes questioned her, and she answered, "All serene, Dick." But I didn't like the look of her, and packed her off, though she wanted to stay. As a matter of fact, she had been severely crushed under the weight of the car.

There remained now the chauffeur and old Jock. But when they were liberated at last they were a frightful spectacle. They seemed to have borne the brunt of the crash. The chauffeur lay with his head staved in, and Jock, though still breathing, was terribly mangled.

They were carried to the house; and as by this time a doctor had arrived, he followed to attend to the patients. When at length Olave and I were able to leave the scene, we were surprised to find Blanche up and awaiting us at the Hall, and Katrina ordered to her bed by the doctor. I could hear Ravin and Flame whimpering outside her door.

Blanche insisted that she was unhurt, though she was pale enough and was evidently suffering. When she found we didn't need her attention she went off to find the doctor and accompany him in his inspection of the patients, and presently she returned with him. He had been attending to Katrina, who needed perfect rest for a few days, and now he was on his way to examine Jock, though from what he had seen of him he didn't think there was much hope.

We all went with him; but one glimpse of the poor, mangled wretch was enough to bring my stomach into my mouth. I turned away in disgust, wondering how Olave and Blanche could endure the horrible spectacle. And no wonder I felt ill. I heard afterwards that an arm and a leg had been completely crushed, and the other leg was useless and would have to be amputated. Also his face, as I knew, had been smashed out of recognition. I had seen myself how his lower jaw hung open, wrenched out at the side with the teeth sticking bare at crooked angles. But the whole thing was too disgusting to linger over in detail. It was just a raw, bleeding distortion, hideous and haunting.

The amazing thing was that he was still alive. The doctor was mightily pleased, and declared he would be able to patch him up all right. He rubbed his hands as though anticipating a pleasant afternoon's work. As for me, I thought a fellow had better be dead than live a patched and legless trunk. But I hadn't the heart to say a word. And meanwhile, the doctor left us to make arrangements for his being taken to hospital.

Well, we spent a sad enough evening. For my part I was unsettled because Katrina lay in pain. But Olave and Blanche were more concerned over Jock.

Olave kept on repeating, "He mustn't live like that, he mustn't live like that. It'll be frightful."

And I tried to set him at ease by declaring, "Well, whatever the doctor says, I don't see how he can."

He turned to me quickly, "Honestly," he cried, "do you think he'll die?"

"Well," I answered, "both legs, isn't it, an arm, and goodness knows what beside."

"Yes, yes," said Olave, "it's horrible. He can't live like that."

"But he will," said Blanche.

We both turned to her. "What do you mean?" Olave asked nervously.

"I saw the will to live in his eyes," Blanche said.

"The will to live," exclaimed Olave, "in such a state! Good God, if I were mauled like that I hope I should have the decency to die outright."

I hardly recognized Olave; he seemed so unusually perturbed and shaken from his serenity.

"After all," I put in, still trying to ease him, "he can't live or die merely by willing to."

"But he can," said Blanche very quietly.

I turned and looked at her, and saw in her eyes that strange, deep light I had learnt to know and half to fear.

"Oh, it's silly," I said, shifting in my chair heavily, merely to make a disturbance.

"No, Dick," said Olave, "it's not silly," and he was speaking more quietly and calmly. "He may feel he's needed."

"He does," said Blanche.

"Good God!" I cried, feeling a growing uneasiness at Blanche's short, significant answers, "You seem to know a mighty deal, Blanche."

But she didn't take any notice of my outburst, except to say, "He's Katrina's protector, you know."

"Well," I jerked out, for I felt an unpleasant jump of fear at her words.

But she wasn't looking at me; she was looking at Olave. And for his part he was studying her seriously. At length he said, "Blanche, there's something you know. What is it?"

"No," she answered slowly, "there's something I feel; I don't rightly know. I can't know unless Jock can tell me. And I don't think he'll ever be able to speak again." She paused a moment, and then went on more quickly,

"To tell the truth, there seemed to me to be a message in Jock's eyes. I don't think he'll die till he's delivered it somehow. He's seen something."

Olave started. "Perhaps," he said, and broke off into, "We've never asked how the accident came about."

"Yes," said Blanche, as though he had answered her question, "I think that's it. Jock saw."

There was a long, tense silence while Olave and Blanche seemed to be saying things to each other that I couldn't fathom. At last Blanche said, "I'll go to him to-night."

"Will it be any use?" Olave asked.

"I think so," she replied. "At any rate, it's a chance." And she added, "And then he can die at his ease."

The thing had passed beyond me. And as a matter of fact, I had been following a line of thought of my own. Blanche's words, "He's Katrina's protector," had set me thinking. It seemed to me now that even patched up and legless, Jock's life was worth preserving, provided the doctor could really make him presentable again. For somehow the picture came to me of Ravin and Flame whining helplessly, terrified to follow Avery's trail; but I saw old Jock striding on undaunted. I thought perhaps he was like myself, too dense and stockish to be made the butt of fancy trickery.

And so Blanche's saying, "Then he can die at his ease," shook me into a protest. "Look here," I said, "if the man can live, give him a chance. Don't go bothering him about things to-night."

Blanche must have read my thoughts, for she looked at me with a serious smile and said, "We'll find another guardian for Katrina."

"Well," I said taken aback, and repeated, "give him a chance, anyway."

"But, Dick," said Olave, and I could see he was troubled, "honestly, is it right for a man to live in such a state? If it's just that he's hanging on because he's got something to say, surely it's kinder to let him say it and pass off at ease."

"But it's silly," I cried. "Do you mean to say that when you get caught in a motor smash you refuse to die because . . ." I couldn't finish. The thing was so obviously absurd. Olave looked rather helplessly to Blanche.

"I shall go and see him," was all she said, and she left the room.

Olave and I were left alone, and naturally we argued the thing out over and over again from beginning to end. It was so obvious to me that the man was alive because he had the vitality not to die under the shock. But Olave had set his trust in Blanche, and refused to be shaken from his faith.

"Blanche is always right," he said. "It's so easy to explain the inexplicable by mere reference to natural laws, and so forth, which after all explain nothing. I find that Blanche has hit on a clue which answers riddles that science doesn't realize are even puzzling."

So we waited for her, and at length she returned, her eyes shining.

We both gazed at her, for there- was a meaning in her look. And Olave bowed his head. I turned feebly from one to the other, wondering how he could read her unspoken message, which to me was unintelligible.

"It was so," she said. "It was Avery."

"What!" I shouted, springing to my feet.

She went on. "He couldn't speak. But I could read it there. He had seen him."

Olave raised his head with a question in his eyes.

"He wanted to live," said Blanche. "He feared for Katrina."

Since I had risen I was unable to move. Something held me in a suspense of expectation. I felt that Blanche was going to say something that would change my life for me, so strained was the sense of dark forces at work at the mere mention of that hated name.

"I told him," Blanche went on, "that I . . ."

"Yes?" said Olave.

Blanche faced him very gravely and said, "I promised him I would protect Katrina."

Olave rose and took her by the hand and said, "Then you must come and live here, Blanche."

And still I was spellbound, unable to move or speak. What was this terrible menace threatening my beloved one?

But those two had no eyes for me. They stood silently facing each other. And Blanche said, "Poor Jock! Still he wanted to live. I suppose it is a wrench. But it couldn't be, could it, Olave?"

"No," said Olave, "no."

Then I found my voice. "Is he dead?" I cried.

Blanche nodded.

"But how?" I gasped.

"Dick," she said, "he'd done his work. Only selfishness could make him want to live after that. And so . . ."

"Well?" I said.

"So I told him to die."

"You . . ." I gasped. But the look in her eyes was something I had never seen, and I turned away feeling heart-sick and weary.

All I knew was that there was a danger menacing Katrina. And one defence had gone. Old Jock was dead.

CHAPTER XI

A few days later, when the inquest was over, Blanche declared she must return to Chalk Ridge. I wasn't too well pleased, because I thought I should have to accompany her, and Katrina was only just beginning to get about again, so I hadn't seen very much of her.

"Need you go just yet?" I asked.

"Yes, Dick, it's urgent," she said.

"But why?" I pressed.

She merely said, "Gaveston."

"Gaveston?" I repeated.

"Dick," she said gravely, "you don't realize yet how much depends on Gaveston. I tell you he's got to win his battle. Don't you see," she cried, gripping me by the shoulders, "that's where I've got to meet Avery? If he beats me there . . ." She threw out her arms and dropped them to her side.

"All I know is," I answered rather moodily, "that I don't understand anything about it. It all seems to me a stupid piece of tomfoolery. Still, if you must go, you must."

"Yes," she said.

"I suppose you're taking Olave's two-seater," I went on.

"Yes, he's coming with me," she said.

"What?" I cried. "But I thought you wanted me to drive you."

She looked at me a moment, then laughed gaily. "Oh, that's the trouble, is it? Poor old thing. No, you stay here and look after Katrina. You see," she became more serious, "after what's happened I don't think I should trust even you to drive me."

"Olave, of course . . ." I began banteringly.

"No, nor Olave," she cut in. "I shall drive myself."

"But, good God; why?" I asked.

"Oh, just to practise my nerve," she answered lightly.

"And I suppose Olave's going with you for ballast," I said.

"If you want to know why Olave's going with me," she replied, "you must ask him."

But I didn't need to ask him. He came up at that moment and told me he wanted to speak to me. Blanche left us together.

Olave began without preliminaries, looking me straight in the eyes. "I expect you know what I'm going to say, Dick. I've asked Blanche to marry me, and she has consented. I want to run over and see your mother, if I have your permission."

Well, I suppose I had guessed what was in the air, but this abrupt way of notifying me of the thing rather took my breath away.

"Good heavens," I exclaimed, "but this is simply splendid."

And then at the sight of Olave's grave face watching me as though the fate of the world hung on my words, I fairly burst out laughing, and seizing him by the hand I cried, "I say it's simply splendid, old man."

"You're really glad?" he questioned me, his fingers tightening about my own, and the grave light still glowing in his eyes.

"Glad!" I exclaimed. "Good God, Olave!"

And at that he broke into a smile and said, "Thank you, Dick," and was off in search of Blanche. But in a minute they both came running back, Blanche pulling Olave after her. She dropped his hand as she reached me, and throwing her arms about me, kissed me passionately. "Dick," she said, "Oh, Dick."

At that moment I am sure she was just an ardent-hearted girl, with not a thought in her mind of the perplexing and troubling mysteries which usually enveloped her. And when she turned from me with shining eyes, and put her hands on Olave's shoulders and gazed full into his face, I felt an unaccustomed emotion at the mere human beauty of the picture. She stood so a moment, then with a slow yielding pressed up towards him as his arms closed about her; and with the touching of their lips they seemed to rush into one as though fused by the power of their passion.

There was such a radiant abandonment in the mutual gesture, and yet such a sense of abiding unity, that I felt I was witnessing something strangely sacred like some dim ceremony of forgotten days, and I know not what primal emotions stirred vaguely but joyously deep at my heart.

And when they drew apart Blanche said simply, "We are betrothed."

In an hour they had gone. Katrina had been able to come down to see them off. While she was saying good-bye to her brother, Blanche took me apart.

"Dick," she said, "I don't want you to be alarmed. But keep Katrina in sight during the day. And at night let the dogs sleep outside her room."

"Blanche," I said, "tell me straight now; what's the danger?"

"None at all just yet," she answered. "But there may be."

"But what?" I asked.

"Oh, Dick," she answered, "I don't know. But we must be prepared. That's all."

"That's all very well," I began to fume. "You suggest all sorts of un-canny things, and tell me to be prepared. I tell you, I don't like it, Blanche. What have I got to guard against?"

"Avery," she answered.

"Well, I know that," I said impatiently.

"Then you ought to know as well," she answered me rather sadly, "that I can't say any more. I don't know what he'll do. He's struck once, and failed; but none of us were ready for it."

"Not exactly failed," I said, thinking of Jock.

"Ah," she answered enigmatically.

Olave came to shake hands, and I asked him point-blank, "What's all this worry about? Blanche tells me to be on my guard. Well, what's likely to happen?"

"Nothing will happen here," he said. "It's Blanche we need to de-fend."

"Blanche?" I said. "I thought it was Katrina who was in danger."

"As far as that goes," he answered, "we're all in danger. But Blanche chiefly. At least until this Gaveston business is settled one way or the other."

"Oh, Gaveston!" I exclaimed in impatience.

And they got into the little car and drove away. And with a sudden shyness I realized I was left alone with Katrina. But not quite alone; for Ravin and Flame reminded me that there were a couple of devoted slaves besides myself ready to sell their lives for their mistress.

So for a few days I was installed as Katrina's guardian, and mightily proud I felt. You may be sure I obeyed Blanche, and kept her well in sight during the day. I had no desire to stroll far from her. And at night I saw to it that the hounds slept outside her door. She asked why, and I'm afraid I answered none too truthfully that they had taken up their place there when she was hurt and now refused to go. I think this pleased her; for she threw her arms about them, and called them faithful old things in a way that made me jealous.

She wasn't sufficiently recovered for us to resume our old tramps, but we could stroll gently about the grounds for short spells. And the first time we did so I noticed how she kept turning her head to look behind her. I knew what was in her mind, and at last I said, "Poor old Jock, he won't bring up the rear-guard any more."

She answered me with a little shiver, "You know, somehow I feel sort of cold behind without him there." Then she asked quickly, "Dick, was he terribly damaged?"

"Pretty bad," I answered.

"Too bad to live?" she asked.

"Why Katrina, what do you mean?" I said, wondering how much she knew.

"I mean, couldn't they have saved him?" she explained.

"Well," I said rather guiltily, "I suppose they would have done it if they could."

She sighed and said, "I wish I could have seen him, just to say good-bye."

"Thank God you didn't," I cried, as the picture of the mangled body came into my mind.

She looked at me a moment, and said, "Well, I wish they could have saved him, all the same." And looking behind her again she shivered as she had done before. Then touching me on the arm she said softly, "Dick, I don't like it. Let's go back."

But after this Katrina didn't mention Jock again, though at times I caught her turning her head and trembling suddenly in a nervous way that troubled me. But always when she saw I was watching her she would break out into her fresh gay laugh, and exclaim, "Oh, I am a stupid, Dick. Why don't you scold me?"

And at such moments the almost childlike charm of her radiant eyes and slight little body nearly broke down my resolve to keep silent about my love until she was old enough to know her own heart fully; for it would have been taking an advantage of her innocence and inexperience to speak so soon.

And in a few days Olave returned. My mother was poorly, he said. He wanted to marry Blanche as soon as possible, and of course my mother would come to Hinton Hall where Blanche could nurse her. Also he had a favour to ask, namely that the ceremony might be performed at his own private chapel. It had been so for generations, he said. I must admit that I felt a cold wind go down my spine as I thought of that ghostly place with the white tombs ranged around the walls, and the busts and figures of departed Guthries staring out of niches and corners. But of course I gave my consent, and Olave breathed gladly as though he had gained a great boon.

"We set rather a store by these things," he said in explanation. "It's almost a point of honour with us to be married and buried there."

"Well," I said with a little laugh, "I suppose you can always guarantee the first, but the second might possibly present difficulties."

"It has done before now," he answered. "My grandfather died at sea, and my father who was with him, fortunately enough, could scarcely persuade the captain not to drop him overboard. And then my great-grandfather died abroad. Killed, as a matter of fact, in battle. It was years before his body was brought home. You see, they weren't sure which was his grave in the first place, and the matter of identification was pretty complicated. However, there he is now, lying at peace where he should."

"Well, Olave," I said, "it's very impressive, and all that, and somehow all this ancestral stuff seems to suit you. But for myself I don't think I should bother much where I was earthed."

He looked at me with an amused twinkle in his eyes, and said, "Well, perhaps you're all the happier so. At any rate, you can't go, as I can, and stand before the spot where you're to be buried, and say to yourself, 'Some day I shall lie here.'"

"Good God, no!" I exclaimed; and he laughed outright.

CHAPTER XII

I set off the next morning for Chalk Ridge in Olave's little two-seater, and one of his men came with me to take the car back. Olave said he would remain with Katrina, "just in case."

"In case what?" I asked quickly.

"Oh, she's not recovered yet," he answered easily. "She may need someone to look after her."

I could learn nothing from his tone or his expression, and so had to remain content. But it seemed to me that Blanche was afraid of some danger which hung over Katrina, and of course she had told her fears to Olave. As a last hope of learning something definite I put the question to him at parting, "Olave, tell me now, what's the danger?"

He answered me as Blanche had done; "Avery."

"Yes, I know," I said fretfully, "but that's too vague."

"That's the whole trouble," he answered.

"Well then," I waited for something more explanatory.

He seemed as though he were going to confide in me, but he only said, "Dick, old boy, don't worry. Honestly, Katrina's in no danger as far as I know. It's merely that that sort of fellow usually strikes at one through the womenfolk. And as a matter of fact, it's Blanche he's really up against. But Blanche can defend herself better than the rest of us."

"And so she ought," I exclaimed, "seeing she's the only one who understands the business."

So I drove off, feeling none too well at ease, and too preoccupied in my mind to take much care of my driving.

I was rounding a corner past St. Jude's Asylum when a sudden nervousness seemed to take possession of me. It seemed just for the moment that I was back in the accident of a few days before, with the car swerving round into the drive at Hinton Hall. I suppose it was something in the resemblance of the turn which struck at my memory, and as my mind was busier with its own dreams than with the car, the fantasy that I was in for a smash was so vivid that I foolishly jammed on the brakes. Immediately I knew where I was and released them; but it was too late. The back of the car had swung round with the clamping on of the brakes in mid turn, and as I released them I found the thing rushing straight at the wall of the Asylum. I heaved at the wheel, but something seemed to snap. I avoided the wall by a bare inch, but the car flung headlong across the road, and I found myself tossed like a sack into the hedge. I was somewhat shaken but quite unhurt, and as I tore myself free of the hedge I saw Olave's man dragging himself out of the ditch where he had been thrown. We looked at each other, and then set to examining the car. And then I heard Blanche's voice, "Well, Dick, are you trying to run me over?"

I turned quickly. "Good Lord!" I said.

"Oh, just coming along," she said.

"But where?" I pressed her.

She looked at me as if to ask why I was so inquiring. Then she said, "You missed me by six inches, perhaps."

I knew that our thoughts were the same. But I turned away and helped heave the car out of the ditch, glad to find it undamaged. I told the man to drive it back, and I joined Blanche.

"I've had enough of motors," I cried.

"Well then," she said easily, "come with me to the Asylum."

"I was hoping you were going the other way," I said; and she laughed.

Naturally I questioned her about Gaveston, but more from a sense of duty than from curiosity. The less I heard about the little fellow the better I was pleased. And, as a matter of fact, Blanche wasn't very communicative. I gathered that things weren't going as smoothly as she wished. Certainly her face was strained and troubled as she told me the little she thought it good for me to know.

"He's still not himself," she ended up.

"Still possessed of a spirit," I said rather flippantly. And at that she turned on me more angrily than usual with, "Dick, don't talk lightly about such things. If you can't understand them, then keep quiet."

"Very well, then," I answered, "mum's the word for me."

At the Asylum Doctor Dale was awaiting Blanche impatiently. "Why didn't you drive here?" he exclaimed as they met.

"I thought it safer to walk," she answered; adding with a smile, "but now I'm not so sure."

"Well, come quickly," he said nervously, and led her off. He seemed too preoccupied to notice me, so I followed, not quite knowing what I ought to do. The doctor was talking eagerly. "He's getting worse and worse. To-day he's been positively frightful."

"It's a good sign," said Blanche.

"I don't know, I don't know," he exclaimed fussily, "I don't see that at all."

"It means he's coming round," Blanche said calmly.

"Well, perhaps, perhaps," said the doctor, "but it may mean the madness is getting a firmer hold."

"The spirit, you mean," Blanche corrected him quietly.

"Oh, well then," he cried in irritation, "the spirit, what you will. It's only a term, after all. A silly term; but a term."

We came to Gaveston's cell, and here I was shut out without ceremony, and left to kick my heels at leisure. One or two visitors passed, and probably took me for a madman. I dare say I looked it after the spill I had had. But after waiting an age I was in half a mind to go, but still delaying, was at length rejoined by Blanche and the doctor.

The doctor was looking terribly white with a kind of sickly transparence; and he had lost his talkativeness. But Blanche, though pale, seemed to me transfigured. Her eyes were blazing, almost like a wild animal's at night, but with a fervour not of ferocity but of power. I remembered her looking like that at the play. Instinctively I crept aside and followed as they led the way.

I could hear the doctor muttering, "My God, my God!"

They parted almost without a word. Blanche merely said, "If necessary chain him up."

"He'd snap it like a thread," the doctor protested.

"Never mind, try," Blanche persisted, "and have the door well barred. If he escapes . . ."

The doctor merely continued his muttering, "My God."

Turning to me as though she had only just that moment left me, Blanche took my arm and said, "Now then, come along home, Dick, and tell me all about Hinton."

Well, the walk and the chat, which if I remember rightly became extraordinarily sentimental, were decidedly refreshing after what I had just been hearing. And seeing the glow in her eyes and cheeks and the swinging buoyancy of her step as she spoke of Olave, I wondered why Blanche was sacrificing the charm of her womanhood for all this unhealthy dabbling in occult things.

When I reached home I was staggered to see how my mother had changed. I had heard that she had been failing, but I hadn't expected to find her so collapsed and exhausted as she really was. I glanced quickly at Blanche, and she turned sadly away. But although my mother seemed faded to a mere shadow of herself she was remarkably cheerful.

"I'm very happy," she kept on repeating, "I'm very happy."

But I was wondering how she would ever be able to stand the journey to Hinton Hall. Later, I spoke to her of Blanche's coming marriage, and put the question to her.

She looked at me in a curious way. Then she began smiling very knowingly, and at last put her lips up to my ears and said, "It's a secret, Dick. Promise not to tell?"

"Yes," I said, mystified as to how there could be a secret in her journey to Little Hinton.

She smiled slyly and said, "Well, I shan't go at all."

"Mother!" I exclaimed.

"Shhh!" she said, finger to lips. "You mustn't tell Blanche. She won't get married if you do. You've promised, Dick."

I could see that even this little colloquy was tiring her, so I patted her hand and promised again not to tell Blanche. And noticing the two, I thought my mother was really easier away from Blanche. "Well," I told myself, "poor thing, she's been wanting to die, and Blanche hasn't let her." Then realizing how I had unawares put faith in what the doctor had told me, I called myself a fine fool, and burst out laughing.

But in spite of that, when I spoke to Blanche about my mother's failing strength I asked her if she couldn't do anything, and I knew quite well that I meant couldn't she use her force of will to restore my mother's vitality. And she answered me as though she quite understood my meaning.

"No, Dick," she said, shaking her head slowly, "I can't do anything. I need my strength for another battle."

"But, Blanche," I said, "it's mother."

"Yes," she answered with firmness, "but it's only one woman's life more or less."

I answered angrily, "But that's more important than a madman's."

She looked at me steadily, and said, "Dick, how can I convince you that it's not Gaveston's life that counts? It's something deeper than a life, deeper even than a soul. Oh, Dick," she cried in appeal, "if only you believed your Bible I could explain so easily."

"My Bible?" I said in astonishment.

"I mean the miracles," she explained.

"Oh, yes," I answered, rather nettled, "but that sort of thing doesn't happen now."

She looked at me with a sudden wrath in her face, and cried, "You say that, and it's all happening before your eyes."

Then she seemed to droop, and her anger melted. "I'm sorry," she said, "but I get tired, Dick."

She turned to leave me, but stopped at the door and said very gravely, "Dick, let me tell you. Gaveston is possessed of a devil. It's got to be driven out. If it isn't, it'll take complete possession of him." She paused a moment, and asked simply, "Dick, was Gaveston very strong when he was at school?"

I could have laughed aloud. "Strong!" I exclaimed.

"Well," she said, "it takes three men to hold him now. He's nearly escaped from the Asylum twice. He just bursts the door down as though it were a piece of card. They'll soon have to chain him up, and I doubt if that'll have much effect. If he took a dislike to you, Dick, he'd just drop you out of the window."

In spite of myself I felt a chill at my bones. Blanche was so obviously telling the truth. Her clear and precise tone made the effect of her words more telling than if she had tried to frighten me with theatrical gestures. I knew she was just stating the exact thing as it really was. I tried to shake off the feeling of uneasiness at my heart. "Oh, well," I said, "madmen are like that."

Blanche watched me steadily for a minute, but I couldn't read what was passing in her eyes. Then she asked me slowly, "Dick, don't you realize who is behind all this?"

"Good God," I cried in real alarm, "don't I realize? Haven't I told you often enough . . ." I couldn't find words to continue.

"Yes," she said, "yes. Whether you were right in the past, I don't know; but you're terribly right now. And, Dick," she again questioned me in her slow way, "if Gaveston escapes, if I can't cure him at all, don't you realize whose servant he'll be?"

"Servant?" I said.

"Oh, Dick," she cried in a terrible voice, "can't you see, oh, can't you see? Have you never heard of a familiar spirit? Have you never . . ." But she broke off with her hands before her eyes, and muttering wearily, "I'm tired, tired," she left me.

CHAPTER XIII

With my mother's growing weakness, and Blanche's approaching marriage, life became too full for me to contemplate returning to Oxford. And as a matter of fact I had accomplished my ambition there and had nothing to lure me back, except indeed the happy companionship of the place. But even that was giving way before my desire for Katrina's presence, and while at Chalk Ridge I could drive over whenever I felt inclined.

My mother's health gave me serious uneasiness. It was clear to me that she hadn't much longer to live. And for that reason I was anxious to speed on Blanche's wedding. It seemed to me that once safely married she might find healthier things to occupy her mind than the curing of possessed lunatics. And if my mother died before the wedding, it would have to be postponed for a year. I don't think I put the matter to myself crudely like that, but that's what my thoughts really amounted to.

Blanche still visited at the Asylum, sometimes going there of her own will, and sometimes at the urgent summons of Doctor Dale. What was happening there I didn't trouble to inquire; but I noticed that Blanche usually returned almost prostrated with weariness, and I began to understand why she had no power left to support her mother.

The doctor would drop in now and again. And though my mother showed something of the same aversion for him as she did for Blanche, yet she always seemed to rally in spirit after he had been. I thought probably he was attempting to take the place that Blanche had abandoned.

Sometimes we talked together, and I soon found that he was never tired of singing the praises of Blanche, though always there was a sort of fussy nervousness in his words as though he was rather frightened at her wilful behaviour, but more frightened to take her to task about it. I thought I understood him perfectly. He was just in love with her in a stupid sort of way, although she was plighted to another; and though he knew quite well that he was allowing her unwarrantable liberties, yet he was too weak to refuse her. Now and again he would talk of Gaveston, and from his timid hints I got a certain insight into the battle that Blanche was waging. The doctor, at any rate, took it seriously enough. It was clear to me that the dread of Gaveston escaping was wearing down his nerve. "He's as fierce as a lion and as strong as a bull," he would say in a distressed voice, and would go on, "but that's not all. It's something else. I don't know what. Of course, your sister has her theories; girl's fancies, you know. I don't take much account of that. But I've never seen anything quite like it."

"But suppose he did escape," I said.

"God forbid!" he said almost in a whisper, and wiped his brow.

I was puzzled. "I suppose one could shoot him," I suggested.

"Shoot him?" he cried. "Well, yes, I suppose so," he consented haltingly, and went on, "but I shouldn't like to hold the gun."

I was merely talking to pacify him, and I said easily, "Oh, I dare say I could do that for you." It didn't occur to me till I had spoken that I was making a very light matter of killing an old school chum. And at the thought I remembered Gaveston as he used to be; mild and gentle, almost like a girl. And I think I had been fond of him in a protective sort of way. It had been a pleasure to use my strength to defend him from Avery. His very helplessness had cried out to me to shield him. And somehow I began to think of Katrina, and how my whole soul and body yearned towards her in the same protective desire. But the doctor cut short my meditations with his adieux. And as he went he said, "I know what I was trying to get at. He's like a battery gradually being charged. To kill him would be to release the whole electric force in a flash. I shouldn't like to be by, that's all."

So the time drew on towards the wedding day. But Blanche still continued her visits to the Asylum, and indeed more frequently than before. And she was out late at night again and again, though where she went I didn't know. "Meetings," I said, and was satisfied. But when I saw her visibly wasting I began to feel it my duty to say a word. Indeed, I was frightened by her heavy brow and hollow cheeks. It seemed to me that in a couple of weeks she had grown old. I wondered what Olave would say when he saw her. And yet beneath her thinness and pallor there glowed a deep underlight that told me that her spirit was vigorous yet. "She's just burning herself out," I said to myself, and made up my mind to speak to her.

I had given up waiting for her in the evenings as she stayed out later and later, but with my determination to talk to her I decided to catch her one evening as she came home. I think I had a sort of sneaking thought that she would be tired then and so unable to argue me down. So the next time she went out I sat up, going over and over in my mind what I would say to her. "Surely she will listen to reason," I told myself without conviction. I coursed the monotonous circle of my arguments again and again, till I suppose the repetition made me sleepy. I began to doze, and would waken with a start as my head fell suddenly forward onto my breast. "Surely she will listen to reason," I would say, and stifling a yawn drop off again, to be again awakened with the jerk of my head falling forward. I got up and paced the room for a turn or two, then settled myself more comfortably on the sofa.

I seemed to come racing down through a rush of air to a thud of consciousness. A voice was echoing piteously, "Don't let them touch me, Dick."

I sprang up, exclaiming, "Gaveston!" and looked wildly round the room expecting to see him shuddering somewhere in the shadow. But there was just the faintest sound of a dying moan on the air, as though the last of the wind had fallen; but not a sign of Gaveston.

I even went to the window and peered out, and half wondered whether I ought to go outside and search for him. For my thought was that he had escaped. But all this was a momentary impulse, and with my mind clearing I realized I had merely had a dream. Then I gazed at the clock. The hand stood at two. I rubbed my eyes and looked again. It was certainly two o'clock. "Oh, well," I thought, "I must have missed her. She's in bed and asleep by now."

I switched out the light and went sleepily up to my room. But I stopped short at Blanche's door. For a light showed under it, very clear in the darkness, and there was the sound of talking within. I listened involuntarily, and was frozen to the spot. For though I couldn't distinguish any words it was Gaveston's voice I could hear. He had escaped then. That hideous thing I had seen with the hanging hair and the leering eyes, it was in there, in Blanche's room. I could hear it speaking in an endless drone, a sort of pitiful whining cry. And sometimes there came a wilder note that sent a chill shudder down my spine. I was trying to make up my mind to fling the door wide and rush in, but I couldn't move a finger. I was rooted to the spot, unable even to close my ears against that shrill monotonous voice interminably jabbering. And once or twice I just heard Blanche say quite low but clearly, "You must," at which there would sound a shaken cry, and again the voice would continue its pitiful droning.

At length there came a pause, and at that the spell that held me snapped. I seized the handle and wrenched the door open. There was a shriek and the sound of a body falling with a thump to the floor. Blanche leapt towards it, and when 1 could see what had happened I saw her kneeling over a prostrate woman, loosening the clothing at her throat and forcing some brandy between her teeth.

The woman sighed wearily, blinked her eyes, and stirred as she lay in Blanche's arms. Little by little she came round, while I stood there helplessly, wondering what could have happened. And looking about me I could see no sign of Gaveston.

Blanche took no notice of me till she had laid the woman on her bed, and seemed satisfied that she had come round. Then she came to me and said quietly, "Please go, Dick."

"But what is it, Blanche?" I asked.

She didn't answer, but only said, "Please," gently pushing me towards the door.

"No," I said in sudden obstinacy. "I want to know what's happened. Where's Gaveston? I heard him talking. And who's this woman?"

Blanche faced me in her steady way when she had something particular to say, and then she said very deliberately. "She's the medium."

I gasped, trying to frame the word on my lips.

Blanche smiled and said, "Not now, Dick. Scold me to-morrow if you like. But I must nurse her to-night. You see, bursting in like that you nearly killed her."

I looked towards the pale woman lying on the bed as though she were some unholy creature. Blanche must have read my look, for she laughed quite quietly and said, "Oh, she's harmless, Dick. Her name's Mrs. Wait. You see she has a name just like you and me. She even has a husband. Quite commonplace, isn't it?"

I couldn't understand the exact significance of her gentle irony; but throwing the woman another look I went off to my room, half afraid of the darkness of the landing as I crossed it, and wondering what sort of dreams I should have if I ever managed to get to sleep. But as a matter of fact I was asleep as soon as my head touched the pillow, and I woke so fresh in the morning that the night's strange business seemed to me like a dream itself. And when Blanche came down to breakfast serene and unperturbed I simply couldn't determine in my own mind whether the thing had really happened or not; and so I didn't dare say a word about it.

But I still had it on my conscience that I ought to speak to Blanche. And yet now she seemed to be rallying from her languor, and for a few days didn't vanish mysteriously in the evenings, so I thought I might postpone an unpleasant duty which after all would probably be useless. Then one night she went out again. I thought I would sit up for her, but with the first sign of drowsiness I felt frightened and went off to bed. And I think the memory of that other evening must have preyed on my mind, for twice I woke with just the faintest sense of having heard Gaveston whisper my name; or rather, not so much whisper it as cry it from an infinite distance. But I turned over and went to sleep again. And in the morning I watched Blanche to see if I could spy any signs of the medium having visited her again. But her countenance was inscrutable.

And at last the wedding day approached. As a matter of fact, Blanche had asked me once whether it might be postponed for another month.

I chaffed her in reply: "Is the little girl nervous?" I asked.

She patted me lightly on the cheek, and with a glorious blush exclaimed, "Oh, Dick, I just long for it with my whole soul."

"Well then?" I asked.

"My work isn't done," she replied.

"Oh, that'll keep," I said, and declared that I wouldn't hear of the wedding being a minute later than arranged.

She smiled at me, and made no further protest. I think she was glad to feel that there was no escape for her. She merely said with a comic archness, "Oh, it's sure to be five minutes later. It wouldn't be proper to keep to time. People would say, 'What indecent haste!'" And with that she tripped away from me, leaving me as so often before with that wonder at my mind why this girl should choose to hide her charm behind such a baffling veil of mystery.

On the night before the wedding I went to bed early. For we were to be up in good time the next morning to drive to Hinton Hall for the ceremony. It was to be a quiet affair with practically no guests. I saw that everything was in order, and went to sleep with a glad mind. After this night Blanche would be responsible to Olave for her conduct. Perhaps he would know the secret for bringing her to reason. And then as I dozed off the vision of Katrina came to me, and melted sweetly into my dreams.

But for all that I woke in a strange horror as though I had dreamt of something unnameably evil. There was a clinging constriction at my chest, and I was breathing with difficulty. My chief feeling, I think, was one of numbness. It was as though I were bound about with innumerable threads that held each least muscle from moving. Also I found myself gazing intently on a patch of brilliant white on the wall in front of me. That patch of light seemed to fascinate me. There was something in the cold immobility of it that seemed to hold me with the spell of its own stillness. I lay watching it with wide eyes, waiting for I knew not what. And then I told myself that I hadn't drawn the blind, and the moon was shining full into the room. No wonder I had had strange dreams. And yet I couldn't remember having had any dreams at all.

I was trying to shake off the impression of heavy numbness from my limbs and muster courage to rise and draw the blind, when I became aware of a dark shadow slowly rising into the square of light. If ever I have known the paralysis of utter terror it was at that moment. I seemed to feel a hand pass slowly over the back of my neck, brushing the hair up stiffly. And a horrible, dizzy sickness made my brain swim as though in a faint. But it was only for an instant. As I watched the shadow rise and take shape I became master of my nerve again. Slowly a head formed on the wall, and then a man's shoulders rose into view. There was someone climbing in at my window.

I was thinking rapidly what I must do. There was a revolver in the drawer of my dressing-table, but I didn't think I could get it in time, because I wasn't quite sure where it lay, and if the fellow were armed he would have me at his mercy as I crossed the room. I decided to lie still till he was upon me, and try what surprise would do. So I lay there watching the moving shadow, and reconstructing from it what was happening behind me. Incidentally I wondered why the fellow had chosen my window, till I realized it was the only one that could be scaled from the ground. Well, he would soon be very sorry for himself.

Strangely enough he wasn't making the least sound. He was a cute thief, I thought. And still the shadow moved, slowly, and with infinite caution. And still I watched it, trying to guess at the man's size and probable physique. Suddenly something in the huddled contour of the shoulders made my heart freeze. I knew as surely as if I had been told that this was Gaveston, or rather that frightful caricature of Gaveston that I had seen once, never to forget. He had escaped. And here he was at my window. And the reports I had heard of his enormous strength swarmed back upon my mind. There was no hope, I knew, except in my revolver.

With a bound I was out of bed and across the room. My hand was diving into the drawer when a frenzied laugh rang fiendishly at my very ears, and I was wrenched off my feet and sent swinging with a crash against the wall. Before I could so much as stir, the creature came leaping upon me out of the darkness. I felt two frightful hands seize at my neck like knotted cords, the thumbs digging into my throat like solid bars of iron. Through a black mist I could dimly distinguish the distorted form. I lashed out feebly with arms and legs, but I was like a baby in that relentless grip. And then with a snarling yell of triumphant fury the creature shook me till my head seemed to be flying from my body and all my senses whirled dazedly. In a moment I would have lost all consciousness of what was happening to me.

But suddenly the thing threw me violently off, and flung round with a howl, for all the world as though it had been struck from behind. For my part I lay stupefied and choking, only half aware of its frantic antics. I can't hope to describe them. It seemed to me as though the very spirit of madness had been let loose. Dimly through the darkness I could see it clawing at the air with swift savage snatches as though striking at something that was pressing upon it. And then suddenly it clutched at its own throat, and became a mere whirling and indistinguishable mass as it plunged suddenly out into the moonlight or flung back into the shadow, uttering all the while sharp, guttural cries of rage and pain. Foolishly I lay and watched it, half wondering what its frenzy meant, and too stupid to rise and get my revolver. It seemed to me as though the thing were fighting with itself, and would soon tear itself to pieces.

I suppose all this had only taken a few seconds, though in my confused state of mind it already seemed an age since I had first seen that shadow rising into the moonlight. In fact, I could have believed I was having a bad dream as I lay there watching that hideous dance of madness. But all at once the room was flooded with light, and Blanche stood at the doorway.

At the sight of her the creature made as if to hurl itself at her; but suddenly it seemed to shrink and quail before her gaze, and crouched shuddering, pressed close against the wall, watching her between its fingers. She stepped forward a pace, and the thing was seized with a spasm, and seemed to shrink even closer into itself. Then, slowly, as Blanche gazed at it, it rose, and began crawling towards her, though slantingly as it were, as though it would willingly have fled from her altogether. It passed her, and backed out of the room, still with its eyes fixed to hers, and slowly she followed it as it moved out on to the landing, seeming to guide it with her steady gaze.

And then the wall hid them. Rubbing my eyes I rose unsteadily, and followed. They were disappearing into Blanche's room, the creature still moving backwards and Blanche advancing upon it; both with their eyes intent upon each other. I crept to the door and looked in. Seated on a chair in the middle of the room was Mrs. Wait, her eyes wide open and staring stonily straight in front of her. Her body was perfectly motionless except for an occasional spasm of pain that shot across her features and twitched her fingers in little starts as they lay upon her knees. She was muttering incoherently, though her lips scarcely moved.

Gaveston's body, for I don't know how else to name the thing, had come to a halt at Mrs. Wait's feet. It was crouched down on its knees, peering over its shoulder at Blanche, who was standing before it steadily fixing it with her eyes. For my part I just stood there watching helplessly. The thing had passed clear beyond me.

Then Blanche said clearly, "Gaveston, you must come now."

At this a cry burst from Mrs. Wait, and her face became convulsed with fear. But what set my heart thumping was to hear her moaning in Gaveston's voice, "No, no, no."

"You must," said Blanche.

"No, no, I can't," said the voice.

"You must," Blanche repeated.

"Oh, no, no," came the voice again. "I tried, I tried just now. To save Dick. But he beat me."

"You must try again," Blanche said.

Mrs. Wait moaned sadly, and I saw she was weeping. But gradually her face smoothed out calmly and lost all trace of its pain. Indeed it became utterly expressionless.

But now I glanced at Blanche and saw she was gazing with a terrible intentness at the creature before her. And suddenly there was a frightful shriek, and the thing sprang into the air, and clutching at its throat as I had seen it do before, it whirled round the room, gasping as though half throttled. I seemed to come to my senses all at once, and ran to my room for my revolver. I was back in a moment's time, and met the thing face to face as it came leaping towards the door. I flung out my arm and fired. What happened I don't know, except that I was hurled across the passage, jarred and shaken in every limb, and with a roaring echo at my ears.

When I came round I picked myself up unsteadily and staggered back to the room. Blanche was kneeling over the prostrate body of Gaveston, who lay deathly white with a red stain down his cheek. But what set me peering into his face was that it was the very face of Gaveston himself.

I looked questioningly at Blanche. A wonderful light glowed in her eyes. "Oh, Dick," she said, "look, we have won."

"What does it mean?" I asked.

"Ah," she cried triumphantly, "at the last moment. Dear little Gaveston. He won through after all. And look, even his eyes."

I looked, and the sightless eyes gazed back at me, pale grey as I had known them.

"But, Blanche," I said, "have I killed him?"

"You've saved him, Dick," she answered. "If he had lived he might have lost again."

I looked down at my little friend, utterly at a loss to understand what I had done.

Blanche spoke again. "But, Dick, if you had fired a moment earlier . . ."

"Well," I said.

"I don't know," she answered solemnly. "It was bad enough as it was. But if Gaveston hadn't won through . . . Well, I don't know, Dick."

She left me to attend to Mrs. Wait, who was still sitting in her chair, blinking dazedly about her. For my part I knelt down beside Gaveston and folded his frail hands across his breast. Something he had said, something about trying to save me, still echoed in my ears. What his struggle had been, I didn't know, but it seemed to me that he had made a supreme effort for my sake. Perhaps that was why the thing that had usurped his body hadn't strangled me when it had me in its power. Well, it was all beyond me. But there lay my little school chum, dead, and I had shot him. Yet if I were to believe Blanche I had killed him only to save him.

And suddenly my thoughts were wrenched violently from their course by a frenzied ringing at the bell. I sprang to my feet in alarm. I suppose the thought of the law came to me for the first time. It was Blanche who ran downstairs and opened the door, and following her with my eyes as she left the room I became aware for the first time of the terrified servants crowding at the bedroom entrance. Then I thought of my mother, and sent a girl to see if she had been frightened. And soon there came a hurried sound of feet up the stairs, and Doctor Dale came panting into the room. He knelt down quickly by the body, muttering, "My God! My God!"

Then he rose and said more calmly, "Well, heaven be praised!"

Suddenly he turned to me and said, "You shot him then?" I bowed my head, but he gripped my hand and cried, "It was well done."

I looked up to ask what he meant. I suppose he read the trouble in my eyes, for he said with more firmness than I usually saw him display, "I take full responsibility for this."

"Doctor!" I cried.

"After all," he said easily, "when an escaped lunatic breaks into one's house . . ."

Well, looked at like that I thought I had nothing to fear from the law, and indeed so it proved.

When the doctor had gone I went to my mother's room, and was rejoiced to find that she had scarcely been disturbed at all. I don't suppose she could have heard much even if she had been awake, as her room was well away from the scene of the affair.

In the morning, in spite of what had happened, Blanche and I set out for Hinton Hall, though not at the hour we had intended to. Blanche insisted on driving. I was glad enough to let her do so, as I was thoroughly weary. But for her part, she was radiant, and I wondered what tonic she could have found in a night of such terror and tragedy to give colour and life to her pale and wasted cheeks. But I thought I knew what it was when, swinging out of the drive, she waved her hand with an unaccustomed gesture of exultation, and cried, "Avery, you're beaten, beaten!"

She turned to me and said, "And he knows it. He was here last night all the while, waiting outside."

"What?" I cried.

"Yes," she said, "I felt him. He meant to have murdered us, just to start his career. But his minion has been crushed, and his power has gone."

"Gone?" I asked.

"Of course," she admitted, "he is still Avery."

PART II

Katrina

CHAPTER I

It was in full daylight that I entered the chapel at Hinton Hall for the second time, and I was surprised to find how utterly its first impression of ghostliness had vanished. Perhaps it was that the sprinkling of guests gave a sense of human companionship, or it may have been due to the garlands of flowers festooned along the windows, and crossing under the roof in intricate and airy mazes, and winding up the pillars on either hand. And as I led Blanche up to the altar, from somewhere behind us came delicate and delicious strains of music; like a flight of butterflies, I thought, or a rain of petals. Olave, of course, was awaiting the bride, drawn up very grave and straight, and I knew that behind us came Katrina, invisible to me, but shedding a fragrance that somehow seemed part of the flowers and the music.

The altar was almost severe in its simplicity, contrasting with the lavishness of the floral decorations all around. It was a plain block of alabaster with a gold cross inlaid on the top, and in front the graven sign of the Guthries, a serpent twined about a sword. On either side of the cross stood a lighted candle in an alabaster holder, the flames standing clear and motionless in the still air. And at the foot of the altar stood a vase with three large, white lilies.

The service was simple but beautiful, and most impressive. It gave me the curious feeling that marriage was a mystic thing, lying central in the mystery of life itself. I suppose I had always thought of it as the glorious consummation of desire, but now I began to feel even a little afraid of it, and glancing round at Katrina I met her eyes fixed wide on mine in solemn awe.

The ceremony over, the music burst radiantly out again, and the sense of constraining mystery fell from me, and my heart leapt with a wonderful gladness. Following the bridal pair to the vestry I found myself passing close to the tomb of Olave's father. And then I felt a touch on my arm. Looking round I saw Katrina urging me out of my course, and I stepped aside wondering. But on reaching the vestry she whispered, "You were walking over Olave's grave."

Her words sent a shudder through my heart.

As we went back in procession down the chapel to the swelling chords of the wedding march, I glanced at the floor where Katrina told me lay Olave's grave. A stone slab had been let into the marble, reminding me of the slab on which I had seen the coffin of Olave's father when it had risen so mysteriously out of the dark. I was careful not to tread on it, not only because it seemed to distress Katrina, but because I was half afraid it might sink beneath my feet and let me into the earth. The unpleasant thought made me shiver.

Passing by I noticed it was engraved like the altar with the sword and serpent, as indeed all the monuments in the chapel were. I was rather glad to be out in the open air again, for somehow the place had seemed to become haunted with hovering presences since I had looked on Olave's grave. All the fear and uneasiness I had known when I had entered it that first time had returned upon me, and it was good to see the sun shining again with no suggestion of death or mystery in its familiar face.

Olave and Blanche were unable to leave for their honeymoon straight away as they had intended, as Blanche would probably be needed for Gaveston's inquest. It had been arranged before that Katrina should return with me and stay with my mother while her brother was away, and this arrangement we held to, although the honeymoon was postponed, so as to leave the couple to enjoy their own company undisturbed. The guests left early, and I set off with Katrina in good time, as I didn't want to be caught in the dark. I decided to drive the car myself, promising Blanche and Olave that I would be extremely careful. Katrina sat with me in front, and behind us Ravin and Flame laid their huge bodies on the spring seats, revelling in unaccustomed luxury.

My last vision of Olave and Blanche was one of a pair of radiant lovers waving us adieu. "Now she will settle down," I thought to myself, and turned to smile at Katrina, wondering when it would be my turn to stand at the altar thrilled with the expectation of her coming. The yearning to speak to her at once surged up in my heart. But still she seemed so slight a child, though she no longer wore her hair in a girlish plait, and the melting curves of her body cried out to a man to crush her to him in an ecstasy of desire. But though my heart beat fast with the longing to speak to her, and a strange throbbing at my throat seemed almost to choke me, I kept telling myself it wouldn't be fair. And finally I was decided to remain quiet, at any rate during the journey, by narrowly missing the edge of a ditch; I realized I wasn't paying proper attention to my driving, so I slowed down a little and concentrated my thoughts on the car, while Katrina prattled brightly at my side.

"You're very quiet," she said at last.

"We mustn't have another smash, you know," I answered.

She was silent a moment, then said, "Dick, it was perfectly wonderful the way you saved me."

"Oh, nothing," I smiled back at her, though feeling splendidly proud.

"You must be strong," she went on. "I simply couldn't move, you know. And you just lifted the whole thing off me."

"Oh, well," I laughed, "there's nothing very wonderful in that. It's merely a matter of so much muscle, you know. You've either got it or you haven't."

"Ah, no," she said with a glorious ring in her voice, "it's strength, Dick," and added, "you see, I'm so little."

Somehow her simple words became instantly luminous to me with a wonderful interpretation. It was only the swerving of the car as I gripped at the wheel that brought my mind back to my job.

Katrina was fingering at my arm as she had done after the boat-race.

"You don't mind, do you?" she said, with an unconscious simplicity that I can't describe. And how could I tell her how the little familiarity thrilled along my blood like a running fire? I thought to have declared that my soul and body were hers to do as she wished with, but all I actually said was, "Of course not, Katrina." I didn't even dare to add, "I love it."

So we reached the gates of Chalk Ridge, and I slowed down for the porter to open them, as it was after sunset when they were always closed. The hounds had become weary of their enervating couches, I suppose, and realizing they had reached their destination they bounded out of the car and raced on ahead. And suddenly I saw them stop short and crouch low to earth, whining, and then they turned and came creeping slowly back. The car had only just started forward again, and they jumped in, still growling in a low, ominous sort of way, and Katrina leant over to them and patted and fondled them, and turning to me asked, "Is he here too?"

"He has been," I answered, adding, "it must be an old trail. I expect it clings."

But I knew that Blanche was right when she said Avery had been there the night before, when he had sent his madman in to murder us. And the words came back to me, "Of course, he is still Avery." I wondered whether he were still prowling about, waiting to strike. And what power had he now? What could he do? How could he avenge his defeat? Well, evidently Blanche didn't fear him now or she would never have consented to go away.

With that I was leading Katrina into Chalk Ridge, trying to imagine that she was entering the house as its mistress. The thought was so pleasing that I had no room for any other.

It was my intention to keep the affair of the night before hidden from Katrina. The police business had been rapidly settled during the early hours of the morning. Doctor Dale had smoothed things out, and the whole matter seemed perfectly clear and straightforward. Gaveston's body had been taken to the Asylum, and the inquest was to be held in two days' time. Meanwhile, Blanche's room had been set straight, but locked up by my orders. My mother's inquiries as to the disturbance during the night had been discreetly brushed aside, and indeed she wasn't too anxious to be bothered about anything which didn't immediately concern her. So I thought if I could keep the daily papers well out of the way for a week or so Katrina might remain in complete ignorance of the affair.

But on passing Blanche's door that night I shivered a little. It was my intention to keep it permanently locked, and I felt that now we had a real haunted room. It would have been more than I would have dared to pass a night in it alone. I saw that Ravin and Flame were set on guard outside Katrina's door, and as they passed by Blanche's room they sniffed suspiciously and growled.

I must have been thoroughly tired out, for when I woke in the morning a glance at my clock told me I was a couple of hours after my usual time. I jumped out of bed and drew the blinds. And crossing the lawn towards the house I saw Katrina with her hounds leaping gladly about her. With her hair under her red Breton tammie shining golden in the sun, she looked the very picture of morning. Somehow it seemed to me that she had been up with the lark, tramping the dewy fields, and bathing herself in the fragrant freshness of the dawn. But suddenly I felt alarmed. Blanche had told me not to let her out of my sight. Suppose Avery had been waiting for her; suppose she had met him! The fear was a vague one. I couldn't imagine what Avery should want with her in any case. But still the fear was there. I was turning away intending to dress with all speed, but she had seen me, and came running towards my window waving.

"Old lazy-bones!" she cried. And the hounds took excitement from her running, and raced round her in circles, and bounded up to lick her cheeks.

"Why, wherever have you been?" I said.

"To the morning Star and back again," she laughed in answer.

"And you've brought back the light of it in your eyes," I said, waxing poetical, though by the dancing sparkle in them as they were raised to mine I might have been speaking the very truth.

"Yours are still full of the shadow of the moon," she answered me.

And for a moment we remained so gazing at each other. Then I said, "But you're a real bad girl to have run off alone like that."

"Why?" she asked.

"Oh," I said lightly enough, though I wanted her to believe me nevertheless, "it isn't safe, you know."

"Why, where's the danger?" she asked, glancing about her.

I scanned the countryside for an answer, not daring to tell her the truth. "There's the Gipsies," I said, "in Morton's Dingle, and the old bull over there in Seven Elms Meadow. And then there's the level crossing; you might have been run over."

"Why," she cried delighted, "what a land of lovely dangers you live in. I'm going to chase the Gipsies with my dogs, and tease the bull with my tammie, and then sit on the railway line and hold up the first express."

She ran off laughing, and I called after her, "Wait a mo, Katrina, I'll be down in a minute."

"Oh, no," she cried, "you must come and rescue me in the nick of time."

She was still full of the whim when I arrived down to breakfast. She rather puzzled my mother by a breathless story of how I had fought three giant Gipsies who were carrying her off, and had wrestled with a bull that had nearly charged her down, and had stopped an express train, just as it was going to run her over, by chasing after it and catching hold of the guard's van. I had never seen her in such splendid spirits, and that day was one of radiant laughter. We even visited the Gipsy encampment where an old ragged dame whiningly called us pretty gentleman and lady, and told us our fortunes. It was all very romantic. Katrina was to be carried away and I was to rescue her, and all the rest of it; and the old hag, doubtless taking us for a pair of sweethearts, finished off the story with the happily-ever-after touch. I tossed her a shilling, which she rubbed and spat upon and pocketed with fawning gratitude.

Katrina looked at me and laughed, and said, "How awfully jolly that would be, Dick."

Then with a good stout stile to protect us we stopped to admire the bull. It was known to be a savage brute, and I wasn't going to risk taking Katrina into the field with it. In her usual ardent way she exclaimed, "How splendidly strong he is! And look at his head!"

Then she turned to me and asked, "Is it true that men used to wrestle with bulls?"

"Still do, I dare say," I answered her.

"But how brave they must be, and how strong," she said. She eyed me up and down, and looked again at the mighty brute. I could read her thought, and laughed, "No, no, you needn't think I'm wanting a bout with it." But I felt flattered all the same, and added, "A man who knew how to hit could kill it with a blow."

She looked at me with wonder in her eyes, and said quietly, "What, kill it? That?"

I suppose the bull had spied Katrina's red tammie, for at first it began to eye us fiercely, and then came slowly advancing towards us, its head swinging low and its tail lashing in a growing fury.

"Oh, look," said Katrina, "let's stare it in the eyes, and see if we can keep it away."

But our staring had no effect, and feeling none too easy, in spite of the stile between us, I said, "It's getting angry, we'd better go."

The next day I had to attend the inquest. Jestingly I warned Katrina not to get up to any mischief while I was away, as I wouldn't be at hand to save her.

"Oh, I'll be very good," she promised.

But to be on the safe side I detailed Tom, the biggest of my men, to keep an eye on her.

Although I had taken precautions I don't think I seriously thought there was any danger. And when I arrived back at night I was surprised to find Tom lurking about the drive, waiting for me. He stepped out from behind a laurel bush and said, "Excuse me, sir."

"Why, Tom," I exclaimed, "what is it?" And I felt a horrible fear. "Quick!" I ejaculated.

"Oh, the lady's all right, sir," he said, to put me at ease.

"Well, then?" I asked.

"Well, sir," he went on hesitatingly, "I don't rightly know how to tell you. I couldn't see just what happened, sir. And I'm puzzled like."

"You're sure Miss Katrina's safe?" I asked, still not feeling satisfied.

"Oh, yes, sir," he answered quickly.

"Well, then," I said, relieved, "just tell me what it's all about."

"You see, sir," he began slowly, "it was the bull."

"The bull?" I exclaimed.

"I suppose it had got loose, sir. Broken through the hedge, or summat. Nobody can clearly say, sir. Nobody seems to have seen it."

He had stopped. "Well," I encouraged him.

"Well, sir," he went on, "the lady was in the fields, when sudden-like the bull comes out of nowhere and charges down on her."

"Good God!" I cried.

"Yes, sir," he continued, "that's about what I said. I was taken all of a heap, sir. I couldn't do nothing as it were. And the little lady turns and sees it. And she stands quite stiff, a-staring at it. I've never seen that work yet, sir, though folks say it do. That is, sir, until someone steps out of the hedge. And he walks right up to the bull as it comes full at him. And I couldn't move a foot, sir, no, sir, not if you'd paid me a fortune. And then, sir, I couldn't believe my eyes. I thought to see him tossed up to the sky, and I blinked, dazed-like. But suddenly the bull seems to be taken with a weakness. His legs just crumple under him, and he falls flat with his nose right along in the grass. And the gentleman turns and goes up to the little lady, and I suppose she thanks him. I don't know all about that. But I goes up to the bull, sir."

"Well?" I asked, for he had stopped to wipe his brow. He seemed to be living the whole thing over again, and he was clearly frightened.

"Well, sir," he went on in a lower voice, "it was dead."

"Dead?" I cried.

"Dead, sir," he declared in a hushed tone, "the gentleman had killed it with his eyes."

For a moment I was chilled with a paralysing fear, then I exclaimed, "Where is he?"

"Can't say, sir," answered Tom, "when I looked round he had gone. Nobody's seen him. And the little lady went straight back home, and shut herself up. She won't say a word to nobody."

I didn't wait for more. I rushed into the house and up to Katrina's room. I listened a moment, then knocked gently at the door.

"Katrina," I said.

She opened the door to me, and stood before me very pale and grave.

I couldn't say a word. I just looked at her, glad to see her unhurt, but feeling as though something had come between us. I was looking at her as through a veil.

"Dick," she said quietly, and not in her own bright voice, "can you ever forgive me?"

"Forgive you?" I said. "Why, whatever for?"

"I suppose I ought to have been more careful," she answered.

"But, Katrina," I exclaimed, "it wasn't your fault. And in any case, I'm too glad to see you safe to be able to scold you."

But there was a question I wanted to ask her. I blurted it out all of a sudden.

"Katrina, who was he?"

She looked at me with a strange passion. "Dick, you've warned me against him, and you hate him, but he's saved my life."

There were tears in her eyes. I was dumbfounded. What did it all mean?

"Katrina," I said weakly, "I don't understand."

She became calmer, though evidently struggling against some powerful emotion.

"I'll tell you, Dick, what he said to me," she explained. "He said . . ." but she broke off, and cried, "No, I won't. He meant it for me. You would say it was all a lie. You hate him."

Again there were tears in her eyes. I looked at her in dismay. What on earth had the fellow been saying to her? I had it on my lips to tell her the truth of the Gaveston affair, but it seemed unsportsmanlike just after he had saved her. And, moreover, I didn't think she would believe a word of it just then.

I said simply, "Katrina, if ever I meet him I'll thank him from the bottom of my heart for saving your life. But I tell you plainly that I do hate him, and always will. You can think what you like of me, but that's how things stand."

Something of her old childishness came back to her face, and she said, "Oh, Dick, I don't quite know what's the matter with me. You aren't angry with me, are you?"

"Angry?" I exclaimed.

I thought for a moment she was going to throw herself on my breast and burst into a fit of tears. Her lips quivered, and she gazed at me with a strange yearning in her brimming eyes. I put out my arms towards her, but she slipped back into her room, and gently closed the door.

I waited for a minute or two, and knocked. She said kindly enough from the other side, "Not to-night, Dick." And I went away. And you may be sure I passed a troubled night, questioning what Avery could have said to her to make her behave so strangely.

In the morning she was her own delightful self again. She was hiding behind the dining-room door as I came down to breakfast, feeling jaded and stupid after a broken night. I glanced about the room for her and saw her drawn up very straight, with her finger to her lips.

"Shhh," she said in a whisper, "I've been a naughty girl."

At that I broke out into a peal of laughter, rather stupidly uncontrolled at the sudden revulsion of feeling at seeing her restored to her gay little self.

She said, "Can I come out of the corner?" with such an artless charm that my love seemed to swell at my throat and choke me.

Perhaps she read the meaning of my flushed face, for she came tripping up to me and said more seriously, "Dick, it was stupid of me. I'm sorry."

I told myself that her behaviour of the evening before had been merely the effect of shaken nerves. And yet there was still a shadow in her eyes. Something had gone, or something had come. In spite of her evident desire to set things just as they were before, I could feel a difference. It seemed to me like the touch of a gloved hand when you have been used to the intimacy of the naked flesh.

It was a day or two later when we found ourselves nearing Seven Elms Meadow again. Katrina suddenly seemed to realize where we were, and catching me by the arm said, "Not that way, Dick."

"There's no danger now," I answered. "The thing's dead."

"Dead?" she exclaimed.

"Didn't you know?" I asked.

"No," she said. "But how? Why?"

I looked at her searchingly, wondering what effect my words would have. I said, "It just fell dead when Avery looked at it."

She stood rigidly still. Then she whispered, "He killed it." But I couldn't read her thought.

CHAPTER II

I had seen Blanche at the inquest, and had been amazed at the change which two days of married life had made in her. She seemed to have stepped clear back into childhood again. Her cheeks were full and rosy, and her eyes dancing with a deep delight. She had thrown off the whole burden of the past as she might have tossed aside a cloak. I asked her of Olave, and she pressed her face to mine and murmured, "Wonderful!"

She spoke of the honeymoon to come as though she were to go a journey on a magic carpet, and she assumed easily that when she returned mother would go to Hinton Hall to live with her. I didn't disillusion her on that point, not wishing to break the spell of her content. I didn't see her again before the honeymoon was over, so she heard nothing for some while of the affair of the bull.

I managed to keep the papers out of Katrina's way without much difficulty. As a matter of fact, she wasn't of the paper-reading sort. The fields and the open air were her daily delight. For myself, I was beginning to be tired of seeing the photograph and reading the exploits of a certain "Mr. Bellew who rowed in the Oxford Eight." First he had done Herculean things in a motor smash; then he had rushed in and shot an escaped lunatic who had broken into his sister's room; and lastly, it was on his estate that a rather extraordinary fate had overtaken a bull. Somehow or other I always seemed to gain glory by publicity; but I didn't like it, nevertheless. I suppose I had always suspected people whose names appeared in the papers. They were connected in my mind with divorce-suits and thefts and murders. There seemed something shady about folk who suddenly broke from their obscurity to figure for a day or two in the public eye. Still, things blew over, and "Mr. Bellew who rowed in the Oxford Eight" was quietly forgotten again.

That summer, I suppose, was the most perfectly happy of my life. But I must pass it over, as apart from inevitable visits, or the more welcome inroads of my boisterous chums, it was merely a matter of little daily delights in the company of Katrina; very quiet and very ordinary, but illumined for me with a radiance not merely of this earth. And yet sometimes there came a shadow between us, vaguely disturbing, as though the memory of our little quarrel were still rankling in our hearts. "It's Avery's doing," I said, but I wouldn't mention his name, and I always steered away from any topic that threatened to bring him to mind.

When Olave and Blanche returned I took Katrina back to Hinton

Hall. But I was utterly unable to persuade my mother to accompany us. Blanche took the refusal quietly enough. I think she had quite made up her mind to let that matter take its own course. To tell the truth, I think my mother was really too weak to be moved, and as she was in the hands of a good nurse, who spoilt her magnificently, it would have been cruel to have thrust her back into the guardianship of Blanche.

I had for some time been meditating a scheme which I took the first opportunity to communicate to Olave. I knew my heart well enough to realize that Katrina was the only girl I should ever bother about in this life, but I wasn't so sure of her sentiments towards me. She had been growing a little less free with me of late, perhaps thinking that her childish familiarity was becoming too compromising. I wanted to speak to her, but now the old scruple was reinforced by her growing reserve. Besides, I knew she was almost utterly ignorant of life. Indeed, this made a great part of her charm. But, looking at the matter from a practical point of view, it seemed to me not only fair to her, but wise in every way, to let her spend a winter or two in London. She would see life as it was; she would develop. And if after that I could win her, she wouldn't be a mere delightful plaything, but would have something of the settled steadiness necessary to a wife and mother. Incidentally, I think I was flattering my own vanity in imagination, for the picture I loved to dwell on was that of Katrina tired of the frivolities of London turning back to me with a fuller appreciation of all that I could give her.

So I approached Olave and told him of my wish to stand as a suitor for Katrina, but suggesting that he should send her to his aunt, Lady Bullen, for one winter at least; and for my part, I promised to go to London partly to keep an eye on her, and partly to press my suit among the innumerable rivals that I could see in my mind's eye already clustered about her. And Olave agreed.

Katrina looked just a trifle blank and dismayed when she was told she was to go to London. She looked at me with a question in her eyes. I said, "I'm going too." And the way she clapped her hands was enough to appease the most ravenous vanity. And I must confess I left Chalk Ridge feeling not so much like a general at the opening of a campaign, as a conqueror preparing for his march of triumph.

Well, all this chapter of my life I must dismiss very hastily, as only a little of it has any bearing on my story. Lady Bullen received me affably enough when I first paid court to her, though I must admit she frightened me a little; and the vision of Katrina when I saw her for the first time in the shimmering semi-transparences of ball-room dress, set my lungs strain-

ing at my own tight costume. For to tell the truth, I was a hopeless igno-
ramus in all matters of London life and etiquette. I had loved the sports of
the country too well to sacrifice them to the glittering excitements of the
town. And now I began to realize that I hadn't been educated properly for
this sort of thing. I committed a hundred and one solecisms, and always
felt awkward and ill at ease at the dinner-table and in the ball-room. But I
comforted myself by saying that I was enduring it all for Katrina.

I dare say it was my clumsiness which in the first place made Lady
Bullen turn the cold shoulder on me. For it wasn't very long before I was
given to understand that my constant inroads into her house weren't ap-
preciated. A rare visit was tolerated, but that was all. I found myself being
pushed further and further away from Katrina. It was as though a river of
men in white-fronted shirts, and ladies in every conceivable creation of
costume, were rushing between us with ever increasing force and volume.
And at last I began to be thankful for a passing smile, or the touch of fin-
ger-tips in the press.

Katrina, I must say, showed none of my silly uncouthness. From the
first she seemed to be in her element. Not that she ever became a moth to
the glitter about her, but there was always something in her carriage, her
behaviour, her dress, the very play of her fan and the delicate inclination of
her head, which were eloquent of her purity of breed. I was fascinated
watching her, and found my greatest delight in hiding myself well in some
corner where I might peep out at her unseen, and warm my heart at her
adorable beauty. For though she never lost that freshness of grace which I
had learnt to love, yet she developed a richness and depth which were a
growing wonder to me. But all her simplicity returned whenever we managed to get a moment to ourselves. "Ah, here you are," she would cry,
catching me from behind as I was peering out for her from my hiding-
place, wondering where she had gone.

"Still on guard," I would say, not wishing her to know the real reason
for my sneaking into shelter.

"Why," she would declare, "I believe you think I'm in some terrible
danger, the way you hide and watch."

"Don't you like it?" I would ask.

"Oh, yes," she would exclaim, "I love to feel you're there, Dick."

"You see," I would say lightly, "you haven't got your dogs here to defend you."

And once she shivered a little at that, and said, "No, Dick, and I miss
them." And turning to me suddenly she laughed, "How lovely it would be
if you came and slept outside my door."

I laughed in my turn, and said, "The Old Griffin wouldn't allow that."

"The Old Griffin?" she asked.

"Sorry," I said, "I always think of Lady Bullen like that."

Katrina clapped her hands, and cried gaily, "I shall tell her."

"You won't," I said, feeling really alarmed.

"Oh, well," she smiled at me, "we'll always call her that to each other."

And for a week I had to feast on the memory of that little intimacy.

Another time she showed that I still held the old place in her thoughts by saying, "Dick, do you know I've had three proposals to-day, and two yesterday."

"Is that a record?" I asked.

"So far," she said.

But it cheered me to think that she could talk to me in this way. I was quite willing to bide my time. I began to count the weeks, setting myself a limit before which I wouldn't speak. After this, I thought, Katrina would know her heart; and I wasn't very doubtful as to the issue.

But as the season wore on Katrina showed signs of tiring. The sparkle left her eyes, and her face sometimes looked drawn and sad. I was even selfish enough to be glad of it, for I thought she would turn all the more readily to me when I came forward. But in spite of this I felt rather uneasy, too, for Katrina didn't look merely tired. I thought she was also a little troubled. And then she began to keep away from me. At least so I thought. I no longer felt those little finger-tip touches as we passed. And when she threw me a smile it had a twist in it which I didn't like. Also, I found it increasingly difficult to get an interview with her. The Old Griffin, if she didn't bar the door, at least thrust her own unwelcome presence between Katrina and me. I found myself alone with the old thing sometimes by the hour, waiting for Katrina to come; but she came less and less. I thought I felt the workings of a plot somewhere, and set myself to watch. I could discover nothing except that Katrina was beset even more than at first by rival suitors. It was painfully obvious to me, watching from my corner, that the girl was being badgered and badgered by titled folk. But I wasn't alarmed at that. As a matter of fact, it was part of what I had foreseen; and I was ready for it. I trusted Katrina to follow her heart. It was merely the Old Griffin who annoyed me. I knew she must be pestering the girl to make a conquest of a title. It all seemed clear enough, and ordinary enough. But somehow the explanation didn't satisfy me. There was more in it, and I couldn't fathom the thing.

At Christmas I had a better chance of speaking to her as she went back to Hinton Hall, and of course I drove over once or twice. But she seemed to have become herself again so completely that I didn't like to question her on what had been troubling her in London. "She just needed a rest," I told myself.

I met her at Hinton Hall with her usual bodyguard, and as she saw me she exclaimed, "Now we're complete." The idea that I was necessary to give the finishing touch to the picture was one to set at rest any doubts I might have had.

Blanche was more than ever a picture of happiness and content. She confided to me with a wonderful pride that the early summer would bring an heir to the Guthries. She put her hands on my shoulders and said, "Now are you satisfied with me, Dick?"

I answered, "You made a fine sorceress, Blanche, and you make a better wife. But I dare prophesy you'll make a better mother still."

She laughed gaily, and rubbed my cheeks between her hands.

All this was pleasing enough, but on getting back to London again I found the shadow had fallen over Katrina once more, I began to realize too, that I hadn't the entry into her world that I needed if I were to keep an eye on her. She had become a fine favourite, and no wonder; and I found I simply couldn't follow her in her rising flight. Accordingly, when I did see her, I could notice the change in her more easily than when I had caught at least a glimpse of her nearly every day.

Once when I did manage to get invited to a ball where she was to attend, I succeeded in coming to speech with her. Or rather she came to speech with me. For it was she who spied me out and came to me, not with the old glad cry on her lips, but with a rather nervous, "You don't speak to me now, Dick."

"Good God," I exclaimed, "I don't get the chance."

She stood before me very demure, and smiling rather strangely, occasionally glancing round to see if she were being watched.

"Why don't you call on me?" she asked.

"I do," I said, "but I have to sit and talk to the Old Griffin, and you never come near me. Sometimes," I added, rather spitefully I'm afraid, "I have the pleasure of hearing you at the piano. With a couple of doors in between, of course."

"At the piano," she repeated in a startled voice; then turned away, biting her lip.

I said, "Don't run off, Katrina."

"Well, you mustn't scold me then," she said, and there was a dimness of tears in her eyes.

"Why, Katrina," I cried, "whatever's the matter?"

I glanced about me, and luckily enough there was a conservatory handy. "Come in here," I whispered, "there's something you want to tell me."

She threw a rapid look behind her, and gripping my arm, said, "Quick then."

Once well inside I turned to her and said, "Now then, Katrina, what is it?"

But she had had time to collect herself. "Nothing," she evaded me, "except that I don't see you now."

"That won't do," I said.

"Well, what do you want to know?" she asked rather petulantly, and in a way so unlike herself that I was taken aback.

"Katrina," I said gently, "I believe there's something troubling you. Well, if it will help you to tell me about it . . ." And there I came to a stop.

She was silent a moment, then said, "No, Dick, I don't think it would help."

"Then there is something," I seized on the admission.

She answered more coldly, "It wouldn't help at all for you to know."

I began to feel a chilling doubt at my heart. Katrina had never spoken to me like this before. There was something dividing us; something that I knew could easily be torn aside if only I could say the right word.

"Katrina," I pleaded, "I've made you angry. I've been prying into things that don't concern me. I know well enough I've no right to bother you. It was only that I thought I could help. Perhaps you'd better leave me."

She clutched at my arm, and for a moment I thought she would tell me all, then her hand fell limp to her side and she turned away her face.

"Yes," she answered, and I stood there helpless and watched her go. But suddenly I had an idea. I sprang after her and said, "One word."

"Well?" she turned to me.

"Katrina," I said, "wouldn't it be rather splendid to go for a tramp together one morning, as we used to, early, before all these people are well in bed even?"

Her eyes lit up like the sky under kindling sunshine. "Oh, Dick," she cried, "yes, to-morrow."

So the next morning I had her to myself again. True, there was only the park to tramp in, but it was almost deserted, and in any case the luxury of being up early in the morning had become so rare with both of us that we were like children on a spree. It wasn't part of my plan to talk of disturbing things, so I kept the conversation, as far at least as I had any control of it, to memories and prospects of home; and Katrina kept on exclaiming, "Oh, if only we had the dogs!" And I know, when at last we parted at her door, that she had a glow and a colour in her cheeks that I hadn't seen for many a day.

"Oh, Dick, thank you," she said as I left her, "that was just what I needed. It was like a fresh wind."

I thought I had found out now what I wanted to know. The girl was just tired of her round of gaiety. A day in the country would restore her. She had left her heart behind, as I had hoped she would, and it would be mine for the asking when we returned home.

I should have liked to have repeated the little escapade indefinitely, but it wouldn't have been wise. Besides, it might have lost its effect with frequent repetition. But I decided one repetition would do no harm. I thought I had found my work for the month or so that remained before Katrina would leave for Hinton; it was for me to turn up at intervals with little surprises that would set her heart throbbing again with old memories and longings. So I ran over to Hinton Hall one day and brought back Ravin and Flame, and after some manœuvring I managed to get Katrina to promise to meet me in the park as before. And the brimming gladness of her face as the great hounds went leaping up to her in an ecstasy of welcome was as rich a reward as I could have wished for my pains. But I noticed that the eager joy soon faded from her face. I did my best to rally her as I had done before with memories of home, and she was grateful enough I am sure for my well-meant efforts, smiling frankly at each repetition of, "And I say, do you remember . . ." But there was clearly some disturbing thing rooted too firmly in her mind for my clumsy cheerfulness to shake away. The most I could do was to call up a momentary brightening of her eyes, and at times a happy sigh. Then continually, in my stupid way, I found myself verging on reminiscences which were better avoided, and by my hurried sheering away from them probably only made them the more conspicuous. And always at such moments I noticed how Katrina shivered, and turned from me with a sudden eagerness towards the dogs, till at last I could see only too clearly that there was a forbidden topic that neither of us must mention, and that forbidden topic was something to do with Avery. I tried to tell myself that Katrina didn't like to recall anything which suggested that we had ever quarrelled, though even so, the few words we had had after the affair of the bull could hardly be termed a quarrel. But then there was that other little scene in the conservatory. Once I nearly touched on that, and received immediate warning that it was forbidden. I began to grow seriously annoyed, chiefly because I felt baffled and teased by the hint of mystery in the misunderstanding which was dividing us. At last I blurted out, "Katrina, you're unhappy. For God's sake tell me what's wrong."

Her quivering lip was confession enough to the truth of my accusation. But she wouldn't answer me.

"Come," I pressed, "what is it?"

In my zeal I had come to a halt, and we stood facing each other. I didn't notice whether the park were full or deserted. All I saw was the trouble in Katrina's face.

"It's no good telling me you're happy," I went on. "I should hardly know you, you've changed so. But I didn't bring you out here to talk like this," I changed the theme, "I brought you hoping you might forget whatever it is that's hurting you."

"And, Dick," she said, "it's awfully kind of you. And I'm sorry I'm behaving so badly."

"That won't do," I declared. "I didn't mean to drag in unpleasant things, but since we seem to have stumbled on them we must just face them out. Now what's all the trouble about, Katrina?"

"Dick, I mustn't tell you," she said.

"Then there is something troubling you?" I asked eagerly.

"You keep on telling me so," she replied with a touch of coldness she had shown in the conservatory, and I felt it as a chill at my heart. For it was like a cruel hand firmly repulsing me, as though I were pushing in where I wasn't wanted.

I looked at her for a moment, and was on the edge of a passionate outbreak. But I mastered myself and said, "We've quarrelled twice, Katrina, don't let's do it a third time."

But at that it was her turn to exclaim, "Oh, Dick, we've never quarrelled."

"Not when Avery . . ." I began.

But she broke in with, "Ah, don't talk of that."

"Well then," I said helplessly.

"No," she went on more calmly, "don't let's talk of those things. I expect we think differently. It wouldn't help to discuss them."

"I don't want to talk about them," I said, "I only want to know how I can make you happy again."

She looked up into my face with a sudden return to her sweet childlike confidence, and said almost in a whisper, "Oh, just be my friend, Dick."

Well, what could I do? We turned and retraced our steps, and on the way back Katrina chatted as she had used to do, and was as bright as I could have wished when we reached Lady Bullen's house. But as we were saying good-bye the hounds began sniffing at the steps and growling ominously. I darted a look into Katrina's eyes. She had turned strangely pale. And with the shock of the truth I recoiled a step and exclaimed, "Avery! Here!"

Katrina drew herself up proudly and faced me.

"You've never told me," I said.

"It would have served no purpose," she replied.

Never had I felt so alienated from her. It was in my mind to turn and leave her, for there was something final and determined in her words and bearing that made me feel curiously weak. But the fear at my heart that Avery was drawing his mesh about her urged me to risk everything to save her.

"Katrina," I said, "if we've never quarrelled before we're going to do so now."

"Do you think this is a fitting place?" she asked.

I glanced rapidly to right and left. The street was almost deserted as it was still early morning. But I certainly felt a shrinking at the publicity of the place, and a spasm of wonder that I should be found behaving so in the open. But my fear for her safety broke down all such considerations.

"I can't help it," I cried. "If you'll let me come in we can have it out quietly, if not I shall keep you here till you listen to reason."

"I can't think what's the matter with you, Dick," she said.

"No," I exclaimed, "because you don't know the danger you're running."

"Dick," she said almost scornfully, "I can't stand here and watch you behave like this."

She was moving up the steps, but I caught her wrist, and said, "You'll either stay or take me with you."

She stared at me with wide eyes, and such anger in them as I hadn't thought possible. For a flashing moment it seemed to me that it wasn't Katrina who was standing there, but someone else; someone I had seen somewhere, I couldn't remember where.

"What right have you to treat me like this?" she asked, with a subdued passion.

But I wasn't to be put off. "The right," I exclaimed, "of my love for you. I love you Katrina, I love you."

"Dick!" she said, relenting.

"It's a queer place to be telling you," I went on, coming rather dazedly back to my senses, "and I had meant to have kept it till we got back home."

Her lips were quivering, and she asked almost in tears, "But, Dick, why didn't you tell me before?"

How could I explain? I just said, "Well, you knew."

"But I didn't know," she exclaimed. "You were like a brother," she added, fingering at my arm in the way I knew so well.

I seized her hands and said, "Well, Katrina, I've told you now. I love you. And you . . .?"

But she drew her hands away and said in a frightened voice, "No, Dick, no."

I spoke her name pleadingly.

"You should have told me before," was all she answered.

I was alarmed at I knew not what. "Why," I hesitated, "is it, is it too late?"

She repeated, "Too late," in a way that was neither a question nor an avowal.

"For God's sake," I cried in anguish, "don't keep me in doubt like this. Tell me, Katrina, tell me."

But that baffling look was coming back to her eyes. She was gazing at me in a way I couldn't understand, a tense, almost questioning way, but whatever it was, it was utterly unlike herself.

"Tell me," I repeated in an agony of suspense.

"Later," she answered quietly.

"No, now," I cried, and again seized her hands. But she snatched them from me with vigour, and said, "You have no right to . . ." But she broke short, and added relentingly, "yet."

I watched her in dismay as she turned to go up the steps. But the hounds brought my mind back to Avery, for they flung themselves in her way and would have stopped her.

"Down," she cried, and they shrank from her, looking strangely ashamed.

Again my fears returned, and I put my hand on her shoulder, and said, "Katrina, won't you take warning? You see what they think of him."

"They're only dogs," she replied. But her straight, hard look drove in the sting of the unspoken irony.

"Very well," I said, turning away, "you won't take warning. I shall have to use force."

"What do you mean?"

I meant nothing more than that I would warn Olave and make him take her away. But I answered, "I shall kidnap you and carry you off home."

At that she laughed and clapped her hands with a complete return to her own bright self. "Oh, Dick," she cried, "how lovely!"

I was bewildered, but I said, "You mean it?"

"Yes," she answered, and came tripping down the steps to me. "Look," she said confidingly, "I'll tell you how. Come here to-morrow morning, and I'll be all ready. We can slip away together, and the Old Griffin won't know anything about it. Why, we'll have time to get home and send her a telegram that I'm all safe before she's down to breakfast."

All the burden seemed to have lifted suddenly from my heart. I didn't pretend to understand what it all meant, and I didn't intend to ask in case I should draw down the old shadow again. So I said, "Right, you promise?"

"Promise, Dick," she answered, and added, "That'll let you see that I'm not in danger, in spite of all your fears."

"It'll certainly take a load off my mind," I answered. "Somehow," I went on, "you don't seem yourself in London."

A shade passed over her brow, and I thought I had made a mistake. I put in quickly, "But you'll be all right at home."

She said in a tired voice, "I don't feel quite myself, except when I'm with you, Dick. And even then sometimes . . . Well, I don't know quite what. I believe, you know, that you've taught me to be a little afraid. But I shall be all right after to-night."

Once more she was going to leave me, but she stopped half-way up the steps and faced me with the trouble darkening about her again. I thought she was going to go back on our arrangement, and I said, "You've promised, remember. To-morrow morning." I turned to go before she could go back on her word. But she called after me, "Dick, Dick."

I had to turn again. "Well?" I asked.

She had come right down to the street, and was looking rather timidly up at the windows, I suppose to see if anyone was watching. Then she took me by the arm and said, "Round here."

She led me down a side street and up a little alley. We came to a door which she opened, and I peeped through and saw a smooth lawn well bordered with spring flowers, and with a large greenhouse at the farther end. We had come round to the back of the house.

Katrina was whispering to me. "Dick, I've a better plan. It'll be such fun." But she spoke nervously all the same.

"What is it?" I asked, for she had stopped short.

"Much better fun than the other," she went on. "You must come for me here, to-night." She paused and looked at me.

"To-night?" I repeated.

"At exactly one o'clock," she continued. "I shall be here. But if I can't get away, don't wait. At least not more than ten minutes. But, Dick, don't be late whatever you do," she finished, with a stress of warning.

I didn't like the escapade, and I tried to put her off. "Don't you think it might be rather compromising if we're caught?" I suggested.

"Oh, we must risk that," she answered lightly, "it'll be such fun."

But the thing that was puzzling me was that her words weren't convincing. She seemed to me to be playing a part as though she were trying to make herself think it was fun. I couldn't believe it was just a mere frivolous prank, because such an explanation seemed absurdly out of keeping with what I knew of Katrina. Her childishness was never stupid frivolity. And yet I couldn't see what other motive there could be.

"You don't like it?" she asked me.

"Well, no," I said, "I must confess I don't. If people got to know they might say things about you."

"Well, Dick," she said, "I'll tell you then, I've got a reason."

"Yes?" I asked.

"Ah, I'll tell you the reason when we're safely home," she said.

"All right," I agreed, "here, to-night, at one o'clock. And if you don't come, then to-morrow morning as we agreed before."

"Yes, Dick, yes," she said, and added, "Sir Knight doesn't look overjoyed at the prospect of rescuing his fair lady."

"Rescuing?" I asked.

"Oh, that's what the Gipsy woman said," she laughed. "You see, I haven't forgotten."

"If there were any rescuing to be done . . ." I began.

"Oh, we must make a game of it," she said coaxingly.

"You see, fair ladies don't really need rescuing in this dull old world nowadays."

She opened the little garden door and stepped through. Ravin and Flame naturally enough followed, and she cried gaily, "Ah, you coming too? Come along then, you shall guard the castle gate."

The last I saw of her was the heaven-blue of one eye as she smiled at me through the closing door.

CHAPTER III

I turned away slowly, feeling by no means easy in mind, but clinging for relief from the doubts that assailed me to the thought that at least Katrina was willing and even eager to leave London and escape with me to the healthier atmosphere of her home. Her strange request that I should carry her off in the middle of the night perplexed me; but not seeing any possible solution to the mystery, I dismissed it from my mind, and merely accepted the fact of the thing. And now with the menace of Avery suddenly looming up larger than ever, it became imperative to get Katrina away from London by any means that might offer. So I took a deep breath and stepped out from the little alley. The discordant cry of a milk-boy and the clattering of cans brought my mind back to the realities of daily life. The world was awakening about me, emerging from the mists of dream, where I myself seemed to have been straying, to take on again the shape and colour of day-time actuality. And suddenly the adventure of the night to come appeared to me no more than a thing to be successfully planned and carried through.

I reached my hotel, and while at breakfast a telegram was handed to me. I slit open the envelope and read.

"Mother very ill. Come at once.—BLANCHE."

I leant back in my chair feeling stupidly weak. It seemed as though something had happened to me, and I couldn't quite think what. My mother was ill. She was probably dying. But that wasn't the trouble. There was something else beating deep in my mind, a sort of subdued throbbing, like a pain trying to make itself felt through the numbing deadness of an anæsthetic. And the realization of what it was came to me very quietly. Of course, I shouldn't be able to keep my appointment with Katrina.

Well, I must let her know as soon as possible. After all, I could probably be back again for the morning. Or in any case if I couldn't, I could wire Olave and he would take my place. It would only be necessary to tell Katrina that I couldn't come at night. She must wait for me till the morning.

I rose, intending to despatch the message, but collapsed limply onto my chair. What on earth was the matter with me? I suddenly knew that I was trembling violently. There was a coldness about my brow, and when I put my hands up to my throbbing temples they were wet. I lifted my paper with shaking hands to cover my face in case anyone was looking at me, for it seemed to me that I must be rather a queer spectacle. Somehow I felt that I was deadly pale. Even my fingers were white to the tips, and strangely nerveless.

I began to speak to myself in my own mind, "Look here, what's the matter with you? Are you ill, or what?"

It was as though someone had answered me, "No, you're just in a white funk."

That seemed to set my mind properly functioning again. What was I scared at? Good God! Of course, something might happen to Katrina while I was away. My message might go astray. She might be waiting for me. And then something she had said came back to me; "1 shall be all right after to-night." Why to-night above all nights?

It wasn't my nature to grope about among riddles. My strength had come back to me, and I rose steady enough now. I had to make sure that my message reached Katrina. I sent a personal note by messenger. I sent a telegram. I sent a registered letter, as there was plenty of time for it to reach her during the day. Also I called at the house hoping to speak to her personally, but in that I wasn't successful. However, I thought there was no possibility of all three messages going astray. So with a fairly easy mind I set off for Chalk Ridge, my thoughts gradually disentangling themselves from the worries of London to fix themselves upon my dying mother.

She died within half an hour of my arrival. Doctor Dale was there, and Blanche, of course. The doctor whispered to me, "You're just in time. Your sister couldn't have kept her going any longer."

Poor little mother! But I couldn't feel much regret, for she looked so peaceful and contented lying there, with all the care smoothed out of her face. Blanche took my hand, and said, "She's happy now, Dick."

There were a great many things to be arranged, of course, and it was late in the day when I told Blanche I must be off to London again. A few words explained why, and the look of surprise in her face changed to one of strange dismay.

"Oh, Dick," she cried, "why ever didn't you go at once?"

"Well, I'll be off now," I said.

"But you can't get there by one o'clock," she exclaimed.

"No, of course not," I answered. "I told Katrina to wait till the morning."

Blanche was straining at her fingers in a nervous way. "You ought to have gone before," she repeated.

"Why, what's the matter?" I asked.

"Oh, may be nothing," she replied, "but I don't like it. But you must get the next train," she added.

I couldn't see why Blanche should be so anxious. I told myself that my own queerness of the morning had been due to the sudden discovery that Avery was at his games again. But Katrina merely had to lie low during the night, and I should have her out of it in the morning. And then I felt immensely cheered by the knowledge that she had her hounds to guard her. Really there was no possible danger, for I knew he didn't want to murder the girl, otherwise why had he saved her from the bull? Some darker menace might be threatening her, and probably was, but that would be frustrated in the morning.

Well, calming myself as well as I could with such considerations, I set off for London again, dozing and waking in my corner of the carriage as the train rolled rumbling through the night. Vaguely I noticed the stars in the sky, and the sparks rushing by the window, and the black shadows of trees and houses appearing and vanishing with a little swish as the train cut past. I had travelled on the night express more than once before, and it was all very ordinary. There was nothing to suggest that evil things might be happening while the world slept. I dozed away, and woke again, and always my mind was turning on the meeting ahead. It would be good to take Katrina by the hand and race her off to safety. To-morrow we should be returning this same way, but with the fields rushing by in the good daylight.

Only once, if I remember rightly, was I startled out of my sleep. I woke with a terrible cry ringing in my ears, the cry as of a creature being violently torn away to torment. But I laughed at my fright when I realized that it was merely the train's shrill whistle as it plunged into a tunnel. I looked at my watch. It was a little after one. If things had gone as they had been planned I should have been creeping away with Katrina by now. I felt a sudden desire for the little fingers in my hand, trustful and clinging, and seeming to say, "Oh, how strong you are!" And with that I smiled to myself and curled up again in my corner.

It was early morning when I reached London. I had time to go to my hotel for a refreshing bath before I was due to meet Katrina. Feeling very wide awake, in spite of the night journey, I stepped out on my errand of rescue. I thought of the adventure as Katrina had spoken of it. I was off to save my lady-love from a wicked enchanter. Smiling at the childish thought I reached the house, and commenced a patient promenade at a little remove from it, so as not to arouse suspicion. In a minute, two minutes, Katrina would appear, and I should calmly march her away to safety.

But Katrina didn't appear, and growing impatience changed to anxiety. Sometimes I walked right in front of the house scanning the windows for a sign of her. I noticed the blinds were all drawn. I couldn't see a movement nor hear a sound. In five minutes or so I came back, again eagerly searching the windows for some possible sign from Katrina. And through a chink in a blind I saw a wan gleam of light. That cheered me a little. Someone was stirring then. It wasn't till another five minutes had passed that it struck me as being somewhat peculiar that anyone should choose to dress by electric light when the morning was already so bright. Again I strolled past the house, and this time I noticed a gleam of pale light in one of the reception rooms. I stood stock still for a moment. What on earth . . . There was a mystery somewhere, and my heart went cold. Instinctively I raced round to the back gate where Katrina had told me to meet her. What I expected to find I don't know. I pushed the gate open an inch or two and peered through. There was nothing to see. I pushed it open a little farther, but something seemed to be weighing against it. I just managed to strain it open wide enough to put my head round. And there on the ground were Ravin and Flame lying huddled against the gate, keeping it shut.

"Good dogs!" I murmured, feeling immensely relieved. If there had been any danger during the night . . . But there my thought seemed to freeze, for I caught a glimpse of Ravin's eyes. They were staring wide, but glazed filmily, unblinking and unseeing. I burst at the obstructing gate, and forced my way through. Eagerly I bent down to the dogs. They were dead.

I fell back a pace. Something in their attitudes as they lay huddled there told me how they had died. With one last leap they had crashed the door to, and had fallen dead. But too late. That I knew. The enemy had passed their guard. Gamely as they had died, it had been in vain.

Why I stood there gazing at them instead of alarming the house I don't know. But something seemed to paralyze me from moving. And then I think I went mad. With a shout I rushed for the house, and burst in. Dimly I realized that the lights were all blazing full. Swinging round a corner I tripped and fell over a prostrate figure. It was the butler who lay sprawled across the passage. He growled sleepily as I tumbled over him. But I hadn't a thought to give him. I rushed on and broke into the room where I had seen the light from the street. And there I came to a dazed halt. All about me, lolling on chairs and couches in every attitude of sleep, was a company of ladies and gentlemen in evening dress. At my feet I just noticed that the carpet had smouldered into a hole where a cigar end had fallen from a prostrate sleeper in a chair beside me. And in the middle of the room a little brazier still glowed redly, sending up a thin curling blue smoke that scented the room heavily.

For a moment I stood there too amazed to move, then I let out a howl, and rushed from one to another shaking them back to consciousness. I can't describe how dully and languidly they blinked into slow awareness of their state. All I know is that I was wild with impatience and apprehension before anyone was sufficiently awake to answer my repeated cry, "Where's Katrina? Where's Katrina?" For she wasn't in the room.

Suddenly someone took up my cry, "Why, yes, where's Katrina?"

There was a blank searching of speechless faces. I saw Lady Bullen gazing foolishly about her, and I rushed to her and shook her vigorously by the shoulders, still shouting, "Where's Katrina?"

She made a ridiculous effort to draw herself up with dignity; as though it had been a wax thing that had begun to melt, and springing up with a frightened scream she ran from the room, as well as her clinging dress would allow her, calling thinly, "Katrina, Katrina!" I followed her as she stumbled up the stairs, regardless of appearances, and even pressed in after her as she bustled into Katrina's room. The bed had not been slept in, but it showed that Katrina had rested there, for the coverlet was disarranged. And on the floor were some torn scraps of paper. I flung Lady Bullen aside, and stooped to examine them. They were my messages. She had received all three. They lay in a little torn pile on the carpet by her bed. A vision came to me of the girl in a strange dismay reading and reading that repeated phrase, "Can't come to-night. Meet me to-morrow. Dick." And I turned my eyes to the crumpled bed, and could almost see my little sweetheart tossing there in a fretful anguish at my disloyalty to her. But I rubbed my eyes to clear them of the picture, for I knew it was a time for action not for sentimentalizing.

I turned to Lady Bullen and said fiercely, "Well, where is she?"

She flung out her arms and dropped them limply to her sides. "Gone," she faltered.

I raced downstairs again. There was an animated discussion going on among the aroused sleepers as I entered the room. I cut into it sharply, "Look here," I cried, addressing no one in particular, "I want to know what this means. Where's Katrina?"

There was a sudden silence, and a drawling voice began, "And who may you be, if it's not impolite to inquire?"

I saw it was all useless. "I'm off for the police," I said.

At that the ladies set up a startled chattering, but I slammed the door and sprang for the street. There was a constable in sight, and I hailed him.

He came up at the double, and I called to him, "Just prevent any of these people from quitting," for there had begun a panic-stricken rush from the room. He was in time to hold them back, while I 'phoned Scotland Yard.

But all the details of that matter I needn't go into. It caused a fair scandal at the time. The inquiry showed that there had been nothing worse than a foolish tampering with spiritualistic things. There had been some sort of society clique, very secret and select, that had made a hobby of such matters, under the guidance of Avery. He had been their priest. And I dare say the fellow had skill enough to hoodwink such a pack of brainless dupes. I knew he could do a trick or two that would hold weak minds in amazement. Well, he seemed to have succeeded pretty well. Hysterical women referred to him as a saint; one or two declared it was the second coming of Christ; and when the hunt was out after him they whimpered primly of martyrdom.

All that sickened me. I didn't go into it in detail. I knew just enough to picture to myself the kind of thing that had happened. And all the time, I knew, Avery had merely been weaving his net about Katrina.

It was to have been some kind of test of his power, the inquiry showed. He had declared he could will anyone of his flock to follow him, though all the rest should try and prevent him. He had picked on Katrina, because, he had laughingly said, she believed in him the least. She was to be surrounded with a guard, if she wished, but he would have her away from them. He even stated the time when she would follow him. One o'clock . . . Well, it was all too painfully clear what had happened. The fellow's power must have been enormous. He had sent that whole household to sleep, had drawn Katrina out to him, against her will I must believe, and had killed her hounds as they had tried to save her.

Of course, everybody said he would bring her back again. But I knew better. Scotland Yard seemed to share my view, and the most skilled detectives were set on his track. But they found just nothing.

For my part I turned to Blanche. I was wildly angry at the imbecile stupidities of these tom-fooling idlers, and I whipped up my anger and kept it in a blaze to prevent the harrowing fear that clutched at my heart from numbing my reason. I knew I must keep all my faculties clear and alert if I was to find and save Katrina. The word rescue came back to my mind, and with it a mocking thought that the old Gipsy woman had been more of a prophetess than she had known herself to be. I hoped her prophecy would come true. At any rate there was the need for rescue now, but success was another matter.

I took express to Chalk Ridge to consult with Blanche, and suddenly remembered that my mother was dead. It seemed ages ago that she had died. But there she lay unburied. The funeral was to take place in three days' time.

In the hush of my darkened home, and under the shadow of my mother's death, my anger left me, and I began to realize what had taken place. Katrina was in the clutches of Avery! However I tried to envisage the meaning of that in all its possibility of horror, the plain statement of the fact was more appalling than my most lurid imaginings. My little Katrina in the hands of that man!

Blanche was comforting, but her face was drawn, and her lips were thin and white. "We shall save her," was all she said at first. She repeated it quietly again and again, and then changed it to, "We must save her."

She was looking right out far away. She seemed to be seeing things.

"Yes, but how?" I was asking.

My thought was that my mother's funeral would hold me at home inactive for the next few days. The fellow could be over the Atlantic before I could follow him. And in any case I had no clue.

The alarming significance of the situation took a tightening grip of my mind. "Blanche," I exclaimed suddenly, "we're helpless."

"I have allies," she answered me steadily. I thought I remembered her having said that once before. I couldn't think when.

"We shall need them," I said bitterly.

Olave was sent for, as Blanche said I might need to be away on the trail any minute.

"But where is the trail?" I asked blankly.

Even the hounds were dead who might have set me on the man's track.

"That's for me to find," she answered. She went to the window and raised the drawn blind, looking far out. "And don't be alarmed, Dick," she turned to me assuringly, "I shall find it all right. But it's for you to follow."

"Give me a lead . . ." I began.

"Dick," she cut in, "you know this is serious, don't you?"

"Good God, Blanche," I said with a little laugh.

"Ah, yes, of course," she turned from me, "but you don't know how serious." She paused, and then turning her eyes on me again she said slowly, "Dick, it may mean killing."

Some obscure association of thought made me blurt out, "Mr. Bellew who rowed in the Oxford Eight . . ." I stopped and said, "Killing?"

I looked to Blanche who seemed to have grown suddenly fatigued. "Good Lord!" I said to myself, "she'll be a mother in a month or so."

One by one the complications of the situation were forcing themselves on my mind as I came gradually out of the bemused confusion of thought and feeling which I had been thrown into by the shock of the disaster.

"I say," I ejaculated, "we shall have to be quick."

"Every day is precious," said Blanche, but she didn't mean what I meant. I realized all of a sudden how absolutely dependent I was on her aid. In a month she would be unable to help me.

"You show me the trail," I said, not asking myself how the task was to be accomplished. I just took her at her word. She had allies. I remembered now that she had said that when she was pitting her strength against Avery for the salvation of Gaveston.

Well, the battle had passed into a second phase; and the prize now was infinitely more precious. Suddenly I felt a surging agony at my heart, and crying bitterly, "Katrina! Katrina!" I ran from the house. A motor was driving up to the door. It stopped and Olave jumped out. We gripped each other by the hand without speaking a word.

CHAPTER IV

I was for leading Olave straight away into the house to join Blanche, so that we might fix on some plan of campaign, but he turned back to the car, and I saw for the first time that he hadn't come alone. A lady was getting out, and he held his hand to her to help her. She raised her face as she stepped down on to the gravel, and I recognized Mrs. Wait. Olave introduced us. I was rather taken aback, and I think my confusion must have been noticeable, for Mrs. Wait smiled rather wanly, and withdrew the proffered hand; but I recovered myself, and mumbling an apology took the hand as it drew back.

She smiled more cheerfully at that and said, "I'm not really very wicked."

My thought was that I had never seen quite such a timid little woman. There was nothing about her to suggest wickedness. Rather she seemed to me as ordinary a specimen as one would wish to see of the uncertain little soul whose whole aim in life is to steer away from all possibility of disturbance. There was a question in my mind as well as to what her part was to be in the coming battle.

I wasn't left long in the dark. Blanche, of course, took Mrs. Wait to her room, but it was scarcely a couple of minutes before they rejoined us downstairs. Blanche beckoned me aside and said, "Are you going to stay, Dick?"

"Stay?" I repeated, not taking her meaning.

"You can see what's going to happen, can't you?" she explained.

I looked blankly round. Mrs. Wait had drawn a chair to the centre of the room, and was evidently waiting some signal to be seated. Olave was by the window, and had his hands on the cord of the blind.

"Do you mean . . .?" I began in dismay.

"There's to be a sitting," said Blanche.

I threw a startled look at her, and was suddenly aware how changed she was. The married Blanche that had seemed to me so full of lovely, womanly charm had vanished completely, and the old Blanche of the Gaveston days had usurped her place. She stood up before me, tense and determined, as she had used to do in the days that now seemed so far away. I felt then as I hadn't felt before the vital nature of the issues that waited on the battle in which we were about to engage. And a foolish sense of my own utter weakness to cope with the thing made me feel queerly faint. I tried to speak but couldn't frame a word.

I think Blanche read what was passing in my mind. She drew a chair up near the door and said, "If you want to go just slip out quietly."

"Look here," I pulled myself together and managed to say, "is it, is it anything fearful?"

Blanche looked as though she would have laughed, but the seriousness of the thing prevented her. She said lightly enough, "My dear Dick, it's just as simple as you could wish."

I had mastered my first stupid shrinking, and said, "Well, just tell me what to expect."

She hesitated a moment as though deliberating, then answered, "Well, I'm going to try and get father to help me track down Avery."

"Father?" I exclaimed.

"I dare say Gaveston will help too," was all she answered.

"I don't understand," I cried.

She said, simply enough, "Hadn't you better just sit quiet and listen? You'll learn in a minute or two."

So I sat down. Blanche gave a sign and Olave drew the blind, and the room became dim and shadowy. Mrs. Wait disposed herself in the chair, letting her head sink deep into a soft cushion, and laying her arms along the arms of the chair. Blanche stood before her, slowly moving her hands; and presently stepped softly away and seated herself at a short remove near to Olave.

I looked towards Mrs. Wait. She seemed to have fallen asleep. But after a little her breast began heaving uneasily, and her lips began to move and a confused muttering and murmuring came from them. Then suddenly there was a clearly enunciated word, "Feefie," and a child's voice began speaking, "Feefie sees a stranger. Feefie afraid."

Immediately Blanche took up the conversation, "You mustn't be afraid, Feefie. Now, just listen."

But there came a petulant, childish complaint, "But Feefie is afraid."

Blanche spoke out sharply, "Listen, Feefie; there's no time for nonsense. I want to speak to father. At once."

"But . . ." the voice began.

"At once," Blanche repeated, with emphasis.

"But it's so long," said Feefie, whoever she might be, "Feefie hasn't seen him."

"I must speak with him. Now," was all Blanche said.

There was a little indistinguishable noise, a kind of fretful sniff, and then for a little there was silence. For my part I couldn't understand what on earth was happening. I don't know what I had expected to happen; but with the memory of that night in my mind when I had heard Gaveston speaking through the lips of Mrs. Wait, I had at least expected to hear my father's own voice. I looked across to Blanche, and raised my brows in sign of inquiry. She walked quietly over to me.

"Who's Feefie?" I asked in a whisper.

"The control," she answered.

"The control?" I said questioningly.

Blanche looked at me with a little playful smile quivering at her lips. "To put it in your lingo," she said at length, "she's the one who pulls the wires from the other side."

"Look here," I began, but Feefie had started speaking again, and Blanche went back to her seat.

"Here's daddy," she was saying, "and Feefie can see someone with him. Feefie not seen her before."

"That's all right," said Blanche, "it's mother."

"Feefie thinks daddy very happy," the voice went on. "He's smiling at Feefie."

"All right, Feefie," said Blanche, "that'll do. Now I want to speak to father."

"Yes, yes," said Feefie, and after a pause she began again in a slightly altered voice, "Is that you, Blanche dear?"

"Yes, father," Blanche said, "and is that mother with you?"

"Yes, dear. We're very happy now," came the voice. "But you haven't called me for a long time. It seems rather strange."

"I want your help, father," said Blanche. "We've lost Katrina. Where is she?"

At this there was a confused muttering for a moment, and then came the voice of Feefie, "You did say Teena, didn't you, Blanche?"

"Ka-tri-na," Blanche repeated very distinctly.

Again there was a slight murmuring, and Blanche repeated, "We've lost Katrina, father. We don't know where she is. You must help us find her. It's desperately urgent."

"I'll try," came very faintly, and then Feefie seemed to interpose with her own comment, saying in a sort of confidential whisper, "Oh, Blanche, what have you said? He shakes his head, like this. He's frowning. Feefie thinks he's hurt somewhere."

Blanche cut in rather sharply, "I want to know what he says."

The answer came hesitatingly, "Near; she's near."

"Where?" asked Blanche eagerly.

"M, M," Feefie went on, "I can see an M and R. Feefie can see M and R. No, no," she broke off querulously, "Feefie can't make it out."

"Look again," said Blanche.

"Daddy making such faces at Feefie," the answer came. "What is it, daddy? M, R, another M. Daddy shakes his head. N; is it N? Yes, yes, yes; he nods, like that. There's M, R, and N. Feefie can't see any more."

"You must," Blanche exclaimed.

"No, no, no," came the fretful protest. "Daddy tired."

"Father," Blanche called.

"Blanche dear," the answer seemed to come from very far away, "you haven't called me for so long. It all seems very strange now. And I must pass on now mother's come over. She says good-bye. We both say . . ." Then suddenly Feefie seemed to break out in her own voice, "Oh, daddy, he's going, fading, I can't see him. Blanche, why's he fading like that? Feefie's lost him in the mist. Just his eyes, and they look so sad. Feefie see his eyes. Yes . . . No . . . Daddy's gone right away."

There was silence in the room for a minute. I looked to Blanche. She had risen and was gazing very fixedly at Mrs. Wait. Then she said slowly, "Feefie, you must find Gaveston for me."

There was such an outburst of childish petulance at this, that I felt I wanted to laugh. And yet Blanche took it all so seriously, as though she were indeed talking to a child actually before her. All at once the whole thing seemed to me a monstrous piece of tomfoolery. I wondered how I could have sat there so long listening to such extravagant nonsense. Yet Olave had no smile on his face, and Blanche clearly believed she had been talking to her father, and was even now forcing some unwilling child who called herself Feefie to go and find Gaveston. And Gaveston was in his grave!

There had come another pause. My intention was to have Blanche out of this. That timid little woman in the chair must be deeper than she seemed. She had Blanche and Olave dancing to her wires. I wondered what they were paying her. I rose and crossed over to Blanche. "Look here," I said, "this is all rot, Blanche."

"I told you you needn't stay," she answered.

"I'm going to wake her up," I declared, taking a step towards Mrs. Wait.

Blanche gripped my arm, her eyes blazing; and Olave rose sharply and held me back.

"Well," I repeated, "this is all rot."

"You'd better leave us," said Olave, "you don't understand."

"Feefie!" I ejaculated in scorn. Then an idea came to me. "Last time," I said, "I heard Gaveston speaking in his own voice. If that was really father speaking just now, why didn't he speak himself? There's no consistency in the thing."

"You forget," said Blanche, "that Gaveston hadn't passed over." For my benefit she added, "Not really dead."

At that I turned and left the room, and as I closed the door behind me I heard that ridiculous childish prattle begin again.

I was angry. This way of dealing with the calamity that had so suddenly overtaken my darling seemed the most futile trifling. For the scene I had just witnessed appeared increasingly stupid the more I thought of it, till at last I could scarcely believe that I had actually sat and listened to that fantastic dialogue. Even now, with the knowledge of later events to steady my judgment, I can't remember ever having heard anything so utterly unreal and unreasonable. Children at their most extravagant games of make-believe would seem sane by comparison. And at the time, beating about in my fretfulness to express my sense of disgust at the thing, I could think of no other way of describing it than as mere silliness. It seemed, indeed, just silly. But what angered me was that all this while Katrina lay in the power of Avery. How was I to find her?

I spent a hectic quarter of an hour trying to get a trunk call through to London. Eventually I succeeded, but it was useless, Scotland Yard hadn't got a clue. They couldn't understand the business. Avery and Katrina had just vanished. Well, they wouldn't have been so surprised if they had known what I knew of their quarry.

I roamed from room to room, unable to settle to anything. Then I strode out into the grounds, still asking myself how on earth I was to get on the track of Katrina. And in spite of myself those three letters, M, R, and N, ran through my head. I had grasped enough of the Feefie business to understand that Avery was supposed to be somewhere near, at a place presumably containing those three letters in its name. But there was no such place. I went over in my mind every village and farmstead within a thirty mile radius. There was no such name that I could recall. As, of course, I knew there wouldn't be, because all that affair was just silly tomfoolery; the kind of tomfoolery that had lost me Katrina in the first place, and wasn't likely to win her back for me now. So, at least, I told myself, cursing myself for a fool whenever I found my mind beating about for the name with the three letters.

And always, like a background of gloom to my enraged thoughts, was the knowledge that upstairs, lying very white and still, was the dead body of my mother. I went back to the house and sat beside her for half an hour, trying to steady my mind and cool my anger. Feeling more subdued I went downstairs again. I stood for a moment outside the door where Blanche was still talking with her precious Feefie. I could just hear the shrill, querulous voice, and I turned away in disgust. They were at it yet.

I strolled a little way from the house, but soon returned upon my tracks. It wasn't safe to leave the place. There might come a message for me at any moment. Where from, I didn't know. I had begun to give up hope of Scotland Yard being able to do anything. And now I knew what Blanche meant by her allies. Allies, indeed! She was being fooled finely by that insignificant little woman with her prattle of Feefie.

I took to a restless pacing up and down in front of the house.

It was some while later that Blanche joined me.

"Well?" I said, coming to a pause before her. I had meant to say a thing or two to relieve my feelings, but the sight of her tired, pale face made me restrain myself.

"Nothing just yet," she said wearily.

"Blanche," I exclaimed, taking her by the shoulders, "you must stop this business. It's tiring you. And just now you know you've got to look after yourself."

"It's unfortunate," she said weakly.

"Well, then, stop it," I said.

"No," she answered more firmly, "I must see it through."

"But, look here," I said peevishly, "it's all rot in any case. There's no call for you to wear yourself out for a stupid fad."

Her eyes took on a harder look, and she answered me steadily, "Dick, it's just no use at all your trying to bully me like this. I know perfectly well what I'm doing. It may seem nonsense to you. It must do. If you want me to explain, I'll do so. If not, well just leave me alone. It'll take a little time. Gaveston's not used to things yet. But he knows where Avery is, and he'll get his message through in time. And in any case, Dick, it's a tiring enough business without having to quarrel with you."

I made one last appeal. "It's not for my own sake," I said. "I was thinking . . . Well," I blurted out, "you must think of your responsibility to your child."

"I'm responsible to Olave for him," she said.

"Oh, well," I threw at her, and walked away.

But Mrs. Wait seemed to have taken up her abode in the house. I avoided her as well as I could, and she seemed to avoid me. No wonder, I told myself; for I thought I was the only one who could see through her humbug. And yet I couldn't twist my picture of her into anything else but that of a timid, shrinking little thing, afraid almost to be seen, and terrified when spoken to. It seemed impossible that she should be the cunning trickster that I told myself she must be. So I steered away from her, not liking things I couldn't understand. And whenever I knew there was a sitting in progress I gave the house a wide berth.

So the day of the funeral came, and my mother was quietly lodged in her long home. And Blanche and Olave left for Hinton Hall, taking Mrs. Wait with them, much to my relief. Blanche told me to stay at Chalk Ridge, for all she knew was that Katrina was in the neighbourhood. She might have a message for me at any time.

I shrugged my shoulders incredulously, but refrained from saying anything to displease her. She gave me one parting piece of instruction. "There's a hut in the mountains," she said, "which has something to do with Avery's hiding-place."

"Well, that's not near here at all events," I answered.

"No," she said, "but if we miss him here we must find him there."

"A hut in the mountains," I couldn't help saying, "that's not much of a clue."

"More will come," she declared.

"Oh, well," I tried to put an end to the useless talk. But she was searching my eyes in a way I had learnt from of old. And presently she said very solemnly, "Dick, when you get there what are you prepared to do?"

"When I get where?" I asked, not liking the way she spoke.

"Well, when you find them," she changed her question.

"Why," I said, "I shall, I shall . . . Good God! I don't know," I began to fumble for some conception of what I should do. "It all depends," I ended.

Still Blanche was fixing me with those dark eyes of hers. "Dick," she said very solemnly, "I should advise you to kill him."

I fell back a step and laughed rather stupidly. I didn't know what to say. I think I stuttered something about murder not being in my line.

"Yet you must kill him," Blanche repeated.

"Look here, Blanche," I cried, feeling strangely shaken by her whole way of speaking and looking at me, "this is all mighty unpleasant. You talk a deal about believing your Bible and all that, yet you want to send me out on an errand of murder."

"I do believe my Bible," said Blanche, "and I know that Christ cursed his enemies, and withered the fruitless fig-tree with a word. And see here," she went on, touching a pendant on her breast, "this is the sign of the Guthries; the serpent for healing and the sword for killing. When there's an evil thing in the world the sword's the only remedy."

"Well," I said, still trying to laugh to mask my strange nervousness, "I can't see myself deliberately murdering a fellow in cold blood; but if he gives me an opening, well, I suppose there's no one I should more gladly put a bullet through than Avery."

"That's how you saved Gaveston," said Blanche. And until she spoke no memory of that affair had crossed my mind. I felt suddenly nerveless.

"Yes," I muttered.

We said good-bye. But I threw off the oppressive weight at my heart when I gripped Olave's hand, and was able to say, "Look after her, Olave, don't let her get tired. I know how weary she can get if you let her."

"Thank you, Dick," was all he said.

CHAPTER V

Looking back I can't understand how I endured the agony of these days as patiently as I did. I suppose it was merely another case of my stolid, blunt nature serving me as a defence. For knowing in whose hands Katrina had fallen, and having no clue as to her whereabouts, I ought to have been prostrated with anxiety. But as a matter of fact, for the most part I was merely thoroughly angry. A sort of stupid rage kept me in a state of fuming annoyance with everybody and everything. I tramped out for long walks, with the dim thought in my mind that I wanted to get to some place whose name contained those three unintelligible letters. Yet whenever I caught myself consciously crediting that absurdity, I cursed myself furiously.

I tried to reconstruct in my own mind exactly what had been happening in London to put Katrina into the power of Avery. I thought if I could work at the problem from that point of view I might get some clue at least as to Avery's purpose. For it baffled me to think what he could want with the girl, unless his motive were mere revenge; in which case, I told myself, we should soon hear from him with some monstrous ultimatum. But for the life of me my imagination couldn't picture the past with any kind of coherence or probability. I could go no further than the police inquiry had done, which had merely exposed the folly of an idle clique, whose sole purpose had been to find some new and thrilling game to ease their boredom. There had been hypnotisms and mesmerisms, and trances and planchette-writings, and dabblings in all the absurdities of spiritualistic trickery. And Katrina had been caught in the middle of it, merely because Lady Bullen had been dupe in chief. Well, I understood now why she had been so averse to my company.

But this didn't explain the puzzle that was really worrying me. It was the behaviour of Katrina herself that I couldn't understand. I could see now, looking back on the affair, that she had been frightened. She had known that that night was to decide her fate, and that was why she had planned that extraordinary elopement. She must have been afraid that she wouldn't be able to resist Avery's spell upon her, and so had called me in to protect her. But why, I asked myself again and again, didn't she tell me long before what was happening? Why had she kept the whole thing a secret from me? There was a dark fear at my heart that perhaps her own inclination was not so averse to Avery as I would have wished. But always I argued down that doubt by telling myself that she had summoned me to carry her away to safety at the very moment when Avery was to have put his utmost power to the test.

And here my imagination, strangely enough, did give me some kind of picture of Katrina's struggle. For somehow that crumpled coverlet and the torn messages on the floor brought vividly before me the tormented girl fighting down the charm that was rising about her, and crying out against me for deserting her in her time of need. I could see her reading in an agony those messages of betrayal, tossing upon her bed, and calling on me to come and save her; and at the last tearing the papers into shreds as the spell grew too strong for her, and creeping away to her doom.

I could see all that in my mind, though I wasn't given to such fanciful imaginings as a rule, and the vision distressed me. But when I let my mind play about her actual state I couldn't call up any kind of scene at all. The whole thing was just a blank to me. All I knew was that I had got to find her and rescue her.

But how? And again and again, I ranged over all possible means of coming on her trail. But there seemed not a sign. The police couldn't help me, and I began to think they never would be able to. Some other agency was needed to track down a man like Avery. And then I turned to Blanche. But all that Feefie business seemed too preposterously absurd to give me the help I wanted. I found myself going over that broken scene in my mind, and trying to explain it with some kind of logical connectedness. Feefie "pulled the wires from the other side." Blanche had been kind enough to translate into my own lingo the meaning of a control. I supposed she was the medium in the spirit world, just as Mrs. Wait was the medium in this world. But why was a medium needed? If all you had to do was to talk away as though you were actually in the presence of the departed spirit, why couldn't you do it anywhere, and without the need of others butting in? I dare say such questions seem absurd enough to people who profess to understand the matter, but those were the questions which constantly rose to my mind, and made the affair seem paltry and ridiculous. And then the whole idea of speaking to someone who was dead as though he were in the room with you, and pretending that he was answering your questions, seemed so tame and petty and altogether unworthy of the vast mystery of death. I might have been convinced if there had been something really mysterious, even frightening, in the procedure; but there was no suggestion that there was anything supernatural in it at all. It was all too utterly commonplace for words. And then that absurd child's prattle . . . I simply couldn't force myself to put any faith in the thing, and yet, inconsistently enough, I kept looking to Blanche to give me the guidance I needed, and incidentally kept my revolver always about me, mindful of her warning.

So the days passed for a while, but I kept no count of time. And my only solace was to keep my muscles in trim, ready for use, I told myself. For I couldn't bear to think that my strength was to be of no avail. I remembered how Katrina had rejoiced in it, and I swore I should put it at her service yet, though often enough I asked myself of what use was muscle in such a fight as this. I felt like an unarmed man facing a battery of guns. And I think that feeling of helplessness against odds was the most maddening I had to endure. The consciousness of fitness was no longer the bounding delight it had been, but merely the sober realization that I was ready for the battle when it should break.

I liked to haunt the spots where I had spent happy moments with Katrina. The one place I avoided was Seven Elms Meadow where we had looked upon the bull. The memory of that episode was disturbing. I felt even a twinge of jealousy; for it was against the bull that Avery had displayed his prowess. Well, he had saved Katrina's life, and I ought to have been thankful to him. He certainly had a power. And yet it was that very power that had broken down Katrina's last guard. Thinking of the bull I remembered with a spasm of anger the murdering of Ravin and Flame. They had been faithful to the last. They had tried to save their mistress, but he had killed them. And somehow the picture I had now of Katrina was a lonely and forlorn one. She stood by herself, a little dot on the landscape. There was no huge following shadow, and no leaping dogs at her side. Her body-guard had gone. She was defenceless and alone. Whenever my thoughts came round to that I clenched my fists and stamped in an unavailing fury.

One day my wanderings brought me face to face with the old Gipsy woman who had strayed a little from the encampment. A sudden impulse made me accost her. I suppose I was feeling particularly sore against my fate just at the moment, and I blurted out, "I don't think much of your fortune-telling, mother."

She answered me in a whine, "The pretty gentleman must be patient. He hasn't come to the end of the road."

Something in her eyes made me cry out, "Why, what on earth do you know about me?"

She continued in her fawning whine, though there was more assurance in her voice as she answered, "Would he rescue the little lady and not lose her first?"

I was going to question her, but it suddenly occurred to me that of course she knew all the gossip of the district.

"I suppose you think you can get another shilling out of me," I said angrily, and turned away. But she clutched my arm, and I faced her again.

There was an enigmatic smile wrinkling at her lips, and her eyes glowed strangely bright for such an old crone.

"The pretty gentleman can keep his shilling," she said. And there she paused.

"Well, what do you want?" I asked impatiently, impressed by something in her manner in spite of myself.

"He would give me his hall and lands to know what I know," she went on.

I was certain that she was just playing with me, banking on the disappearance of Katrina to make me think that she really could look into the future, and so weedle some more money out of me. And yet I couldn't tear myself away from her. I had to stay and listen.

"Well, what do you know?" I asked.

She shook her head, and shuffled her feet.

"If the pretty gentleman will come with me," she began, looking up at me with a dark amusement in her eyes.

"Where to?" I asked.

She pointed with a shaky hand to the encampment. "To the Cuckoo's Home," she said.

She took a step or two, and I was making to follow, when the absurdity of the thing struck me afresh. I stood still and said, "Look here, mother, you haven't got a baby to deal with. Now just tell me what all the mystery's about."

She shook her head and walked on, mumbling, "Then the little lady must break her heart."

I sprang after her, questioning her volubly; but she would say nothing. And in this way we came to the encampment, where I stopped, feeling a fine fool, for it seemed to me that I had suddenly become an object of immense interest to this dusky clan. All about me were faces gazing and fingers pointing, and heads nodding together in rapid chatter. I felt horribly uncomfortable, and felt my face flushing hotly. I gripped the old hag by the arm, and said as authoritatively as I could, "Now then, tell me at once what you want with me."

"It was the gentleman who followed me," she answered with enigmatic impudence.

I would have marched off in a huff, but at that moment she hobbled up to a dilapidated tent, and drew aside the dirty canvas that was raggedly slung across the entrance. The shadowy figure that I saw within, drawn up very straight, sent me, after a gasp of surprise, leaping towards her with the cry on my lips, "Katrina!"

CHAPTER VI

I ducked beneath the flapping fringe of the low doorway and had her in my arms, exclaiming, "My darling, oh my darling!"

She had been standing stiff and alert as one does when the whole body is listening, but at my clasp she seemed to fall limp, and I let her sink gently onto a pile of rough bedding, though I would rather have held her to my breast.

She sat there weakly, with her arms around her knees, and her face half raised to mine as I stood above her in the darkened tent. "I kept telling myself," she said in a toneless voice, "that you would come."

"Katrina," I cried, "have you been waiting for me? Long?"

"I kept saying, 'He must surely come,'" were her words; but there was no answer in them to my question, and no expression to interpret her thought to me.

"Katrina," I said more quietly, feeling that all wasn't well, "it's over now. I've found you. Let's go."

"It was the last chance," she went on, still not heeding what I said. "She wanted to bring you before, but I wouldn't let her go. But this was the last chance. I had to see you."

"See me?" I exclaimed. "Of course. Well, let's go."

I put my arms down to her and would have raised her, but she didn't respond by the least movement. She weighed like a piece of dead matter in my arms, and I set her down again.

"What is it?" I cried in alarm. "For God's sake, Katrina, tell me what the fellow's been doing to you."

At last there came a sign of animation to her face. She passed her hand across her brow, and her lips trembled as though she wanted to cry. "Dick," she said faintly, "why won't you say good-bye to me?"

"Good-bye?" I repeated in dismay.

"Oh, Dick, Dick," she exclaimed more passionately, "I did want to see you just once more. I wanted to say good-bye. Why do you stand there like that? Why won't you speak to me?"

"Speak to you?" I could do nothing but echo her words stupidly.

"Don't you know," she said slowly, "that we shall never see each other again?"

I just breathed her name in a whisper of dismay.

"Didn't you know?" she repeated. And suddenly she broke out into a mirthless peal of laughter, which sank into a sob and stopped abruptly.

I stood there utterly at a loss. What did it mean? She had collapsed into a huddled heap, her head drooping low beneath her shoulders.

"Aren't you going?" I heard her say faintly.

At that I realized that I had got to do something. "Katrina," I said sternly, "I've come to take you away." I bent down and caught her round the waist, but she put out her arms and strained herself from me with amazing strength. I fell back in confusion.

"You've got to come with me," was all I could say.

She answered me with spirit, "Dick, how stupid you are. I can't come with you."

"Whatever do you mean?" I asked weakly.

Her voice sank again to its first toneless pitch. "Oh, Dick, I told you. I just wanted to see you again and say good-bye." And before I could answer she asked again, "Don't you understand?"

"No, I don't," I replied with some heat. I knew that if I were to break through the baffling estrangement which was somehow holding us apart I must assert myself as one must when treating an hysterical patient.

"I don't understand," I repeated. "All I know is that you're coming with me. Now."

Again I laid my hands on her. She didn't attempt to resist me. But in a voice utterly colourless she said, "Of course I'm not coming with you. You came to say good-bye."

"For God's sake," I cried, "get that stupid idea out of your head There's no good-bye in the affair at all. You're coming with me."

"But it's all so silly," she answered me dully.

I tightened my grip of her. "Come," I said sharply.

"It's too late," she said and there was something in the slow, dull, matter-of-fact way she spoke which sent a chill to my heart. I nearly let her fall. Her words had a finality about them which no amount of blustering or argument could brush aside. So convinced did I feel that she was speaking the naked truth that I set her back on the bedding and turned to go.

"Good-bye," I said.

Then with a sudden sense of yearning at my heart I turned to her again. It was absurd to surrender her like this without a blow struck. And she lay at my mercy. I merely had to pick her up and carry her away to safety.

"Katrina," I exclaimed, "I think you're making me mad. I didn't come to say good-bye."

"You've said it once," she answered. "It'll be more difficult the second time."

"There won't be a second time," I declared. "You're coming with me now."

"You see, that's silly," she said.

And for the life of me I couldn't make the plunge and whisk her away as I knew I ought. She was so lifeless, so inert, as though already we were far apart and all she had to do was to sit and mourn for me. There seemed to be invisible bars between us, or rather unseen fingers that pressed me away from her whenever I would have drawn near. I tried to throw off the impression that was settling about me that she was lost to me, that we belonged to different worlds, and that I couldn't stretch out a hand to save her. For gradually it seemed that although she was sitting there at my feet, yet she was really leagues away, with a great water washing between us. It was her presence that was the unreal thing, not the distance that divided us. I felt as powerless as one in a dream who would pluck a flower but cannot move his hand.

So I stood for awhile in silence, with this horrible impression of ineffectiveness growing upon me and numbing my faculties. I couldn't shake it off. It was closing me about. I tried to break the spell by speaking her name. But it sounded far off, as though another had whispered it through a thick curtain.

She began to speak again, still in the same slow quiet way. "If you had taken me with you before . . . But that was a long time ago. We should have been very happy, Dick. But you should have taken me before when I was waiting for you."

I made a desperate effort to shake myself back to reality.

"Come now," I said.

"You didn't tell me, you know," she went on. "You didn't tell me you loved me, Dick." Her voice became broken with a little whimper, and immediately I was on my knees beside her. But she sprang up and cried out terribly, "Oh, Dick, why did you betray me?"

Then she sank back upon the bedding, shaken with sobs.

I put out my arms to her. "Katrina," I said desperately, "I've come to you now. Look, here I am."

She rocked herself to and fro, while I tried to steady her, still saying, "I'm here, Katrina; I've come to take you away; to live with me for ever."

She grew calmer again, and I heard her say, "Good-bye, then."

"It isn't good-bye," I insisted.

"Yes, it's good-bye," she repeated with dull composure, the storm of tears having swept past.

I rose impatiently, wondering what on earth a fellow ought to do with a girl in such a state. For I thought Avery had turned her wits. And looking down at her I suddenly saw she was smiling, wanly enough, but smiling. "I'm quite happy," she said simply.

She looked and spoke more like herself. I thought there was still a chance. "Come, then," I said.

She shook her head.

"I'll make you," I threatened her.

"You could have made me once," she answered.

"Why not now?" I asked, laying my hands on her shoulders, and determining not to let her go this time.

"Because I love him," she said; and I fell back as though I had been struck, repeating feebly, "Love him?"

Something of the wildness of tears came back to her as she cried, "Yes, I love him. You always hated him. You know you did. But I love him."

A horrible suspicion was darkening at my thoughts. Could it be true that she had gone with him willingly? I cried out in dismay; "Katrina, for God's sake tell me the truth. He forced you, didn't he? Tell me he forced you."

"You see, you didn't come," was all her answer.

"And if I had come?" I asked.

"But you didn't," she evaded me.

"Yet you wanted me," I pressed her.

"You didn't come," she said once more in a tone so expressionless that I was utterly baffled to know what she meant.

I hesitated for a moment, again half turning to go, for what could I do in the face of that "I love him."

"Good-bye, Dick," she said, "you've been a dear boy. It's a pity, isn't it? But you must go."

That brought me back to her, and again I declared that I was going to take her with me.

"Ah, no," she said, as one might speak to an importunate child.

If only she had resisted me I should have known how to treat her. But this perverse assumption that we had merely met to say good-bye paralysed my will. And all of a sudden I found myself on my knees launching out into a passionate appeal. What I said I don't know. But I eased my mind of many things that I had been thinking of Avery. I warned her of the danger she was in. I told her something of Gaveston, and the wickedness that had broken his life. "You can't love him," I ended.

But all I received for my pains was, "Yes, I love him."

"But, Katrina," I went on, "he's just got you under his spell. He can make you do and say just what he wants. You can't love him."

It was useless. She seemed to take no notice of what I was saying. She went off into her own thoughts, and said, "Now you must go. He said I could say good-bye; just that."

"He said so?" I cried; and added, "Why, where is he then?" It hadn't occurred to me till that moment that he might be near. I sprang up repeating, "Where is he?"

"Do you want him?" she asked.

"Where is he?" I merely asked again.

"Why do you want him?" she avoided the direct answer.

Why, indeed? At that moment I think I could have killed him without compunction. I drew my revolver from my hip pocket, and said, "That's why."

Katrina gazed at me in a strange silence; and just then a gleam of sunlight fell through a rent in the doorway full upon her face. There was a fierceness about her brows that I couldn't have thought possible if I hadn't seen it, and a look of hate about her whole face that appalled me. And suddenly I stared deeply into her eyes. The blue of heaven had dulled to the colour of storm. But the expression passed as rapidly as it had come, and I thought I had imagined the whole thing. She dropped her eyes and said wearily, "Well, put it away."

I slipped it back into my pocket, saying, "That's where I keep it; always ready." She glanced at me quickly, and once again her gaze fell. I felt strangely confident all of a sudden. Perhaps the feel of the weapon and the sense of power that it gave me had brought me back to reality. For the last time I stooped to take a grip of her and carry her away with me if she wouldn't come of her own accord. "Now then," I said, "we must go."

"Good-bye," she answered.

"Katrina," I said sharply, "are you coming with me, or must I carry you?"

"Just neither," she replied.

"We'll see," I said, tightening my arms about her. She lay limp and unresisting as I began to raise her up.

"Because," she said, "I'm married."

I suppose I ought to have dropped her with a cry; but as a matter of fact I set her down very deliberately, and said, "Of course that's not true."

But it was true. And all my passionate outcry against the monstrous horror of the thing couldn't avail against the naked fact of it. What we said after that I don't know; but I remember striding back home alone, cursing the blue heavens and all the world of men.

CHAPTER VII

There was a telegram waiting for me when I reached home. I opened it list-lessly enough, and read,

"Morton's Dingle.—BLANCHE."

I looked stupidly at the curt message, feeling bitterly that it was of little use to me now. And even if it had come earlier it wouldn't have helped at all. Katrina was lost to me. And deep in my mind there was another thought which was crueller still. She was lost to herself. I couldn't put the thing vividly enough to my tortured heart; to say that her life was blighted, ruined, utterly smirched and spoilt, didn't express the heavy horror that beat throbbingly somewhere deep within my soul.

I glanced again at the unavailing message as I held it limply in my nerveless fingers. So limply that it slipped and fluttered to the floor. I stooped languidly and picked it up. "Morton's Dingle." And suddenly those three mysterious letters seemed to stand out clear from the rest of the name. Why, what a fool I was not to have thought of the place before! But my mind had been busy with towns and villages. And then in a fume I told myself that it was just a coincidence. Yet in spite of myself I felt a re-turn of hope, a sort of dim stirring only, but enough to bring my mind back to realities again. For I had been under a cloud, pushing blindly through a baffling weight of fog which had obscured the familiar face of things and distorted all my thoughts and feelings to monstrous and fantas-tic shapes of nightmare. I began to ask myself where I had been, as though I had suddenly awakened to find I had been wandering in my sleep. All that strange business in the shadowy Gipsy tent seemed far away and ut-terly unreal, and I had to hold to certain vivid memories of it to persuade myself that it had actually taken place. For already it seemed as remote as the last dream on waking. I could almost see it visibly slipping back into the night to merge shadow-like with the shadows; and the voice of Katrina speaking came to me sleepily and thin.

I had wandered up to my bedroom, I suppose with some idea of changing for dinner. Looking from the window I could see the Dingle with its gaudy caravans and untidy tents. I could distinguish the one where I had met Katrina. "It's true," I cried, "it's true!"

And then the whole thing surged upon me in frightful clearness. But especially I seemed to hear that fatal, "I'm married." And then would come, "I love him," and somehow that seemed more full of menace still. What was there to be done? What could I do but accept Katrina's verdict, "It's too late."

I found myself crumpling the telegram into a ball, and that set me thinking of Blanche again. Of course I must let Olave know. The thought only just came to me. I went downstairs and got out my car and set off for Hinton Hall. And once started, the speed of the racing hedgerows on either side, and the rush of the air about me stirred me into life again, and I began to wonder whether everything were so hopeless as it seemed. However, I must break the news to Olave without delay, and take counsel with him as to what could be done. The thing began to seem more and more urgent as the road spread out behind me, and so I was distinctly annoyed to find myself held up at the level crossing by a tedious goods' train that seemed to have all eternity before it. However, with the falling of the night I reached Hinton Hall, and had delivered the fatal news.

"Where's Katrina?" Blanche asked me quickly as I jumped out of the car; for my coming had been expected, and they had been listening for me.

"It's no use," I said. "She's married."

"But where is she?" Blanche asked again.

"Can't you understand?" I answered her. "She's married."

We entered the house in silence.

Blanche began as soon as the drawing-room door closed behind us, "And you mean to say you haven't brought her?"

"How could I?" I said.

"You've left her behind?" she went on, as though there were something unbelievable in my conduct to which she couldn't reconcile herself.

Olave spoke. "Let's get it all clear," he said quietly. "Tell us your story, Dick." So I told everything that I could remember of that extraordinary scene in the tent.

There was a moment of silence when I had finished, then Blanche said, "And still I don't understand why you left her behind."

I felt irritated and said rather sharply, "I'm not used to running off with people's wives, Blanche."

"Oh, Dick," she answered me, "you supernal fool. Is this a time to stand on pride? Do you mean to say you're not willing to sacrifice a trifling convention when Katrina's whole life's at stake? Don't you see that the only way to save her is to carry her off bodily?"

"Well," I answered weakly, "somehow I couldn't. She wouldn't come."

"Wouldn't come?" cried Blanche. "What's the use of brawn and muscle if you can't handle a child like that?"

I began to feel fretful at the attack, "I tell you I couldn't," I repeated. "There was something that baffled me, I couldn't get my will to work. I wanted to carry her off, but there was something that wouldn't let me. I can't explain. It was just like that; I couldn't."

"Oh, Dick," Blanche said more quietly, "if you'd guessed what was at stake you'd have broken through all that."

"It was my fault," Olave put in, "I should have gone."

"You couldn't have done anything," I declared. "I didn't realize it at the time, but now I can see that it wasn't merely that she didn't want to come. There was something between us, a feeling in the air . . . Oh, I can't describe it," I broke off, "but it had me beaten."

"Now you're talking sense, Dick," said Blanche.

"It seems to me," I exclaimed, "that I'm talking infernal nonsense; and yet that's how it was, all the same."

"So he's married her," said Olave. "Why?"

"Why?" I cried. "It's about the worst blow he could have struck, I reckon. He's got her to keep, and we can't get her away from him. We've just got to sit tight and hear from time to time how he's bullying her. . . . Good God!" I ended, "it's beyond picturing. It's horrible."

"It's worse than horrible," said Blanche.

For a minute there was silence, and for my part my mind was in a frenzy of crude imagination, busy envisaging the tortures Avery had in store for Katrina.

Blanche began again. "You've got to go back and get her, Dick."

But at that the fact of the marriage rose up formidably in my mind. "But I can't," I said.

She answered me very solemnly, "You're saying to yourself, 'She's married,' aren't you, Dick?"

"Well," I began.

"I tell you," she went on, "you've got to get her away from Avery. And if marriage stands in your way you've got to sweep it aside. And if life stands in your way you've got to sweep that aside. I've already told you it may mean killing."

"Well," I answered, "that's cleaner than the other thing."

"Incidentally it's more effective," she said, "as long as you make sure."

Again there was a pause, and Blanche repeated, "As long as you make sure." Then she asked with a strangely ominous voice, "Dick, is it possible that you don't know why he's married her?"

"Why," I answered, "it seems to me a pretty effectual revenge."

"Revenge?" she repeated.

"After all," I continued as the thought came to me, "he's only got to murder us, and he'll have a tidy little inheritance."

"Do you think Avery cares for such things?" she asked.

"Most people do," I answered. "And he was a pretty penniless beggar at school. Besides, having tortured us through Katrina, it would be a nice diabolical way of torturing her through us."

"Really, Dick," Blanche exclaimed with amusement, "I hadn't credited you with so much imagination. But still," she became more serious, "that may be just a trifling part of his plan. But can't you see deeper than that? Honestly, can't you see any deeper?"

Her searching gaze full into my eyes frightened me with an unnameable dread. "What?" I asked in a whisper.

"Have you forgotten Gaveston?" she said in a tone of terrible meaning.

"Gaveston?" I answered at a loss. But suddenly the truth burst upon me. "You mean . . ." I cried, and broke off with, "Oh, Blanche, her eyes, her eyes!"

It was her turn to question me.

"Changed," was all I said. But I seemed to be looking again into that beautiful face distorted with a sudden spasm of angry hate, and the heavy menace of the eyes clouded over with the colour of storm.

"We must go back at once," said Olave. "There may be time."

The night was already dark about us as we started, with the headlights glaring straight out into the blackness which seemed like the very gulf of evil that had swallowed my darling. Somewhere in the mirk of the darkness ahead she lay closed round with a horror of threatening doom. And at her side was that evil thing that had already stained and scarred her, and would slowly poison her to the very soul.

The shocking memory of Gaveston as he crawled into the moonlight through my window sickened me with horror. But mercifully it was beyond me to picture to myself what frightful transformation might yet disfigure Katrina's clear, fresh beauty. Just a glimpse of it I had seen, enough to chill me with the sense of impending calamity. But what the final desecration of that radiant loveliness was to be, I hadn't the power to imagine. All that I knew was that a terrible menace hung over her, and I must snatch her away before it fell.

The racing car couldn't go swiftly enough for me. I fretted and fumed with the tedious journey, while Olave sat steadily at the wheel gazing intently out into the darkness. But at last we reached my country. We cut over the level crossing, and I heard the far warning whistle of a coming train. We rounded a bend, and a car came swinging into view. It rushed towards us and flashed by. But our streaming headlights had flooded it for a moment as it passed. A dark figure sat crouched at the wheel, but I had no eyes for him, for inside I had seen Katrina.

"Olave," I cried in a frenzy. But he had seen too; and I felt the brakes go home with a grinding jar. The great car came to a halt, and with difficulty Olave turned it about in the narrow road, while I tore at my fingers in an agony of impatience. And then we were away again, racing back on our trail. We swung round the bend where we had met the other car, and the road layout straight before us. I strained my eyes into the darkness, and just on the fringe of the lamp-light I could make out the shadowy form of the fleeing car, with the rear light staring back at us like a wicked red eye.

Then suddenly shattering the night there sounded a shrill blast, and through the high hedgerows I could see the twinkling lights of a train, with a column of fire and a shower of sparks whipped back from the funnel. And ahead I could hear a shouting, and could just make out the dancing figure of a man, waving desperately. And then I saw him closing the gates by the crossing. I felt a sudden leap of exultation, for Avery's car wasn't over. But it hadn't stopped, and then with a gasp of dismay I saw he was dashing for the opening. And when the gates had swung to he had gone. But we were barred from passing. Olave drew up in the nick of time, while the express thundered past, and the gate-keeper mumbled incoherently about broken necks.

But the race was lost. It would be needless describing our night-long hunt. Avery had vanished. And utterly weary and dejected we came back to Hinton Hall in the chill of the morning, beaten.

CHAPTER VIII

I can't possibly describe all the course of the long hunt that followed. All the guidance and leadership came from Blanche and Olave. I did nothing but follow. The whole drift of the thing was beyond me. I don't know how much faith I put in the broken scraps of direction that seemed to be coming through from "the other side," as Blanche always expressed it. But after all there was no other clue, and to bide inactively at home was out of the question. The only relief to the gnawing dread at my soul was in violent action. If Blanche hadn't sent me speeding hither and thither to rummage in odd and out of the way corners of the country I should have gone of my own accord.

I only took a languid interest in the actual clues that we were supposed to be following, so I can't give any definite details of the affair. But the kind of thing that happened was usually the same. We had a few disconnected letters to piece into a name somehow. Some of the letters we could take as being correct, others were uncertain, and others purely conjectural. Then we were given fragmentary descriptions of the place we were looking for. Sometimes Blanche showed me the thing in writing, having taken it down verbatim during the sitting. The sort of thing I remember ran something like this.

"I can see a valley. The mountains are very high to the right. Very bare and steep. There are patches of heather. There's a thin stream trickling through a cut in the rocks. Above I can see a single tree. It looks very old and weather-beaten. Only one branch still leans out from it. It's frightfully twisted and ugly."

Sometimes other details were added to the picture, which in its general outline was always the same. I remember one such addition. "I can see steps cut in the rock. Three steps. They go up and disappear." And again there was something to the effect that the path fell suddenly out of sight. Then there was a little hut, quite hidden. It was black and old. There were the marks of feet outside the door.

Blanche told me it was Gaveston who was communicating with her. She was full of praises for the little fellow. "He's finding it frightfully difficult," she said. "There's opposition. But he's won his battle once and that makes a difference." But I didn't understand in the least what she meant.

Once she explained herself more clearly. "You see it's his old enemy he's up against."

"You mean Avery?" I said, not following her thought.

"No, no," she answered. "The other enemy. The thing that . . ."

"Don't!" I cried. For suddenly the twisted ugliness of his face as he leered up at me in the cell came back with frightful distinctness, and for a moment it seemed to me that it wasn't Gaveston I was looking at but Katrina herself.

I clutched Blanche by the arm, feeling sick and faint. "Blanche," I said weakly, "will Katrina come to that?"

She didn't answer me, but patted my shoulder as one soothes a child. And indeed I fell into a chair and burst out sobbing as though my heart were broken. Never before had the full significance of the thing come to me so clearly, though I had told myself again and again what I must expect if I couldn't rescue Katrina in time. But it had never appealed to my imagination before, it had merely been a piece of formless and colourless knowledge. Now I felt it at my heart like the touch of death, for I had seen it, and the impression wouldn't leave me. I couldn't call back into my mind the picture of Katrina as she had been in her fresh and buoyant girlhood, a little year ago. Always I was haunted by the nightmare horror of her distorted face and figure, huddled and leering and hideously evil.

The police had been set on the track of the Gipsies, for it looked as though they knew something of Avery's movements. But either they were perversely obstinate or genuinely ignorant, for not a thing could be learnt from them. It puzzled me to conjecture what they had to do with Avery in any case. I hadn't asked myself at the time how Katrina had come to be waiting for me in a Gipsy tent. Indeed there were many things that I had taken for granted then which now looked so absurdly improbable that I could hardly bring myself to believe they had actually happened. That feeling of powerlessness, for instance, that had paralysed my will, and sent me away from the interview alone as though there were nothing more for me to do, seemed now a monstrous foolishness. I could see the reason now of Blanche's amazed questioning when I had come back without Katrina. No wonder she couldn't understand how I had allowed her to slip back again into Avery's power, for I couldn't understand the thing myself. It seemed so obvious to me now that the only thing to do was to steal her away by any means of fraud or force. Yet now that my folly was a puzzle to myself it was Blanche who explained it. "That was part of Avery's revenge," she said.

"Revenge?" I cried. "But why did he risk it? Suppose I had run off with her?"

"I expect he knew you couldn't," she answered.

"Well, next time . . ." I said.

"Ah!" Blanche exclaimed shortly, and went on, "He has a fine sense of warfare; has Avery."

"I don't call it warfare," I cried hotly.

"But he does," she said. "And after all, it was an effectual blow."

"If you mean that it hurt . . ." I began.

"And still does," she put in. "It's the kind of thing to rankle. Avery's a master of poison."

"Poison?" I said.

"Spiritual poison," she explained. "That's the only kind he deals in. After all, it's deadlier than strychnine."

"So," I said, "it was just one of his little torturing games, was it?"

"Ever heard of Tantalus?" she asked. "It's the sort of thing that happens in a dream," she went on. "You can touch a thing but can't grasp it, and it melts away from you."

"God God!" I cried, "that's just how it felt at the time."

"That's how he meant it to feel," she said. "He was working the thing. He must have hugged himself hugely."

I looked at her blankly. "So I've just been finely fooled?" I asked.

She looked at me steadily. "I dare say next time you'll be on your guard," she said with meaning.

I felt the revolver at my hip.

"And the Gipsies?" I asked. "What was he doing with the Gipsies?"

"I should have thought there was a distinct affinity," she replied. "And of course they know more about him than they pretend."

"You think that?" I said sharply.

"Of course," she repeated simply.

"Yet the police can get nothing out of them," I said.

"Nobody could get anything out of them that they didn't want to tell," she answered. "And remember," she added, "these are Gipsies, Romany Gipsies, not mere tramps."

"Where's the difference?" I asked.

She smiled rather amusedly, and said, "Just the difference between, shall we say, a man like Avery and a common conjurer."

That set me on the track of the Gipsies myself. Indeed I had made one blustering onslaught into their encampment already, but had been met with blank headshakes and chattering denials, and in impotent anger had turned from them and set the police to deal with them instead. Now I would go to them in a different spirit. If it was true that they could put me on Avery's trail I must use every means of conciliation to win their confidence. Full of good resolutions I drove back to Chalk Ridge, and without delay walked over to Morton's Dingle. But there was nothing there except an indescribable litter of ashes and rusty pans and discarded gear of all descriptions. The Gipsies had flitted. The Cuckoo's Home was empty.

It was only during our wandering together that I came into much converse with Olave. For the most part he was wordless on the whole affair, but I could see by his face and manner that there was a force of will beneath his reserve: compelling him forward with a resistless energy. Blanche seemed to issue the instructions, and I talked and fretted about them, but Olave set to work to carry them through quietly and firmly with a set purpose not to be diverted from its aim. Sometimes we would start out at a moment's notice with some fresh clue; more letters probably that promised to bring us nearer that mysterious hut with its disappearing path, its three steps, and its single tree. And sometimes we set out after laying in stores for a long journey, and on such occasions usually taking Mrs. Wait with us, to explore some new tract of country in the mountainous north. When opportunity offered, Olave and Mrs. Wait would vanish together, and return with some further direction to right or left, or still further ahead. I guessed there had been a sitting, and Gaveston was supposed to be giving instructions for the path. But I never asked to attend the sitting, and I wasn't invited. I couldn't get Feefie out of my mind with her ridiculous prattle.

But we never spotted that single tree, though many a single tree set us climbing wearily up broken tracks only to be disappointed at the last. And always we seemed to come to a halt sooner or later with nothing to guide us. At such times I noticed Mrs. Wait seemed thoroughly weary, and Olave would say, "We must go back, Dick. We need Blanche with us. I haven't the power."

And returning from one such expedition we were greeted with an unaccustomed sound in the house. Olave stood for a moment listening, then bounded upstairs. He returned very solemn, but his face was lit with a wonderful glow.

"It's a boy," he said.

"A boy?" I asked. Then suddenly I realized that an heir had been born to Hinton Hall and the estate of the Guthries. I seized Olave by the hand. "Splendid," I cried, "splendid!"

"It's just wonderful," he said.

"Blue eyes, of course?" I asked, for that seemed to me the badge of his race.

"With an underglow of violet," he said.

He took me down to the cellars, and very carefully he chose a bottle of rare old port, dusting away the cobwebs lovingly.

We returned and solemnly faced each other across the dining-room table, and Olave filled the glasses.

"To Urcelyn Clonmel," he said.

We clinked glasses and emptied them to the health and prosperity of the new-born heir.

And for a while, of course, there were no more sittings, and consequently no further clues. And I returned to Chalk Ridge alone.

CHAPTER IX

I was nearing home when I almost ran into an old beggar woman. She was cutting twigs from the hedgerows, and just as I raced up she lumbered across the road. I jammed on the brakes and swerved towards the hedge, where I narrowly missed her brat, who was half hidden there, busy breaking off sticks. It was with the merest margin that I steered through, cursing quietly. And then in the mirror I caught the face of the old hag looking back at me. I stopped short, for it was the Gipsy woman of Morton's Dingle. Somehow I felt I had something to say to her, though for the moment I couldn't quite remember what it was.

I jumped out of the car and turned to her. She was standing stock still in the middle of the road, her arms locked behind her, supporting her bundle of stolen firewood. Her boy was gaping wide-eyed from the hedge, not recovered from the shock he had just received.

The old woman's enigmatic grin of mock deference confused me. I couldn't get an idea clear in my head. I knew that some while since I had gone hunting for the Gipsies only to find they had flitted, but why I wanted them I couldn't think. So I mumbled out something about taking more care another time, and would have got back into my car again and driven on. But that puzzling grin held me there, and I couldn't pull myself away.

"The pretty gentleman has forgotten the Egyptian woman," the crone began in her usual whine.

"I remember you too well, mother," I said, and felt easy again now that I had found my voice. And of course I knew then what had been on my mind when I had gone to find the Gipsies that time. Blanche had said they knew the secret of Avery's hiding-place.

The woman was muttering something about the kindness of pretty gentlemen who didn't forget old women, but I cut her short with a blustering, "Look here, mother." Then I remembered my good resolution to go tactfully about the business, so coughing down my exclamation and forcing my face into a smile I tossed her a coin and said, "Have the cuckoos come back to their home, mother?"

"The cuckoos are flying north," she answered me with meaning beneath her whine.

"North?" I cried.

She began shuffling towards me, looking up at me from under her bent brows. I felt she had something to say, and waited in a strange suspense for her to speak. She came quite close to me, and searching my eyes began in her obsequious drawl, "Would the gentleman wish to know what the old woman can see in his eyes?"

"The gentleman would like to know whatever the old woman can tell him," I answered, thrusting my hands into my pockets and jingling my money significantly.

She began a little cackling laugh, very dry and throaty, and said, "It isn't the bonny clink of gold that can buy the truth, my dearie."

I blushed in some confusion, and to cover my awkwardness, said bitterly, "No, lies are sweeter and make a better bargain, I reckon."

"The gentleman is very wise," she said with another little cackle.

I was getting impatient, and would have brought her to the point with a direct question, but I could see she was meditating some confidence, and I knew I couldn't hasten her, and might even spoil things if I butted in; so I endured her scrutiny as well as I could, and at last merely asked, "Well, mother, what can you see?"

Her answer set my heart thumping. "I can see a wee black hut," she said, "high up in the mountains."

"Yes," I said, on the edge of expectation.

Her smile became more significant, even somewhat contemptuous, as though I were a stupid, dull sort of creature that needed to be helped and guided.

She went on, "I can see a rock, and a little path."

"And three steps," I blurted out, "and an old gaunt tree."

She fell back from me as though I had struck her, and her face darkened with sudden anger. But immediately the smile came back to it, still mocking and puzzling, and turning away she said, "The gentleman doesn't need the old woman. The gentleman is very wise."

I took no notice of the irony in her voice, but caught her arm and said, "Come, mother, that's not all. What more can you see?"

"The gentleman doesn't need the old woman," she repeated.

"Look here," I said coaxingly, "you mustn't get angry with me, mother. You put the picture in my eyes, I saw it."

"And what else can the gentleman see?" she asked.

"Nothing, mother," I exclaimed, "nothing."

She looked at me doubtfully. Then she said, "Look again. Now what can the gentleman see?"

I pretended .to be searching her face, and said, "A valley, and a little stream."

"The gentleman has been there," she said.

"Never, mother, never," I protested.

She laughed quietly to herself, still watching me in doubt.

To calm her I said, "Perhaps in my dreams."

"And what has he heard?" she asked.

"Heard?" I repeated.

"Hasn't the gentleman heard voices?" she continued.

"No," I said, "no, I've heard nothing."

"Listen, then," she commanded me. And we both stood motionless.

"No," I repeated after a pause, "I can hear nothing."

"Let the old woman lend him her ears," she said. "Now listen. Can't he hear a music? Doesn't it cry on the air? Whoooo!" She sent her voice out in a soft wail that fell on a dying hum. "Can't he hear it?" she said, pressing up to me and gazing with strange intentness into my eyes.

It must have been the wind, of course, but for the moment I thought the sound I heard was a dim echo from far away of some strange instrument vibrating mournfully on a lingering last note.

"What is it?" I said, almost in a whisper.

"He hears it?" she asked me expectantly.

"What does it mean?" I said.

For answer her face took on a look of far away intentness, her eyes fixed on vacancy, her lips parted as in sleep; and slowly she began tottering forward, step by step, hesitant and uncertain, but as if compelled by some unseen power. Then all at once she came back to her normal self, and with a little dry laugh, said, "Doesn't the gentleman know what it means?"

She seemed to me to have been walking in her sleep. And then the word trance came to me; and all at once I knew. It was as if I could hear Avery's violin as he had played it at school, wailing hauntingly out of the distance. In a flash many things fitted themselves into my mind. I remembered that day when I had first learnt that Avery had gained an entrance into Hinton Hall. I had heard music in the house, which had stopped suddenly as my coming had been announced. And I remember too, waiting more than once for Katrina at Lady Bullen's, and had merely heard the faint tinkling of her piano from the music room. Was that how the fellow had woven his spell about her?

I looked down again at the Gipsy woman. She was smiling very knowingly. "The gentleman has heard," she said.

"If only the gentleman could follow the sound," I cried, "he'd be a happy man."

"He must find a guide," said the woman.

"And where can he find a guide, mother?" I asked, looking her straight in the eyes.

She didn't answer me, and in my impatience I took her by the shoulders and said again, "Where can he find a guide?"

She became all cringing beggar woman once more, and said piteously, "How should the old woman know?"

"Look here," I said, "what's the old woman doing here, anyway? If the cuckoos are flying north why is the old woman flying south?"

At that she chuckled and answered, "The gentleman is very wise."

I thought she was going to desert me at the last, having led me so far. I wondered whether this too were a part of Avery's plan of revenge. Had he sent the old hag to tantalize me like this with teasing hints as to where Katrina was hidden, and suggestions as to what was happening to her, merely to leave me baffled and blinded at the end? For the moment I could have shaken the old creature till her bones had rattled in her bag of withered skin, but I knew that would merely seal my fate. I tried to control my anger, and said as gently as I could, "The gentleman is very weak, mother. He needs to be shown the way."

"And what will he do at the end of the road?" she asked.

"He will rescue the little lady," I cried, "as it was told of him he should."

Suddenly her eyes glowed darkly, and she asked in a tense whisper, "And what will he do to the bad man?"

"Kill him," I said impulsively.

I would have taken the words back, but she dropped her bundle of faggots and clapped her hands in wicked delight. I was at a loss to understand her antics. What possible grudge could she have against Avery that the promise of his death should rejoice her like this? Well, that wasn't my affair. Evidently she had been led to help me by some desire for revenge. She hobbled across the road to where her boy still stood watching me with great round eyes. She took him sharply by the shoulder, and began chattering volubly into his ear in a gibberish that I couldn't understand. He nodded his head from time to time in a vacant sort of way, and languidly pulled at a stiff fringe of hair that hung straight and dark over his forehead. Presently the two came across to me, and the old woman, thrusting the urchin under my nose, said, "This is the gentleman's guide."

"This?" I said in dismay.

"What would the gentleman have?" said the woman. "He knows the way."

I looked down at the staring brat. He didn't seem to have a grain of common sense in his whole make-up. His face was about as vacant as a piece of physiognomical composition as I had ever seen.

"You know the way?" I said to him blankly.

He screwed up his eyes and nodded his head.

"Where?" I asked.

He pointed north.

"Is he dumb?" I turned to the woman.

"The pretty gentleman wouldn't have a tongue to follow him?" she said with a knowing expressiveness. "Caspar tells no tales," she added darkly.

All of a sudden the affair seemed mightily absurd. How did this woman know of Avery's hiding-place? And how could this dumb brat guide me there? And what was the motive that underlay the thing?

I turned to the woman with the question on my lips. But the coincidence of her reference to the little black hut in the mountains jerked me back to my faith in her, and I merely said, "Good-bye, mother."

I bundled Caspar into the car, and took my place beside him at the driving wheel. "Look here, sonny," I said, "when we come to a branch road, you just point the way. See?" He nodded, and pointed ahead

I had intended to drive back and pick up Olave first, so I said, "No, this way." But he shook his head violently and pointed straight on. Well, after all, I reflected, it might be better to leave Olave out of it. Blanche would want him with her for a bit. And if the boy could really show me the way to the elusive hut, I reckoned I could manage the affair alone. So I set the engine going, and the car began to move.

Just then the old woman put her head up beside me and said, "The pretty gentleman said he would kill him."

"Ha!" I cried. "And why do you hate him, mother?"

"Hasn't he stolen the secret of Egypt?" she replied.

She fell back, and I saw her in the mirror shuffle off like the veriest vagrant. As for me, I jammed down the accelerator and raced away towards the north.

CHAPTER X

We had travelled far by nightfall, and it was only the fear of running short of oil and supplies that made me draw up till the morning. Then provisioning the car we set off once more, and were soon beyond the verge of civilization, winding up narrow stony paths, where the car could scarcely get wheelgrip on the loose, steep tracks. But I knew her power, and had already had some experience of this kind of going in my various journeys with Olave.

I couldn't have located my position on the map, but I was cheered to recognize here and there a familiar land-mark, which showed that we were in the country where Olave and I had already followed the mysterious guidance of Mrs. Wait. The coincidence strengthened my staggering belief in the expedition, for again and again the mocking doubt came to me that the whole thing was an extravagance and a fraud. There seemed no sense in it anywhere. And yet I supposed if anyone knew of Avery's hiding-place it must be the Gipsies, seeing that he clearly had some kind of association with them, otherwise how was it that I had met Katrina in their encampment? But the memory of that meeting seemed now so unreal and improbable that I asked myself whether I had not dreamed the whole thing, and indeed whether I were not still dreaming, and would soon wake to find the affair a monstrous nightmare?

As my thoughts came round to that over and over again, I smiled grimly to myself with a sort of dark satisfaction that at least I should have the pleasure of shooting Avery in my sleep without the disagreeable consequences which the actual killing of him would occasion. And indeed, I can best explain my whole conduct at this time by saying that all the while I seemed to myself to be dreaming, or acting a part in a play, rather than consciously performing a task in the world of reality.

That feeling grew upon me with the increasing wildness of the country, and the fading away behind me of all the sounds and sights and memories of my normal life. The wild bare crests of the hills; and in the distance, and ever growing nearer, the jagged spurs of the mountains cutting up into the clouds; and the little noisy splashing rivulets, so unlike the placid streams of England; and the wild clamour of the birds; and the treeless slopes, and the spaces of purple heather; all formed a picture in my mind so strange and unreal that it was difficult not to yield to the suggestion of dreamland fantasy which made the journey seem like a vision or a story, rather than a living fact. And yet, at times, the truth of the thing broke upon me in flashes of startling clearness; and then I had the feeling which I had experienced before, of waking suddenly to find I had been walking in my sleep. At such moments I wanted to turn back, for I seemed to have been caught making a supreme fool of myself. I simply couldn't credit the preposterous assumptions that underlay the affair. But in spite of all I didn't turn back, though I fretted at my own simplicity at pursuing such a phantom trail. And when I gazed at the saucer-eyed, fish-mouthed, wordless Caspar, I could have laughed aloud at the grotesque absurdity of the situation. And sometimes I did laugh, and Caspar would turn his vacant face to me with, if possible, a blanker blankness, emptying it of all expression except dumb questioning as to the meaning of my outbreak.

"All right, Caspar," I would say, "you wouldn't appreciate the joke, old man. But it's frightfully funny, all the same."

He would merely shake his head slowly, and point straight on.

But after such a fleeting glimpse of actuality the strange oppressive atmosphere of dream would close about me more heavily than ever, and I wound on over the broken track steering mechanically, and with the feeling somewhere deep within me that the car would drive itself if left to its own devices; if indeed, it were not already driving itself, and my interference were an unnecessary labour.

Then there were times, too, when the meaning of the expedition was borne in upon me suddenly with vivid distinctness. In a flash I would see the black little mountain hut and the one gaunt tree. And at such moments I would scan the slopes eagerly, half expecting to see the slender path winding up to the rocks and the falling stream. I think it was the wind which put such thoughts into my head; for sometimes when I heard it wailing over the barren spaces I seemed to catch a dying echo of some strange fall of melody which brought my thoughts back to the old Gipsy woman telling me to listen, and all the memories I had of Avery's haunting tunes. There was something, too, that I always found myself hunting for in my thoughts whenever this illusion took possession of me; some memory of Katrina, something she had said. And at last I hit upon it. It was on that morning when I had driven over to Hinton Hall to find Avery's shadow darkening the place. She had spoken of him with trouble in her voice. "He plays the violin, you know," I could hear her saying, "and somehow it seems to go right into my soul."

It was memories such as this, I think, which held me to the track if ever I were in doubt as to the sanity of my behaviour. For the dreadful fate that threatened Katrina braced my purpose to try all means, fair or foul, sane or insane, to deliver her. That was the supreme urgency that impelled me forward. All else had to bow to that. I could face ridicule, if it meant that I had at least been following even the merest shadow of a chance to find her. The clue was the thing to cling to, however unreasonable and improbable it might seem. And at all events it was better to be doing something, than kicking my heels at home in fretful idleness. So if ever I did feel that the venture was frivolous and vain, I told myself that at least I would see it to an end before I abandoned it. And yet I believe that in spite of all my doubts I felt certain, deep within me, that I should arrive at length at this mysterious hut hidden away among the mountains.

The time came, of course, when the car had to be abandoned, and the journey pursued on foot. The boy pointed out to me a convenient shelter in an arching hollow under a rock that hung over the dwindling track. I steered it in, and we left it there; and shouldering our knap-sacks we set off up the steep mountain-side, the boy guiding me unhesitatingly, though I couldn't see the least hint of a trail. We clambered upward uneasily for an hour or more, then reaching the crest, Caspar suddenly ducked his head, and dragged me down. He was pointing over the valley that lay below us. Cautiously raising my head I looked across. Up the slope on the far side was a lonely tree, with one branch spread out like a great raised arm with the hand and fingers drooping. The thing looked to me for all the world like some wicked old witch at her incantations. And catching the red of sunset was a thin line of water cutting down the mountain-side like a gleam of blood. But there was no sign of a hut. I was just going to question Caspar when I saw a faint blue wreath of smoke rising from under the tree, and the impression of witchcraft was increased tenfold. For it was as though those drooping fingers had sprinkled a magic powder on a slowly smouldering fire.

I tried to shake off the silly fantasy and bring my mind down to working actualities. Straining my eyes in the fading light I could make out a barrier of dark rock behind which the smoke was ascending. The hut, then, was hidden beyond.

"Come, Caspar," I said.

But he shook his head frantically.

"All right, you stay here then," I thought I had interpreted his meaning. But he held me with one hand, and with the other pointed behind us to the light still glowing in the west.

"Wait till it's dark?" I asked.

He nodded.

"But we'll lose our way," I protested.

He pointed to where the fall of water broke into the valley. I took his meaning. All we had to do was to find that, and clamber up beside it as well as we could. It would bring us to within a stone's throw of the tree.

So we sat there and made a hearty meal, but without lighting a fire, although it was mighty cold; for I was afraid of its light betraying us to Avery. Though I told myself that he probably knew all about the expedition already, if indeed, he hadn't planned it, purposing to get me into his power.

I turned to Caspar with a sudden sense of suspicion. Was this to be the end of the journey? But his inanely inexpressive face told me nothing. But I determined that if possible I would leave him behind. He had had the sense to bring me to within sight of my goal, and if it were his purpose he would doubtless have the cunning to drive a knife into my back.

But how to get him to stay behind if it were his plan to follow? That puzzled me. At last I had an inspiration. "Caspar," I said as lightly as I could, "you'd better cut some of this heather and make a fire to show me the way back. But give me time, of course."

He shook his head and pointed to himself.

"No," I said, "you stay here."

But he wasn't to be persuaded. And my suspicion deepened. It seemed to me more imperative than ever to get rid of him. I eyed him askance, even wondering whether I hadn't better tie him up till I had Katrina safely back in the car. But I thought I would keep that as a last resort. Meanwhile, I tried another stratagem. It seemed clear enough that if I waited till it was dark I wouldn't be able to shake him off at all. Even if I thought I had done so he would be able to creep after me without being seen. So I wondered whether after all it wouldn't be safer to make the attack immediately. The slope beneath me was in deep shadow, as the sun was setting behind me, and only a lingering gleam still held the crest of the farther slope in a pale glow. By the time I reached the valley all would be in shadow. And I tried to imagine a shape moving on the mountain-side beyond, to determine whether I should be able to distinguish it. I thought not, even if I knew exactly where to look. So I decided if I could send the boy away on some fool's errand I would push ahead myself without waiting for him to return..

"How much longer must we wait?" I asked casually.

He held up three fingers.

"Three hours?" I asked.

He nodded.

I yawned. Then feeling in my pockets I let out an oath. "Where the. deuce is my pipe?" I exclaimed.

I fumbled for it in all my pockets two or three times over. Then looking down by the way we had come I said with affected annoyance, "Well, I must go back and get it."

I rose. But Caspar fell to the trap. He jumped up, pointed to himself, nodded his head eagerly, and set off down the slope where he couldn't see me in any case, even if he looked back for me. Peering cautiously after him I was amazed to see the speed and ease with which he leapt down the rocky way. It seemed to me that he would have time to get to the car and back again before I could reach the hut. So I crept from under cover, and crawled over the crest. Looking back once again, I saw Caspar already far on his journey, moving a dim, black shadow among the rocks. I told myself I must be quick, as he would put on all pace to overtake me when once he found he had been deceived, and there was no pipe at all for him to find. For, of course, I had it on me.

I took a direction as well as I could by the silhouette of the tree against the skyline, and set off down the slope, slipping and stumbling in my haste, but at length reaching the valley where a shallow, gravelly stream prattled away into the darkness. I looked up to see if the tree were still in view, but the night was falling rapidly, and I couldn't trace a sign of it. So I listened for the sound of the water falling into the valley stream, and making my way to it knew I was on the right path. As I struggled upward in the dark I remember wondering how Avery had managed to get Katrina up such a difficult way. For there seemed no suggestion of a track. It was all sheer climbing. And it seemed tedious enough, for I had nothing to tell me how I was progressing, nor whether I were nearing my goal. And it was with a strangely sudden effect that I caught the life of that arm-like branch against the night sky. It seemed unexpectedly huge, looming suddenly above me, and for a moment I stopped in dismay, for it hung over me like a threat of unknown evil.

I shook off the unnerving impression, and cautiously took bearings of my position. The place was wild and rocky, as I knew, not by any sight of it, but by the experience of the climb; and rising darkly beside me were two great shapeless shadows, which I guessed were the rocks I had seen from the farther crest behind which the smoke had been rising. So I crept carefully towards them, and at last touched them, and steadied myself on the uncertain ground. I groped about for some time, wondering whether I had to skirt them or climb over, when suddenly I seemed to come upon a little path. The earth was firm and well trodden beneath my feet, and glowed faintly through the shadow. I tried to trace it, but it seemed to lead away from where I had come. And then I knew what had happened. Caspar had led me up by an unused track. The real path lay on the other side. It was a good manœuvre, as Avery wouldn't be so likely to keep a look-out this way. But still I hadn't found the hut I was seeking. Then suddenly the whole picture as Blanche had repeatedly given it to me rose in my mind. Here was the path that disappeared. I felt the rock for the three steps, knowing that they were assuredly there. As, of course, they were, though steeper than I had pictured them. And they brought me to a little platform which gave on to a narrow passage between two great boulders. I stepped forward with infinite caution, feeling the winding rock-wall on either side, and shuffling with my feet for each step before I rested my weight there. And at length I found the path ended suddenly, but feeling down with my foot I soon discovered that I had merely come to a falling stairway, more easily negotiated than the first one for now I knew I was inside the barrier, where there wasn't the same need for disguising the way.

Reaching the bottom, I paused a moment to listen and take my bearings. But not a sound could I hear, except the falling of the mountain stream outside. I moved forward a step, and immediately became aware of a dim square of light. A window, I knew; though either the light was very low or the blinds very thick, for it was the faintest suggestion of a light imaginable, and only seemed clear to me because of my long groping in the darkness. I began to move towards it, when I saw a shadow pass into it, and remain outlined against it. My heart gave a glad leap, for I knew it was Katrina.

I waited breathless, trying to make up my mind what to do. I suppose the obvious thing was to find the door, burst in, shoot Avery if he were there, seize Katrina, and make away with her. But although all that passed rapidly through my mind, I couldn't bring myself to stir a muscle. Again that haunting sense of dreamy-like unreality was undermining my will. Katrina's shadow stood there like the emanation of a dream. I lost touch with reality, and felt I had to wait for something to happen, as the matter wasn't in my hands at all. A greater will than mine was shaping the thing, and I had merely to look on.

The shadow was growing larger, as though it were moving towards the light, and yet it was strangely distinct. Then suddenly the blood went cold along my veins, for an outstretched hand had touched me. I caught the white gleam of the fingers as they withdrew into the darkness, and I heard a faint, indrawn gasp. Then immediately I realized what had happened. The shadow wasn't behind the window at all; it was between me and the pane, it was there just before me.

I shot out my hand quickly, and breathing a faint "Hist!" I felt my fingers close round Katrina's arm.

A shudder went through her at my touch. I felt her arm vibrate beneath my fingers. But I drew her towards me, whispering, "Katrina, it's Dick."

At that she jerked at my hand as though to free herself; but I held her the firmer. And then with a little stifled cry she fell forward on to my breast.

"Come," I said; and a great joy flooded my heart as she yielded to my lead without a murmur.

I had touched the stairway with my foot when she said, "I thought you were Avery come back."

"Is he away?" I asked.

"I thought so," she answered.

"Then you're coming with me, Katrina?" I said.

"Oh, take me away, Dick, take me away," she whispered brokenly.

And then behind me I heard a low laugh. Katrina stiffened, and suddenly jerked herself free of me.

"What is it?" I said in alarm.

"Who are you?" she breathed fiercely in a strained voice. "Who are you? What do you want with me?"

"Katrina!" I said at a loss; and tried to take her again by the arm. But she shook me off and hissed, "Why will you come between me and my husband? I love him. I tell you I love him. Go away. You hate him. You always did. But I love him. Go away."

Again I heard that low and evil laugh. Avery had returned, I told myself. Then I remembered Blanche's words. I must get Katrina away at all hazards. I struggled against a sense of dreaminess which I felt was stealing over me, paralysing my will and dimming my perception. I remembered the meeting in the Gipsy tent, and knew that I mustn't be caught napping like that again. There was just one thing for me to do, to seize Katrina and carry her off.

I stumbled towards her in the darkness and threw my arms about her, determined at any cost to get her safely away. But just as my arms closed round her there came a low throbbing from the darkness somewhere in front of me. And suddenly it rose on a run to a crying wail, and sank as swiftly to a vibrating drone which seemed to fill the air with a strong pulsation rather than with any definite sound. I felt Katrina shudder in my arms as though her whole body had been sharply shaken; and then for a moment I didn't know what had happened. For at my very ears there was a shrill, inhuman howl of frenzied laughter, and I felt myself hurled violently against the rocks. It was with a sense of utter dismay that I realized that it was Katrina herself who had suddenly sprung upon me, beating at my face with her hands, and biting at me savagely, screaming all the time in a sort of laughing sob too frightful to describe. Recovering myself I tightened my grip about her, and tried to drag her back to the stairway; but she fixed her teeth in my arm, and I felt them meet through the flesh. For a moment the pain made me reel dizzily with a sense of sick faintness at my heart, and before I knew what had happened I found myself dragged forward and thrown violently to the ground. There was a sudden brightness which dazzled me, and the sound of crashing woodwork told me that I had been hurled against the door of the hut, bearing it down in my fall. I tried to rise, and immediately became aware of a hunched figure springing at me out of the darkness, and again I was in a whirling vortex of battle. I knew that that dark hunched figure was Katrina herself, though the glimpse of her as she came was utterly unrecognizable. And yet I didn't dare to handle her gently. It was almost more than I could manage to hold my own against her. But I strained my strength to the uttermost, and at length seemed to be getting a mastering grip of her. But now her teeth were at my very throat, and her arms were locked about me like bands of iron. With one arm still about her to hold her firm, I caught her jaws in my other hand, forcing them open, and slowly straining her head backwards. But it was like wrestling with a wild beast. My muscles seemed to be cracking under the force of my pressure, and dimly I wondered how I was to come out of the encounter alive, let alone carry Katrina with me.

Then all of a sudden she slipped under my arm and sprang free of me. She uttered a frightful laugh, and in her hand was a revolver. I felt involuntarily at my hip. It was my revolver she had taken, and she was pointing it at my heart, still laughing hatefully. And as I stood before her, utterly at a loss to know what to do, I could see the horrible transformation that Avery had wrought in her. But it wasn't merely the hideous wreck he had made of her loveliness that dismayed me; it was that the face I was looking at now was the face of Gaveston as I had seen him in Blanche's room that night.

For a moment we eyed each other, Katrina from under lowered brows, with her shoulders hunched up high like a cripple's. And she was steadying the weapon in her shaking hand. I knew my only chance was to time her action, and to fall flat as she fired. And I remember at this moment becoming aware of that throbbing music again, for indeed it rose to a sudden violent scream which was taken up by Katrina like an echo. At the same instant I fell flat with a roaring detonation deafening me, and the sound of a sharp cry ringing in my ears. With a leap I was on my feet and had thrown myself at Katrina, wrenching the weapon from her hand. But she collapsed in my arms, and would have fallen to the floor if I hadn't supported her. Her head fell back and lay utterly limp. Her eyes were closed, and her face deathly pale. But in spite of my fear for her I felt a shooting spasm of joy to see her own sweet face again, and not that frightful thing of ugliness that had leered at me a moment before.

How the change had come about I didn't stop to think. I laid her gently on the floor, and looked about me for some water. There was none in the room. I turned to a door behind me, which stood open and seemed to lead farther in the hut. Strangely enough I gave no thought to the possibility of Avery's being in there waiting for me. My whole concern was for Katrina. The room was dark, and I struck a match. I caught the shine of a tap, and groping about I found a cup, and was soon back bathing Katrina's brows and trying to restore her to animation. But I couldn't call a trace of life back to her face. In an agony I felt her pulse, and drew a deep breath of relief to feel it throbbing faintly.

I was still busied over Katrina when I felt a touch on my shoulder. Swinging round I was amazed to see Caspar. I sprang up, gripping my revolver. I didn't know what he wanted with me, and his presence made me suddenly aware that I was in imminent danger from Avery.

"Well?" I said sharply.

Caspar began making signs, pointing to his breast, and then making motions as though he were dragging something across the room. I didn't understand, and shook my head. He walked to the door and beckoned me to follow. After a moment's hesitation I did so, still gripping my revolver. He noticed this, and pointing to the weapon opened out his hands and smiled. He flashed the light of a torch into the dark room where I had just been, and pointed to the floor. I looked in sudden horror at a dark wet patch at his feet. I put my finger down and touched it. It was blood.

I turned to Caspar with the question on my face, "What does it mean?"

He pointed back to Katrina, and went through various antics which suddenly became clear to me. Katrina had shot Avery over my head as I had fallen.

"Dead?" I asked.

Caspar nodded and grinned widely, and I knew then that he was really an ally, not a decoy.

"Where?" I said.

He led on through another door and out into the open air again. He stopped after a few paces and laid his hand on my arm, drawing me back.

Then flashing his torch at my feet he lit up a yawning space in the earth. He pointed downwards significantly. Then stooping he picked up a pebble and dropped it into the chasm. I didn't count the seconds, but it seemed an age before a very faint plop told me that it had struck water. And somehow that brought me back to the full reality of the situation. I was horrified rather than relieved. Avery was dead. But the thought appalled me. For the violent manner of his death, and all the ghastly business of Katrina's madness and my frenzied struggle with her, sickened me to nausea. I caught hold of Caspar to steady myself, and tottered back into the hut.

Katrina was still lying white and motionless on the floor. In a daze I stooped and raised her in my arms. She lay there quietly enough now. I walked out into the darkness, forgetful of Caspar, only knowing that I must get Katrina home as soon as possible. The darkness of the night about me didn't give me any uneasiness. I was beyond all that. I stepped on as though the way were perfectly known to me, and was soon outside the barrier rocks that hid that black and evil hut. I hoped they might hide it to the trump of doom.

In a little I became aware of Caspar again, for he had joined me and was lighting my path with his torch. It wasn't till then that I realized what an improvident fool I was not to have thought of an essential like that even. This blank-faced boy had more wits in his little finger than I had in my whole head.

We were some way down the slope when the sky was lit up with a bright red flash, and immediately there followed a splitting roar from behind us. I turned round to see a mass of black wreckage tossed in fragments amid a lurid, red glow, and almost instantaneously the vision had gone. Caspar began capering about like a mad thing.

"What is it?" I asked.

He heaved up his hands as though scattering a load of refuse high into the air.

"Ah," I said, "blown up."

He pointed to himself, nodding vigorously.

I was dazed and weary when at length I reached the car. Katrina was breathing easily, but was still unconscious. I laid her tenderly on the soft cushions, and wrapped her round well with warm rugs. Then motioning Caspar to jump in, I took my place at the wheel, and in a dream set off slowly down the broken track, with the headlights streaming out before me, making the rough path look tenfold more menacing by filling the hollows with deep black shadows till it seemed that every yard of the way was yawning with crevices and chasms.

It was with a sense of wonderful relief that I caught the first light of the morning whitening in the east. I seemed to be steering out of the land of nightmare into the world of day. I looked back towards Katrina. She was lying motionless. I stopped the car to see if all were well with her. She was sleeping peacefully, with a look of wonderful contentment in her face. I went over her and kissed her reverently.

Jumping back into the car I missed Caspar. I looked round for him, but there was no sign of him anywhere. I called, but he didn't come. And then I began to realize that I hadn't noticed him beside me for some while. Well, he must have slipped off under cover of the night to rejoin the cuckoos who were flying north. I drove on without him.

How many miles I covered that day I don't know, but it was with nightfall that I reached Hinton Hall, and handed over my precious capture to Olave.

As for myself, I turned into bed without undressing, and slept solidly till high noon, when I woke feeling very stiff and sore, and with a raging agony at my damaged arm.

CHAPTER XI

A good hot bath and a poultice on my wound went far to restoring me to some sense of comfort; but better still was the report that Katrina had regained consciousness and was doing well. But it was clear that my presence wouldn't tend to calm her, so I thought I had best return to Chalk Ridge without delay. I merely stayed at Hinton Hall to put Olave in possession of the facts, and to take counsel with him as to what should be done. Blanche was still in bed, of course, and I was told I mustn't bother her with any disturbing matters, so I left Olave to communicate to her whatever he though advisable.

Talking the thing over with Olave I began to realize that I had put myself in an awkward fix. In fact if by any chance Avery's body were found I might find myself up on a charge of murder. For I hadn't the least intention of letting Katrina's part in the affair be known. I had even falsified that part of the story to Olave, saying that I had shot Avery myself. I didn't suppose for a minute that Katrina would have any clear memory of what had happened, and I didn't want to risk her hearing the truth. And as for Caspar, well, he had appeared on the scene after the shot had been fired.

After some deliberation it seemed best to notify Scotland Yard that Katrina had been found. If they asked questions I would tell them that the Gipsies of Morton's Dingle had put me on the track, that I had found Katrina while Avery was away, and that she had returned to her home with me. As for Avery, I decided to maintain an utter ignorance of where he was or what had happened to him.

For a while I was distinctly uneasy and apprehensive. I didn't know how far Scotland Yard would push their inquiries. But as a matter of fact the thing blew over without much trouble. After all, there was no charge against Avery. He hadn't committed any crime, and so unless his relations began to make a stir about him, wondering where he had vanished to, nobody had any cause to hunt him out.

But that didn't end my difficulties. In a week or so I was back at Hinton Hall taking counsel with Olave once more as to how Katrina was to clear herself of the entanglement of her marriage. For if Avery was dead, her hand was free. But his death couldn't be proved without the risk of serious complications. There was the possibility, of course, of getting the marriage annulled, as Katrina had clearly been forced into it against her will. There would have been sufficient evidence forthcoming from Avery's

London clique to have proved his amazing hypnotic power. Or again Katrina might eventually free herself from him by bringing up the charge of desertion, if she were willing to wait long enough. But in any case the question would inevitably arise, Where is Avery? I didn't know what relatives he had, but even if they made no move, yet search of some sort would be made for him, and suspicion might be aroused. It seemed best to lie low for a while till the affair had been forgotten, and then see what was best to be done. But meanwhile, Katrina remained in name the wife of the fellow, and I fretted to see her free of him so that I might try my fortune with her.

As the summer wore on I began to see a little of her. Gradually she grew more like her old self, but I knew she would never be the bright charming girl she had been. There was a wanness and a vacancy in her expression now which was infinitely pathetic, but I would have given anything to have restored the dancing colour to her eyes and the bright freshness to her cheeks. I didn't dare speak to her about what had occurred. Indeed, I had been warned not to hint at the subject. But sometimes she would look at me with a question in her face, and I knew she was trying to puzzle out what had happened. It was clear that she hadn't any clear memories of the affair, but that she was struggling in her mind to unravel some disturbing riddle that was teasing her. Once she said to me, "Dick, I've had such a frightful dream."

I was taken unawares and said, "Tell me."

"But that's the trouble," she said, passing her hand across her eyes, "I can't remember it. I can't get it clear."

"Oh, well," I said, trying to take her mind from the thing, "dreams are stupid affairs. Don't bother about it."

"But, you see," she went on, "it comes again and again. I can't drive it away. And sometimes it seems so real I think it's happened." She suddenly turned to me and cried, "But it hasn't happened, has it, Dick?"

"Of course not," I said, "it's just a dream."

"Then why are things so strange now?" she went on. "Why is everything so different? Why don't you speak to me as you used to? And why do you look at me like that?"

"Why, how?" I asked, for I didn't know what to say.

"You used not to look at me like that," she said.

I merely hung my head. I was utterly at a loss how to turn her thoughts away from the disturbing matter.

She began to speak more gently. "Once, Dick, you said something to me. I've forgotten where. Was that a dream too?"

"Katrina!" I turned to her impulsively. But it was useless. How could I speak of my love to her? I thought I had better leave her and never see her again. Always there would be that reproach in her eyes. Why are you so different? Why have you changed?

And then she asked me with a sudden break in her voice, "Dick, have you grown tired of me?"

At that I did take her hands in mine, and pressed them to my lips. Then I rose sharply and walked away. It was more than I could endure. But although I knew quite well what my duty was I couldn't tear myself away from her, and again and again I had to bear the stabs of her questioning reproach. But it was worse to know that I was wounding her by my strange aloofness which she couldn't understand.

In dismay I went to Blanche, who was up and about again, and had assumed full charge of Katrina.

"What am I to do?" I asked her.

"It'll be all right," she said quietly. "I shall tell her soon."

"Tell her?" I cried.

"Of course," she replied. "She must win through by her own strength."

"But," I stammered, "is it necessary, Blanche?"

"Absolutely," she answered. "She'll never be herself till she has learnt to face the truth. So long as she thinks it all a dream she'll always be puzzled and uncertain. And if," her voice became full of meaning, "if the attack returns she won't be able to fight it off unless she's learnt to face up to the truth of the thing."

"But how should the attack return?" I asked, for her words had sounded almost like a threat.

"I said if," was all she answered.

I knew there was no getting round Blanche in that mood, so I merely mumbled, "Oh, well, you know best," and went off.

But when I returned to Hinton Hall a fortnight later I found Katrina wonderfully altered. There was a deep, serious look in her eyes as she received me. She held out her hand in a strangely grave way, and said, "Dick, I know everything."

"What do you mean?" I asked.

"It wasn't a dream," she said.

"Oh, well," I blurted out, "let's forget all about it, Katrina."

"I want you to forgive me," she said.

"Forgive you?" I cried.

"I've hurt you, Dick," she went on. "I know I've hurt you. I wish I could make it up to you. But I didn't mean it, you know I didn't mean it."

"Katrina," I repeated, "let's forget it all. Let's pretend it hasn't happened."

"If only I could, Dick," she said sadly. "But you see it's gone right into my heart. I don't think I can ever get it out quite. There's something there I'm afraid of. Something lurking there. I shall never feel quite certain of myself. Do you know, Dick," she smiled faintly, "even now . . . I must confess it . . . I feel a sort of wicked wish to, to . . . Well, to fly at you. You know, like a cat. There," she ended on a sigh, "now I've told you. Now. you know what I am."

For a moment I felt weak with horror. Then I put my arms about her and said, "Oh, my darling, I daren't think how you have suffered. But it's over now. All that'll go. And I love you, Katrina. I know I oughtn't to tell you, but I can't help myself. And some day things will all come right again."

She put up her lips and kissed me. Then suddenly pushing me away she gazed at me wildly and said in a startled whisper, "Oh, Dick, take me to Blanche."

There was a frightful dark shadow rising in her eyes. I caught her by the arm and raced her off to her room, sending a servant to find Blanche. By the time she arrived Katrina was struggling violently in my arms, snarling like an enraged animal. But she kept her face averted from mine, and I could only guess at the hideous distortion that was taking place there.

Blanche dismissed me summarily, and what happened between the two I don't know. But it was some while later when Blanche rejoined me downstairs where I was waiting with Olave to hear her report.

Her first words sent a fear to my heart.

"Dick," she said, "you haven't done your work. Avery isn't dead."

"Not dead?" I gasped.

"Where did you shoot him?" she asked.

"I don't know." I answered. "It was dark." Then suddenly I remembered Caspar's description of the thing in his dumb show. "Just a minute," I said quickly, "it was in the breast."

"No use," Blanche declared. "You must find him again, and shoot him in the head."

"Good God!" I exclaimed.

"It's the only safe way," Blanche went on.

"But look here," I broke in, "he was chucked down a pothole. I don't see how he could get out of that alive even if he were only wounded."

"It doesn't much matter how he's done it," said Blanche. "The fact is that he's back again at his infernal tricks." She added, "Besides, he's got friends among the Gipsies."

"Enemies," I corrected her.

"Friends too," she said. "And I dare say if you went home you'd find the Gipsies back in Morton's Dingle."

"I'll go and chase them out of it," I declared.

"No, you're wanted here," she said. "You'll have to do duty for Ravin and Flame."

"How do you mean?" I asked.

"Sleep outside her door," was the answer.

But I don't intend to describe the whole course of the battle that followed. The memory of it is like a desecration of my love for Katrina. For to see her under the power of whatever the evil thing was that possessed her, her body horribly deformed and contorted, and her face twisted to a mask of hateful hideousness, is a thing that I would like to erase from my mind for ever. For it haunts me like a terrible dream, or frets me rather like a disloyalty lurking at the very heart of my devotion, for I feel as though I am betraying her in my soul whenever that evil memory forces itself into my thoughts. It is enough to say that not once nor twice I found myself locked in a sudden desperate struggle with her, just as I had done in the mountain hut. Sometimes the attack caught her during the day, but usually it came at night, and it was well that I was on guard outside her door or she would have broken through to Avery in spite of locks and bolts. For her strength at these times was amazing, and her fierceness more amazing still. But I was able to hold her in check long enough for Blanche to work her back to calmness.

All this while Blanche was the girl I had known in the Gaveston days. Master Urcelyn, I'm afraid, was left in the charge of the nurse-maid, as all Blanche's strength was given to the contest she was engaged in. And this might have had disastrous results. For three times, at least, Olave found the girl wheeling the baby from the house in a dazed sort of way, without in the least knowing where she was going to. And perhaps this would be the place to enlarge on the strange series of accidents, or rather escapes, which befell Blanche herself at this time, and yet they were all things of such minor account in themselves that it seems difficult to connect them with Avery, except that they were continually occurring. For one day it would be the cook who would nearly capsize a bowl of scalding water over her; and another day the gardener working in the conservatory would dislodge a heavy plant from a shelf within an ace of her head; and once it was my own clumsiness, I remember, while hanging a large portrait of Urcelyn over the mantelpiece in her room, which nearly put an end to the list; for I was holding it for her to see, and she was just approaching to give it a last tilt into position, when somehow the great thing slipped from my hands and smashed down on her shoulder. And as it happened, Olave was just coming into the room at the moment, and it was his quick clutch at the thing which diverted it from Blanche's head, for Olave in his quiet unobtrusive way always seemed to be where he was wanted.

It was continuous little accidents of this sort, together with a fear that the baby might somehow be stolen away when we were off our guard, that made this a time not merely of uneasiness on Katrina's account, but of unbroken nervous strain. It was clear that Avery was hovering near. Sometimes it seemed that he must be in the very house, watching everything, and seizing on each least opportunity to strike, however insignificant the blow might be. But though Olave used to vanish at times, and I knew he was scouting round for Avery, yet he never seemed to come upon his trail.

Blanche's surmise that the Gipsies had returned to Morton's Dingle was true. Olave made an expedition to them to learn what he might of Avery. He learnt exactly nothing of what he was seeking, but incidentally he heard that the old woman who had set me on the trail was dead. Caspar, too, had vanished. As far as he could piece out the hints and evasions of the Gipsies, who were evidently trying to put him off with lies, it seemed that the old dame had been poisoned and Caspar quietly got rid of in the mountains. There was nothing in the way of proof that this was so, it was merely the eagerness of the Gipsies to clear themselves of any suggestion of foul play which made the suspicion likely. Blanche declared it was clearly the case. Avery had friends among the Gipsies more powerful than his enemies, or at least they were more afraid of him, and would rather side with him than against him. How he had been brought back to life we knew we would never rightly learn, but Blanche said it was clear enough that Caspar had fallen in with the tribe up north before he could rejoin his mother, and the doings of that night had been wormed out of him, and a rescue party had gone to Avery's deliverance.

But what puzzled me was how the fellow could live through such an experience.

"With a man like Avery," said Blanche, "life is a matter of will."

"But there must be a limit," I declared.

"There is," she answered. "You should have shot him in the head."

I had heard that before, and it didn't help matters to say what I should have done.

"I don't see what difference it would have made," I grumbled.

"No, Dick," she said, "I don't suppose you do. But it is so, all the same. You see, if the brain's disorganized the will has nothing to work upon. You might as well try and play a fiddle with all the strings broken."

Well, the fight went on for some weeks, till the attacks became weaker and less frequent, and I began to think we were winning through at last. In her sane moments Katrina realized what was happening, and sometimes she thanked me in a piteous sort of way as though I were a kind of guardian spirit. "If you weren't so strong . . ." she said.

"It'll soon be over," I tried to comfort her.

"No, never quite," she said.

"Oh, come!" I cried cheerfully.

And once, after a particularly tempestuous night she noticed the scars and bruises on my face. She put her fingers up and touched them, and suddenly broke out sobbing. And after that she always searched my face and hands to see if she had wounded me in her madness. And to see her bite her lips while the tears gushed to her eyes was a thing that caught at my heart like a wrenching pain.

"Don't," I pleaded with her, "don't, Katrina. You know, I'm wonderfully proud to be able to help you at all. And when it's over . . ."

"Ah, then . . ." she cried, and threw her arms about my neck. But immediately she drew away and said, "Oh, Dick, I had forgotten. I belong to another."

At that I gripped her firmly by the shoulders and said, "Look here, that's all nonsense. If you belong to anyone at all, it's to the man who can save you, not to the man who would destroy you."

She looked at me sadly and said, "I should like to believe that."

I didn't press my advantage. I knew I must bide my time. So I said nothing further. But after a pause she added, "And yet, you know, Dick, I thought I loved him."

"Ah, you thought," I emphasized the word.

"No, Dick, no," she shook her head slowly, "I did love him."

"And now?" I asked.

She didn't answer me directly, but repeated an old cry half brokenly, "Oh, why didn't you tell me before, Dick. I would have come to you."

I didn't attempt to defend myself. I merely said, "I'm sorry, Katrina."

"There," she cried more gaily, "how ungrateful I am; and after all you're suffering for me."

She reached up to me and kissed me with a passion.

And it was interludes like this which touched with sunshine the evil gloom of these dark days. But always the shadow swept back again, and it was hard to believe that it was the same girl who at one time would be talking to me as to a lover, and at another struggling with me like a demon of hell.

"Will it never end?" I asked Blanche wearily one morning after a night of tumult.

"It is ending," she said.

"It may not be quite so bad," I agreed. "But when will it be over?"

"I don't know," she said, "but it will end."

"Well, that's something," I said.

"You see," she went on, "Katrina has got fight in her. She's not like Gaveston. She's bound to win."

"She's a brave girl," I exclaimed.

"If we could have got her from Avery sooner . . ." she said, but stopped with the sentence unfinished.

And suddenly the battle ended. Strangely enough the Gipsies vanished at the same time from Morton's Dingle. "He's gone with them," we told each other, and for my part I began to think that the fellow must be a Gipsy himself.

Still, we were on our guard for a while, though Blanche declared the danger was over, Katrina had thrown off the last three attacks by her own unaided strength. "He's wise enough to know when he's beaten," said Blanche, and added, "Of course, he'll find another victim somewhere else."

"Well, we're free of him," I exclaimed, and Blanche turned a steady gaze upon me which somehow made me feel uncomfortably ashamed of the selfish expression.

So life became quiet again. With an ease that had puzzled me before, Blanche threw off that tense purposeful manner that had seemed to wrap her about as by a garment during the whole episode, and became once more the radiant wife of the honeymoon days. And Master Urcelyn came suddenly into the foreground of the picture, and was made a rare fuss of, Blanche smothering him with mouthing kisses as unashamedly as the veriest mother of them all, and Olave quietly observing the pair with a glow of wonderful pride in his eyes.

Yet my heart was still unsatisfied. There was a gulf between Katrina and myself that promised to be difficult enough to bridge. She was still Avery's wife. And it wasn't easy to see what was the best way of breaking that ugly tie. Especially as Katrina had some strange objection to the tie being broken at all.

"He's my husband," she repeated in a way that puzzled me.

"But he forced you to marry him against your will," I said.

"I don't know," she answered. "But I promised him, didn't I?"

I thought she would overcome her scruple sooner or later. I knew she loved me, and would gladly marry me if she were free. Well, that was something. Meanwhile I had to possess my soul in patience, and feed on her repeated, "I'm sorry, Dick, I wish I could believe that," whenever I insisted that she didn't belong to Avery at all, that he had merely stolen her, and had no claim upon her. And then I told myself there was no immediate urgency. She was only seventeen, though somehow it seemed monstrous that such a child should have endured so much. And when I saw the lingering trace of storm still dulling the sky-blue of her eyes, I gnashed my teeth in a fury of hate for the man who had set that smirching stain upon her loveliness. She was only seventeen. Well, there was plenty of time before us. The knot might cut itself. Meanwhile, I could but bide my time and wait for what might happen.

But I didn't know that the next thing to happen would be the European War. Nor could I foresee how it would entangle us once again in Avery's snares, and bring to a head the struggle in which Blanche had already defeated him twice.

PART III

Olave

CHAPTER I

This isn't a war story, and I don't intend to say anything about my life as a soldier; but the thing happened, all the same; and though even a mere summary of my doings would be clean out of the course of my narrative, yet without the war my tale would not have been what it is. In fact, I think it would have ended with Avery's second defeat, because I don't believe the fellow had any intention of renewing a conflict where he had already been twice worsted, especially as he had the whole world before him if he wanted to find an easier victim. Though, of course, if he had found a victim and worked his will upon the wretch he would have had an ally to second him if he had wished to break another lance against Blanche; and what the result of such a struggle would have been I don't intend even to try and imagine. But if I were to take Blanche's view of the thing it would have been something altogether beyond what I had already seen. Still, that's only Blanche's view. I don't know how far I put faith in her extravagant hypotheses. Her talk of being possessed by spirits, and all her communicating with the dead, are beyond me. I don't even pretend to understand them. Certainly Avery had a knack of undermining one's nerve and driving one into an evil kind of madness; and I believe if I had been tied to his company for a few weeks I should have gone as mad as ever Gaveston or Katrina did. And then, too, I must confess he had an unholy power over animals. But what it all amounted to I never pretended to know, and even now I haven't any settled theory of the thing. I can only tell the story according to the actual facts. The explanation, if indeed there be one, must shift for itself.

And then, in any case, it isn't worth while bothering about what might have happened, because as a matter of history the war did break out, and the things that I am going to relate did occur.

The only incident bearing on my story which has anything to do with active service happened during the fourth winter of the war towards the beginning of the great Ypres offensive. Olave sent for me one day to help him identify some poor smashed beggar who seemed to have been hit by about a dozen shells all at once. He was pretty frightfully mangled, and utterly unrecognizable. Though I had become reasonably inured to horrors by now, yet the sight turned my stomach. Olave had a wonderful nerve for this kind of thing. He carefully freed the body of the clotted mud and the torn clothing to try and find some possible mark of identity; but it was all useless. There were letters in the fellow's pocket, but it was completely impossible to decipher a word of them under the filth that caked them over; and there was an identity disc too, but that was cut and twisted, and gave no information. Even when the roll of the killed and missing was made out it wasn't possible to fix a name to him for certain, as so many lay out still in No Man's Land, and wouldn't be collected till after the next push.

Olave seemed worried over the thing, though I'm afraid I was more callous. "After all," I said, "there are thousands of others who can't be traced."

"Yes," said Olave bitterly, "missing; believed killed." And suddenly he broke out, "It isn't good enough, Dick."

"It's certainly hard luck," I admitted.

"You see," he went on, "there'll be people in Blighty wondering what's happened to him. They'll hang on to the belief that he's been taken prisoner. And when the war's over they'll wait and wait for him to come home."

"Oh, well," I tried to put an end to the pathetic story. I preferred to keep my mind clear of such things.

"Sentiment, isn't it?" Olave continued, and suddenly nailed me with, "Suppose it were you, or me."

I hadn't anything to say that. I know I had rather an unpleasant picture in my mind of my own broken body tossed into a nameless grave. . . .

Olave broke into the ugly thought. "We must find some better means, Dick."

Then I had a bright inspiration. It was that very morning that I had seen a fellow amusing himself in the trenches tattooing his hand.

"Wait," I said, and went to find him.

He was busy with his dinner, as it happened. He said he hadn't got much in the way of paints and tools with him, but he could manage to do something simple.

I went back to Olave and told him of my idea. "I've seen fellows," I said, "with a whole fox-hunt on their backs."

Olave smiled. "That should be fairly obvious," he said.

"For myself," I went on, "I should think a pair of crossed oars might do. What about you?" To tell the truth, I was rather taken with the idea of the thing.

Olave wasn't so enthusiastic. "It mightn't help very much," he said.

"It would be something though," I answered.

"Well," he said, "I'll see the man."

"And what's the sign to be?" I asked.

What he answered me was for a long time a perplexing puzzle. That he did answer me I felt certain, and as I lay tossing, for how long I don't know, in a feverish delirium, I seemed to be fumbling about in my mind for what Olave had said. For it was just then that a shell caught the dugout, and nothing had any meaning for me till some weeks later when I began to come back to some sort of dazed realization of where I was and what had happened.

That slow returning to consciousness was a miserable business. I chafed at the dull confusion of thoughts and memories that seemed to be tangled hopelessly in my mind. There was nothing clear, nothing to cling to. I knew that there were heaps of questions I wanted to ask, and one particularly; but I couldn't frame them. All I could say was, "Where am I?" I was told to lie quiet, and promptly turned over angrily on my side and let out a wild curse that so startled me that I broke into a stupid giggling. But I remember how one day the question suddenly came to me. I leapt up in bed and cried, "Where's Olave?"

I think there was a bit of a scene, because I have a sort of recollection of fighting half a dozen people who seemed to me to be keeping me away from Olave. I called them murderers, and other things that don't look well on paper, and I knew what I was doing, that was the queer part of the business. And yet I couldn't help myself. I was frightfully aware that they had taken me from Olave and had him in some terrible dungeon where he was being slowly tortured to death.

I tried to be reasonable. "Look here," I said, "you can do what you want with me; but tell me where's Olave."

"She's well enough," somebody said.

"She!" I cried, and burst into an uproarious guffaw. "Oh, you fool," I shouted, "you prize idiotic fool!" I don't remember anything in my waking life that amused me half so much as that. little misunderstanding.

I don't know exactly how long after this it was that Blanche seemed to appear from nowhere. I suppose I had been moved to England at last. Somehow I became almost immediately myself again, and learnt that Olave was well enough.

"They've let him out, have they?" I asked.

Blanche seemed to understand quite well what I was talking about. "Oh, yes," she said, "didn't you know?"

That seemed to clear my head. I looked at Blanche with the sudden fear at my heart that I had been making a monstrous fool of myself.

"I say, Blanche," I said, "have I been saying things?"

"They won't be brought in evidence against you," she smiled back.

"Good Lord!" I muttered, with a sort of dim memory of shouted oaths and curses echoing in my mind.

"Dick," Blanche said, taking my face between her hands, "shall I tell you something to comfort you?"

"Do," I replied.

"Well," she went on, "it's a good sign of character to say bad things in delirium."

I laughed. "I don't understand that," I said.

"And I don't intend to enlighten you," she retorted.

I took it that she was either trying to set my mind at ease, or else it was merely another of her mad ideas.

But it was good to know that Olave was still unhurt. Yet it was better to be master once again of one's faculties and it was a glad day for me when I was able to return to Chalk Ridge. Especially as I was told I should be fit in a few months to join my battalion again.

And about this time the Ypres offensive came to a halt.

CHAPTER II

I found a letter from Olave waiting for me when I got home. He had heard from Blanche that I was to be discharged from hospital, and had written to congratulate me on my recovery. "It's constitution that does it," he wrote. That made me smile, and I determined to show it to Blanche as an example of Olave's heresy; for Blanche would have put it down to will. I was expecting Blanche the next day. She was to bring Katrina and Urcelyn with her to spend a few days at Chalk Ridge. She said she knew that otherwise I should be dashing over to Hinton Hall before I was fit. I pictured to myself a little debate on constitution versus will. I should quote Olave as my authority and myself as a case in point.

This passed through my mind quickly as I glanced through the letter. But the amusing fancy was whisked right away when I came to an unexpected mention of Avery. It was the first I had heard of him during the war. Olave had seen him. I looked back to the date of the letter. It was three days before the end of the offensive, which the morning paper said had now won its objective.

All the old evil associations that had gathered in my mind about the name of Avery came crowding back into my consciousness, and for a while I read the letter without understanding a word. I turned back to the first mention of him, and studied the thing more carefully. "I just got a glimpse of him," Olave wrote, "but it was unmistakable. I don't think he saw me; but then you never know how much a fellow like that has seen. His eyes seemed to sweep past me like a dark searchlight, if you can imagine such a thing. A black gleam, and they had gone. He's a colonel; full rank, too; and seems to be a fellow of some importance. Red tabs, and so forth. From what I can gather he's got some devilish invention he wants to try. He's been fixing up something in No Man's Land half the morning. (By the way, if this letter gets opened I shall get into a fine row!) I must do him justice, and say a word for his pluck. I think the Bosch have got an idea that there's something unpleasant hatching out in the mud there, and they've been dropping things all about him for some while now. It was the same yesterday; but he doesn't seem to trouble about that kind of thing. Perhaps he's immune from shell-fire, under the special protection of Heaven!" Of Hell, I commented to myself. The letter went on, "We attack to-morrow morning, for the last time, I hope. And knowing what I do I'm pretty thankful that Avery's for us and not against us. I shouldn't like to come up against some unexpected devilry of his in the middle of No Man's Land."

All this set me musing, and I wondered whether after all I would mention Olave's letter to Blanche. I didn't like to think of the possibility of his meeting with Avery out there where so many things might happen with never a witness to tell of them. I was uneasy, and felt I shouldn't rest happily till I had heard again from Olave to say he was well out of the battle.

I read his postscript twice before I realized what I was reading. "I've followed your suggestion," he wrote, "and had that tattooing done. Only just lately, though. There didn't seem to be time before."

That sent my thoughts racing back to that last talk with Olave. What was it he had said when that shell came? Still I couldn't get my memory on the track of the thing. I answered Olave's letter, promising him more when I had seen Urcelyn and Blanche, and I asked him to let me know what sign he had had tattooed upon him.

And the next day I was to see Katrina again.

Naturally, I had seen little enough of her during the war. This was my first long spell in England after the first training was over. And that hadn't taken very long. I had seen her in snatches during my scanty leaves home, but it was seldom enough that I had been able to get on to the theme which alone interested me. Abroad, of course, it had been so easy, even for an unimaginative fellow like myself, to picture wonderful home-comings, and delicious confessions in the moonlight. But actually faced with Katrina I found it quite another matter. There was a barrier of reserve between us. Words didn't come easily, and again and again I found myself outward bound with nothing said. I couldn't make out whether she were deliberately heading me off the forbidden subject, or whether it was merely my own hesitant awkwardness that stood in the way. For her behaviour was puzzling. Certainly she wasn't happy, yet I couldn't persuade myself that she was hungering for me to speak.

But during my last leave I had managed to come to a clearer knowledge of her heart. Perhaps it was that she had been franker with me, and altogether more like her old self as I had known her in the days of the golden girlish plait and the leaping hounds. Also I think I took heart from seeing her eyes clear again of the last trace of leaden storm which had dulled their beautiful blue. For indeed it wasn't till the summer of this year, three long years after the disappearance of Avery, that Katrina really became herself again. The shadow of harassing care that had gloomed her brow so long had gone. I returned to find her almost as I had known her first, except that she had become somewhat more grave and serious; and that was only natural seeing in what days we lived, not to mention her daily companionship with Blanche.

Seeing her restored, and clearly delighted to meet me again, I took heart to speak to her; and yet it wasn't till the last day that I managed to say what I wished. For now it was her gaiety which hedged me from her as before it had been her sad reserve. When I tried to bring her down to a serious facing of our situation she laughed me away from it; or if there were no other escape for her she would defend herself behind Urcelyn, racing the little toddler away for a game. I would find them hidden behind a bush, and Katrina would say very solemnly, "Here's Uncle Dick with the big eyes," and Urcelyn would scream with laughter, though just where the joke lay I couldn't make out. Still, in the face of such odds it was impossible to press my purpose.

I caught her at last, though, at an unguarded moment. I plunged without warning. "Why do you run away from me, Katrina?" I asked.

She didn't pretend to misunderstand me. "Because it's safer," she said.

"Well, you've got to stand and fight now," I declared.

She looked at me quite steadily and said, "I had quite intended to, Dick, at the right time. But it might have spoilt your holiday, earlier."

"You had quite intended to?" I repeated her. "You mean, you intend to fight me?"

She gave me a look of inexpressible tenderness. "Oh, can't you see," she cried on a note of wonderful appeal, "that I'd surrender if I could? Unconditionally," she threw in.

I suppose I ought to have been content with that. I couldn't have hoped for a more naked expression of her love for me. But somehow I was chafed by the continual thwartings I had been forced to submit to, and I refused to be appeased.

"You can surrender," was all I said.

"I wish you'd show me how," she answered, with a tone of weariness in her voice.

She dropped listlessly into a seat, and at once I was on my knees before her. Her words had blown my smouldering annoyance to a flame of longing. I caught her by the wrists and pleaded with her in a way altogether unworthy, not only of her, but of my own love for her. I babbled easily of divorce, and so forth, as though marriage were merely the chance partnership of a dance. She could throw Avery off, as one might discard a servant, and wed me instead. I can see now that I was just carried away by my own selfish desire. There wasn't a consideration in all my heart for Katrina's own feelings in the matter. I suppose I assumed that she yearned for me with the same abandonment of desire with which I yearned for her. And so for the moment I really saw nothing dishonourable or degrading in what I pressed so ardently upon her.

She heard me to an end without an interruption. She didn't even draw her wrists free. But when I had finished, she looked very sadly into my eyes and said, "I wish you hadn't spoken like that, Dick."

"But, Katrina," I continued blindly, "we love each other. What other bond is there so sacred?"

"One's word, Dick," she replied.

That steadied me somewhat. But I went on, "But if the word was forced upon you . . ."

"If," she repeated. I realized then that I had come no nearer my end than I had three years before.

I rose and said rather sulkily, "Yet you love me."

At that she rose too, and was suddenly crushed against my breast. And it was her lips that sought mine in a pressure of passion.

She drew away from me slowly, and looking at me with pleading in her eyes said, "You wouldn't want me to say more than that, would you, Dick?"

She seemed to be waiting for the answer as though great. issues depended on it. I felt utterly shamed, and could scarcely murmur a word. I turned away muttering, "I'm frightfully sorry, Katrina. You must forgive me."

She caught me by the arm and held me back. "Dick," she said very decidedly, "there's nothing to forgive. Please believe that. You mustn't think I don't prize your love. I prize it more than I can say. But you see, it's too good to spoil."

I just crushed her hand and let it drop. I had nothing to say.

"But isn't it?" she pressed me.

At that I cried out, "All I know is, you're too good for me, Katrina. I'd better take myself off."

"Not like that, you old stupid," she exclaimed. And once again we embraced.

"There," she said, "now it's all clear, isn't it?"

"Except the end," I answered.

"Ah!" she said sharply. And a little shudder seemed to shake her, and I thought I caught again the trailing edge of cloud darkening in her eyes. But I had no time to undo what I had done, for Blanche had come upon us. And with nothing further said of any consequence I had gone back to France.

Well, it was with the memory of all this in my mind that I awaited Katrina's coming. I knew now that I had behaved shabbily. I had drawn the girl to an exposure of herself which wasn't so much a gratification to my vanity as a condemnation of my selfishness. I couldn't help feeling elated at her more than frank confession of her love; but so completely had she abandoned herself to me that I felt ashamed that only so could my selfish hankering for her be appeased. Yet so beautiful had her yielding been that it served to place her the higher in my adoration, while it sunk my own respect for myself lower than I cared to confess.

So it was with a fine sense of upright resolution and chivalrous purpose that I looked to meeting her again and setting all straight between us.

CHAPTER III

She came with the morning. But it wasn't till the afternoon that I found myself alone with her. She seemed delighted to be back once more at Chalk Ridge, and trotted me from room to room, refreshing her memory of every little nook and corner. "And you know," she said gaily, "there's not a thing been changed for four years."

"You see, I've been away," I explained.

"And everything's been kept in order for the return of my lord," she bobbed me a curtsy.

"Ah, well," I laughed, "I'm a rare old conservative, and they know my habits."

"And when a thing isn't just where it ought to be, somebody gets a scolding," she said.

"Usually," I admitted.

She looked at me saucily for a moment and broke into a bright peal of laughter, then turning to Blanche she said, "Is he such a frightful tyrant, really?"

Blanche looked very solemn and said, "He mustn't be crossed, you know."

I believe they had got some little joke to themselves which I didn't quite tumble to.

It was after lunch that Katrina said, "I've inspected everything indoors, and find it quite in order, so now you must take me out, Dick, and show me round all the old rambles."

"Right," I consented, "And I don't suppose you'll find anything changed there either."

Blanche elected to stay at home. It may have been from consideration to me, or the reason she gave may have been the truth. She said she must attend to Urcelyn. Why he needed any attention I don't know, because he seemed to sleep for the better part of the afternoon. But Blanche wasn't an ordinary mother. She had ideas as to her duties, and seemed to have precious little time to give to anyone or anything if it meant her being separated from Urcelyn.

Well, I didn't attempt to dissuade her; the prospect of a walk and talk with Katrina was too good to be resisted.

We said little enough for some while. Katrina seemed to be enjoying herself immensely, though she merely expressed her satisfaction by her buoyant stepping and alert attention to everything about her. Now and again she would just say, "Ah, here it is," or "The same old spot." And I was content to let her enjoy her thoughts in silence without needless comments from me. I was only too glad to feel that the place had such a hold on her affections, though it was bitter to know that if all had gone as it should have done she wouldn't have been tramping at my side as a stranger.

It was with a slight sense of dismay that I realized she was heading for Seven Elms Meadow, for I had thrown the reins of leadership into her hands. I tried to steer her away, but she understood my action, and said, "No, let's go there, Dick." She added after a little pause, and in a more serious tone, "You see, it doesn't matter now that I've got over all that nonsense."

I looked at her quickly, repeating, "Got over it . . . Nonsense?"

We stepped on together for a few minutes without a word said. In fact it wasn't until we were leaning over the stile where we had once surveyed the bull that Katrina spoke again.

She said slowly, "Dick, I thought we had cleared things up, but we hadn't. It would be better if we could be quite frank, wouldn't it?" She turned her face full on mine as she spoke.

"Katrina," I blurted out, "there's a lot I've been wanting to say. I behaved like a cad last time . . ."

"Stop," she said sharply. She gave me her hand and went on, "You mustn't say things like that. I just won't listen."

I tried to interrupt her, but she shook her head, "No, I tell you I won't listen. It's I who have behaved badly, Dick."

"You!" I protested.

"I want you to know everything," she continued, and looking up at me with trouble in her eyes she repeated, "Oh, Dick, I want you to know everything."

She seemed to be waiting for me to give her permission to speak.

"Katrina," I said hesitatingly, "of course, you can tell me anything you'd like to, but I think I know all I want to know. You love me. You've told me that. I forced you to; brutally . . ."

"No, no, no!" she cried. "You didn't force me. Besides, I think I had told you that before." She smiled up at me wonderfully, and added, "And I'll tell you again and again, just as often as you want me to."

We kissed each other.

"There's nothing to be ashamed of in that," she said gravely. "But it's something else that I want to tell you. It's . . . it's . . ." Then it came out

with a sudden cry, "It's that I haven't been true to my love for you. I let
Avery come between. Because you know, Dick, I had loved you long before I met Avery. But I did love him, Dick. That's what I wanted to confess to you. I've been afraid before. I've just sort of hinted at it. But I loved
him, Dick. Really loved him, I mean. I want you to understand that, because it may change your feeling towards me."

I spoke her name, but she ran on in the same troubled voice, "Ah, let
me finish, I shall feel easier. You see, there was something about him, different, you know. His eyes . . . And then music seems to float me right
away. If I had never met you, Dick, I could have followed him gladly to the
ends of the earth." She gave a deep sigh, and ended softly, "Now you
know."

For a moment I didn't quite know how to tell her how completely un-
changed her confession had left me. I began to stutter a few words, and
then blurted out, "I don't care, Katrina, I don't care a snap of the fingers.
It's so utterly clear to me that the fellow practised his infernal tricks on you
just as he has done on others."

"No, no," she said wearily.

"Yes," I insisted. "I know. I was at school with him. I've seen some of
his handiwork. He just victimized you. Surely you must realize that by
now."

"Yes, after he got me into his power," she said. "But you see, it was
my own fault that he ever got me into his power. I was willing to go."

"Yet you wouldn't have gone if I hadn't failed you that night," I said.

"That was just a last feeble flutter of resistance," she replied sadly. "If
you had come I should have gone with you. But even so it was my own
fault. I think I let myself get rather angry with you for not coming. You
see, you didn't say what was keeping you away. And I believe I could have
resisted. But I didn't really want to."

"Well, I just don't believe it," I declared. "I've been under Avery's spell
myself. He makes you think you're doing something you're wanting to do.
And all the time you're just obeying him. I know, though he's never actually
caught me out. And then, the way he treated you after he got you . . ."

"Yes," she cut me short with a sudden cry, and her face hardened
strangely, "Yes, now, of course, my eyes are opened. I know him for what
he is. I'm his wife; I can't forget that. But I shall never be his victim again.
And yet," her face softened, "I still believe there are possibilities of good in
him . . ."

"Don't believe it," I broke in. "It's just there that he finds the weak
spot where he can strike. He caught Blanche the same way. Others too, I

don't doubt. He's just utter black through and through. But it's no use calling him names, the ordinary sort of thing doesn't apply to him, he needs a vocabulary to himself."

After that there was a long pause, while I chewed savagely at the thought that such a man should be allowed to touch and stain the life of such a girl as Katrina.

"Well, then, you see how it is," Katrina said at last.

For a moment my old weakness was upon me, and I said, "But, Katrina, do you mean that you intend to stand by him to the last? Are we to let him come between us, for all our lives it may be? It's simply preposterous."

I had caught her by the hands, and was speaking with a passion.

She steadied me with a look.

"I'm sorry," I said. "I won't trouble you again. But it's frightfully difficult. It just makes a ruin of our whole lives."

"It does," she said. "Things happen like that sometimes. I can't think why."

We turned away without another word spoken. I thought at that moment that it would be good to be back in the firing-line again, with death busy in the air.

I had always hoped that when Katrina had quite fought down her madness she would immediately set herself to win back her freedom. That had seemed to me the obvious thing to do. Even Olave had assumed that she would do so. It wasn't until I had begun to find her averse to it that it had occurred to me that perhaps there was something in such a course repulsive to a girl of her nature and upbringing. Now, of course, it was painfully clear to me that she wouldn't contemplate the thing for a moment. Her vow remained sacred, even though it might have been won from her by guile. She was evidently obsessed with the idea that she had gone to Avery of her own free will, and had merely discovered too late what kind of man he really was. If I wished to persuade her to sue for a divorce I would first have to get that idea out of her head. But as a matter of fact, I respected her scruples too much to try and argue against them. It was only in moments of sudden passion that I had pleaded with her to take the dishonourable course. And I had repented of such moments. Even now, when I thought I had quite steeled myself to the inevitable, my weakness had found me out. It was only Katrina's own straight directness of purpose which made it possible for her to treat me as a lover, and yet never overstep the line she had set between us.

It was with some such thoughts as these beating in my mind, with a

feeling of exaltation struggling with a hopeless bitterness of disappointment, that I walked on with Katrina, speechless for the most part, and at
length with the falling of the early winter twilight turned back home.

Nearing the house I saw someone approaching us through the dusk. It
was a messenger, one of Olave's men. He was in motoring gear, and in his
hand he had a little paper. He brought it to Katrina, saying to me, "Mrs.
Guthrie told me to bring it straight out here, sir. She said I should meet
you."

"You're from Hinton Hall?" I asked.

"Just come, sir," he answered. "I had orders to bring anything along
that looked urgent. It's from the War Office."

At that I turned sharply to Katrina. She was gazing at me, but what her
eyes were saying I couldn't read in the dusky light. She held the paper out
to me. I read it dazedly, rubbing my eyes. At last I got the meaning clear.

Avery had been killed in action.

For an age, it seemed, we stood there without a word, gazing at each
other.

"Of course it isn't true," I said at last. It seemed too silly for words.
And yet with the memory of Olave's letter in my mind I knew there was
nothing more likely. But the thought I had was that a fellow like Avery
didn't get killed. It seemed too simple an ending to such a story as he had
already made of his life.

"It's true, Dick," said Katrina.

I tried to read her meaning in her expression, but it baffled me. I
wanted to crush her in my arms; there was such a leaping gladness at my
heart. But something in her voice restrained me.

The messenger said, "Do you want me, sir?"

I had forgotten him. "No," I said, "no." And he went.

That brought me back to reality again. Avery was dead. I read the official notice once more. This sort of thing could be trusted. The shadow had
gone. The burden had fallen away. Again I looked to Katrina with the
yearning at my soul straining mightily towards her.

She said simply, "It's my husband who's dead." Then I knew why I
mustn't break into a shout of triumph.

"I shall ask you to come to me some day," she went on. "You'll come,
won't you, Dick?"

I just said, "Yes, Katrina."

We went quietly into the house. I wanted to tell Blanche the news. She
wasn't about. I was rather glad because I thought I should like to tell her
with no one to witness the exultation which I knew I couldn't keep out of

my voice. I went to her room, and knocked. After a moment's waiting I knocked again, and presently she opened the door to me.

"Avery's been killed," I said, holding out the note.

She took it, but didn't read it. She was looking at me strangely. "Come in," she whispered at length. "Quietly!" There was no expression in her voice.

She tip-toed to Urcelyn's bedside. The little fellow lay sleeping, with his hands thrown carelessly across the coverlet. His lips were pouted to an adorable prettiness, so that I could have caught him up and kissed him like a very girl.

"Isn't he beautiful?" said Blanche, again in that expressionless whisper.

Strangely startled I turned to her and muttered, "Why, whatever's the matter?"

She drew herself up very straight, and slowly handed me a paper. It was the counterpart of the one I had just shown her. In a terrible alarm I took it from her, but I didn't dare look at it.

"Good God!" I whispered, "don't say . . ." but I couldn't shape the words.

At length I turned to the fatal note in my hand. Stupidly I read, "Missing; believed killed."

I knew those weren't the words I could see, but they were the ones that forced themselves into my mind. I could hear Olave speaking them as he had done in the dug-out. I strained at the paper through an obscuring mist, but couldn't get the thing clear. But after all, what did it matter? The meaning was all too plain.

"Olave!" I said faintly.

Blanche fell on her knees by the little cot, and sobbed against the pillow.

Urcelyn opened wide eyes, and with a mischievous chuckle thrust his fat little fingers into her hair.

CHAPTER IV

My convalescence dragged on miserably enough. There was nothing to make me want to linger in England. For the time, I knew, Katrina had gone right out of my life, and I felt that it wouldn't be for a good while yet that she would call me back to her. I had an idea that she would wait till the war ended, if it ever did end, or perhaps she had set some limit in her own mind, a year it might be. But meanwhile there was the tedious interim to fill as best I might.

And yet it wasn't the prospect of a weary waiting that made me chafe to be in action again. It was rather the fretting uncertainty with regard to Olave. I searched the casualty lists day after day, but after the first notice of his being missing I came upon no further reference to him. It was some consolation to see Avery's name gazetted among the dead, and yet, somehow I half expected to find that the thing was a mistake, and feared every day that it might be denied.

Of course, I wrote to my colonel and to my chums in the field asking for any particulars they could furnish. But it didn't help very much. If anything, it convinced me in my own mind, though I wouldn't confess it to Blanche nor yet to myself consciously, that Olave was dead. The actual facts I could get hold of were slight enough. The colonel told me something about Avery; he had messed with him the night before the attack. "Queer fellow," the letter described him, and went on into a rambling yarn of Avery, making some poor, dazed Bosch outpost leave his funk-hole and come wandering across to the English lines. Evidently Avery had done the thing to amuse the mess. The colonel said he thought he must be some kind of conjurer. In any case, he had had a pretty good mine ready for the Bosch, and a nice little scheme to trap them. But something had gone wrong somewhere. The letter described Avery in the hell of a rage about it. He had gone rushing out to set things right, but the Bosch had charged and had captured his little emplacement. Olave had led the counter-attack, and had cleared the position in fine style. But then something had happened, nobody quite knew what. "All the world seemed to be in the air. Deuce of a gaff," said the letter. And when later the English attack had passed beyond, there was a fine tangle of dead and wounded. Avery had been killed outright. Later, in answer to another letter of mine, the colonel said there could be no possible doubt about it. "Half his head was blown away," the letter said. "You needn't hold out any hopes to the widow, if that's your trouble." The colonel didn't know how his bluff statement rejoiced me. I didn't want to hold out any hopes to the widow. And here was just the thing I desired. "Half his head . . ." I remember Blanche telling me that I should have shot him through the head.

The only doubt that still persisted in my mind was that perhaps after all this wasn't Avery. There might have been some coincidence in the names, merely. Yet when I read again the various letters I had received from my chums, and from the colonel, too, there seemed absolutely no reason for such a doubt. The single story of the Bosch outpost should have been enough to reassure me, even if there hadn't been fifty other details in the various descriptions of him to set my mind at rest. This was Avery right enough, I kept telling myself, and he was dead all right. But still the doubt wouldn't be argued away. I suppose it seemed too silly that the thing should end so easily. The death didn't correspond to the life. Avery, I felt, would make more of a stir before he let himself be wisked out of the world like that. And yet, the facts were all in my favour. And Katrina had received official notice of his death.

Strangely enough, where there was room for doubt I felt none. There had been a number of unrecognizable bodies found after the explosion. In fact, the bodies couldn't be numbered correctly, because they had been scattered in fragments impossible to sort. And then, too, the wounded had been cleared before a proper count had been made, and even some of the wounded had been unrecognizable at first, and had gone down the line without a number or a name. So there was always the hope that Olave might be living, but at present too badly wounded to identify. But somehow, I couldn't think it was so. I felt strangely certain that Olave was among those others who had been left unknown on the field. And stupidly enough, my mind went back to the motor smash and the mangled body of old Jock. I could hear Olave saying, "If I were mauled like that, I hope I should have the decency to die outright." I remembered how perturbed he had been that evening, and I couldn't shake myself free of the thought that he had felt some dark presentiment of his own fate. I even had the fantastic picture of him in my imagination, proudly wrenching himself free from his shattered, but still-living body, leaving it to lie there a forsaken derelict.

And yet I couldn't help beating back in my mind for the memory of what Olave had said to me just before I had received my own packet. What was the mark which was to distinguish him? I mentioned the matter in my letters abroad. But it didn't help at all. Somebody remembered something about it, but not what the actual sign was, nor where on his body it had been tattooed. And the man who had done the thing had been killed. I fretted myself into a fine fume about it. This might be just the one detail that was wanted. Meanwhile, Olave had either been buried in an unknown grave, or was lying in some hospital without a name of his own. And suddenly the memory came to me of his own grave at Hinton Chapel. Would he be the first of the Guthries, I asked myself, to fail at the last tryst?

All this bothered me more than I cared to own, and perhaps hindered my convalescence. And even when I managed to tear my thoughts from the puzzle there was still a dull pain at my heart for Blanche's sorrow. She bore up wonderfully, though I think she had no more hope than I had myself. "I must remember I am his wife," she would say proudly, when I knew she was on the verge of breakdown. But sometimes she was unable to repress the grief, and would cry brokenly, "If only I could be certain. . . . This suspense is horrible."

She came to see me, for with Katrina's ban between us I didn't dare visit Hinton Hall. And I think I learnt to admire Blanche during those few months of terrible uncertainty more than I had ever done before. Her strange battling with Avery had passed beyond my comprehension. I had only been able to guess dimly what strain of nerve and steadiness of purpose it had entailed. But here was a human grief that I could quite well estimate. I had known something of the same sort of thing when Katrina had been carried off by Avery. And watching the girl in her trouble I knew she was superb.

For the rest I never learnt full particulars of the stunt that Avery had been engaged in on that fatal morning. As a matter of fact, nobody could tell me much about it. It was assumed that there had been some sort of mine because of the frightful explosion that had resulted. But the colonel hinted that there were other things behind it, if only one could get at the heart of the mystery. "There was some kind of electrical outfit," he wrote. "He tried it on me. Very weak, he said, but I went deuced dizzy. I reckon he had got a trump card there, if things hadn't gone wrong. But it's a queer business altogether. Queer fellow, too. Sort of conjurer, I should say."

And I never learnt any more than that; though I felt pretty certain, knowing my man, that the Bosch had escaped lightly, and we had lost an instrument of war which might have smoothed out our path in many an unpleasant corner.

I missed all the immense battles of the German offensive, but I was back in France in time for the great last act. It was shortly before I left that Blanche visited me. She was obviously troubled at something, and contrary to custom she hadn't brought Urcelyn with her. I was afraid to ask her what the matter was, for I thought I could guess. And yet, the shadow in her eyes didn't seem to me to be mere grief. If Olave were dead after all, I wouldn't have pictured her looking like that. So I waited for her to speak, not caring to put the blunt question, "Have you heard anything?" Though as a matter of fact, I didn't think she could have done, because I had scanned the papers pretty carefully, and hadn't come across any further mention of either Olave or Avery.

"When you get back, Dick," she opened the subject, "I want you to make very careful inquiries . . ." she broke off.

I waited a moment and asked, "What about?"

"There's something I can't understand," she said. "It's about Avery."

"Good God!" I cried, "don't say he's still alive."

"I want you to find out his grave," she said, "and, as I say, make very careful inquiries." She handed me a paper. "Here are the official War Office particulars," she said.

I glanced at the name of the cemetery. I knew the place. It was between Ypres and Poperinge.

"Right, if I can get there," I promised. "But what's the trouble?"

"That's just what I don't know," she replied.

"You're not very explicit," I prompted her.

"Sorry, Dick, but I can't be," she answered with a faint smile.

"You're afraid he isn't dead after all," I pressed her.

"Perhaps," she admitted. "But I can't understand."

"Look here," I cried, "this is horrible. For God's sake tell me what's troubling you. Why don't you think he's dead?"

She didn't answer me for a moment, but passed her hand slowly over her brow in a way I knew from of old. I noticed then that she looked fagged out. I told myself she had been up to her old games. "I suppose you've been seeing Mrs. Wait lately," I said rather roughly.

"Certainly, Dick, I have," she answered me steadily.

"Ah," I exclaimed.

"You see, that's why it's so difficult for me to tell you anything," she went on. "You don't believe in these things."

"No," I said, "I don't."

She smiled with faint amusement, and said, "You seem to forget the hut in the mountains. However," she went on rapidly, as I started at the reference, "we'd better keep off debatable ground. All I can say is that there's something very funny about the whole thing. Frankly, I can't find out whether Avery is dead or not." She added quietly, "Nor Olave."

"If it helps you at all," I said, "I can tell you that Avery most certainly had half his head blown away. I've made very exact inquiries on my own account. You can have the letters, if you like."

"Thanks, Dick," she replied quickly, "I should like to see them."

I hesitated, remembering there were things about Olave in them. She might get the idea into her head that he had been horribly mangled and disfigured, and had been tossed into some unknown hole.

"There are things you mightn't like to read," I suggested.

"Oh, I want to know everything," she cried. "Let me have them, Dick."

I unearthed the packet and gave them to her. She began running them through quickly, and I left her at the task. When I returned I found her deep in a reverie, with the letters fallen to the floor.

"Any clearer?" I asked, stooping to pick them up.

She seemed to come back slowly from very far away. "I don't quite know," she answered at length. "I think I begin to see. I'll let you hear later. Although you are such an unbeliever," she added with that faint smile which had before played wanly about her lips and eyes.

And the next day I crossed over once again, and was soon with my battalion, and forgot all the doubts and anxieties that had troubled me in England, because life was very full in these days, and there was no room in one's head for anything except the urgent matter of the moment.

It was later, when the war was over, and we lay idly at rest, that the old problems came back to me; and once more I found myself fretting over the disappearance of Olave, and Blanche's dark hints that perhaps Avery was still alive.

At the first opportunity I beat back on my tracks to Ypres, and soon found the cemetery. It was a more difficult matter finding the grave in that little forest of wooden crosses, but I tracked it down by the date. And at length I stood before it. If faith were to be put in names and inscriptions, here was Avery's grave for a certainty. "Colonel Avery Booth," I read, "Royal Engineers." I studied the name, letter by letter, as though half expecting to see them change before my eyes. But there was no possibility of mistaking it. It was as clear as daylight.

How long I stood there, I don't know, but suddenly the thought came to me that after all, this told me no more than the official announcement of his death, and not nearly so much as the accounts I had had of him in the various letters I had received. If I could dig up the earth and examine the body that lay buried there I might be able to settle my doubts. But there was nothing in a mere name to prove that there hadn't been a mistake.

Unsatisfied, I turned away. I noticed a pioneer at work a few graves off. Idly I strolled up to him, and he straightened a bent back and saluted me. I wondered if he could tell me anything. At length I asked him if there were any records of the burials to be seen. He scratched his head and said he didn't rightly know. He directed me to the officer in charge. But he looked as though he would like a good gossip, and I thought I might learn something useful. "If there's anything I could tell you, sir," he suggested with an obvious desire to yarn.

Well, I let him yam, and eventually asked if he remembered Colonel Booth who had been buried there. He seemed to have some hazy recollection of the name. I took him to the grave, and memory came back to him in a flood.

"Ah," he cried, "red tabs. Yes, sir, I remember burying him all right. Sowed him up neat, sir. Brother? Cousin?" he looked up at me inquisitively.

I gathered that he was rather proud of having had the burying of a staff colonel. No wonder the thing lived in his memory. But though I questioned him pretty closely I couldn't get anything more out of him. He seemed to want to impress me that everything had been done handsomely for the staff colonel. Evidently he took me for a relative, and thought he might get a fat tip. The idea amused me, and I played up to it.

"Yet you don't seem to have done much for him since you buried him," I said, pointing out the unweeded and flowerless grave, which by contrast to the graves around looked more desolate than if it had been alone by the wayside; for it was clear that the cemetery was well kept for the most part, nearly all the graves showing some tribute of autumn flowers, though now the frosts were beginning to get them. But Avery's grave seemed utterly neglected. Even the few weeds that grew there looked shrivelled and withered.

The fellow began shaking his head, and exclaimed, "Yes, sir, that's so, sir, but it's not my fault, sir. It's the women does it all, sir. They come from the village, three or four of them, and stick in these here flowers. I does the weeding as a rule. But they say they won't grow here, sir. I've told them . . ."

"What do you say?" I cried.

"I say I've told them hundreds of times . . ." he began.

"No, about the flowers," I cut in.

"About them not growing?" he asked. "Truth, sir, though you mightn't believe it. You ask them." He pointed to a group of women in a far corner of the cemetery, and then began whistling and shouting to them. "You just ask them," he repeated. "Truth, sir."

I took his insistence to mean that he was afraid the tip wouldn't be forthcoming if he couldn't prove his point. And still he called and waved to the women, till a couple of them eventually came over to us. He accosted them vigorously, "Tell the orficer about this here grave. Flowers, plenty, all no grow. *Vray, wee?*"

The sudden burst of clatter from the two women was enough to convince me of the truth of the thing. I couldn't make out much of their words. They seemed to be tumbling over themselves to express their utter lack of comprehension of the mystery. They opened their arms wide in token of being completely baffled. "Plentee flowerrs, yess," they had sown, but the "officer no bon." They came back to that again and again.

With the feeling that there was something unholy about the place, I distributed largess and turned away. I didn't want to examine any records now. The barren grave in the flowering cemetery seemed to me the strongest proof of what I wanted to know. I refused to listen to the idle chafing of reason, and the insistence of common sense that there was merely something unhealthy about that patch of ground. A gas shell might have fallen there. Anything might account for the coincidence. But contrary to custom all this was as nothing to me. I felt rooted to the conviction that the thing was only explicable by the evil poison that lay buried beneath.

CHAPTER V

It was in the early months of the next year that I got my discharge, and crossed homeward for the last time. Knowing that I was coming Katrina sent me the summons I had been longing for. It was simple enough, just, "I should like you to come to me, Dick," written clearly on a folded slip of paper and tucked into a letter from Blanche. So reaching London I took train for Little Hinton without deviating by Chalk Ridge.

As I had hoped, I was able to come to speech with Blanche before I saw Katrina. Though I had told her of what I had seen and heard at the cemetery, and though the evidence for Avery's death seemed beyond all possible doubt, yet her letters had been unsatisfactory, and in spite of myself I couldn't quite clear my mind of a shadowy uneasiness that persisted in lurking there and refused to be dislodged. And I wanted to know how far I was justified in pressing my suit upon Katrina while the death of Avery still seemed, to Blanche, at any rate, a matter of uncertainty. Also I wanted to know whether Katrina herself had any doubts on the subject. Blanche, in her last letter, had said that she had told Katrina nothing as there was no need. But quite what Blanche's grounds of suspicion were, I didn't know, and for all I could make out, Katrina might have doubts of her own, irrespective of Blanche.

Then, too, I was puzzled at Blanche's saying there was no need to tell Katrina anything. It seemed to me that Avery's being alive or dead concerned Katrina more than anyone else. Blanche had written, "To Katrina he is dead, so you needn't worry, Dick." But that didn't explain anything to me. And again she had said in her elusive way, "He is dead, all right, but he hasn't passed over." But that didn't help either. So I wanted to see her and have the puzzle cleared up before I met Katrina, as otherwise I shouldn't know how I stood with regard to the girl.

Blanche drove to the station to meet me, so I was able to have a good talk with her before entering the house. The first thing I noticed was that she was dressed in black. The shock was sharp, for there only seemed to be one possible explanation. She looked very weary and wasted, too, as though she had been watching late at night. I couldn't help blurting out, "Good God! have you heard?"

She wrung my hand very hard and turned her face away. It wasn't till the motor had started that she answered me. But her face was serene enough now, and she said, "Yes, I have heard, Dick."

I sat speechless.

After a pause she said, "Don't grieve for me, Dick. I know now. It was the suspense I couldn't bear. And I have a great consolation."

At that I broke out, "It's all too utterly cruel, Blanche. I can't see what consolation there is, and I can't preach any. I don't see why these things happen."

I knew while I was speaking that it was a strange way to offer comfort to the girl, and it seemed stranger still when she began to console me as though the loss were mine, not hers; for she said in a soft voice, "You must think of what you still have, Dick. Katrina's waiting for you at home."

"Good God, Blanche," I cried, "it's you I'm thinking of . . ." But I couldn't say any more. The position seemed too absurd.

"You needn't think of me, Dick," she answered me. "I'm wonderfully happy. Really I am. But, of course, you can't know all about that."

"You don't look happy," I said. But turning to her, I saw all the weariness had gone from her face, and she was smiling with a wonderful contentment. "At least you didn't when I first saw you," I added.

At that the shadow came back to her, and she said, "But, it wasn't for myself I was worrying, Dick, I could be quite happy if it weren't for something that still baffles me."

"Avery?" I asked.

"Yes, that," she answered, "and something else too. But I needn't bother you with it."

"If it's anything to do with Avery," I said, "you'd better tell me all about it. I want to know just how things stand. Is he alive or dead?"

"Why, dead, Dick," she answered.

"Then, what's all the fuss about?" I asked, puzzled.

A tone of weariness came into her voice as she answered, "When I say 'dead,' I'm using your language. He's dead enough to leave Katrina free. That's clear, isn't it?"

"If he's dead enough . . ." I began, but broke off with an exclamation of disgust. It all seemed so ridiculous. "He's either dead or not dead," I went on. "I don't see that there's any other alternative."

"All right, then," she said, "we'll say he's dead. And you needn't bother about him any more." She added, "He's really buried too, if that helps."

I seemed to be plunged into deeper mysteries than ever. All this talk about being dead enough . . . I felt a little angry. Blanche was keeping something back from me. And I knew why, though she hadn't told me. It had to do with her spirit-raisings, and I didn't want to hear anything about it. Especially as she didn't seem at all clear in her own mind what the matter was. And then the thought came to me that she had probably been speaking to Olave himself. That was her consolation. A pretty thin one, I thought, but I was devoutly glad to feel she had any sort of consolation at all. Otherwise her loss would have been shattering. I even felt an illogical gratitude to the fantastic humbug which had brought comfort into her desolated life.

"Have you told Katrina anything of all this?" I asked at last.

"Nothing," she said.

I hesitated for a moment, then asked, "And you honestly think I can go to her . . ." But I broke off in sudden shame, and muttered, "I'm sorry, Blanche, I'm a selfish brute."

At that she put her arms about me as she had done in the old days, and murmured, "No, dear, no, there's nothing I want so much as to see you two happy. Honestly, Dick. And I shall be angry with you if you haven't made all arrangements before the day's out."

She pressed her face to mine, then drew back from me and smiled radiantly full into my face.

"I don't understand," I muttered. "All I know is, I'm so intent on my own happiness that I can't properly realize what you've got to bear."

"If you'd only believe me," she said, still smiling. "I tell you I'm quite happy, Dick. You don't know. And it's Katrina you've got to think about, not me. She's suffered far more than I have. And now you can make it up to her."

"You're a real brick, Blanche," I said humbly, "but I don't know that I feel like speaking to Katrina while . . ."

"I turn my back on you," she exclaimed, doing so. And I even laughed.

"Well, well," I said, "if I must, I must."

"The noble self-sacrificing youth!" she cried gaily.

"But, honestly," I said, growing serious again, "is it all straight? Is it above board?"

"I wouldn't send you to her if it weren't," she replied.

And with that I had to be satisfied.

Our talk returned to Urcelyn, and Blanche rattled into a gay recital of all his marvellous sayings and clever tricks, till at length the motor swung us round into the drive and up to the Hall.

I found Katrina waiting for me in the music room. She was standing by the window as I entered. I paused at the door, and gazed in a rapture of expectation at the little figure framed against the light. The longed-for moment had come.

"You sent for me," I said, lingering out the sweetness.

"Yes, Dick," she answered simply.

I went to her, and taking her hand pressed it to my lips. There was a delicious silence while we looked deep into each other's eyes, but what I read in those pools of blue was something so inexpressibly wonderful that it seemed like a desecration for a fellow like me to lay unsanctified hands on such a loveliness. With a troubled sense of my own unworthiness I stooped and kissed her gently on the lips, and the next moment we were breast to breast, and all was spoken.

CHAPTER VI

Raising my face at length I found myself gazing abstractedly through the window out across the space of lawn to where the wall of woodland, still black and leafless, closed in the view. The stirring of a shadow struck at my attention, and whipped my mind back to the day when I had rushed to the pane to see Avery's figure vanishing into the woods. I blinked away the mist that dimmed my sight, and strained my eyes to the spot where I thought I had seen the shadow. There was nothing. But the inopportune recollection had troubled my content.

Katrina was watching me, and looking down into her eyes I tried to smile the frown out of my face.

She drew a little away from me and said, "I know what you're thinking."

"How beautiful you are," I replied.

"Do you have to look away from me to think that?" she asked roguishly.

I knew how to answer talk of that sort.

"But honestly," she said more seriously, "I had a reason for choosing this room, in fact this very spot. It's symbolic, Dick."

"Ah," I smiled back, "you've been living with Blanche."

"Yes," she admitted, "and I've learnt a lot, Dick. Symbols can be very expressive, you know."

"And what's the symbol here?" I asked.

"I don't think I'll tell you," she answered, "you look as if you're going to laugh."

"There," I said, straightening my face, "now expound, my Lady of Mystery."

She looked at me very solemnly for a while, and then said, "Well, Dick, standing here with me, and looking out to the woods, doesn't it remind you of something?"

"It does," I admitted, "something I'd like to forget."

"You can do better than forget," she said. And after a pause she went on, "You see, I wanted to make a clean break from all that. And he was in here with me that day, you remember. And I was thinking how wonderful he was. The music . . . But I've told you of that. And then I heard you come. And immediately I knew he was nothing to me. I just left him and ran to you."

"And that was the proudest moment of my life," I said.

"Well," she went on, "I wanted to go back to that and begin all over again. Because afterwards I forgot. We saw him disappear over there." She pointed out to the woodlands. "See, there he goes," she said, and with a silly sense of alarm I glanced quickly at the spot where she was pointing, half expecting to see him merging into the shadows. "Well, we'll let him go," she continued, "and this time he won't come back."

She turned to me impulsively and kissed me. The little play was ended, and I laughed delightedly. It was so charming and simple and so altogether like Katrina that I knew I should never forget the least detail of it. It was as though her love for me had been wrought into a clear, living picture which I might always carry with me.

Then Urcelyn found us, and romped us away for a game.

It was later in the day when Katrina took me to the chapel. We entered it from the vestry, and were immediately at the spot where Olave's grave should have been. The slab of stone on which I had nearly stepped on the day of the wedding still lay in the marble floor, but now it was inscribed with Olave's name. And behind it stood a large block of marble, very much like the one which rested on his father's grave. It hadn't been there when I was in the chapel last. It was evidently this which Katrina wanted me to see. She pointed to an inscription upon it. I leant forward to read it, for the place was only dimly lit by the falling glow of sunset. "Here lies . . ." I made out, and started back, "I don't understand," I exclaimed. Then I turned to it once more and read the simple inscription through.

"What does it mean?" I whispered.

"This is his grave, you know," she answered me in the same hushed voice.

"But," I said in perplexity, "wasn't he killed in France? How is it . . ." She understood the question without my finishing it.

"Yes, yes," she answered, "but he will come."

"Come?" I repeated.

Then another question rose in my mind.

"But when did you hear of his death?" I asked.

"Blanche told me just a week ago," she answered.

"Well then, all this," I pointed to the marble block, "not much time wasted."

"Oh," she explained, "Olave had that put there all ready."

"Olave!" I exclaimed.

"Dick," she said solemnly, "I believe he knew. But in any case he meant to leave things ready. Olave was like that, you know."

"Yes," I agreed, "Olave was like that."

"It's the same as father's," she began. But at that I fell back a step. I had the picture of myself treading on that slab of stone and sinking into the black earth, while the marble cenotaph came sliding over my head.

"Let's go," I said. I felt I had laid in a store of unpleasant matter for a nightmare. And looking around the white and shadowy place it seemed more haunted and sepulchral than it had done when I had first entered it that evening with Olave. Somehow the thought of a grave ready hollowed and inscribed for a corpse that was yet to lie there, seemed more horrible than the knowledge that beneath the monuments that stood about the walls there actually lay the bodies of the dead.

I drew a deep breath of the clean air as soon as I stepped into the open. Then I heard the sound of someone coming. Katrina drew me into the shadow of a tree, and Blanche and Mrs. Wait passed us by and went into the chapel.

"What, that woman!" I muttered.

"Doesn't she look tired?" said Katrina.

"I didn't properly see," I answered. "But I wish she wasn't here."

"She looks faded to a shadow," Katrina said, not heeding my exclamation. "Blanche doesn't have pity."

We were indoors again before it occurred to me to ask where Olave was buried, and whether Blanche had applied for the removal of his body.

"But she doesn't know," Katrina answered me.

"How do you mean?" I asked.

"You see, he was missing," she replied.

"Quite," I said, "but now that she's had news of his death they must be able to tell her . . ."

"Dick," she broke in, "hasn't Blanche told you?"

"Told me?" I asked. "What?"

"Why, all about it," she said.

"She's told me that she's heard," I answered.

Katrina watched me for a moment in silence, then turned her eyes away. "Well, you see, Dick . . ." she began, but broke off. There was evidently something troubling her which she found rather difficult to say.

I waited, letting her take her own time.

"Dick," she said at length, facing me again, "you must understand that Blanche has her own ways of learning things."

"Good God!" I exclaimed. "Do you mean . . ." But I couldn't frame my thoughts in words. "All that Mrs. Wait business," I threw out as the best I could do to express myself.

"Blanche has spoken to him," Katrina said. "To Olave," she added, to make sure I had understood.

I looked sharply at the girl. She had spoken with such a simple acceptance of the thing that I thought she had been caught in the same net.

"Surely not you too," I said.

"Yes, Dick," she replied, misunderstanding me, "I've spoken to him too."

"But surely," I broke out, "you don't believe in all that bunkum, do you?"

She looked at me in dismay. "Dick, you're not angry with me, are you?" she asked, laying her hand on my arm.

"Of course not," I said rather ungraciously, patting her hand, "but these things are dangerous, you know."

"Because it's not bunkum," she continued her own thought. "I don't pretend to understand it all, but it's not bunkum, Dick. Really, we spoke to each other. It was Olave, I'm sure of it. Though it was rather faint and uncertain; the way he spoke, I mean. You see he hadn't been well."

"Not well!" I cried. "I thought he was dead."

"Yes, of course," she said, and went on quickly. "Oh, I can't explain properly. You must ask Blanche. I'm just making it all sound silly. But you see, he had rather a nasty passing. Blanche says it takes some time to recover from that sort of thing. They have doctors on the other side. They see to you. Oh, I don't know," she broke off with a little laugh, "No wonder you say it's bunkum. It sounds it when I talk about it like that. You must get Blanche to explain. But after all, we're in this world a good time before we quite know where we are."

"Yes," I said, "but we never remember where we came from. If we came from anywhere."

She looked away from me, biting her lip.

I felt we were treading on the fringe of a quarrel, so I turned back to the original theme, and said, "But has Blanche had no other notice of Olave's death than what she has learnt through Mrs. Wait?"

"That's all, Dick," Katrina answered.

"Then for all we know he may still be alive," I said.

She shook her head, while I muttered to myself, "Really, it's preposterous."

It seemed clear to me that Mrs. Wait was imposing on Blanche. She had decided that it would be safe enough now to assume that Olave was dead. And on such evidence Blanche had had the tomb inscribed. She had even written, "Here lies." That sent my mind whirling to another problem.

"But she doesn't know where he's buried, then," I exclaimed.

"No," said Katrina.

I opened my hands and let them fall to my knees.

"But she will know," Katrina added. "She must know."

I thought I knew of what she was thinking. My mind went back to Olave's saying that it was a matter of honour for a Guthrie to be buried with his ancestors. But he was missing; had been missing for more than a year. The prisoners were being returned, we should have heard by now if he had been captured merely. And if he had been killed his body would have been identified before this if it would ever be identified at all. Yet Blanche had written, "Here lies." . . .

"We won't talk about it any more," I said more cheerfully, trying to ease the unpleasant atmosphere with a yawn and a smile.

Blanche joined us at dinner, but Mrs. Wait didn't put in an appearance. I presumed she was staying in the house as she had done when we had been hunting for Katrina. Looking at Blanche's pale, drawn face I guessed that Mrs. Wait had retired to her room, readier for bed than for company. And somehow I remembered Katrina's little expression, "Blanche doesn't have pity." I glanced at her again. There was something about the set and expression of her face which made me think of a queen of old time imposing her sovereign will on a multitude of slaves. There was something too of Beatrice Cenci as she had performed the part years ago. I don't know why the memory of that came back to me just then, but we were a silent party, and my mind seemed busy with a host of half remembered things.

It was after dinner that I took Katrina by the hand, and leading her up to Blanche, said, "I've obeyed your orders."

"I could see that," she replied, smiling back at us. "You'll be very happy."

When we were retiring for the night, and Katrina had already left us, I took the chance to say a word to Blanche.

"You're looking frightfully tired," I said, by way of a beginning. "You must take care of yourself."

"I will, Dick, I promise you," she said, "when I've put everything straight."

"Things will straighten themselves," I told her, not quite knowing what to say.

"No, Dick," she answered me firmly, "not tangles like these."

"You may well talk of tangles," I exclaimed, seeing my opening. "Really, I don't understand you, Blanche." I went on into a confused harangue about the inscription on Olave's tomb, trying all the while to steer

clear of anything that might sound unkind or tend to emphasize her be-
reavement, but probably in my clumsiness prodding her wound with every
word.

She heard me patiently to an end, and merely answered, "I shall find
him, Dick. I must find him."

Katrina's words. I knew where she had learnt them.

"And I want you to help me," Blanche went on.

"I wish I could," I said, "but honestly I don't think there's much
chance."

"But you see, Dick," she explained, "there's something that you know,
something that will give me the clue I want."

"Something that I know?" I questioned blankly.

She came close to me, and said slowly, "Olave's been trying to tell me,
but I can't make it out. It's a sign."

"Good God!" I muttered.

She put her hands on my shoulders and said coaxingly, "Come, Dick,
tell me. What is it?"

"But Blanche," I began, "I don't understand. How could you know of
it?"

"Never mind," she said, "just tell me what it is."

"I'm sorry," I answered, "but honestly I've forgotten."

"You must remember," she said, looking straight into my eyes.

"I wish I could," I exclaimed in annoyance, "but I've been trying to
remember ever since . . . for over a year. I can't get on the track of it. It's
bothered me a lot."

"You must remember," she repeated, still fixing me with her eyes.

For a moment I thought it had come to me. But just then there was a
burst of hammering at the front door and a terrible ringing of the bell.

CHAPTER VII

We both stiffened, listening alertly. The clamour continued till the door was opened. There was a confused noise in the hall, and Doctor Dale broke in upon us. He looked round quickly, and seeing me, said, "Ah, you here, good; I didn't know." He spoke disjointedly, puffing somewhat. "Sorry to frighten you," he added, trying to smile. He collapsed onto a chair, and threw open his overcoat, which in his hurry he hadn't taken off. He had his hat, too, in his hand, and seemed to become awkwardly aware of it, looking about him for somewhere to put it. I took it from him and laid it on a chair. "Thanks," he mumbled, "thanks. Bit of a hurry. No need, I dare say. Didn't know you were here." He shook out a huge handkerchief and mopped his brow. Then recovering himself somewhat, he beamed wanly at us and said, "I suppose you think I'm mad. But it seemed urgent. I had to come and warn you."

All this while Blanche had said nothing. She had remained standing, watching the painful struggles of the doctor to calm himself. Now she came forward and said, "Well, doctor, just make yourself comfortable, and then let's hear what the matter is."

The doctor rose, and I helped him to remove his coat.

"Ah, that's better," he said, bracing himself and smoothing down his hair. He made as though to sit down, but first said, "Everything's all right here, I take it?"

"Quite," Blanche assured him.

"Good," he said, sitting down. "But I thought I'd better come and make sure."

I was getting impatient. "Well, doctor," I addressed him, "what's it all about, anyway?"

"Escaped lunatic," he answered me.

"Another?" I couldn't help exclaiming. I glanced at Blanche, and felt a sudden chill of alarm. She was standing motionless, her eyes fixed wide on Doctor Dale, and all the colour gone from her face. The doctor was watching her too, and I noticed he shuffled uneasily under her stare. He blinked and bit at his lip, then trying to smile, he said, "Oh, nothing to be alarmed at. Really, nothing. . . ."

Blanche cut in coldly, "So I gathered from your manner of entry."

He opened his hands and wrinkled up his brow, then turned to me and said with a stupid snigger, "But you see, we have Mr. Bellew with us.

He knows how to settle escaped lunatics. Eh?"

He rubbed his hands nervously. But at Blanche's sharp pained cry of, "Doctor!" I saw him start and wince as though from the cut of a whip. And I too felt as though a sudden hand had gripped me, and a shudder went through me as she cried terribly, "He won't have the settling of this one."

Her hands were pressed to her temples, and for a moment she swayed to and fro, her head thrown back and her teeth set.

I thought she would have fallen, but I couldn't stir from where I stood. And then she seemed to recover her composure. Her hands fell to her sides and she bowed her head. "No," she repeated quietly, "not this one, doctor." She raised her face and looked him steadily in the eyes.

He seemed utterly at a loss, and began mopping at his brow again, muttering, "Well, really, you know, really . . ."

There was an uneasy pause. I gazed from one to the other. I think they had forgotten me, for they both seemed taken aback when I said, "For God's sake let's know what all the fuss is about."

"Ah, yes, quite," said Doctor Dale. "An escaped lunatic . . ."

"I know that," I cut in. "But what I don't see is how it affects us. Do all escaped lunatics inevitably gravitate our way?"

"You see, Mr. Bellew," he explained, "we followed him as well as we could, and traced him as far as the wood here. He's probably hiding in the neighbourhood. So I thought I had better warn you."

"And is that all?" I asked.

"That's all," he said.

"Well . . ." I began to wonder what the excitement was about. Then glancing at Blanche I cried, "That isn't all, doctor. You're keeping something back."

He looked helplessly to Blanche. I knew what his questioning gaze meant. He didn't know whether he would be doing right in telling me what underlay the business. For it was clear to me by now that there was a secret between these two which was dark to me.

I strode up to him and said gruffly, "Look here, there's something in the air. I want to know what it is. If there's any danger threatening us I'm the one to deal with it."

I thought a little bullying might help to unseal his lips, but I had mistaken my man. He seemed to grow sulky, and said, "If you want to know more you must ask Mrs. Guthrie."

I walked away from him. And again there was an awkward pause while Blanche and the doctor seemed to be conversing with their eyes.

I sat down to await what might come of it all. I had made up my mind not to leave them together, as I felt a sort of obstinate desire to get to the heart of the mystery. If they intended to talk they would have to do so in front of me. And then, too, I didn't know what the danger was, nor what it involved. Katrina might be implicated, and if so I was determined to take things into my own hands. I knew something of the strength and devilry of lunatics. I had nearly been killed by one. And the thought of one prowling in the neighbourhood was unpleasant enough in itself. But added to that was the feeling that there was something particularly frightful about this one. The doctor's frantic bursting in upon us, and Blanche's terrible cry when he had suggested that I could shoot the creature, had shaken me uneasily.

It was Blanche who broke the silence. She said, with quiet decision, "You'd better tell us all about it, doctor, from the very beginning. Dick ought to know. And then I'm still very much in the dark myself. There are things I haven't managed to unravel yet. You can probably help me."

She sat down as though prepared to listen to a long story.

The doctor drew a deep breath, and crossing his legs and sticking his thumbs into his waistcoat, said, "Well, I've been wanting to tell you. It will relieve me to get it off my mind. We've had a pretty bad time, you know, and it's worried me." He paused, then began again with emphasis, "Avery Booth, you remember . . ."

"What?" I cried, "Avery?"

Just then the door opened and Katrina stood on the threshold. The doctor started up in confusion, and bowed to her awkwardly. Blanche said, "Come in, Katrina."

"What is it?" she asked, looking round in inquiry.

"The doctor's going to tell us a story," said Blanche. "It will interest you."

"No," I cried, breaking from the sudden horror that had numbed me. I rose quickly and went to Katrina. "Go back to bed," I said. "It'll only trouble you."

Katrina looked from me to Blanche. Then turning back to me she smiled and said, "But I'd rather stay, Dick. I heard you speak . . . that name."

I tried to urge her away, but she shook her head. So I drew up a chair for her, and leaning over the back, prepared for the story with a sickening sense of apprehension at my heart.

The doctor looked round at us and with a shrug began again. "I'm afraid I've been raising expectations," he said, "but I haven't much to tell. It's merely the story of a war lunatic. Shell-shock case, I suppose. And little wonder, the fellow was nastily smashed. Both legs off, face too horrible to be seen, body all twisted. So forth. He wears a mask, always. In fact, we keep him covered from head to . . . I was going to say 'to foot,' but he ends half-way. He's really too appalling a sight to endure. You couldn't even get used to it. Of course, I've had to attend to him at times . . . I still dream. He's like that, you see, so we keep him covered. That is, if he lets us. He's frightfully strong. I suppose the strength of his legs has gone to his arms; something like a blind man becoming extraordinarily keen of hearing. And he seems to take rather an unholy delight in exposing himself. People simply scream when they see him. I can believe the old yarn of the Gorgon now. Only yesterday, he set on one of the attendants. His mask fell off, and the man saw his face. He just went sick."

"For God's sake stop," I broke in.

"Sorry," he said, "but I had to give you the picture. You see that's the one that's escaped. He's about here somewhere."

"Very well," I said, "if I meet him I'll know what to do."

"I hope to God you'll meet him then," the doctor cried impulsively. "I shan't sleep easily while he's still above the earth."

I was taken aback, not expecting such an outbreak.

"He's thoroughly evil," he explained. "He's not a mere lunatic. He seems to know what he's doing, and takes a devilish delight in it. In fact," the doctor turned to me, "I seem to know what people mean now when they say, 'ugly as sin.'"

That jerked my mind back to his mention of Avery. I felt my heart leap and set off with a heavy thumping. "Go on," I said, my throat feeling strangely dry, "let's hear the worst."

But the doctor was again holding a mute discourse with Blanche. His brow was raised as though in inquiry.

"Yes, go on," I thundered.

"Well, then," he resumed, "here's the extraordinary thing."

He sniggered as though to set us at ease. I laid hold of Katrina's hand, feeling that at last the climax had come.

"You see," he said, "a lunatic is merely a weak-minded person who has yielded to a fantasy. It's usually easy enough to understand why. A charwoman calls herself the Empress of China . . ."

"Oh, cut that out," I exclaimed impatiently.

"Well," he turned to me, "this fellow chooses to call himself Avery Booth."

Katrina pulled her hand free from mine, and sprang to her feet. "It's my husband," she said. "He's still alive."

Blanche came quickly across to her, and I tried to get possession of her hand. "No, Dick, no," she cried. Blanche led her from me, and they sat down together. I collapsed on to the empty chair.

"Go on," said Blanche to the doctor. Her voice sounded toneless and hollow as though she were performing a task that had been imposed on her. I looked towards her. She had one arm about Katrina, and had the girl's hands clasped upon her lap. But her face was turned to the doctor. I couldn't read from it what was passing in her mind. Her brow was smooth and her lips steady, but her cheeks were very pale.

"Go on," she said again.

"Yes, but how?" he asked. "You see, it's all such a puzzle. Because it isn't Avery at all. If it were Avery then there'd be no reason to keep the fellow at St. Jude's. He was sent to us from hospital because he insisted on calling himself Avery Booth, but when inquiries were made it was found that Avery Booth was dead and buried. All that was gone into pretty carefully. There couldn't be any mistake about it. So he was handed over to us. He must have met Avery somewhere and taken to him, and now he's got the idea that he's Avery himself. It's just understandable, I suppose. A weak-minded fellow might conceive rather an admiration for a man of Avery's power. So there it is."

I began to breathe more freely. "But isn't there anything to identify him by?" I asked.

"Well, yes, but it leads nowhere," he said uneasily. "There are bits of evidence, but they don't tally."

"What evidence?" I asked.

He began to shift in his seat, and obviously to evade me answered, "Well, for one thing, he seems to know all sorts of things about Avery which it's unlikely that anyone except Avery himself could know. Things which have been examined and proved, I mean. In fact, there are some things that I know for certain were secrets between Avery and me. And if he isn't Avery, how's he got to know them? But he isn't Avery, because Avery's dead. That's the puzzle."

I thought over that for a minute, then asked, "But are there no physical signs to identify him by?"

"I tell you, he's smashed," he answered.

"But his eyes?" I suggested.

"Ah!" he exclaimed. "There again. I should know Avery's eyes in a million."

"Well?" I waited.

"Well," he answered, "they are Avery's eyes all right."

"Good God!" I said.

"Black," he went on. "But it isn't only their colour. It's . . . well, it's everything about them. If you've ever seen his eyes you'd know."

"Yes, I know," I said.

Then Blanche asked very clearly, "But were they always black?"

The doctor didn't answer her for a minute. Then he exclaimed, "Yes, since he's been with me. But . . ."

"But before?" she asked again.

"I don't know," he said slowly, as though his mind were busy with a thought. He was gazing very fixedly at Blanche, and I heard him mutter several times, "My God!"

Again there was silence for a while. Though my thoughts were in a confused tangle I seemed to see by glimpses something of the reason of Blanche's strangeness when she had spoken to me of Avery. She had told me that Katrina was free, but had hinted that there was still something unsettled and mysterious about Avery's death. She had probably heard about this lunatic. But I couldn't get anything clear in my mind. The glimpses of understanding faded before I could focus them. There was a sort of floating confusion of disunited ideas in my head, but I couldn't find the necessary view-point which would show them in their right relation. All I knew for certain was that Avery's shadow had fallen again between Katrina and myself, and I wondered whether it would ever lift, for now it wasn't merely as if the man himself were keeping us apart; there was something subtle, something preternatural and incomprehensible, which baffled me, and left me struggling ineffectually as though with an image of vapour.

I became aware of Blanche speaking. I must have missed part of what she said because I had become wrapped in my own thoughts. What I heard was, "There is a sign."

I didn't know what she was referring to, but my mind went back with a jerk to Olave and the mark he had had tattooed upon him. And suddenly I remembered what it was. Without thinking how utterly irrelevant my exclamation must seem, I cried, "Yes, the sword and the serpent."

The doctor sprang up as though I had struck him, and still gripping his chair in one hand he gazed at me with wide eyes. Then swaying slowly he fell back into his chair, exclaiming faintly, "My God! My God!"

"Why, what on earth . . ." I looked at him in wonder, utterly unable to understand his emotion.

Blanche went up to him and said, "That's quite enough, Doctor Dale. I'm very much obliged to you. Of course, you'll stay to-night."

She rang the bell, and before I could recover enough to ask what it all meant, the doctor had said good-night, and was being shown to his room.

"What is it, Blanche?" I asked as the door closed behind him.

She looked at me with that deep gaze of hers, and said quietly, "The story will soon be ended, Dick."

I looked doubtfully across at Katrina, who was standing away from me, with her hands clasped at her breast. Blanche went to her and led her up to me. She took our hands and joined them, but Katrina drew hers away, and said, "No, not yet, Dick. I don't know. I don't know."

Blanche looked at us, then dropping her arms to her sides she bowed her head and went from the room.

I was left alone with Katrina. For a moment I felt a surging desire to claim her for my own, to plead with her to put aside all thought and memory of Avery, to tell her he was safely buried where he couldn't rise to divide us. But the words sank dead at my lips. I took her hand and kissed it, and saying good-night stepped aside for her to pass.

Before going to my room I took a turn outside. The night was very dark, but in the east there was the glow of the rising moon. The air was still, and everything spoke of a wonderful peace. Drawing a deep breath I went inside again, feeling soothed and relieved. The calm and quiet of the night were like a promise or a blessing. I went upstairs to my room.

But a sudden thought sent me to Blanche. I knocked at her door. She opened to me. "Have you a revolver?" I asked.

"You won't need it, Dick," she answered.

"It was useful last time," I pressed her.

"But this is different," she said. I went back to my room with the spell of the quiet night broken in my heart, and the old uneasiness fretting me more distressingly than ever.

CHAPTER VIII

Shut in by myself, a stupid nervousness began to take possession of me. I paced my room knowing quite well that I was too shaken and restless to think of sleeping yet awhile. So much seemed to have happened that day to disturb me; the excitement of the return to England, the emotional stress of the meeting with Katrina, and more unsettling still the strange circumstances that had enveloped in mystery the revelation of Olave's death, culminating in the sudden bursting in upon us of the terrified doctor with his talk of Avery and the escaped lunatic. Never had I felt myself so utterly adrift amid shifting uncertainties. I found myself harking back in an inconsequential way first to one then to another of the exciting incidents of the day till at last everything became confused into one blurred picture. At one moment I was repeating something particularly delicious that Katrina had said to me, and the next I was living again that horrible moment when the doctor had let loose upon us the name of Avery.

And always I felt a fear hovering at the back of my mind, and trying to analyse it, I suddenly realized it was due to my being unarmed. If anything happened I should be powerless to meet it. Why anything should happen, I didn't ask myself, though I did feel about among my fears for what might happen. But I couldn't come upon it. It wasn't the escaped lunatic, for when the memory of the creature lurking in the neighbourhood came consciously into my thoughts, I laughed it away. I didn't suppose for a moment that there was really anything to fear from the fellow, whoever he was and however powerful he might be. And yet it troubled me to be without a weapon; but when I tried to get on the track of the thing that was disturbing me, I couldn't run it to earth. I suppose it was just the sum total of all the strange occurrences of the day that had combined to throw me into a fine state of nervous upset.

Feeling angry with myself I pulled off my clothes, switched out the light, and threw myself on the bed. But though I turned from side to side, and one by one threw off the blankets which seemed to be stifling me, I couldn't get a wink of sleep. My head was in a whirl. And that made me angrier still, because of the unusualness of the thing. As a rule disturbing thoughts fell from me like ripe fruit as soon as my head touched the pillow. Even in the days when Katrina had been missing I had slept soundly enough. Again and again I asked myself what was troubling me. I went through the experiences of the day, item by item, and told myself that there was nothing to keep me awake. True, there might be work for me on the morrow, unpleasant work, perhaps. For there would almost certainly be that lunatic to hunt down, for one thing. But that was only an added reason for me to get a good night's rest.

Then the question seemed to come from nowhere, who was the lunatic? By the sickness at my heart I thought I had come face to face with the real cause of my fear. Who was the lunatic indeed? Was it Avery? But as soon as I put the question like that I felt reassured. Not only had I satisfied myself that Avery was dead and buried, but Blanche had definitely told me it was so, and the doctor, too, hinted that an official inquiry had been made into the matter as well. There could be no doubt on that point. Well, who was he, then? I told myself it didn't matter in the least. As long as he wasn't Avery he might call himself what he chose. So I turned over again and determined I would keep awake no longer.

I had heard that one way of sending oneself to sleep was to take deep breaths until the temples began to throb. I tried it, and felt the blood begin to thump at my ears. A sort of warm singing silence seemed to grow out of the heavy pulsing and cover me like a soft robe. Then suddenly I was frightfully awakened by a violent knocking and ringing. I sat up in bed with the echoes buzzing in my ears. I listened, but the house was deathly still. Not a murmur of the shattering clamour lingered in the air. "Good God!" I muttered, "I've been dreaming."

I lay down again and dug my head viciously into the pillow. At any rate I had been to sleep. The thought was consoling. If I had succeeded once I might succeed again. I began to breathe with great lungfuls. And then I was falling into a deep black hole in the earth. Something came down over my head. I started up, beating wildly at the clothes which had got tangled round my face. I turned over, and felt myself suddenly seized from behind by two powerful arms and whirled violently off my feet. And as I jerked back to consciousness I seemed to see a masked cloaked figure creeping stealthily away.

I got out of bed and switched on the light. I felt I couldn't stand any more of this sort of thing. I felt I would go mad if I continued to have such dreams. The night was chilly, so I pulled on some clothes, and taking down a book set myself to read. But, of course, my mind wandered from the page. I tried to fix my attention on the story, but a few consecutive words were all that I could take in. The sentence faded before my eyes half read.

I tossed the thing away and commenced pacing the room. Looking at my watch I found it was still not one o'clock. I shook the thing and listened to hear if it were going. I could have sworn I had been prisoned in that place for hours. Yet I suppose I hadn't been undressed for more than half an hour at the most. I felt frightened. If the whole night were to drag itself away at such a leaden pace I thought I should be raving long before the morning.

It was little enough comfort to have the room lit. I had the sense of things behind me, pacing with me as I strode from door to window. I kept turning quickly to try and catch them at their game, but they were too quick for me, and whisked round me as I turned. I dropped into a chair and called myself a thundering fool for yielding to such crazy fantasies. "Just the way to make things worse," I argued against it in my mind, and the next moment leapt from my chair and grabbed fiercely behind it for something that I felt was lurking there. Of course, my hand clasped air. I pulled the chair away. Just nothing. But I didn't dare sit down again. And during my pacing I kept a watchful eye on the suspected chair.

Then I began to suspect other things. I stooped to peer under the bed, but swung round suddenly to see what it was breathing on my neck. Then I opened the wardrobe door, and for a moment had a terrible scare, for the hanging clothes gave me the impression of someone drawn up alert and waiting. That made me ask myself what I would do if I should actually see a face looking at me as I peered under the bed or behind some piece of furniture. The cold shudder that the thought gave me prevented me for a while from indulging in the fantastic game. But then the window curtains began to fascinate me. I turned from them, only to wonder what was on the other side of my bedroom door. And so at either end of my path I was tortured with the teasing desire to fling open the door, or tear aside the curtains. On the whole, the curtains tempted me most. They swayed and swelled and subsided so noiselessly and stealthily that it seemed as though there were a moving thing behind them, hesitating to throw them aside and leap out. I went up to them and twitched them suddenly apart. I found myself looking out into the moonlight. For, in spite of the brightness of my room, the air was silvery with moonlight, though I couldn't see the moon. For my window faced west, and the shadow of the house lay black beneath me, though the lawn lay white beyond. I gazed out into the night, straining for a movement, but everything was still. My fancy distorted the bushes and the trees into images of fear, but all the while I knew them for what they were, checking them in my memory.

Then on the landing outside my door I heard the least creak.

It was all that I wanted to steady me. I turned about, feeling suddenly calm. I knew that something was going to happen, and I welcomed it as a relief to my tortured nerves. I went to the door and opened it. The light of my room lit up the balcony and the empty space beneath the dome, and shone across to the door of Katrina's room which lay opposite. I looked out, but there was nothing to be seen. I left my room, pulling the door to behind me, and the darkness closed me in. Very quietly I made for Katrina's room, feeling my way round by the balustrade. And outside her door I came to a halt, listening.

But all was silent. And though I waited there longer than I could reckon, I couldn't hear a sound. Disappointed, I made my way back to my room. Before I reached it I was shaking with terror of the dark. All my calmness had deserted me. I had been braced for action, and finding nothing to be done, my fear had returned upon me. My fingers stumbled upon the switch of the dome light, and suddenly I was out of the dark. For a moment I was startled, but it was good to be in the wholesome light once more, and with a gasp of relief I moved on again to my room.

And so the long misery began all over again. But now it wasn't merely my own room that I paced so restlessly. I made excursions round the balcony, listening intently behind each door. Sometimes I thought I could hear the sound of breathing, and sometimes there was nothing but the shrill singing of the silence in my ears. And back to my room I came, only to start out once more. And always I was tempted to go farther afield where the long black corridor led to remoter parts of the house.

Returning to my room for the third time I looked at my watch. Half-past one! At that a sweat broke out all over me. I felt the night would never end. It was almost more than I could do to restrain myself from waking up Blanche to share my vigil with me.

And still I was fascinated by what I felt was happening across the landing. I couldn't keep away from Katrina's door. There was a deepening conviction in my mind that something was taking place there, something evil and terrible. I didn't attempt to shape it in my thoughts, though flying images chased through my head from the hideous dreams that had already alarmed me. And standing there, listening for some sound that might tell me what was happening, or some least little cry for help that would justify my breaking in, I couldn't help thinking of the days when I had slept on guard there. But even that wasn't so bad as this. And yet with my ear pressed to the panel I couldn't hear a sound. But whenever I turned away I seemed to catch dull mufflings of movement that drew me back to my post again, feverishly uncertain.

By this time I had given up any attempt to control myself. It was useless telling myself I was merely playing the fool, yielding weakly to empty shadows and imaginings. I was prepared to laugh at myself on the morrow, but meanwhile the sense of dark happenings had become too real to shake off. And I thought I had located the centre of terror. It was behind that door, where Katrina lay.

More than once I had my fingers on the handle, closing about it ready to fling the door wide. But something restrained me. I think it was the fear of being premature, of scaring the evil thing, whatever it might be, before I could catch it at its work, rather than any scruple of startling Katrina, which held me back, listening, straining my ears to interpret each least stirring of sound.

And at last it came clearly and unmistakeably. My senses were alert and my fear gone. I flung the door open and broke into the room. There was a splitting scream. I rushed across to the window where Katrina was framed darkly against the full glare of the moon. She was leaning half out, and in another moment would have fallen. I caught her in my arms, and she collapsed in a swoon upon my breast.

I had hardly laid her on the bed before the room was flooded with light, and Blanche stood at the door, and in another moment Doctor Dale had joined us, too. Katrina lay moaning brokenly while I knelt beside her, and then recovering consciousness she opened wide eyes full upon me. It was clear that she was at a loss to know where she was or what had happened. She lay for a while gazing at me blankly, then seeming to remember something of what had occurred she tried to raise herself up and speak, but fell back to the pillow muttering incomprehensibly.

Blanche was standing over her. She laid her hand on the girl's brow, and Katrina looked away from me to her. "What is it?" Blanche asked in a steady voice.

But Katrina was still unable to speak. She shook her head feebly and closed her eyes.

"Katrina," Blanche spoke sharply, and Katrina opened her eyes with a frightened start, and looked up at her with what seemed to me a growing comprehension.

"What is it?" Blanche repeated.

There was another space of silence while the two gazed at each other. Then all of a sudden Katrina sat upright clasping her hands together and staring wildly before her. "Avery!" she cried. Then she shook her head violently and exclaimed, "Don't ask me. Oh, don't ask me."

"You must tell me," said Blanche.

Katrina covered her eyes with her hands and muttered, "But I want to forget, I want to forget."

"What about Avery?" Blanche persisted, with what seemed to me needless cruelty. I would have interrupted, but for the knowledge that Blanche intended to have her way. It was evident in her expression.

Katrina threw an appealing gaze at her, and clasping her hands convulsively cried, "But it was horrible, horrible. At the window. I saw him. Slowly . . . He came in and stood by me. He . . . *Ugh!*"

Her voice broke on a sob of disgust, and I threw my arms about her. Her broken phrases had given me a picture of the whole thing. My memory went back to a similar experience of my own. I could see the black form creeping up into the moonlight, and Katrina spellbound with horror watching it slowly frame itself against the window.

I felt her body cold against my arm, and she was trembling violently. Then a spasm seemed to shake her whole frame, and she whispered, "I saw him."

No one spoke.

She gazed round at us vacantly, and suddenly cried, "I tell you, I saw him." She gave a frenzied laugh and dug her hands into her eyes.

The doctor was muttering, "Oh, my God!" I knew what Katrina meant, though I couldn't realize the full horror of it. The creature had taken off its mask.

Then Blanche said, "There, that's enough." She gently urged the girl to lie down again, and motioned me away. I went from the room with the doctor, for Blanche dismissed him, too. Outside I turned to him and asked hoarsely, "What does it mean?"

He was dabbing at his perspiring face. "Hell knows," he exclaimed.

"But is it Avery?" I pressed him.

"Don't ask me," he pushed me aside. "Don't ask me anything. I don't want to hear anything about it. I've had enough of it, I tell you. It's getting on my nerves. It's driving me mad. I'll never have a decent night's sleep again." He was hurrying off, but I held him back.

"Look here," I said sharply, "this is your business, I reckon. Here's one of your lunatics broken loose again. It's your job to explain what it means. Why has he chosen this house to break into? And Katrina's room . . ."

He cut me short with an angry, "I don't want to hear anything about it." He clapped his hands to his ears.

I pulled them away and exclaimed, "But you're going to answer me before I let you go. Is this Avery? That's what I want to know."

He turned upon me and cried viciously, "Haven't you said yourself that he chose this house and . . . and his wife's room. . . ."

"Stop!" I shouted. I felt I could have knocked him to the floor. Instead, I flung away from him and strode back to my room. My intention was to get on some thicker clothes and go and hunt for that abominable thing. I could not think of it as a man. The doctor's description of the legless trunk with the powerful arms and the distorted face had somehow made me think of Old Jock's mangled body. I had the impression of something loathsome and inhuman, bestial and soulless.

But it wasn't merely the horror of such a creature having appeared to Katrina and unmasked itself before her that made my heart sick, it was the significance of its having selected Katrina as its victim. The doctor had given me the answer I had dreaded to hear. "His wife's room. . . ." The words echoed in my ears like a mocking refrain. In spite of all that Blanche had told me of Avery's being dead and buried, in spite of her reassurances and my own investigations in the matter, I knew now that Avery was alive, and that this was none other than Avery himself. I felt an urgency to track him down and to settle him once for all. There would be no mistake this time. Then I suddenly remembered I was still unarmed. But Blanche must have a revolver of Olave's somewhere in the house. I had forgotten for the moment that she had already refused to let me have one. I pulled on my coat and made for Katrina's room.

As I opened the door I seemed to see again the girl leaning from the window as I had found her when I had first broken in. The fancy passed in a flash, but I seemed to see now something I hadn't seen then. There were two arms locked about her forcing her through. Avery had come to carry her away. If I had waited another moment she would have been lost to me.

Blanche turned as I entered. She motioned me to be quiet. I looked to Katrina. She was asleep. But her lips were moving uneasily, and her face was bitterly unhappy.

I tip-toed to the bed. "I want a revolver," I said.

Blanche shook her head.

"But it's Avery come back," I insisted.

She looked me in the eyes, and again shook her head.

"I tell you," I began again, "he mesmerized her, and was carrying her away with him. She was half out of the window."

"Yes, I know," she said.

"Well, then . . ." But my expostulations were cut short. A wail seemed to rise from the heart of the house and came ringing down the corridor. Blanche pulled me quickly out of the room, and closed the door behind her. I suppose she was afraid of Katrina being awakened.

The noise was on us now. It was Urcelyn's nursemaid who came running up to us in wild disarray, crying unintelligibly.

Blanche caught her by the arm and steadied her. "Well?" she asked.

The girl was blubbering hysterically. "Gone," she cried, "he's gone. Urcelyn . . ." She collapsed to her knees, clinging to Blanche, and sobbing in choking gulps.

I looked at Blanche in stupid dismay. She was drawn up straight and rigid, and in her eyes blazed a fire that terrified me. She stood speechless, her breast heaving, but her face white and set like a statue's. I didn't dare speak her name. She walked away from me and left me standing there gazing after her.

The girl clutched at my arm and would have raced out into a tearful story of what had happened. But I knew what had happened without being told. I shook myself free of her, and she fell away from me with a moan. I turned and raced down the stairs and out of the house.

I knew that if I found Avery I should kill him without scruple. Even in my rage against him I was sane enough to realize that now he was my lawful prey. A lunatic, an outcast, a public danger . . . The expressions ran through my head like shouts of laughter. He was delivered up to me. He was mine to catch and kill.

But morning found me still vainly hunting for him. He had melted into the night, and not a trace of him could I discover.

CHAPTER IX

During the days that followed Blanche was almost unapproachable, and I was left to take what action I thought best in the matter of recovering Urcelyn. At first, of course, I told Blanche what I was doing, and asked her what else there was to be done. I thought she would send me scouring the country as she had done when Katrina had been kidnapped. But she didn't seem to take any interest in my movements. When I told her I had set the police on Avery's track she broke into a scornful laugh. When I asked her where I should search for him she said, "Don't." I couldn't understand her behaviour, unless it was that she was driven half mad by anxiety. Her face was like an unchanging mask, for I could read nothing from it except a burning determination to win back her child. That was clear enough, but whether she were hopeful or otherwise I couldn't read a sign to tell me. There was never a trace of any passing or surface emotion, but always there was the white, set grimness that I had seen come over her when the nursemaid had run screaming to her with the news of Urcelyn's disappearance. It was as though her spirit were ever at white heat, and her eyes were filled with the fire of it. I was glad to avoid her, for I felt utterly useless, and it seemed to me that my presence merely irritated her to an intenser pitch of anger or indignation, or whatever it was which set her lips into such a hard, thin line. Looking at her sometimes I thought her face was the cruellest thing I had seen. The girl looked capable of cold and calculated murder, and I wondered what she was planning for Avery when she should win him into her power.

That she was busy day and night weaving some subtle scheme I could guess well enough. At times I caught a glimpse of Mrs. Wait creeping wearily up to her room. I knew she had come from some exhausting sitting with Blanche. Once I saw the pair coming from the chapel, evidently the sittings took place there; but what Blanche hoped to gain from them I didn't ask myself. If I thought anything it was that she was trying to learn where Avery was hidden, and perhaps she would soon have work for me. If she came upon his track, I guessed she would send me after him. I think it was this, even more than any desire to be near Katrina, that kept me lingering at Hinton Hall, when I should have felt mightily relieved to have been at Chalk Ridge away from Blanche's uncomfortable presence. But I stayed on, day after day, expecting that at any time she might send me racing off on Avery's track.

But the days wore on, and nothing seemed to happen. Katrina had recovered pretty well from the shock of that terrible apparition, but her treatment of me was rather puzzling. She kept away from me, and I gathered that now that Avery was alive again—for it seemed to me that he must have risen from the dead—Katrina felt it best for us to part. She was obviously uneasy in my company, and I didn't attempt to press myself upon her. But on the other hand, I didn't want to desert her if she really wished me to stay. Thinking I might have misinterpreted her avoidance of me, I asked her plainly one day whether she wanted me to go.

She looked timidly up into my face, and the tears started to her eyes. She laid a hand on my arm and said, "That's rather unkind."

Of course, I was all protestations that I merely wanted to know what she would have me do. She turned away from me and faltered, "I think, Dick, you ought to go."

That was all I needed. I raised her hand and kissed it, and turned and left her.

Then I sought out Blanche. If she had no use for me it was clearly my best plan to quit. I came upon her at length, having waylaid her as she left the chapel.

I opened the matter without preliminaries, saying, "I'm thinking of going home, Blanche. Do you want me here?"

"No, Dick," she answered without hesitation.

"Right," I said, turning away. But I stopped to add, "Of course, if you need me I'm at your disposal."

"I won't need you," she said.

Somehow I was piqued to know what her plan of campaign was. She was keeping it mighty secret, and I felt she ought to have taken me into her confidence. I think it was her abrupt acceptance of my offer to leave her which brought my curiosity to a head.

"Look here," I said, "you don't tell me much, and you don't seem to be making much headway. Haven't you got a clue yet, or what?"

"You needn't worry, Dick," she said.

"That's all mighty fine," I cried, beginning to bluster. It annoyed me to see her standing there so straight and frigid with all her thoughts masked away from me behind that inscrutable white countenance.

"I tell you it's all right," she said.

"All right?" I cried in amazement.

"Yes, Dick, quite all right," she repeated.

"Well, then," I said feebly, "it doesn't seem so to me, that's all."

She took a step nearer to me, and said, "But you see, Dick, you don't understand."

"No, I jolly well don't," I exclaimed.

She looked me full in the eyes for a moment, then turning away said, "But it wouldn't help to tell you."

"Look here," I broke out, catching her by the arm, "I don't suppose I should understand if you did tell me, but at least you might let me know where Avery's hidden. I expect you've found out that much, haven't you?"

"Yes, I know that," she said.

"Well then . . ." I exclaimed. It seemed preposterous.

It was my turn to fling away from her, and her turn to hold me back. She said very slowly, "I could have Urcelyn back to-morrow if I wished."

I waited for her to continue.

"But you see, there's a condition," she went on.

"Well?" I asked.

"I must give Katrina in exchange."

I fell back in dismay. Yet I must have been dull indeed not to have guessed as much before.

"Does she know?" I faltered at length.

"No," she said, "and she never must know."

"Ah!" I exclaimed relieved.

There was another pause. Then I said, "Well, it seems to me that you'd better put me on Avery's trail and let me settle the fellow."

"That would be disastrous," she exclaimed with fervour.

"Why, how?" I asked, taken aback.

Again she drew near to me, and said, "Why will you ask these questions, Dick? Why must you know things you can't understand?"

I shuffled uneasily. I didn't like the look in her eyes.

She went on, "Very well, then, let me tell you. Urcelyn will come back to me." She paused, and added in a voice that thrilled me, "Olave will bring him."

"Olave!" I exclaimed.

"Yes, Dick," she said.

"But good God, Blanche," I cried, "what on earth do you mean? Olave? He's . . . Are you going to raise him from the dead?"

She stared in my eyes with her face right close to mine, and said, "Have you ever heard of Lazarus?"

With that she turned swiftly away and left me in my stupefaction. I looked after her with an unspeakable fear at my heart. It seemed clear to me that her troubles were turning her head.

I determined to leave for home the next morning, and accordingly set out soon after breakfast.

But it wasn't pleasing to find, on my arrival at Chalk Ridge, that the Gipsies had once again settled themselves in Morton's Dingle. There seemed to me a sinister connection between their presence there and Avery's reappearance. I jumped to the immediate conclusion that Avery was in hiding with them. And it wasn't long after my arrival before I was tramping down to the encampment with the intention of raising hell's delight.

Yet I came away having achieved nothing. The cringing of the wretches, and the squalid misery of their encampment, disarmed my determination. Feeling all the time that they were imposing upon me, I couldn't bring myself to believe that such a despicable crew could possibly do any serious mischief. They seemed to have no spirit, no force. They whined and fawned and pleaded, till in disgust I turned away and left them masters of the place. I knew I had behaved weakly, and was angry with myself. I even said I would go the next day and turn them off without listening to what they might say. But I knew perfectly well that I had no intention of doing any such thing. So they stayed.

And then the days began to drag themselves out more wearisomely than at Hinton Hall, for though I was free from Blanche with her ghostly face and bright, wild eyes, yet now I was at the mercy of my own disturbing thoughts, and with nothing but the boredom of my own company to take my mind off things. Again and again I puzzled over Blanche's cryptic reference to Olave and Lazarus, but always I told myself that the girl was driving herself crazy with her absurd fantasies. The more I thought of that scene, the more it seemed to me that it was the dawning light of madness I had seen in her face. The way she had stared at me, with her eyes blazing full into mine, came back to me again and again. If I shut my eyes I would see her looking at me with her face not an inch away. And always I said to myself, "The girl's mad."

And yet I couldn't have sincerely believed that it was madness which had made her behave in such a way, for if so, I wouldn't have waited idly at home expecting every day to hear from her that Urcelyn had been restored, or at least to receive a summons from her, or orders to be away in pursuit of Avery. I must have trusted her deep in my heart, for I didn't attempt to go behind her and make investigations on my own account. And sometimes I was puzzled at my own inactivity. It fretted me to be idle when there was such an evident need for action. Yet there I stayed at home, doing nothing, but chafing at heart at the weary and ineffectual delay.

It was some days after my return home that I received an urgent call from the Gipsy camp to visit them immediately. It was a scrubby little brat of a boy who brought the summons. He tried to explain that the Gipsies were grateful to me for leaving them in peace, and in recompense for my kindness wanted to do me a service. Of course I sent the brat bundling, with an angry refusal to have anything to do with the cursed crew. Yet, somehow, shortly after he had left me, protesting vociferously against my suspicion, my mind altered. After all, there was nothing else to do. If there were any trouble it would be a relief. So I pocketed my revolver and set off.

The boy had arrived before me with my message, which seemed to have caused consternation in the camp. At any rate, when I broke in on them unexpectedly, I found the whole clan gathered into a wildly chattering group. But at the sight of me they split apart, ejaculating incomprehensibly, and I was more suspicious than ever. I thrust my hand into my revolver pocket and stepped up to them. "What is it?" I asked severely.

Nobody ventured to explain, but fingers were pointing to one of the tents, and it seemed to me that I was expected to enter. I made a step towards it, and heads nodded me to proceed. Clearly there was somebody hidden in that tent who was supposed to be of interest to me. Suddenly my mind came on the meaning of the thing. I didn't stop to ask whether the Gipsies were acting in faith or not, but I guessed that it was Avery who lay concealed there. It might have been a trap, or perhaps for some reason or other the Gipsies really wanted to betray him to me; I didn't stay to argue that out. With a quick step I walked to the tent and threw aside the curtain, drawing my revolver as I did so. A black figure rose from the bedding on the ground. I raised my revolver swiftly, but fell back with a cry when I saw Katrina.

Then dropping the curtain behind me I entered the tent.

"Katrina!" I exclaimed.

She didn't say a word, but stood facing me steadily.

"What is it?" I asked at length.

"Dick, why didn't you tell me?" she said.

"Tell you?" I didn't understand.

"You knew," she said, "you must have known!"

"But what?" I asked.

"The price," she answered me.

"The price," I questioned. Then the meaning came to me. Blanche had told her of Avery's condition.

"But that's impossible," I cried, trying to take her by the wrists.

She drew back angrily, and said, "No, Dick, you mustn't touch me. I don't belong to you. I must go to him. It's the only thing to do. These people will take me."

"But it's madness," I exclaimed.

She backed farther and farther from me in the little tent, gazing at me the whole time. At last she cried, "Oh, Dick, I didn't think it of you."

I tried to keep calm. "Katrina," I began, "I don't know what you mean, but I tell you frankly I don't intend to let you fall into Avery's clutches."

"You'd let him murder that child," she cried, "because you're too selfish . . ."

"Murder?" I repeated.

"It's worse than murder," she retorted fiercely.

"I'm sorry," I said, "but I don't intend . . ."

"Dick," she cut me short passionately, "do you want me to tell you what I think of you?"

I opened my hands weakly. "I'm sorry," I said again.

She was glaring at me now with undisguised anger, her breast heaving with such indignation as I had never seen in her before.

"There isn't a word for it," she said at length.

Talking seemed to me to be utterly useless. She had made up her mind to sacrifice herself for Urcelyn, and my conduct seemed to her to be that of a selfish coward. So much at least I could read in her behaviour. But I hadn't any intention, nevertheless, of giving in.

"Aren't you going?" she broke the silence.

"No, Katrina," I answered.

Suddenly she threw herself on her knees before me and cried, "Oh, Dick, you must go. Please go. Can't you see, it's for the sake of Urcelyn. We must rescue him somehow. If I had known before I would have gone at once. And I don't think he can hurt me now. I can stand up against him. I know how to be strong. And after all, he's my husband."

She gripped my hands fiercely. I tried to raise her up. "No," I said.

She sprang away from me again, and said in a low voice, "Then you're a cad, Dick."

"Yes, Katrina," I said.

There was another pause; and at length she asked in a calmer voice, "Why won't you let me go, Dick?"

"For one thing," I said, "because I don't think it would be any use."

I couldn't understand why Blanche had told her of the thing. But in any case, I didn't believe for a moment that Avery would keep faith, even supposing the exchange were agreed to.

"We could try," she said.

"It would be too dangerous," I answered.

"Are you afraid, Dick?" she asked.

"Afraid for you," I said.

She watched me in silence for a moment and asked, "What do you intend to do?"

"Wait for him and kill him," I replied, "unless you'll come away with me."

"He won't come while you're here," she said.

"Then that's another reason for my waiting," I retorted. Again she came up to me, and laid her hand on my arm.

Her anger seemed to have melted. "Dick," she said, "I'm sorry I called you . . . that. But really you must leave me. I must go to him. These people can take me. They're sure to know where he is. And you see, perhaps I'll be able to get a message through. You may be able to rescue me after all."

"No," I declared emphatically, "I don't intend to let you out of my sight. Blanche should never have told you," I added gruffly. Katrina's obstinacy was getting on my nerves.

"But she didn't tell me," she answered.

"What?" I cried.

"I heard," she said.

I didn't stay to ask how she had heard. I broke out hurriedly, "Well, she told me. And she told me not to tell you. She said you mustn't know of it. She wouldn't hear of your . . . of what you want to do. She told me so herself. She says Urcelyn will come back. She says other things that I don't pretend to understand. But in any case, she doesn't want you to sacrifice yourself like this. You mustn't do it. Really, you mustn't."

Katrina caught me by the shoulders. "But, Dick," she said, "is that true? I thought Blanche didn't tell me because . . ." She broke off with a cry, "Oh, Dick, then I needn't go back to him?" She pressed herself to my breast looking questioningly up into my face, and repeated, "I needn't go back to him?"

"Of course not," I said.

Her body went limp, and she sank down on the bedding, and burying her face in her arms sobbed with relief. And I didn't realize till that moment the utter fear and loathing she felt for the fellow. I didn't dare touch her, so humbled did I feel as the meaning of her sacrifice dawned slowly upon me.

"You must come back with me," I urged her gently.

She rose, and wiping away her tears smiled up at me. Then leaning on my arm she followed me from the tent.

The Gipsies watched us in silence as we walked away from the encampment.

"I didn't think they would have betrayed me," said Katrina.

"Thank God they did," I exclaimed. And turning I scattered what coin I had about me into their midst.

There was a sudden clamour as they fell to gathering the bounty.

It was some minutes later that Katrina said thoughtfully, "Avery must be losing his power."

"Yes," I replied, "last time I left you behind."

"Ah," she said, glancing quickly at me, "but I didn't mean that."

I drove her back to Hinton Hall. Blanche didn't seem to have discovered her absence. Nothing appeared to have changed, and once again I returned to Chalk Ridge alone.

Saying good-bye to Katrina I asked her how she had found out about Avery's ultimatum. She shook her head, and said, "Ah, I just heard." Before I could speak again she added, "It was silly of me. Prying, you know. And Blanche is commander-in-chief of this campaign. I'll remember that in future."

As the car moved off she said. "And you remember it too."

CHAPTER X

I heard occasionally from Katrina. She seemed as puzzled as I had been at Blanche's strange behaviour. She half hinted that it might be well if I came back to Hinton Hall to keep watch over things. I wrote and said I would go at a word, but she answered that after all she didn't think Blanche wanted me there. For herself she said I knew well enough whether she wanted me or not, but now it was rather a matter of prudence than desire. I felt she was right. It was hard enough to bear the separation from her even at such a distance, but it would have been far worse to have had her daily company with the knowledge galling me that she wasn't mine, that perhaps she never would be mine. For I knew that until Avery were dead without any possibility of doubt she would never consider herself free.

I began to wonder whether Avery could ever be dead without any possibility of doubt. It seemed to me that he had the power of rising from the grave at will. And I told myself that if he knew he were to die he would vanish to some unknown corner of the world so that we should never know what had become of him. I had given up all idea now of trusting in the official account of his death, and even in the investigations which the doctor said had been made into the matter. The bare and barren grave took on a new significance for me. The evil that poisoned the earth from flowering wasn't merely the body that lay buried there, but rather the unholy mystery of its resurrection that polluted the very soil into sterility. I found myself seriously believing the fantastic notion, and made no struggle to free myself from such distempered imaginings.

Katrina's letters became more frequent. Sometimes I received two a day. They were really notes telling me of the state of affairs at Hinton. More than once I nearly made up my mind to drive over and risk Blanche's displeasure. As far as I could make out the girl was killing herself slowly by the merciless strain she was putting on her nervous powers. And Katrina, too, betrayed signs of uneasiness which I didn't like. She said little enough about herself, but I thought I could read between the lines more than a suggestion of shadowing fear. Once she referred to the time when I had slept outside her door. Her words were, "I should feel so safe, Dick, if you were there now." But she added, "That's silly, isn't it?" And another time there was a reference to my strength quite in her old manner. It sent my memory back to her as she had been when I had known her first. "I love strong things," I could almost hear her saying. And I thought of how well she had been framed in those days with the great hounds and the huge figure of old Jock. Now she seemed pitiably defenceless, and if she had let fall a single word that I could have construed into a summons, I would have been with her without delay.

Sometimes I half wondered why I never heard of Doctor Dale now. As far as I could make out he didn't seem to be stirring a finger in the matter of his escaped lunatic. I couldn't quite make up my mind to call on him at St. Jude's. For one thing I didn't like the place. And then I didn't know how he would receive me. He seemed to have been pretty well shaken by the whole episode, and by what I could gather he had been having a bad time before we had had so much as a hint of Avery's being alive. Then he had rushed off early in the morning after the disappearance of Urcelyn. Evidently he wanted to wash his hands of the whole thing. I called to mind how he had tried to shake me off when I had questioned him on the meaning of the affair. His wild behaviour settled me in the conviction that he had had as much as he could bear, and wouldn't be much use to me.

So the days wore on, and nothing happened.

It was one evening that I noticed from my window that there were no caravans in Morton's Dingle. At least, as far as I could make out in the dimness of the twilight, there was nothing there. I was dressing for dinner at the time, so I decided I would take a stroll that way after dinner to make certain. I remembered that once before with the disappearance of the Gipsies Avery had disappeared too. I wondered whether history would repeat itself. My thoughts on the matter were very idle, for it wasn't until half-way through dinner that I remembered how the Gipsies had betrayed Katrina's presence to me. If they were still in alliance with Avery they wouldn't have been likely to have done that.

Then without any connection that I could trace there came into my mind the sudden phrase, "The cuckoos are flying north."

I sprang up from the table, leaving my dinner unfinished, and rushed off to the Dingle to see if the Gipsies had really gone. The place was completely deserted. I strode back home in a fever of excitement. What I was busy telling myself was that Avery was in hiding in his hut in the mountains. I couldn't understand why I had never thought of that before. Perhaps it was the sense of his being in the neighbourhood that had kept the thought from me. But now I was convinced that he was working his schemes from his mountain retreat. I would go at once and hunt him out, and settle him for ever.

I didn't waste time over any elaborate preparations. I made sure that I had my revolver with me, and a supply of ammunition. Also I fired a couple of rounds to satisfy myself that the weapon was in working order. Then I drove away into the night.

I needn't describe that journey in detail. At first my excitement kept me alertly awake, but with the coming of the day I began to feel the want of sleep. Still I pressed on, though towards noon I felt stupidly drowsy, and more than once must have nodded at the wheel, for with a jerk I seemed to come back to consciousness to find myself nearly into a cart or a wall. Eventually I drew up, wondering what I had better do, for I felt I should never get to my destination in this way. But in a moment I was sound asleep, and woke later with a start to find it was evening. There was a strange dizziness in my head, and somehow I didn't feel master of myself. Mechanically I set the engine going and drove on. It seemed to me now that the affair wasn't in my hands. I knew I ought to put up for the night, and set out fresh again the next morning. But I couldn't make up my mind to break the journey. The car was running so beautifully that it seemed easier just to let it run. And besides, I was getting to the edge of civilization now, I should soon be on the slopes that led to the mountain of the mysterious hut. Dimly I was surprised at myself for knowing the way so well. I never had to hesitate at a turning. The car seemed to be like a living thing that knew the path by instinct. The night gathered round me, but I made no halt. I switched on the head-lights, and drove on into the dark. The purring of the car was like the undercurrent of a dream. In fact I seemed to be in a land of dream, unreal, fantastic, yet perfectly familiar.

Through the long night I climbed steadily. There was never a break in the monotony of the journey, and the sense of dream-like unreality became more oppressive than ever. But I made no struggle against it. I yielded to the fancy that I was being guided on my way. There was a presence about me controlling me, even controlling the car and impelling it onward.

Then slowly a strange thought seemed to be forming itself in my mind. There was a dim stirring of memory that I couldn't quite understand. I seemed to be living over again some age-old experience. Somewhere or other in the remote past I had been drawn forward in just such a way. There was a voice, too, trying to make itself heard. It sounded very faint and distant, and yet I could feel a kind of warning in it. Suddenly it was all clear. It was Gaveston saying, "Dick, take care."

With a start of fright I realized what the memory was which had been stirring in the depths of my mind. It was in just such a way that I had been lured at school to leave my bed and set out on an aimless wandering. For a moment I had the intention of stopping the car and turning back, but the thought came to me that the analogy was all wrong. I hadn't set out on an aimless wandering, nor had I been compelled to it against my will. I pressed down the accelerator again. It was merely the want of sleep, I told myself, which had made the journey seem hazy and fantastic. And it was the loneliness of the night around me which had given me that old impression of being lured on to some enterprise against my will. I knew perfectly well what I was doing. It wasn't Avery who was drawing me into the net, it was of my own will and purpose that I was on his track to hunt him down.

And yet at times during the night, as my drowsiness got the better of me, I had the feeling more than once that Avery was leading me on to some trap he had prepared for me. "Dick, take care," I heard Gaveston repeat. "Very well," I said to myself, "I'll take care." I fingered my revolver. Even if it were by Avery's will and not by my own that I was seeking him out, I told myself that the end would be the same.

The air was hazy with the coming of the morning when I reached the hollow by the wayside where I had once before hidden the car. With a feeling of grim satisfaction as the adventure seemed to be closing in I drew up under cover, then making sure that I had my weapon handy I set off up the slope. When I reached the top and looked across the misty valley I could just distinguish the witch-like tree standing up darkly against the rim of grey light that lay along the farther ridge. Almost without a pause I was climbing down towards the valley, and was soon groping in a blanket of mist that rose about me from the little stream that I could hear chattering beneath. Reaching it I made for the fall, and began the ascent. As I rose out of the mist I found the air already much brighter about me. The tree above me was clear enough against the sky. For a moment I thought I saw a figure moving. I stopped to watch, but it must have been an illusion. I climbed on again.

I moved with greater caution as I drew nearer the old tree. Sometimes I paused to listen, but I couldn't hear a sound. I thought there was a thin curl of smoke coming from behind the rocks, but I couldn't be certain. At last I reached the tree, and creeping round to the three steps was quickly tip-toeing through the narrow passage that led into the enclosure. Descending the stairway at the end I put my head around the rock, not knowing in the least what to expect. But my heart thumped with excitement as I saw a Gipsy tent standing where the hut had been. There was a little fire smouldering dully as though it were being left to burn itself out. All around lay fragments of charred and sodden wood, and other indescribable refuse. The remains of the hut, I told myself, remembering the explosion. But all that was merely a fleeting thought. My mind was fixed on that tent. Who was inside it? Was it really Avery? And was Urcelyn with him?

I crept up to it with infinite caution, still hesitant and uncertain. Then I heard a distinct sound from within.

That settled me. I strode up to the crazy tent and flung aside the curtain. It was some minutes before I recognized the ragged youth I saw there as Caspar. He was eating his breakfast, but at the sight of me he stopped with the bowl half raised to his lips. Then he rose slowly, and suddenly seeming to recognize me began gesticulating wildly. I didn't know what on earth he meant. I was too dazed to try and understand. It suddenly seemed to me that I had been finely fooled. I had been looking for Avery, and I had found this dumb lout instead. I thought he had been done away with long ago. I even said to him, "I thought you were dead."

He shook his head vigorously, and I laughed at the energetic denial.

"Oh well," I muttered, and turned away. It was quite clear to me that Avery wasn't there. I began to understand what had happened. But Caspar caught me by the arm. There was something he was trying to tell me in his inexplicable dumb show. I watched him for a moment, and shook my head.

"If you can tell me where Avery is," I said wearily, "I should be infinitely obliged." To tell the truth the shock of disappointment had brought on a heavy weight of sleepiness. I didn't quite know what I was saying.

"Has he been here?" I asked, though knowing quite well what the answer would be. He shook his head. I began to move away, and he followed. But he blocked the passage out before I could reach it, and went through an elaborate pantomime. I was too tired and spiritless to interrupt him. And indeed at last some kind of comprehension began to dawn upon me. His acting must have been pretty clever, because in spite of myself I knew that what he was trying to tell me was that Avery had never returned to the hut; that he, Caspar, had waited for him there; I had the impression of years passing over while he waited; it seemed too that his intention was murder; he pointed significantly to the yawning chasm, which I noticed now for the first time, down which Avery had once been thrown . . . But it didn't interest me. I pushed past him, and made my way out.

Dimly, as I clambered back on my trail, I was aware of Caspar following me. It was well for me that he did so. For when I reached the hollow in the rock the car was gone.

It was Caspar who guided me during two terrible days of racking anxiety over the mountainous tracks back to civilization. Without him I should have been lost, for my mind had become utterly fogged. I don't think it was merely the need of sleep which made me stumble blindly forward without knowing where in the least I was going. There was some evil influence at work stupefying my wits. I couldn't think, I couldn't reason. I don't know to this day where I slept, nor whether I ate a morsel of food during the whole journey. All I am certain of is that Caspar must have led me by a quicker path than the road I had taken. But it was rough, and my boots weren't made for mountaineering. I remember how bruised and weary my feet were. And that's about the only physical distress I do remember. As a matter of fact, it was a kind of relief to me, for it kept my mind away from the terrible fear that was torturing me. Avery had fooled me; I knew that well enough, in spite of my bemused brain. He had got me out of the way so that he could carry out his devilries undisturbed. All Katrina's hints of danger crowded back upon me. I could see now that she had been menaced all the while by some lurking evil, but hadn't told me of it. I ought to have stayed at Hinton Hall. Blanche was too intent on her own schemings to know what was happening to Katrina. And what might have happened to her during my absence I didn't dare guess. But I knew that Avery must have been at his old games again. Failing to win the girl by holding Urcelyn as a hostage, he had turned back to his earlier method. I had a frightful picture in my mind of Katrina's sufferings. I could see her struggling against the strangling madness which Avery knew so well how to coil about her. Perhaps she had even fallen a prey to it, and was back in his power once again. Well, it was a relief from such nightmare thoughts as these to feel the dragging pains at my feet holding my mind down to my own physical misery.

It was wonderful to be in a train once more, and to feel I had touched civilization. Whether the journey were fast or slow I didn't know, for I was in a deep sleep as soon as I was settled in the carriage.

Mechanically I got out at Chalk Ridge, though I should have gone straight on to Little Hinton. I was at home before I realized what I had done. Then I seemed to wake up. The first thing I noticed was that Caspar had vanished. I didn't even know whether he had got into the train with me. However, that didn't matter now. I changed my clothes, attended to my damaged feet, and feeling generally refreshed got out my motor-cycle ready to set off to Hinton Hall. A telegram was brought to me before I started. It had come two days ago, I was told. It was an urgent message from Katrina for me to come to her at once.

I was almost insane with anxiety as at last in the failing light I raced up the drive at Hinton Hall. I flung the cycle from me, leapt up the steps, and began hammering wildly at the door. It was opened to me almost immediately, and I burst in. Katrina came running towards me. "Oh, Dick," she cried, "why didn't you come?"

I was too relieved to say a word. I felt faint and weak with the sudden revulsion of feeling. I swayed, and fell forward towards her.

She steadied me, asking, "What's the matter, Dick?"

I pulled myself together. "Is all well?" I asked.

"Oh, it's been terrible," she cried, "terrible!"

I suddenly drew her to me and looked into her eyes. But the hall was dusky with evening, and I couldn't be certain. But what I thought I had seen in them was that leaden shadow of storm dulling their beautiful blue.

"Katrina," I exclaimed, "he's been trying . . ."

"If you had been here," was all she said.

"But you beat him," I answered.

"It was Blanche," she said. "Oh, Dick, she's splendid."

"Blanche?" I repeated.

"But it's tired her, Dick," she went on. "I'm frightened. I don't know what's happening. She looks as if she could just lie down and die. You know, as I might lie down and sleep. Like that."

"Where is she?" I asked.

"In the chapel, I expect," she replied. "She seems to live there."

"With Mrs. Wait, of course," I said.

Katrina nodded.

"That woman!" I exclaimed.

"She looks like a ghost," Katrina said.

"Look here," I cried, "I'm going to put a stop to all this." I began to move away, but Katrina caught me by the arm and said, "No, Dick," in such a terrified voice that I looked quickly at her in a startled dismay.

"Why not?" I asked.

"You mustn't," she said.

I paused irresolute. "Well, then," I began again, "at least I'm going to investigate, and find out what's going on."

I think she would have held me back, but my mind was made up. I led on to the chapel, and she followed. I made my way round to the vestry entrance, thinking that there I might see without disturbing Blanche. Once more Katrina would have interposed, but I opened the door quietly and slipped inside. She turned and left me.

Only a curtain screened the chapel from me. I pulled it open the merest slit, and peeped through.

Immediately I saw Blanche standing up very straight in front of the altar, for the two candles were lit, drawing my attention to them at once. But it wasn't easy to make out much else in the dim light. A little way down the aisle I could distinguish Mrs. Wait who was seated facing Blanche. The light from the high windows caught her open eyes, making them stare glassily. They seemed fixed on me, and I half dropped the curtain to hide them away. The whole picture seemed spectral and ghostly. There wasn't a sound or a movement. The dim columns, faintly luminous in the twilight, the marble monuments of the dead, and the heavy black shadow of Blanche thrown down the chapel by the candlelight, seemed a fitting frame to those motionless figures.

Presently I noticed Blanche was moving her arms in a slow, rhythmic swaying. It was the huge waving shadows in the roof that I saw first. And then I heard a faint stirring at the far end of the chapel. Straining my eyes into the dusk I caught the glimmer of a moving figure. It seemed to be advancing slowly up the aisle. Almost before I realized it was so near it had passed Mrs. Wait. I gazed at it, fascinated, as it advanced towards Blanche. Then with a sickening fear I understood.

It was a little squat thing, covered entirely in a black cloak. There was a mask over its face. It moved forward with a swaying lurch, for its arms reached to the ground, and it swung itself along on its knuckles. It was Avery.

It seemed to have its face raised to Blanche, who, for her part, was gazing intently down at it. She took a step forward arid I heard her say very quietly, "Olave."

Suddenly there was a frenzied scream, and the creature seemed to be taken with a paroxysm. It clutched at its throat and fell to the floor writhing horribly. Blanche stepped quickly forward, and stood staring down at it. Mrs. Wait, I just noticed, was stirring uneasily. Then I turned away in disgust, listening to the strangled moans of the wretched thing as it rolled and struggled on the floor.

What it meant I didn't know, unless Blanche were just mesmerizing the creature by sheer force of will. But I didn't think that was possible with such an adversary as Avery. Two pictures seemed to mingle themselves in my mind with what I had just seen; Blanche as Beatrice Cenci staring down her betrayer; and Gaveston just before I had shot him, wrestling against his madness.

I didn't venture to look again till the sounds of struggling had subsided. Then once more I drew aside the curtain and peeped through.

I could scarcely believe my eyes. Blanche was on her knees before the hideous thing, clasping it in her arms. The mask had been half torn from its face during the mad fit, and the cloak was hanging about it in shredded tatters. It was enough to show me something of the twisted deformity of the abominable thing beneath. And Blanche was hugging it in a passionate embrace!

Presently she drew away and slowly rose to her feet. I gazed in sudden stupefaction at the creature's breast. For the cloak hung open, and the light of the altar candles fell full upon it. Distinctly I could see the tattooed sign of the sword and serpent.

Then the thing began slowly moving my way. I think it was only the extremity of my fear that held me to the spot. But my alarm subsided only to give place to a stupefied amazement. For it had turned aside to Olave's tomb. It lurched on to the graven slab, and slowly began to sink into the earth.

But suddenly its madness seemed to come upon it again. With a shrill scream it caught at the floor and would have swung itself out of the black hole into which it was sinking. But Blanche stepped swiftly up to it, and glared down at the struggling thing.

They were only a couple of yards from me, and I could see the whole drama. The creature made one desperate effort to break the spell that was overpowering it. Seizing its mask it tore it off, that so its hideousness might frighten Blanche away. I would have run screaming from the place had I not been fascinated by the thing's eyes. They were jet black; and though the rest of the face was utterly unrecognizable, yet the eyes were the eyes of Avery.

And still Blanche stood above it, staring it down. Its struggling slackened, it seemed to shrink and quail before her eyes, and shuddering sank back into the darkness. And the heavy marble block came sliding over the place, while a thin, lost cry seemed to vibrate like an echo from another world.

For a moment Blanche stood there silent and motionless. Then suddenly she broke into a cruel, hard laughter, but checking herself abruptly, she threw her arms across her face and flung herself down against the tomb, sobbing terribly.

I hesitated whether to go to her or not. Something of the enormity of her deed had made itself clear to my appalled understanding. She had called back Olave's spirit to wrestle with the evil thing that had usurped his derelict body, only to send him wandering again when his victory was complete. Well, she had done right, I thought. Such a thing couldn't be allowed to live, whether it were Olave or Avery. But it seemed to me best to leave her alone with her bitter triumph. It would have been cruel to have thrust myself upon her at such a time. I gave her one last look. She was kneeling silently with her arms flung over the tomb and her face pressed to the cold stone.

Quietly I left her, and went back to the house. And there I found Katrina with Urcelyn. She had come upon him, she said, outside the chapel. The boy didn't seem to know what had been happening to him. He was sleepy and fretful, so I sent for his nurse and had him packed off to bed.

Katrina wanted to know what had happened. I thought it best to tell her the truth as far as I knew it. I told her all I had seen.

For a long while we sat in silence. I heard a step outside. I thought it must be Blanche. I opened the door. It was Mrs. Wait dragging herself painfully up the stairs. That made me feel uneasy for Blanche. I went back to the chapel. She was kneeling as I had left her. I went up to her and touched her shoulder. She was dead.

It was a year later that Katrina and I were married. The ceremony in that ghost-haunted chapel was more of an agony than a delight. The knowledge of the tragic contents of the tomb at my side took all the glory from the music. It was with a sense of throwing off an ugly disease that I left the chapel never to enter it again.

www.ingramcontent.com/pod-product-compliance
Lightning Source LLC
Chambersburg PA
CBHW061438030726
47503CB00005B/1462